RELENTLESS SOULS

RYAN KIRK

WATERSTONE
MEDIA

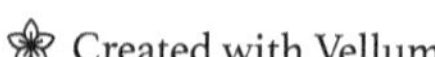 Created with Vellum

For Jeremy

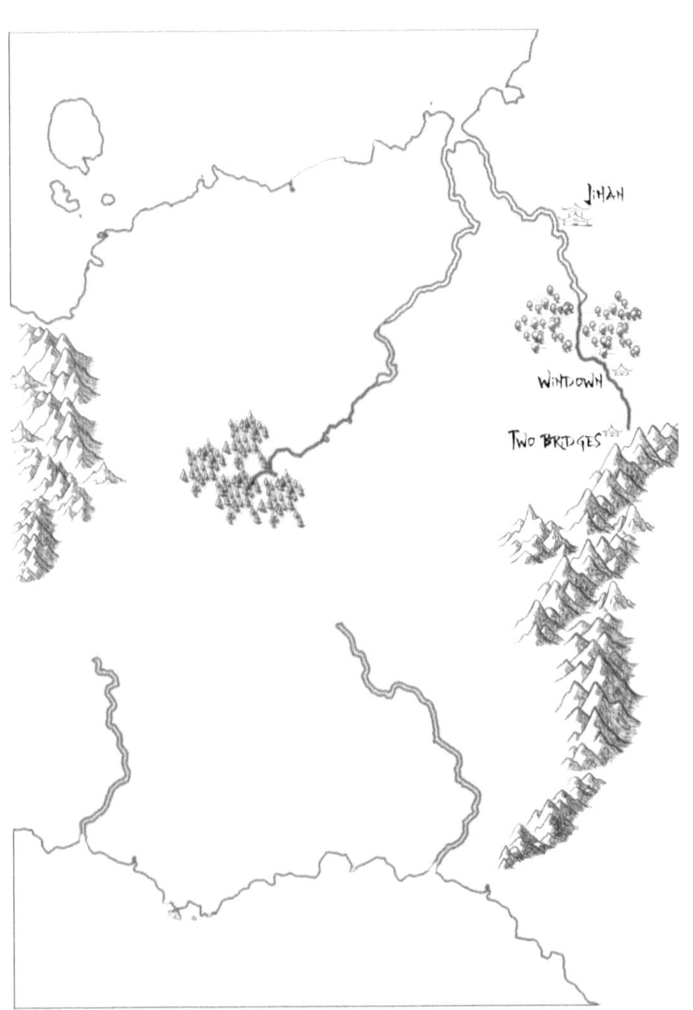

JIHAN
WINDOWN
TWO BRIDGES

PROLOGUE

The stiff breeze flapping through Jian's white robes portended a storm. After a lifetime of training, his heightened senses easily detected the subtle changes that indicated a changing of the weather. Above him, puffy clouds sprinted across the sky as though to escape the onslaught. The air, which had been humid and sticky all day, now held just a hint of a chill, cooling what little skin he left exposed to the breeze. Jian expected a thunderstorm to echo within the valley tonight.

He was certain of his prediction, and already looked forward to the rain. Not only would the storm bring the promise of relief from the heat, it also served as a metaphor. Rain washed everything away, including all the mistakes of the past. While he didn't feel particularly guilty at the moment, the morning after a storm always felt like a fresh start, something the world could always use more of.

A powerful storm would also distract him from the thoughts running through his head. He'd been away from the monastery now for weeks, and he was disturbed by what he had learned. Although definitive answers still eluded him, he felt another storm brewing in the future, a storm aimed directly at the heart of all he held dear. He needed more information, but the outlines of a conspiracy were already taking shape; and if his hunch proved correct, they faced a foe more ruthless than any living monk had confronted before. Jian prayed he was wrong.

As Jian crested a small rise, he looked down at the town of Two Bridges, the village that he had called home for as long as he had known the word. It was a small town with only a few hundred residents, but it was where he had spent his childhood, before he joined the monastery in the mountains above. Now that he had seen more of the world he understood just how small of a town it was, but that didn't decrease his love for the place one bit. It held both sorrow and joy, the key ingredients for a worthwhile life. If anything, on trips to the capital, like the one he'd just taken, he felt an acute longing for the simpler life he'd grown up with. Those who were born and raised in the city looked down on the towns and villages that surrounded them, but in Jian's opinion, they didn't know what they were missing.

His easy steps carried him to the outskirts of town, where a group of boys played catch with a small ball. When they saw him, they shouted and pointed in excitement. While they'd all certainly seen monks before, Jian understood that his white robes were not a common sight. Their voices sounded happy, but he thought he noticed a twinge of nervousness among them as well. They would've heard stories from their parents and would be just a little afraid. Most citizens feared the monks and their powers, powers the people didn't understand.

If only the citizens knew how little the monks knew about their own powers, Jian thought. We're all like blind men, groping around the proverbial elephant, desperately trying to understand the power we control.

Jian felt no particular rush to return to the monastery. So long as he arrived before the storm developed, he should be fine. The news and information he carried was important, but nothing that couldn't wait for a few minutes while he played ball with the children. Their mission in the monastery was to make the world a better place. That mission was a lot easier when children grew up having positive experiences with his kind.

He smiled and bowed to them as he approached. He laughed as they all stopped their game and bowed to him as well, their forms sloppy and unrefined, but earnest. When they brought their heads back up he could easily see the worry on their faces. There was no reason for them to be so afraid of him. He unfolded his arms and brought his hands out from underneath the folds of his robe. He held his hand up as a target and said, "It has been a long time, but give me a throw."

The boy holding the ball looked terrified, as though he had just been asked to jump off a high cliff, but he wasn't going to disobey the request of a monk. He wound up and threw, a small leather ball poorly aimed. Instead of heading towards Jian's hand, the ball sped towards his face.

He had just enough time to register the look of abject terror on the boy's face before he moved his hand quickly and caught the ball in midair. The well-worn leather slapped against his palm, stinging his hand. He smiled again, trying to ease the boy's fear. "You have a strong arm. Who thinks they can catch my throw?"

One of the boys, who Jian believed to be the leader, stepped forward and held up his hand as a target. The boy looked to be perhaps a year or two older than the rest. In fact, he looked almost old enough to be spending more of his time helping around the house. Jian didn't recognize him but decided to give him a little test anyway. He tossed the ball, snapping his wrist and making sure to give it a fair amount of speed. The older boy didn't even hesitate. He snatched the ball out of the air with a triumphant grin as though he had slain a terrible monster.

With that, the awkwardness broke and Jian reveled in the game of catch with the boys. By the time he left, each of the boys was smiling and waving, new friends that he told himself he should visit again as soon as his duties allowed.

He passed through the town, taking an easy pace and allowing his eyes to wander over the buildings and establishments that he knew so well. While he had just been through town a few weeks ago on his way from the monastery, it was still an experience to be able to walk through it and notice the changes. He was no different than the other monks. He did not leave the monastery often enough, did not spend enough time out in the world among the people they were supposed to protect and serve. Training and study took up more time than it should, especially with all the new discoveries as of late. The town had changed considerably since he was a child growing up in its outskirts. For one, there were no longer just the eponymous two bridges across the river. Instead, there were now three, with the newest one running through a commercial district that had been expanded in recent years.

Some days he remembered his childhood so vividly it seemed like no time had passed at all, and yet when he returned through town he saw just how much had changed since he left. As the sun was still high in the sky, Jian decided he would take a break and enjoy a small meal. There was a street vendor in the commercial district whom

Jian visited whenever he came through. Although Jian didn't remember the heavyset man's name, the man had been serving some of the best fish in town since Jian was a child.

Jian was ashamed when the man remembered his name. "Jian! It is good to see you once again. Would you like the usual?"

Jian gave the man a grin. "Please."

A few minutes later, a bowl of rice and fish sat in front of him, a feast by his monastic standards. He bowed his head deeply and thanked the old man profusely as he dug in.

When he finished the meal, scraping up every last grain of rice, he decided to head straight to the monastery. Even if he climbed the trail at a slow pace he would be back in time to report to the abbot and still make evening meal. It would be good to see his brothers once again.

As he left Two Bridges, he walked through one of the older sections of town, a place that now only housed the poor and the destitute. He passed the seediest tavern in town, the Old Goat, pausing for a moment as he did. He could feel Lei, his brother, inside, the power of his life force distinguishable even from this distance. His brother's strength, wild and untamed, burned like a bonfire to Jian's senses. Lei's power was still incredible, even after years without training.

When he last came through town, Lei had also been in the tavern. After asking around, he found that most people agreed that was where his younger brother spent most of his time.

Jian considered going in and visiting with his brother. No doubt Lei was currently drunk, but they had been drunk together before, so it wasn't something new and unusual. He wondered if his brother was sober enough to know that he was standing right outside on the road.

Jian felt a gathering of energy from inside the tavern. The force was hostile and angry and was definitely aimed at him. That was as much of an answer as he was ever going to get. His brother not only knew he was outside, but was happy to attack him if he dared get closer.

Jian's stomach twisted as he thought about the anger his brother carried, feeling the guilt of his own actions and how they had brought them both to this place. The sensation was familiar, strong enough to almost make him vomit the delicious meal he'd just eaten.

What would he give to spar with his brother one more time, the way they had when they were younger? He considered the question frequently, and his answer depended on the day. Today, he was almost willing to give up his monastic lifestyle.

Almost.

Jian took a deep breath, exhaling his frustration. Perhaps his brother couldn't forgive him today, but there would be other days. Other opportunities. Jian wouldn't allow the situation to continue much longer if he could help it. He would make things right with his brother, no matter the cost.

Jian gave a bow in the direction of his brother. The gesture felt feeble and empty, but he couldn't think of anything else to ease the pain that his brother felt. The energy inside diminished and Jian turned to walk away, leaving the town and the memories of his mistakes behind him.

Two Bridges nestled in a small valley between a series of hills and a mountain range. Leaving the town behind him,

Jian began trekking up the mountainside toward the monastery high above. His legs, well-conditioned from long hikes in the mountains, took steady strides up the path even as he gained altitude and the air thinned. He welcomed the burn in his muscles as a distraction from the pain in his heart.

After he put about a mile between himself and the town, he stopped to rest where the different paths that crisscrossed the lower altitudes of the mountain met. From here, there was only one way up to the monastery and Jian would hike it all in one effort. But here was a beautiful viewpoint looking out on the valley below. He could see the place where his house had once stood and all the landmarks of his childhood. He thought about how the decisions he and his brother made when they were so young had made such a lasting impact on their lives.

He looked up the mountain. The monastery was still a few miles of switchbacks and climbing away, so it could not be seen from here. As much as the past affected them, it was only the present and the future that mattered. The past couldn't be changed, but the future was yet unwritten, and if Jian had anything to say about it, few children would have to suffer the challenges he and Lei had experienced growing up.

With a newfound sense of resolution, Jian began the final section of the ascent. His long legs ate up the ground quickly, and before he knew it he was at the signpost that indicated there was only a mile left to the monastery.

The only warning he received was the surge of energy building above him. He wasn't sure he had ever felt such a large increase happen so quickly. His body, sensing that he was in danger, acted of its own volition. He leaped forward into a roll, just in time to feel the wave of energy crash behind him. The attack blasted off a section of the path, sending broken rocks tumbling hundreds of feet below.

Jian didn't understand. He'd never been attacked before, not outside of the training they practiced in the monastery. The energy needed to cause that type of damage to the trail was impressive, obtainable only by monks who had achieved the higher ranks of their order. Who among them would attack him out here on the path?

He furiously pushed the questions away. Answers could come later, but he needed to defend himself. The attack had come from above, and Jian assumed that his attacker was one or two switchbacks higher.

Jian felt another surge of energy building, just as strong as the one before. He cursed himself for not having had the forethought to stand up and keep moving. He lay on the ground, as easy a target as had ever existed. Instinctively, he summoned his own energy. Against the force he had just dodged, he wasn't sure he would be able to summon enough energy in time, but his life depended on success. If he couldn't block the energy, perhaps he could deflect it. His hands made the sign, fingers dancing an intricate pattern that told of years of practice. He thrust out his own energy, shaped as two planes coming together above him, a large invisible axe head with his body underneath the wedge.

He finished just in time. Another wave crashed down from above, and the impact against his own pointed energy jarred him, shaking his bones. The attack split in two, crashing into the path on either side of him, digging deep furrows in the stone. The energy had again been more than enough to kill him.

After the attack passed, Jian knew he couldn't afford to make the same mistake twice. He scrambled to his feet and sprinted up the path toward his attacker. He turned around one switchback and came across a man dressed in nondescript traveling clothes. He looked thoroughly unremarkable, even though most of his features were hidden by his clothing and his hood. The only attribute Jian noticed was the man's hands dancing an intricate pattern, focusing energy in the ways that only the monks knew.

Wanting to conserve his own energy, Jian dove behind a large boulder on the side of the road. Another energy wave leaped toward him, crashing against the boulder with unbridled fury.

The boulder was thick enough to take the abuse, though. It cracked and groaned but held. Jian guessed the stone could take one more blast before becoming ineffective as cover. Hopefully by then this man, whoever he was, would be tired enough for Jian to defeat easily.

Jian felt energy being gathered once more, again with incredible strength, determination, and speed. Whoever this man was, he was no amateur. He had trained at least as long as Jian. But there was a reason Jian had been the one sent out to hunt down news of a secret conspiracy. He wasn't necessarily the strongest monk, but his control over his gift was second to none. When it came to a fight, it wasn't always the strongest warrior who won, but the warrior who possessed the greater control over his energy. So far, Jian hadn't found an attack that he couldn't block given enough time to focus his energy, but for all he knew the other man was still holding back.

This time, the energy gathered by his assailant felt different. It was tighter and more focused than any of the attacks that came before.

Jian moved his head, thinking he should glance around the boulder to see what hand signs the man was using to form his attack. Perhaps the movements would reveal some clue as to the identity of the opponent he faced.

Just as he did, though, the energy was released, and Jian couldn't believe what he saw. A small hole, not much wider than Jian's thumb, appeared in the rock where his head had just been. Jian cursed. There was only one attack that could punch through a boulder and remain that tightly focused. Whoever was after him knew the Dragon's Fang. Jian knew of it, and even knew the gestures used to focus the attack. But even if he could contain the energy of the technique, which he thought unlikely, he would be immediately dismissed from the monasteries. A monk would never use such a style. The move was as taboo as using weapons.

Again, Jian's instincts took over. His opponent knew the Dragon's Fang and could summon it quickly. No boulder in the world offered him enough protection. He would need an entire mountain to protect himself, and that didn't seem likely. Jian couldn't risk a prolonged engagement with this assassin. He needed to strike and finish this while he still could. He stood and bolted from behind the stone.

As he ran, Jian focused his own energies, using two different focal points, one for each hand. It was a skill that very few had the ability to perform, and Jian planned on using that hard-won ability to finish this fight.

At a full sprint, Jian thrust out one of his hands and released the energy he'd gathered there. It was a focused attack, the energy spiraling toward the strange assassin in a tight beam. It was nowhere near as tight as the Dragon's Fang, but it was still a substantial attack. A direct hit would kill. Normally, Jian opposed violent solutions, but he did not think a peaceful resolution likely here.

Jian saw the other man make a quick sign for a barrier, and his attack pounded against the shield. He had two choices: he could continue pushing against the barrier, hoping to overwhelm and crack the man's shield, or he could try again with another attack from his other hand.

The signs the man used to make the barrier were simple but effective. The shield was wide and covered the entire space between them. A second attack would do no better, so Jian focused on putting more of his energy into his first attack. The two energies met and swirled, each one wrestling for superiority. Eventually, Jian realized he wouldn't break the barrier without a concerted effort. He released his energy to save his stamina.

Even though his attack hadn't harmed his opponent, it had distracted the assassin long enough to allow Jian to get in close. Hand-to-hand combat was Jian's specialty, and no matter how strong this man was, Jian was certain he would seize the victory if he could reach the other warrior.

Jian sent a flurry of quick blasts in the direction of the man, who stepped around each of them with ease. The only success Jian accomplished was knocking the hood from the man's head, revealing a cleanly-shaven scalp and a menacing glare. The man had dark-green eyes that burned with hate, as though he believed Jian was responsible for all the pain in the world.

The assassin released his own flurry of punches, and hands, wrists, forearms, and elbows met in a dizzying pattern. Throughout the fight, Jian attempted to gather what energy he could, hoping that he could release a blast far too close to dodge. Across from him, the man was doing the same.

The battle felt even, neither of them able to obtain the opening they wanted, but Jian felt that he was just a hair faster than his opponent. His guess was proven when he finally created an opening in the man's otherwise impenetrable defense. Jian made a quick focusing sign with one hand and brought his palm toward the man's torso.

Too late, he realized that the man had made an almost identical gesture. With a start, Jian released his energy, hoping that his attack would land before his enemy could release his energy. It was no use. Both released a wave of force into the other's attack point-blank, and the concussive power of the energies pounding into one another threw them both backward. Jian landed hard, barely managing to roll over his shoulder and back onto his feet. Above the path from him, the man had kept his feet, aided in part by being pushed uphill instead of down.

Jian summoned his energy again but held onto it. Unless he had a clear opening, there was no point in him expending his valuable stamina. His opponent was too good, the fight harder than he had expected, harder than he'd ever imagined. In the monasteries, he had no equal.

The man up the hill from him seemed unperturbed by the energy Jian had gathered, effortlessly matching it with his own. He cracked his neck and looked down at the monk. "I was told you were strong. But I had no idea that the fight would be this enjoyable. You are almost as good as me."

Jian saw no point in trying to speak with the enemy. It would just be wasted breath, and he needed to catch his. They could speak when the man was appropriately subdued.

His heart sank when the man reached behind his body and revealed a small dagger. Somehow, Jian knew exactly what he was in for. A weapon by itself didn't mean much, and in the hands of a civilian, Jian wouldn't have had even a hint of hesitation in attacking. But somehow, deep in his gut, he just *knew* that this man had trained his gifts with a weapon. Among the monks, such training was a sin even greater than performing the Dragon's Fang. It seemed fitting that the greatest challenge Jian had ever faced would be so closely related to the mistakes from his past he regretted every day.

Perhaps this was his path toward redemption. Perhaps this was his chance to make things right between him and Lei. After all, what were the odds that this assassin would be proficient in the very skill that had brought his brother such grief?

Assuming the assassin knew how to use the dagger with his power, the only way Jian could imagine defeating him was to get in close. The dagger would still be a weapon, but at distance the focused attacks the man could achieve with the edged weapon would be the difference between the two of them. Charging an assassin with a dagger wasn't a wise decision, but it was the best he had.

Jian flashed a one-handed sign at his opponent, sending a burst of energy towards the man's face. As he expected, the assassin blocked it easily, but Jian had never hoped to score a direct hit. He had only wanted to distract the man for the precious few seconds he would need to get in close.

For the briefest of moments, Jian thought his gamble had paid off. As the assassin regained his balance, Jian closed the little distance that remained between them. It was almost too late when he realized that a collected force of energy rested in the assassin's open hand. The hand released the power and Jian was forced to spin away from his opponent in a desperate bid to avoid the strike.

Instinctively he prepared to deflect a stab from the dagger. At this distance it was the attack that almost any warrior would use. But here, Jian's instincts betrayed him. The assassin didn't try to close the gap and stab out with the dagger. Instead, he took a step back and let Jian spin past him so that Jian now had the upper ground. The dagger made one quick gesture and Jian felt the energy spring from its tip in a razor-sharp line, whipping towards him. Having no other options, Jian continued his spin, hoping desperately that his momentum would carry him out of the way of the attack.

He had no such luck. While the attack missed his center of mass, it did cut into his torso and the underside of his left arm. For a moment, he thought he had been lucky, but then he realized that the cuts were so sharp he didn't even feel the immediate pain. When his entire left side flared in agony, he stumbled and fell to the ground.

To his left, on the edge of the path, the sound of rock sliding against rock caught his attention. His eyes darted in that direction and he watched the top of a boulder slide off and down onto the path below. The attack he'd almost dodged had cut clean through the rock like a scythe through grass.

That was why weapons were never permitted for those who could control their energy. That blast, as far as Jian could tell, had been relatively controlled, and there was still no telling the damage it could cause. It could conceivably have traveled onward for miles.

The assassin wasn't interested in giving Jian the opportunity to reflect on the strength he faced. Crushing force slammed into his body, pressing him firmly against the ground. Jian cursed at himself. How could he have been so foolish as to drop his guard, even for a second? The force was so strong he couldn't even move his fingers, and he was unable to focus his energy in any way. The assassin stood above him, one arm fully extended in his direction. That was the arm this crushing force emanated from.

"It was well met," said the assassin. The dagger traced a

small intricate pattern that Jian didn't recognize.

With a strength born of desperation, Jian unleashed all his energy in the general direction of the assassin. Without the ability to focus the energy using hand signs, he wasn't sure what chance he had against the other man's strength, but he refused to lie here and die. Too much depended on him, and he now regretted that he had passed up the opportunity back in town to make things right with his brother. He refused to die with the chasm that remained between them.

He wasn't sure if he caught the assassin by surprise or if the assassin was distracted trying to maintain two separate flows of energy at the same time. Whatever the reason, Jian's last-ditch effort succeeded. The assassin lost his focus as he stepped backward, struggling to keep his feet as he was pushed down the path.

Ignoring the flaring agony in his side, Jian stood and faced his enemy. He couldn't hold back anything against this opponent, not any longer. Summoning everything he had, he focused his power into each hand, using the patterns he knew would give him as much focus as possible. He pushed everything he had and everything he was into his outstretched palms and unleashed the first attack as the assassin found his balance. Jian saw the assassin's open hand gathering energy as well.

The assassin snapped his dagger and again energy sprang out of it, blocking and negating Jian's attack. But he wouldn't be deterred. Jian released the attack from his second hand, once again throwing everything behind it. The assassin finished focusing his energy just in time, releasing it just before Jian's attack would have blasted him from the mountain. This time, Jian wouldn't let up. He grunted and strained, forcing all of his will into the energy he projected at his opponent. He could feel his body and his soul acting as a conduit for the force they didn't truly understand.

Down the path, the assassin replied in kind, sweat streaming down his forehead. Jian continued pressing, pushing as hard as he could. If he relaxed for even a moment it might provide the assassin enough time to use the dagger. He needed to keep every bit of the assassin's attention on his attack. More importantly, he needed to win this duel. His left arm was burning from the effort of even being held up, and Jian wasn't sure how much longer he could fight at his full power.

He didn't even see the movement of the dagger, unwilling to accept that his own strength could be outclassed by such a tremendous degree. The actual energy the assassin expended wasn't that great, but focused by the razor's edge of the dagger, it was more than enough. The assassin's aim was true, and a tiny gash opened up in Jian's abdomen. It cut through his internal organs and sliced his spine clean in half as the energy cut through his body, burying itself in the mountain behind.

Jian immediately lost control of his legs and fell backward. He didn't even have time to curse before the assassin was in front of him. With nothing left to give, Jian had the opportunity to observe the assassin closely. He was pleased to see that the man also looked the worse for wear. His eyes were sunken in his sockets and sweat poured off his shaven head. Jian's strength had almost been enough.

But what really caught Jian's attention was the look on the man's face and the hatred that still burned in his eyes. Jian had only once before seen hatred like that, the hatred that had burned in his brother's eyes the day he'd been kicked out of the monastery.

Jian wasn't afraid to die. He had been raised as a warrior

monk, and acceptance of death was a necessary part of the process. His beliefs gave him strength, but that didn't mean he didn't have regrets. He thought of Lei, drinking his life away in the Old Goat below, oblivious to his brother's murder high above.

Jian saw his opponent quickly make a sign with one hand, and he was detached enough to think that the assassin really had excellent skill. His focusing gestures were as perfect as any that Jian had ever seen.

Jian tried to summon what energy he had left, but it was just the barest protection of a shield that had no chance against the onslaught of pressure that crashed into him. The path below his body buckled, the rock cratering and dropping him into it. The fall wasn't more than a foot, but it was enough for him to lose his focus and drop what little remained of his shield. The pressure crashed into him and once again he couldn't move, couldn't even breathe as his lungs and ribs collapsed under the forces crushing him.

The assassin had put away his dagger and with his other hand was making the signs that Jian recognized as being the Dragon's Fang. Despite being the intended victim of the attack, Jian couldn't help but be impressed by the strength of his opponent. To be able to exert such force with one hand while still having the mental focus and will to create a Dragon's Fang with the second was a truly impressive gift. Had his brother continued training, he might have been able to do it, but Jian wasn't sure. He watched calmly as the assassin completed the gesture and aimed it directly at his head. At least, he thought, it would be quick. He closed his eyes and focused on his brother's face, back in the days when they had both been happier.

Back when they'd been together.

I'm sorry, Lei.

1

———

Lei felt near his hip for the small bag he'd recently acquired. He was comforted by the sound of the pieces of silver clinking together. Every few steps he let his hand brush against the bag, just to reassure himself it was still there and still full. It had been too long since he'd had an honest job, and the silver would go a long way toward clearing some of the bad blood between him and many others.

The town of Two Bridges slowly settled into its evening routine. The sun was setting below the mountains, casting long shadows over the squat homes and shops. The heat of a late summer day had faded and a breeze had picked up, the cool air drying the sweat from Lei's skin. The mountains painted a majestic backdrop against the orange hues of sunset.

Such beauty made him uncomfortable, but he couldn't exactly explain why. His life felt out of place among such sights, as though he was an observer, a step out of pace with the rest of the world. Shaking his head at his own foolishness, he stepped through the door and into the tavern.

The Old Goat was as close to a home as he had. He'd given away almost every single one of his possessions to pay for drink, and although he still owned a small hut in town, he did little more than sleep there. What good were possessions anyway? He had learned the hard way how easy it was to lose everything. The simpler life was, the better.

His entrance into the tavern was met with an angry glare from the bartender. He'd hoped Daiyu would be working, as she took more pity on him. Truthfully, she was the only reason he wasn't beaten by the entire crowd of regulars every time he stepped in. Lei had only taken a few more steps before the bartender raised his hand. "Unless you've got money, turn around and step out. I won't have your trouble here tonight."

Flashing a mischievous grin, Lei pulled out the purse of silver and tossed it toward the barkeep. "That should be enough to clear my debt and keep me going for a while."

The bartender dumped the silver on the bar, and even in the dim light Lei could see his eyes darting over the pieces, mentally counting them with the speed that came from a lifetime of practice. Sliding his hand across the counter, the barkeep collected all the silver and returned it smoothly to the purse. "Looks like it will indeed. You thieving now?"

The bartender's tone made it clear he didn't care if Lei was. Ignorance was easy to plead, and the triads owned the place anyway. Silver was silver, and it was always good here. He was merely curious how much trouble the money might cause him.

Lei sat down at the bar, his typical stool empty as usual. "No. Cleared some trees for one of the old men up the mountain."

"That's a lot of silver." The barkeep was clearly skeptical.

Lei shrugged. "They were big trees."

The barkeep looked at him for a moment, and Lei wondered if he would accept the money or seize some other excuse to eject him. Ultimately, the money was too good to turn down, and Lei didn't usually cause *too* much of a ruckus. The bartender poured a tall cup of beer from the barrel behind the counter. "Enjoy, but I don't want any trouble."

"I've been good lately."

"And I would like to see you keep it that way."

Lei raised his glass toward the bartender and then poured half of it down his throat in one long swallow. Damn, but that tasted fine.

He had told the bartender the truth. He had finally found work, clearing trees and chopping wood for a new rice paddy high in the foothills. The work had been hard and miserable, but the old farmer paid well. Until that first pour of beer slid down his throat, Lei hadn't been sure if any amount of pay was worth the labor he'd provided, though.

His muscles were sore, and cuts, both small and large, covered his body. He'd worked from morning to night for several days, throwing himself into the work with an abandon he hadn't managed for years. He couldn't explain what had come over him, or the anger that he'd attacked the task with, but he did feel a hint of pride for finishing the job, the first he'd finished in some time. More than once, he'd been tempted to quit early and demand payment for the unfinished project.

He took another long pull from his cup and felt the influence of the alcohol as his mind and body started relaxing. Honest living was occasionally worth it, he decided.

He was on his fourth cup and starting to feel quite tipsy when a stranger came to the door. Lei supposed he wasn't a stranger, exactly, but he was the sort of man one never expected to see in a tavern, especially not a tavern with as poor a reputation as the Old Goat. The inn down the street was where upstanding citizens drank their beer and discussed the news of the day, as pointless as that was. The triads ran the Old Goat, so you only came here if you didn't want questions and didn't mind a fight or two.

The visitor's white robes stood in stark contrast to the dusty and grimy clothes that most of the patrons wore. Where others slumped over chairs or leaned back with their feet up, the monk's rigid posture was decidedly foreign.

Lei remembered the monk. He remembered all of them from his time in the monastery. This one was a few years older than him and had been a decent enough man. Too righteous for his own good, and more concerned with advancement than anything else in life, but decent enough. Lei and he had never gotten along, but Lei never really got along with anyone up there. What was his name again? Taio? Yeah, that sounded about right.

Taio locked eyes with him, and immediately, in the pit of his stomach, Lei knew what had happened. There was only one reason for a monk who wasn't his brother to come here and search for him.

His stomach churned and Lei suddenly felt sick, as though he was about to throw up all the beer he'd just finished. He tried to stand up and leave, but suddenly his legs refused to obey his commands. They felt as though there were no bones or muscles inside, just an emptiness ready to collapse at any moment.

The monk stepped towards Lei, his face a mask of serenity, the same mask that so many of the monks wore every time they left the monastery. The same mask that made so many people uncomfortable around the monks, as though they were different species trying to live in the same land. Lei knew better. He knew that the monks felt the same anger, sorrow, and laughter that the rest of them did, but the average citizen would never know it. Lei had never gotten the hang of managing his emotions, but Taio? Taio looked like he had mastered it.

Taio sat down on a stool two away from where Lei sat. He looked calm, but Lei's instincts, even after four beers, were sharp as ever. The training one received in the monastery never really faded, no matter how many years passed. He saw how Taio kept himself out of arm's reach, and he saw him pay particular attention to the sword hanging at Lei's hip.

Taio's gaze returned to Lei's face, and Lei tried to stare at him impassively, as though daring him to say anything about the sword.

The monk wisely decided to leave well enough alone. He opened his mouth to speak, but Lei stopped him. "Jian is dead, isn't he?"

Taio looked taken aback, but he quickly recovered, although his eyes narrowed in what appeared to be suspicion. "Yes. He died two days ago on his way back to the monastery."

A surge of emotions washed over Lei. He gripped his cup tightly, trying to force himself to act more disinterested than he was. "What happened?"

"He was killed."

Lei's head jerked around, all pretenses falling away. "Who was strong enough to kill Jian?"

Taio looked to the left and to the right, doing everything in his power to avoid Lei's piercing gaze. "We're still not sure who killed him. The evidence from where the body was found indicates a battle of two masters."

Lei turned back and sipped at his beer, to hide his emotions as much as to quench his thirst. Someone had killed his brother, and that meant they had to be good. Jian had been one of the best warriors in the monastery, if not the best, and that had been years ago. His trajectory had only gone up since then, if one believed what little news made it out of the mountains.

The monk cleared his throat, trying to get Lei's attention. "The abbot believes that it would be appropriate for you to come up for your brother's passing ceremony. It is scheduled for tomorrow night at dusk."

That surprised Lei as well. "The old man would let me return to the monastery?"

"Only for the ceremony, but yes. And you can't bring that," the monk said as he gestured towards Lei's sword. His gaze and tone of voice indicated that he thought the sword was little better than a plague.

Lei considered. Two days ago, he had felt his brother as he walked through the village. Jian had even come close to stepping into the tavern. But Lei hadn't wanted his company then and had pushed him away. That must've been right before he died.

A small seed of guilt tried to plant itself, but couldn't find any fertile soil in his heart. He was sad his brother died, but Jian had been dead to him for a long time now. This just made it final.

Lei called for another drink. "Tomorrow night? I'll need to check; if I'm available I'll see if I can make it. But I can't promise anything."

Taio's face twisted in anger. "Jian was your brother!" His voice was a loud whisper as he struggled to contain his emotion. "He was one of our best, and he deserves your final respects."

Lei took another swig of beer and laughed. Even after all these years, there still wasn't anyone better at angering a monk than him. He noticed that the rest of the room had gone completely silent, a considerable accomplishment. He'd seen conversations happening with fistfights in the background here. Lei might be no stranger to angry monks, but it was a sight that terrified most citizens, even those that frequented the Old Goat.

The bartender stepped in, trying to avoid disaster. "Lei, you promised me there wouldn't be any trouble."

Lei could feel his own anger boiling just below the surface, but he didn't dare let it escape. He had made that mistake one too many times already. He gave the bartender his best offended look. "I'm not causing any trouble. I'm just sitting here drinking my beer. It's probably what I'll be doing tomorrow night, too." He gave a pointed glance at the monk. Taio stood up and put a hand on Lei's shoulder.

Everywhere in the bar, there was a sudden intake of breath. Chairs scraped against the wooden floor as everyone backed away. Unlike the monk, the rest of the bar patrons were regulars, and they knew what came next. Lei didn't bother to look behind him. He knew the expressions that were painted on their faces. Each and every one of the regulars would be debating between going home or waiting for the fireworks to start.

Taio, to his credit, was observant enough to realize that the atmosphere in the room had abruptly changed. He looked around at the other patrons and back at Lei.

"You'll be wanting to take that hand off my shoulder," Lei said with a menacing growl.

He felt the monk summon his energy as he stepped

back. He made one simple focusing gesture with his hand and Lei could feel the energy focused there. The monk was only a heartbeat away from attacking.

"Are you sure you want to do that, Taio?" Lei stood up slowly and faced him. "I seem to remember the last time we scuffled, and it didn't end so well for you."

To his credit, Taio didn't back down. If his additional years in the monastery had taught him anything, it was courage. Or, more likely, Lei thought, the monastery made him believe that he was invincible. Apparently he hadn't learned anything from Jian's death.

He felt other energies gathering outside the tavern. He counted three others and he frowned. Four monks, just to get him to attend his brother's funeral? His alcohol-slowed brain struggled to find the reasoning behind that decision.

"The abbot asked us to escort you up to the monastery tonight," said Taio.

Lei scanned the room. The others didn't know what kind of danger they were in. Without the gift, it was impossible to know what the monk was doing. They didn't know that Taio and his three companions outside were essentially ready to destroy the building at a moment's notice. None of the monks individually were that strong, and Lei thought he could take them, but there was something more at play here. He just didn't know what it was yet.

"So," he said, "that's how it's going to be?"

Taio was starting to sweat. He'd been keeping his energy focused for some time now, and the effort had to be draining, but Lei liked to believe that some part of that sweat was fear of him.

He supposed it wouldn't be that bad to go see his brother's body off. More importantly, he didn't want to destroy the Old Goat. It was the only place that extended him credit anymore, and he liked the atmosphere. He looked around at the dingy interior, the chairs that looked like they were about to break, and the bartender who looked like he should've quit a decade ago. Well, maybe not the atmosphere. But the line of credit was nice.

"Very well," Lei said. "Lead the way."

Taio repeated, "You're going to need to leave the sword."

Lei shook his head. "That's between me and the abbot. We'll deal with that then."

Taio looked as though he was about to press the issue, but then he seemed to realize it was probably the best deal he was going to get. He nodded and released his energy gently. "Fair enough."

2

———

Fang stumbled into the small village, his side burning with every step. Not for the first time, he wondered if he had made a mistake in refusing to return to Two Bridges. His injuries, sustained while fighting the monk, were more severe than he realized, and there was a part of him that worried that perhaps he had gone too long without treatment.

No, he was certain he had made the right decision. Returning to Two Bridges was too risky. Granted, the town was large enough that he was fairly certain he wouldn't have been discovered, but after news of the monk's death reached the village he had little doubt people would be searching their memories for anyone unusual or out of place. Even though this small village was higher up in the mountains, he was sure it would be days, if not weeks, before news of the monk's death reached them. By then it wouldn't matter if others knew of his identity or not. All their plans would've come to completion.

Knowing he had made the right choice didn't make walking any easier, though. His master had told him that the monk was talented, but Fang had never expected him to be as strong as he was. For a few moments during that fight, he had actually wondered if the monk could win. He hadn't experienced that sensation in a very long time, not since he was a young boy at the monastery.

Inside the village, Fang got directions to the house of a local healer. According to the chatty elder, the healer was an older man, a widower who lived alone in a house apart from the village. Fang couldn't believe his good fortune. It was almost too good to be true.

Fang passed through the village without attracting much attention. Even though every step stabbed into his side, he was no stranger to pain. He masked his discomfort and walked through the village as though he had business farther down the road. He bowed politely to those he passed but said nothing. He gave no reason for anyone to remember his passing.

On the other side of the village he found the healer's house with little difficulty. It was a two-story building, large by the standards of the village. The walls of the house had been freshly painted, indicating that even though the man lived alone, he still cared about the state of his home. It boded well for his practice.

Fang knocked on the door and was let in by the old man himself. Despite his advanced age and graying hair, the old man moved easily. His hands looked strong, and as Fang watched the man carefully, he could see no trace of a tremor in the doctor's hands.

Fortune continued to be with him. The doctor had no one in the house. The housekeeper had already left for the day, and the silence in the house was complete.

"How can I help you today? Have the challenges of the road caused you problems?" asked the healer.

Fang didn't attempt to be friendly. Such efforts never came naturally to him, and his master had long ago encouraged him to give up trying. "You could say that." Fang lifted up his shirt, revealing his heavily bandaged torso underneath. The cut on his side was deep, and it hurt every time he breathed. Fortunately, the tightly wrapped bandage that he had wound around himself managed to catch and stop most of the blood.

The healer's eyes widened. "What happened?"

"I'm afraid I was attacked on the road. Although I'm capable of defending myself, this particular bandit was able to get past my defenses."

The healer gave a disapproving look. "The roads are not as safe as they once were. I've seen more cases like yours, although I will say that yours looks much worse than most. I suppose most travelers don't put up much of a fight, though."

Fang tried to measure the attitude of the man. "Why are the roads less safe? I thought this area was a peaceful one."

The older man shook his head. "I suppose it's still fairly peaceful, at least compared to the more chaotic environment near Jihan. But this region is also starting to deteriorate. The monks once walked the roads frequently, and their very presence helped keep us safe. But in the last few years, they have confined themselves more and more within their own walls. Those who would prey on the weak are getting bolder as a consequence."

Fang nodded and tried to control his reaction as the doctor gently cut away the bandages. The pain from the clotted blood tearing away from his skin was considerable, and even a few days later the wound was still leaking.

"You're not the first to say that. I travel frequently, and

the same seems to be happening around the empire. It is sad to see."

Their conversation came to a halt as the healer studied the wound on Fang's side. The healer's eyebrows furrowed in concentration. "That's a nasty wound. It looks like it's been open for a few days."

Fang addressed the question in the doctor's voice. "Yes. I was some days away when the attack happened, and it has been painful to move. I did not make it as soon as I would have liked."

The doctor gave a small shrug, indicating his acceptance. "Well, what's done is done. Did you bandage it yourself?"

Fang nodded. "As well as I was able."

"You did a fine job. It's likely that you made this easier for us both." The healer looked over the rest of Fang's torso, covered with various scars. "It looks like you've had some practice."

Fang kept his voice even. "It's been a rough life." He observed the healer carefully. The last thing he needed right now was a physician who asked too many questions before healing.

Fortune was with him once again. The man, although obviously curious, didn't ask any further questions. Instead, he began heating up the needle and gathering some thread. "I take it you're no stranger to this?"

Fang shook his head, and a few moments later the doctor began. The pain was impressive, and Fang gritted his teeth as the doctor sewed his skin back together. He could feel every jab of the needle and could feel the pull on his skin as the doctor brought the separated pieces of flesh back together.

By the time it was over, Fang had broken a small sweat.

He had no shortage of painful memories, but he believed this one would stick with him for some time.

When the healer finished, Fang stood up and slowly tested his mobility. He moved gently, trying to ensure he wouldn't accidentally tear the stitches open. He discovered that the healer had done a remarkable job patching up his body. He nodded his appreciation. There were few men who could've done it better.

As Fang began to put on his clothes, the healer launched into a practiced pitch. "Now, it's not my practice to demand money of people. But as you know, we need to pay the bills, and anything you can spare would be much appreciated."

Fang looked around the house, well furnished and well cared for. "You don't charge?" He gestured around the space, his question unspoken.

The older man gave him a delighted smile. "I have found that what we give to the world we often receive. Healing is its own reward, but there are people who have been able to give much in exchange for my services. But I'm as grateful for every copper as I am for every bag of gold."

Fang felt a twinge of respect for the stranger fate had introduced him to. It seemed he had found another who loved his craft as much as Fang loved his. There were few like them in the world anymore, it seemed.

With a quick, smooth gesture, Fang reached over, grabbed the old man's head with both hands, and gave one sharp twist. The crack was audible, but the old man didn't have time to realize what was happening. His eyes didn't even have a chance to go wide.

Fang caught the body before it could hit the floor. He picked him up and put him over his shoulder, surprised at how light the healthy old man was. After only a few seconds of searching he found the stairs and climbed them, then stood the man's body at the top and pushed it forward. The body tumbled end over end and sat at the bottom of the stairs. With that, Fang left the house, taking care to make sure no one saw his exit.

After he was a ways from the house, Fang stopped to test his movement again. In all of the activity, the wound hadn't opened one bit. The healer truly had been good at his work.

3

L ei convinced Taio, after no small amount of arguing, to let him finish one more drink before leaving. If he was going to climb up that cursed mountain again, he wanted to be good and drunk for it. The hike was no fun even under the best of conditions, and night had already fallen.

As they walked up the path that led to the monastery, the four monks formed a loose circle around Lei. His mind was too unfocused to think much of it, only grateful that each of their torches aided in lighting his way. The five shadows jumped and twisted as they slowly worked their way to the summit. The hike was every bit as miserable as Lei remembered. More than once his mind wandered the well-traveled paths of memory. How many times had he made this journey as a child? More than he could count, that was certain. But every time the past started coming back to him he pushed it violently aside. The alcohol helped.

Even so, at times he thought he could hear old voices on the wind, the monks in charge of his education lecturing him as he walked down the mountain with empty sacks and then again as he struggled back up with food. The past never quite left him alone.

Well over halfway to the summit, Lei stumbled into a small crater. If not for the monks standing close to his side, he would have fallen and his face smacked against unforgiving stone. Thanks to the monks grabbing his arms as he stumbled, he managed to keep his balance, cursing the lack of repairs on the path.

"You haven't done a very good job of maintenance lately, have you? Maybe you should get out more."

His remarks received nothing but silent glares, filled with more anger than he'd expected. Perhaps he'd touched a nerve.

He supposed the monks weren't great at conversation on their best days, and all of them were probably upset about what had happened to Jian. None of them seemed eager to talk. That was fine with Lei. Every time one of the monks spoke he felt a sharp pounding in his head and wished that he'd had enough sense to pound a few more drinks before making this journey, or fill a flask to bring with him.

As they climbed higher and higher, the air became colder. Even though it was late in the summer, the upper elevations never got warm, and night temperatures could be downright frigid. Lei stopped so that he could take a deep breath through his nose. The cold, crisp air of the mountain filled his nostrils and lungs and he breathed out a small sigh of pleasure. Although he had no desire to live this high ever again, the mountain air was something he had always enjoyed.

A bit later, the monastery came into view. The buildings were situated at the top of the mountain, the only habitation for miles. The monastery itself was surrounded by thick stone walls that rose in places to three times the height of a man. Lei and his companions were stopped at the gate, the monks on guard duty concerned about the sword that he carried.

"He can't come in here with that," the guards said. They made no effort to hide the look of revulsion on their faces.

"It was the only way we could get him to come without a fight. Call the abbot, please," said Taio.

The guard looked uncertain, and Lei was surprised they would be willing to disturb the abbot this late. Back in the day the abbot had always been early to bed, and it was a bold apprentice indeed who dared disturb his slumber. The very fact that they were willing to summon him meant he was likely still awake.

Lei tried to remember what the rites of passage for monks were like. In his time at the monastery, he had seen three or maybe four monks pass away from old age and had been involved in the rites himself. But outside of the basic theology he'd been taught, he remembered little.

The abbot appeared at the door shortly after the guard left to summon him. He looked at Lei with a wary eye. "I see that you're still managing to give Taio trouble," he said with a wry smile. The abbot looked much older than Lei remembered.

"Old habits die hard."

"You know I can't let you in here with that."

"I have no other place to leave it."

The abbot considered for a moment. "Would you be willing to entrust it to my care for the time that you are here?"

Lei didn't trust the abbot, despite the smiling face. He didn't trust any of them. But he was tired and the idea of bed was sounding more appealing with every passing minute.

He wouldn't win any fights, not with the abbot. Better to concede this one and go to bed than to be up all night arguing. He untied the sword from his belt and handed it to the abbot, who gave him a bow as though he'd received a holy relic. "Come in. I can see you are tired from your journey, and some rest will do you good."

They stepped into the monastery, and the stiff wind that had been their constant companion on the mountain was suddenly cut to a gentle breeze by the thick walls that surrounded them. It was almost pleasant.

Taio and the others escorted Lei to the guest quarters, a small building with four rooms and a small kitchen. It was actually nicer than the cells the monks slept in, and he was grateful for the courtesy. He'd only slept in the house once before, on his first night in the monastery, so long ago. He ran his fingers lightly over the walls, feeling the well-worn rock, smooth underneath his fingers. He couldn't help it. Despite all of his bitterness towards this place, there was still something about it that he loved. He appreciated the ancient history and the sense of peace that emanated from every wall.

A storm passed over Lei's face, his mood changing with it as he was attacked by memories. They could all go to hell. This wasn't the place for him and never had been. He would suffer through his brother's rites tomorrow, but after that he would leave and never return. That much, he swore.

He lay down on the bed, closed his eyes, and was asleep instantly.

The next morning, he woke to the sounds of monks practicing in the courtyard. As soon as he opened his eyes, he regretted doing so. Although the day was young and the sun was just beginning to peek over the horizon, the small slivers of light that penetrated his room were enough to give him a piercing headache. He remembered that he hadn't had any water to drink the night before, and all his problems would be compounded by the thin air. He groaned and rubbed at his temple, trying to push the pain out of his skull, to no avail.

It had been a long time since he had hurt this badly from a night of drinking. There was the night of the big barfight, but that had been less about the alcohol and more about the fists that had pummeled his body. He cursed the monks again for dragging him all the way up the mountain. He still had so much more money to spend at the Old Goat.

He took a few minutes to attempt to make himself more presentable, but eventually gave up. His clothes were ragged and worn and he wasn't sure a comb had been made that was strong enough to work its way through his long hair. It had been ages since he'd given any thought to his appearance, and he was angry that being in the monastery ruined his streak.

He stepped out of the guesthouse to watch the practice in the courtyard. The number of monks seemed to have diminished since his time there. Of course, there could be any number of explanations. Perhaps a number of monks were out on patrol, or maybe numbers were actually down. He watched their training with interest, memories of his own lessons coming to mind. Some of the kids he saw were good, with a natural inclination to the martial forms the monastery taught. If he was being honest, some of the children there could probably beat him in a fair fight.

Fortunately, he didn't fight fair.

Lei wondered what he was supposed to do for the entire day. If his memory of the rites was accurate, Jian's funeral wouldn't be until sunset, so he had a full day ahead of him.

As he stood there and watched the students switch to

grappling, his memory ran to his time with his brother, and he suddenly felt an urge to see Jian one last time.

A small, hateful voice in the back of his mind told him that it was wasted effort. His brother was dead and that was that. But Lei couldn't listen. Despite everything that stood between them, this would be the last time he would ever look upon his brother. Their rivalry was over, and if survival was victory, Lei had won.

With the outlines of a plan in place, Lei made his way toward the central building of the monastery, where the abbot lived and most of the duties of the monastery were taken care of on a day-to-day basis.

The abbot was already up and about, making him easy to find. Fortunately, he stopped bustling around the moment he laid eyes on Lei. The two of them approached one another warily, as if each was unsure whether he would be greeted as a friend or an enemy.

Lei was beyond caring. What happened in the monastery was in the past. That was all. But from the look in the abbot's eyes, he wondered if maybe the abbot thought differently.

The abbot was the one to break the ice. "I trust that you slept well?"

"I did. Thank you for your hospitality."

The abbot opened his mouth as if to say something more but then stopped. He tried again. "I'm sorry that we must meet again under such circumstances."

Lei shrugged. He would've been fine had they never met again. But there was no point in being rude. Some semblance of Lei's old training still held, deferring to the older man despite his recent personal convictions.

"May I see my brother? I would like a chance to see him before he is wrapped up for the ceremony."

The abbot's eyes fixed warily on him again, and Lei got the distinct impression that he was being judged. Did they somehow think Jian's death was his fault? The two of them hadn't even spoken in years. Eventually the abbot nodded and led the way down to the basement, where the stones kept the rooms cold year-round. Among its other functions, this dark cellar was where bodies were kept before the ceremony of passing.

The abbot stepped carefully down thick, wooden stairs that were worn smooth by the passage of thousands of feet over the years. More than one young monk had fallen down them while bringing food to the kitchen. Fortunately, today the stairs were dry, and the cool air of the basement eased the raging headache assaulting Lei's calm.

Passing through two more doors, they came to a small room with one long elevated table, the candle held by the abbot their only light. Jian was as still as the table upon which he lay.

Lei stopped just beyond the door, surprised by the tug of sorrow and anger as he looked at his brother's body. Jian was taller and stronger than he remembered, his well-defined muscles evident even in death. How many years had it been since they'd seen each other last? Lei was ashamed to admit he didn't even know.

He stepped forward, his eyes taking in the damage that his brother had suffered. Clearly, the fight had been brutal, evidenced by the fact his brother had been cut in two. Additionally, there was a nasty cut on one side of his torso that didn't look like any sword cut that Lei had ever seen. While the cut was interesting, it was nowhere near as interesting as the wound through Jian's head. The hole was small, smaller than Lei's index finger. He had never seen anything like it in person, but he knew what it was all the same. Any monk alive would recognize that attack.

Lei looked up at the abbot. "Jian was killed by the Dragon's Fang?"

The abbot nodded, his eyes never leaving Lei's face. "We believe so, yes. No one in the monastery has ever seen it performed, but it is the only logical explanation. There was no debris in the wound to indicate that it was created by a weapon."

"How many people even know the Dragon's Fang? That has to limit the suspects."

The abbot nodded slowly. "You're right. Here in the monastery, none of us can perform the technique. Besides being taboo, it requires a certain level of strength and precision that no one here possesses. Many believed it was a myth, until now. But the sixth sign clearly exists."

Lei continued looking down at his brother, forcing himself to remember what he saw. His brother deserved that much at least. "Do you have any suspects?"

"Yes. But that is not why I called you here. We will catch your brother's killer, have no doubt of that. You are here to grieve, not to investigate. We would be honored if you would light the fire tonight."

Lei considered the offer. As his brother's only surviving family, lighting the fire was an honor reserved for him, but he was still surprised that the monks had allowed him to return to the mountaintop.

The small, hateful voice raised itself once again, reminding Lei of how poor his relationship with his brother had been. But the way he figured it, lighting his brother's fire so that his spirit might pass into the afterworld was the greatest and last gift he could offer. He could never forgive his brother, but he could forget him.

THE REST of the day passed uneventfully. Lei was given permission to wander around as he saw fit, but after a short period of exploration he decided the monastery held little of interest to him. He had lived this all before in a previous life. The events and routines that would seem unusual or interesting to a visitor served as little more than reminders of the world he had been forced to leave behind.

Some of the monks he knew from his time at the monastery were willing to talk to him, but the conversations were short. He knew what they had become and what their daily lives looked like. There was little news he was interested in learning, and he suspected there was nothing they could say that would surprise him in the least. Likewise, he had little doubt they all knew he had taken to drink and working on random jobs down in the village. There was no mystery from either party to keep the reunions interesting. And more than a few monks looked as though they would rather see him anywhere but inside their home.

The memory of the monastery was long. He hadn't been inside its walls for years, but many of the faces and expressions he encountered were the same as the day the doors closed behind him the last time.

Despite the hostility that swam just beneath the surface of the monks' behavior, he was treated with the respect a visitor to the monastery could expect. By monastic standards he was fed well and lacked no comforts. In truth, it was the best he had eaten in some time. Nevertheless, he was eager to return to Two Bridges and resume his daily routine.

The pounding in his head was a stark reminder of what

he was missing. With the silver he'd given the barkeep, he would be able to drink for days, but there wasn't anything fermented to be found at the monastery. If only Taio and his companions had given him a little more time, he would've thought to bring some with him.

It was no matter, he thought. At the very least he would be able to return to the village by tonight or tomorrow morning. Then he could mourn his brother's death in his own way. Even the thought of a drink helped the headache recede.

Preparations for the funeral began late that afternoon. Without anything else to occupy his time, Lei volunteered to be part of the group assembling the pyre. Picking up and moving the heavy logs and branches quickly helped him to break a sweat and shake off the constant chill high up on the mountain. His help was gratefully accepted, even though many of the monks wouldn't meet his gaze.

After a time, it almost became a game for him. How foolish was it that they would hold on to the mistakes of his past for so long? To him, it defied all reason, and he enjoyed doing what he could to torment the monks that he assisted. He stared at them constantly, waiting for them to meet his gaze. As they worked, the monks attempted to steal glances at him, only to realize he was already staring at them. Their eyes darted back to the ground quickly, as though they'd been caught misbehaving. Lei laughed to himself every time.

After the pyre was created, supper was served, and Lei's spirits sank. After the meal was over the funeral would begin, and he would be lighting his brother's body on fire, releasing the soul within. His hands began to tremble and he put down his chopsticks so as not to betray his emotions.

He took a few shuddering breaths while he tried to control himself.

Fortunately, the other monks weren't paying much attention. They focused on their own meals and largely ignored him.

After supper, the abbot and the other monks gathered in the courtyard where the pyre had been built. As Lei approached, the abbot motioned for him to come near.

The service began as soon as the monks were gathered. As with any routine in the monastery, the funeral began with a round of rhythmic chanting of the monks. Lei debated whether or not to join in, but his lips moved freely and his tongue formed the sounds of their own accord. How often had he performed these very chants? There was a comforting familiarity to them, unlocking something inside of him he didn't even realize he still possessed.

When the chanting finished, the abbot stepped forward and addressed the assembled monks. "My brothers, one of our own was taken from us far too early. We know that the world wills its way, but as passengers on the journey we can hardly understand. Our faith gives us the strength to bear these difficult trials, but I don't find that it makes the loss of our brother Jian much easier to take.

"Often, at the end of a person's life, it is customary for us to speak of the wonderful attributes of that person. It is useful and beneficial for us to reflect on the traits that made a person's life worth celebrating and worth mourning.

"I don't know quite what to say about Jian. In so many ways he was the best of us. Not only was he incredibly strong, but he cared. He willingly gave every bit of his life to the monastery, a dedication that even I am not sure that I match. I have little doubt that had he lived he would have become the next abbot once my spirit passed on to the next realm."

Lei looked around, watching the other assembled monks giving slight nods of affirmation. Some had tears running down their cheeks. It figured that after everything, Jian would be so well loved. And what about Jian's younger brother? No one would shed a tear for him if he died.

"There's no overstating how hurt this community is by the loss of one of our leaders," the abbot continued. "Jian was the rock we could always count on to stand firm and point us in the right direction. More than once he came to me and persuaded me to see the world the way he did."

The abbot looked as though he was about to shed a few tears himself, and the cynic in Lei wondered if the tears were real or if they were just a well-rehearsed part of the performance.

"We know through our training and senses that our souls are connected in ways too complicated for us to understand. But we know it is a sin to return the body back to the dirt from which it came, and so through fire we release a soul to the other side. When that soul leaves, it takes a little bit of us with it. I know that today, a good part of my soul travels to the other side with Jian."

With that, the abbot finished his speech and looked out over the crowd to see how well his message had landed. Lei had to give the abbot credit. Even though he hated his brother, the speech had made him feel the loss of Jian. The abbot nodded to Lei, who advanced toward the pyre with his torch.

While Lei's right hand held the torch, his left hand wandered over his brother's sternum. Closing his eyes, he let his hand rest on his brother's body, feeling the faint energy of the soul within. There wasn't much left, but it would be enough. He gave a nod of approval to the abbot, who gave him permission to light the fire.

Without a second thought, Lei ran the tip of the torch around the wood his brother lay on. Thanks to the oil that had been poured on the wood, it lit easily, quickly becoming a bonfire that reached twice as high as Lei stood.

At first, Lei didn't feel anything. For all of the abbot's final words, he felt no different than if he was standing at any other fire.

There was no warning when the wave of grief washed over him and sent him to his knees. All of a sudden, it occurred to him that it was his brother's body on the fire, the last relative he had in this world. Possibly the last person that cared about him. Yesterday he had felt lonely, but now he knew that he was truly alone. There was no one left who truly cared for him, no one for him to turn to and seek comfort from. Even surrounded by monks, he felt as though he was the only person in the world. Tears broke through the mask he tried to maintain, and his shoulders heaved as he allowed the sobs to escape.

After a few minutes, he thought he felt a light yet comforting hand on his shoulder. He looked up, expecting to see the abbot, but no one was there. No one was within ten paces of him. The entire monastery was giving him the space to grieve. But the touch had felt so real, as if there had been someone there watching over him. The feeling was at once reassuring and comfortable.

Just as suddenly as the grief hit, it disappeared. There was no gradual fading, no residual ache. Just like that, it was gone, as though it had all been imagined. Even stranger, the feeling that he was alone also vanished. Lei felt more at peace and at ease than he could remember feeling at any time in his recent history.

He didn't know why he felt better, but for now he accepted it. He assumed there would be waves of grief that would come later, just as he had experienced when their parents were killed.

As soon as he felt it was respectful to do so, Lei turned around and left the funeral. There was nothing left of his brother's ashes, so there was little else for him to do. But as he approached the gates he realized that they were closed. That was unusual. The night was still young and he had hoped to return to the village that day.

His head complained, but he saw little reason to pick an argument with the monks. He would allow them to serve him breakfast tomorrow morning, and then he could take off to properly mourn the loss of his brother. There was a certain tavern down in Two Bridges that still needed his patronage.

4

—————

The journey to his master's house took Fang several more days. He was eager to return, but all the same he did not hurry. His mind was heavy with thoughts, and he was something of a slow thinker. He'd always believed the important questions in life should be answered in their own time, after due consideration. Nothing served that philosophy better than when he was out in the world, walking the roads with his mind empty, observing the grandeur of nature. Even though he rarely thought consciously about whatever problems were currently bothering him, a solution always presented itself by the end of a walk.

The journey itself gave him no reason to rush. Autumn was slowly coming, and at higher elevation some of the maples were beginning to turn from green to hues of orange and red. It would be weeks yet before the forests looked as though they were burning with color, but the first hints were already there.

He breathed the cool air deeply, inhaling the scent of the late-season wildflowers and the piney smell of the evergreens that clung to the shallow dirt of the mountains. Here, away from the stench of cities and towns, one could breathe freely.

He was excited about the near future. His master had been planning their actions for years, and Fang had trained harder than he ever had in his entire life to ensure that he could be an instrument of his master's plans. Perhaps now, with the final obstacle removed, he would finally be judged worthy of training directly under his master.

The home he eventually approached was a run-down shack deep in the woods, away from any well-traveled path. It was the sort of place no one stumbled upon unless they were looking for it, which was exactly the reason it had become their temporary shelter.

Fang knew that his master had homes in other places. Although much about his master remained a mystery, Fang understood that he possessed an uncommon degree of wealth. There was no way he could afford their project otherwise.

Fang took off his sandals and washed his feet before entering the hut. As decrepit as the building looked from the outside, the inside was spotless, mostly due to Fang's own efforts. The master couldn't be troubled with meager household chores. He needed time to study ancient texts and to compose letters to the others who followed his instructions. Fang had no idea how large the Order of the Serpent was, but he knew that his master was always busy, locked within his study. Fang imagined that he must be commanding hundreds, if not thousands, of loyal supporters. When all their strength was combined, no empire could stand against them.

Fang entered the house without knocking, but made sure to rap on the door to the study. Even though he couldn't sense his master, he assumed that his master could sense him. Still, it was good manners. The man's abilities were mysterious, and Fang had yet to fully understand them.

His master looked up when Fang entered. "I am glad to see you again, and well."

Fang's master was far older than he was. Although he had never said, Fang estimated that he was about sixty years old. His hair had long ago gone white, and he had a long, silver mustache. His master twirled that mustache thoughtfully as he studied his pupil, bowing before him.

"You're hurt."

Fang bowed more deeply as if to apologize. "I'm sorry. The monk you sent me after was much more talented and stronger than I suspected. It was a challenging fight."

"But you succeeded?"

Fang nodded. "He died from the Dragon's Fang."

His master's eyes widened just for a moment before they narrowed into hard slits. "I thought you hadn't mastered that technique yet."

"I do not believe that I have. My energy could still be focused more tightly, but my signs are sufficient for a weakened version of it suitable for combat. Without it, I'm not sure I could have won."

"Even using your dagger?"

"The monk didn't have the reaction I expected. There is no way of knowing now, but I suspect he had fought against an enemy with a weapon before."

The master silently absorbed all the information Fang reported. He made the younger man go through everything, asking clarifying questions whenever something wasn't clear. The routine was comforting and calming, and Fang learned something from every question, even though he had been the one who lived through the experience.

The practice was yet another area where he was still amazed by the abilities of his master. The man forgot nothing, and even after all the years of their acquaintance would bring up events and details that Fang had long forgotten, connections he never would have made. At times, Fang found the knowledge of his master's memory to be a relief. If something ever were to happen to him on one of his missions, he knew at least that his memory would live on in the mind of another.

When the report was done, Fang was dismissed. He stood up but did not turn to leave. "Master, may I ask a question?"

Fang thought he saw flicker of annoyance pass across his master's face, but it could have been a trick of the shadows in the darkened study. "Of course."

"Given my success on this mission, I was wondering if you might fully induct me into the Order of the Serpent and train me directly in your ways."

Fang had known his master since he was a young man. The master had found him on the streets, performing tricks with his energy to make a few coppers on the street. He had taken him in and given him the teachers and lessons he needed to thrive, but the master never instructed.

The master considered the request. "Not yet. I do believe that soon you will be made a full member of the order, but I do not believe you are ready to learn the techniques that I have to teach you. Mastery of the Dragon's Fang is an important step, but your journey is far from over. However, you should be very proud of your abilities. At this rate, I expect that you will be able to handle my direct teachings within half a year. But you must be diligent in your practice."

Fang's heart soared. To hear that he might have the

opportunity to train with the master himself was a true honor. He thanked his master profusely and bowed to leave.

The master spoke one last time. "Fang, you have done well. Thanks to you, we will bring this government and the monasteries to their knees, and they will never rise again."

5

Lei woke up feeling like a hammer was being taken to his head with every beat of his heart. The high-altitude sunlight shone through the narrow window in his room and his eyes blurred with tears as he tried to focus.

For a few moments, he struggled to remember where he was. His hands groped for a bottle or flask of anything that would ease the pain in his head, but his flailing hands struck nothing but empty air and stone wall. He cursed as his memories caught up with the present.

Outside he heard the sounds of the monks practicing, their feet stomping on the stone floor in perfect unison as they focused their energies. They sounded as though they had purposely gathered right outside his door, every stomp and shout meant only to increase his agony.

A loud knock sent shooting pains flashing inside his skull. His door opened and the piercing morning sunlight made him growl. He hadn't had anything besides water to drink for almost a full day now. How long had it been since he'd been sober for so long?

The door closed again, and as the light dimmed Lei

could see the abbot step in and take a seat across the small room. There was a smile on his face, as though he understood just how much adversity Lei was enduring and enjoyed watching his former student suffer a bit.

"Ahh, I can see you're finally awake. Some of the other monks expressed concern over your wellbeing, and I thought I would check on you once I felt you stirring."

Lei managed to work his way to sitting. "How touching."

"You've fallen a long way since you were a student here."

On another day, perhaps, Lei might have been more charitable. But not today, and certainly not now. "You're the one who exiled me."

The abbot, of course, wasn't perturbed by Lei's accusation. Even when he used to act up as a child, Lei had never succeeded in penetrating the abbot's legendary calm. "My memory of the events seems a little different. You were the one who broke the code we live by. I only did what was necessary."

Lei spat. "You had a choice. You sent me away."

The abbot had the wisdom not to respond. The past was in the past, and both of them could argue the entire day without moving the other an inch. They both knew it.

When the abbot spoke again, the tone in his voice changed. He was more genuine now, the hint of playfulness gone. "I am sorry for your loss, Lei. But I have to ask: did you kill your brother?"

Lei was so shocked by the question, he didn't even get angry. "Of course not. I hated him for what he did, but I would never kill him."

Suddenly, pieces fell into place, and a story took shape that he'd been too inebriated to see before. Now he understood why he'd been summoned in the manner he had, why they hadn't allowed him to leave. His stomach tightened as he realized the danger he had drunkenly walked into. There was a very real chance this monastery would become the site of his execution if he wasn't careful. "You think I did it."

The abbot shrugged. "You are the prime suspect. The Dragon's Fang is the sixth one-handed sign, an almost impossibly hard attack to master, and even practicing it requires an incredible amount of strength. More than most have. Given your tempestuous history with Jian, you can see why many would suspect you."

"Do you believe me?" Lei was surprised to find how desperate he was for the abbot to believe him. Some old habits died hard.

"I do. I never wanted to think you a murderer. I like to think you'd never sink *that* low."

Lei rubbed at his temples, trying to silence the pounding in his forehead long enough to put together coherent thoughts. "You have no idea how easy it is to fall outside of these walls."

The abbot stood up. "You may be right. But you've lived outside these walls you hate so much for years now, and even though you have the strength to succeed at many sorts of crime, you never have. That, and your reaction here today, tells me all I need to know."

"So what about me?"

"What about you? You never liked when I spoke gently to you, so I'll be straightforward now. Although I didn't want you to be responsible for your brother's death, it would have been far easier for us. Now, we know someone else is out there, someone not trained by the monasteries, strong enough to have mastered the Dragon's Fang. Hopefully you can see how that would be a significant concern. You can return to the Old Goat and drink the rest of your life away for all I care. The rest of us have an empire to protect."

Without even a goodbye, the abbot left the room and closed the door behind him, leaving Lei alone with his thoughts. Lei cursed his hangover, then noticed a water skin sitting next to the chair the abbot had sat in. Greedily, Lei took a long pull, the familiar cold, crisp sensation of mountain spring water threatening to pull him back to the past once again.

For a moment, Lei thought about staying, but then shook his head. He had tried that path long ago, and it was closed to him now. Better to return to the life he understood. He took another tremendous swig of water and collected his meager belongings.

Somehow, the stares he received on his way out of the monastery were sharper than before. He wasn't sure if it was his improved awareness, thanks to the lack of drink, or if the monks were actually upset that he was leaving alive. Within the walls of the monastery, the abbot's word was law, a lesson Lei had learned the hard way. If the abbot told the monks to release him, they were honor-bound to do so.

That protection felt terribly thin to him as he left the grounds. He knew his strength, but he was completely unarmed, and hadn't trained since he'd been thrown out the very same doors he now approached. He wouldn't stand a chance against the assembly arrayed against him.

Fortunately, he left without incident. His sword was returned at the gate. The stares of the monks were daggers in his back as he began the descent back to Two Bridges.

Almost immediately he began to feel better. The descent down the mountain was far easier than the hike up, and he was rewarded by gorgeous alpine views with every turn. Climbing up in the dark, then hiding behind the high walls of the monastery, had prevented him from enjoying the majestic snow-capped peaks off in the distance. The monastery was high, but it was on the summit of one of the lower mountains. The higher ones were mostly inaccessible.

As soon as he was out of sight of the walls, Lei paused to take in the panorama. He breathed in the fresh pine air and couldn't help but smile. Part of him felt guilty that he could feel such peace so soon after his brother's death, but the limitless view of the valley below and the mountains above was as intoxicating as any drink.

He continued down the path once he had his fill of the sights. Despite everything he'd just been through, he felt a lightness that translated into his gait, his walk almost becoming a skip at times as he traveled back toward the village.

His positive attitude dissipated immediately as he turned a wide corner in the path. There were signs of destruction everywhere, and his first thought was that he must have been mighty drunk not to notice the damage on the way up. Then his memory dug up the moment he tripped and was caught by the other monks. Looking at the depression in the path, Lei knew his brother had died here.

An acute sense of shame turned his cheeks red, and he was grateful no one else was on the path to observe him. This was where his brother had died, and he had noticed nothing. He had made a joke about road repairs.

Lei collapsed to his knees, momentarily overwhelmed by the flood of emotions. He hadn't felt this much since, well, since he'd been kicked out of the monastery. He'd been so angry at first, but the constant stream of drink had blunted the anger from a sharp knifepoint to a dull ache always sitting in the back of his mind.

Sober, he was angry again, but it was more than that. It felt as though a blade had been driven deep into his stomach and ripped upward through his heart, and the feeling was so strong he actually glanced down to ensure that his entrails weren't sliding out of him.

He breathed fast and hard through his nose, seeking desperately the peace he had felt just a half mile up the trail. But it was nowhere to be found, and his first instinct was to run down the rest of the path, dive into the Old Goat, and drink until his recent line of credit ran out again.

Lei was on his feet and several steps down the path before he remembered the shame he'd just felt. Drinking would allow him to hide from it, but he knew from experience it wouldn't make the feelings disappear. He stopped walking and turned to face the scene of the fight.

Even a single glance told him one indisputable fact: two masters had fought here. Jian had always been talented, and if his strength had always trailed behind his little brother's, his skill had made up the difference. In the years since he had seen Jian, Lei could tell his older brother's skill and strength had both grown. There was no other way to explain the tremendous damage he saw.

Lei squatted down in the middle of the devastation and let his eyes roam the scene freely. At first, his eyes were only drawn to the blood that had congealed on the path. There was a fair amount, and it kept drawing his attention even though it told him little that was useful.

He made himself remain still and gave his eyes and mind time to discover what other evidence he could find. There was plenty to be had.

Both of the warriors had been powerful. The depth of

the craters and the extent of the damage made that obvious, but it was apparent in other ways as well. The path up to the monastery tended to accumulate gravel and dust, but now it was almost completely clear for dozens of paces in each direction. Attacks had been blocked and deflected, and the resulting energy had effectively cleaned the path.

Lei stood up and walked toward the edge of the path, where an outcropping of rock had been sheared neatly in half. He ran his fingers over the cut, noticing how sharp it was. Understanding hit him sharply. This, perhaps more than any other piece of evidence, had been why the monks and the abbot had suspected him. The only way to make a cut this sharp was with the assistance of a weapon, and the monks were never armed. No matter how many years passed, the actions of his past would continue to haunt him.

When he saw the hole in the rock, his breath caught in his throat. The hole was small, not much bigger than one of his fingers. He put his eye to it, amazed by how smooth it was. This was the result of the Dragon's Fang, a move so dangerous no monk was even allowed to study it.

Lei cursed and stood up straight. His mind wandered, and for a moment, he felt like he could replay the entire battle, heartbeat by heartbeat. It was as though he had been here. He felt the panic and the confidence his brother must have felt, and as he closed his eyes, he wondered if he was Lei or Jian.

He shook his head violently and opened his eyes. Just like that, he was back, the man he had always been. The path was quiet, deserted for miles, most likely. The monks would be holed up inside their walls as they often were, and there was no reason for anyone from the town to make the journey up.

The experience shook him. Was this what grief felt like?

He'd never experienced the same when his parents died. For all their animosity, he and Jian had been close once.

He attributed the sensation to a lack of alcohol. The faster he could get to the Old Goat, the faster he could put his brother's murder behind him.

6

Fang dripped sweat as the wood burned around him. The sun scorched the land, reminding everyone that fall hadn't come quite yet. Fang imagined today was one of those days where everyone wanted to rush inside or hide in the shade in a desperate effort to remain cool.

Fang wasn't so weak. He stood, dressed only in his smallclothes, in a tent he had designed solely for training. As tents went, it was relatively small, but it was sufficient for his needs.

He had sealed all of the entrances and windows except for a hole near the top to let the smoke out. He built a perimeter of hot coals, ensuring they remained far enough away from the canvas of the tent so as not to spread fire. As the unbearable heat in the tent built up, Fang began his daily training.

Memories of his last battle still haunted him. Obviously, his master was stronger, but Fang had never seen what his master was capable of. He wasn't worthy, not yet. Although Fang possessed the proper humility in regard to his own instruction, he had always believed himself invincible against the monks. In the limited encounters he'd already fought, it had never been a fair fight. The monks, for all the awe the people held for them, were weaklings, merely dabbling in a power they didn't understand.

Jian had been different. His master had warned him that Jian was well regarded, but defeat had never entered Fang's mind. What could a single monk do against him?

Only after the battle finished did Fang realize how close he had come to losing. Now, in the presence of the master he felt such respect for, that feeling of near-defeat became acute.

His solution was what it had always been. He pushed himself harder. Until he proved himself worthy of his master's training, he could only train himself to the breaking point, over and over. Sweat poured down his shaven skull and burned his eyes as he held a perfect handstand, lowering his head to the ground and then pushing back up. Tremors ran up and down his arms, but he refused to lose his balance and refused to quit. He felt the top of his head touch the dirt and he pushed again. His head came up, but no matter how hard he fought, he couldn't get his arms to straighten. With a final, vicious grunt, Fang collapsed to the ground, careful to avoid the coals.

Ignoring the dirt clinging to him, Fang stood up and worked his way through his more complex forms, the movements almost second nature to him. That familiarity was dangerous. With expertise came a lack of focus. Every time he trained, he imagined it was his first time with a new move, approaching the task like a beginner. His entire body already burned from the combination of heat and exertion, but he demanded perfection. If his pose was off, or if he lost his balance even for a moment, he returned to the beginning of the sequence.

This late into his morning of training, it took him several tries, but eventually he completed the form to his satisfaction. He sat down and crossed his legs, the coals emanating waves of heat all around him as he forced his breath through his nostrils. He began making the signs of his various attacks and defenses, beginning with the most basic shields, then moving to his one-handed signs. He worked both hands at once, weaving defenses with one while doing attacks with the other. Then he would switch.

He completed the round with the Dragon's Fang. He felt the way his energy gathered, wrestled into a tight point, focused enough to punch through any shield or obstacle. Pride coursed through him, knowing he could complete the sixth sign even under these conditions. Fang gently released the energy, careful not to accidentally unleash it. There was no knowing how far the attack might travel.

The Dragon's Fang complete, he stood up and began the whole routine again.

He wouldn't be defeated, ever.

AFTER A QUICK SPLASH in the freezing mountain stream, Fang made his way to his master's cottage. The man was there, deep in meditation. Fang couldn't feel the man's energy, which made him all the more intimidating. If his master decided to lash out, Fang wasn't sure he'd even feel the attack coming. The skill of hiding one's strength was among the first he planned on learning once he was accepted as a full student.

The master opened his eyes. "How was your training?"

Fang bowed deeply. "Good, but I will continue to

improve. I was only able to complete four cycles. On the fifth, I was no longer able to form the Dragon's Fang."

He wasn't sure if the master would be pleased or upset by his progress. Fang had noticed over the years that his master's praise wasn't based on objective progress. Rather, Fang liked to believe he was given exactly the wisdom he needed when he needed it.

"Very good, Fang. I have spoken with the other members, and we agree that upon completion of your next trial, you will be awarded membership into the order. This next trial may prove to be one of your greatest yet, but we all have every confidence in you."

Pride, similar to that he felt when he successfully formed the Dragon's Fang, flushed his face. "I will not betray your trust, master."

"I know. There is an object, several days away from here, which I must ask you to retrieve. It is the last weapon that the monks possess that poses a threat to us. If you obtain it, every path forward becomes victorious. Do you understand?"

"I do. What is this weapon?"

His master stood up from his meditation cushion and walked to his desk. After a brief moment of searching, he found the paper he was looking for. He brought it over to Fang. "This is the last known drawing of it. It has been almost a hundred years since it was last seen in public."

Fang took the paper from his master, holding the delicate material more gently than a newborn. He frowned. "This looks like nothing more than a heart." He had dozens of questions but held his tongue. Experience told him his master would let him know everything that was necessary. Questioning the master was always a risky proposition.

Almost weekly, Fang inquired too deeply and was forced to endure strict punishments.

Fortunately, today was not one of those days. His master nodded. "It is a heart, but it is much more than it looks." Without even the slightest movement that Fang could detect, a long, thin needle appeared in his hand. Fang tried to crush his fear before the master could notice, but failed. The master smiled grimly as he pointed the weapon at the paper.

"See here? A normal heart has four chambers. This one only has three."

"What is it?"

"The monks call it the Silent Heart. It once beat in the chest of a great warrior, but when the monks killed him, they discovered the heart had certain... properties. They preserved it, but the location has been kept closely guarded. I'm not even sure many monks know where it resides. However, it is the only weapon the monks might obtain that could stop us. You must retrieve it first."

"What does it do?"

"It is difficult to say. There are many rumors and legends about it. All I know is this: until I have the opportunity to study it firsthand, you must not allow any of your power to channel through it. Do you understand?"

Fang nodded, and suddenly the needle was at the edge of his eye. He hadn't even seen it move.

"I need to hear you say it."

"I understand."

The master moved the paper, and when Fang glanced back for the needle, he was surprised to find it wasn't there any longer. He knew he was the master's top apprentice, but that never meant he could rest easy.

"Good," said the master. "Now, here is what I've found so

far about where the heart is kept. Although your plan will change as you learn more, I do have some ideas to get you started."

With that, the two of them bent over a pile of papers and maps, planning the most difficult theft Fang had ever attempted. A theft, he realized, where any mistake would almost certainly kill him.

7

At the bottom of the mountain, Lei felt an overwhelming reluctance to head back into town, a feeling he couldn't quite explain. Somehow, the idea of returning to the Old Goat, as comforting as the idea sounded, made his stomach queasy, as though he'd had a bad piece of meat for breakfast.

By pure chance, his gaze fell upon on a small path that broke off from the main road up to the monastery. Although he had passed the overgrown trail hundreds of times in the years he'd eked out a living in Two Bridges, he'd not followed it since leaving for the monastery. Before, even glancing at the path had made his heart race and his fists clench. Now, when he looked at the faded dirt trail, thick with nettle and new growth, he felt nothing at all.

On a whim, he pushed aside the overgrowth that obscured the entrance to the trail, his feet walking the rocky and hazardous path as though they knew each step by heart, as though he hadn't spent the better part of a decade ignoring the trail. His mind split between memory and the present, and at times he thought he could almost hear the echoes of laughter from years ago.

When he stopped, he stood in a clearing, perhaps thirty paces in diameter. The maple trees that had been old ten years ago had only grown thicker and taller since the last time he'd visited. The trees surrounded the open space like an army about to overwhelm its enemies, branches wide enough to stand on looming high above him to provide shade.

He remembered the center of the clearing being sunnier on days like today. But he supposed nothing stayed the same. The world, like the trees around him, grew and aged, overshadowing what had once been bright.

When he and Jian were younger, this clearing had been their secret spot, their place to hide from the world. They had played and fought and talked for entire days here. Looking back, Lei was certain their father had known about the clearing, but had allowed them the illusion of privacy.

The thought of their childish sparring sessions brought a smile to his face, and suddenly his reality shattered into mirror-like fragments. He was in the clearing, but he seemed to occupy several different times at once.

In one shard he fought Jian, their good-natured sparring quickly devolving into a fight with bloody noses and cut lips. When the fight finished, they tended each other's injuries and promised not to tell their parents.

In another shard he heard the shouts from the village, the residents struggling to find the brothers and deliver the news of the accident.

And he was also there the day after, right after he'd seen his parents' bodies. He and Jian were so small, huddled against each other as the sky above threatened more rain. He shuddered, unable to control his grief.

Finally, he returned to the present, finding himself on his knees, tears falling down his face. He wiped them away, trying to remember if he had cried when his parents died. He should have, even if he thought he needed to be strong for Jian. They'd been found by the monks not long after, their powers awakening a few months after the tragedy.

Again, the Old Goat and its comforting embrace called to him, a song that he rarely ignored. Perhaps Daiyu would be tending bar, and at this moment, Lei figured she was the only face that would be sympathetic. She would understand, if anyone did. Perhaps she'd even give them a chance again. He knew it was a dream, but he imagined going back to his place with her after her shift was over. He would like that.

But as soon as he stood, the grief that had weighed on his heart passed like a spring storm giving way to clear skies. What was happening to him? Ever since his brother's body had been claimed by the flames, Lei had felt different, like a stranger in his own body.

Thinking of the times they had sparred in this clearing made him think about his forms, drilled into him by endless repetition a lifetime ago. He was barely aware of taking the first stance of the first form he was ever taught, but he settled into it as though he'd been training just the day before.

The first move came easily enough. He stepped forward, his right fist striking forward as his left came back into the ready position. His right fist came down in a block as he snapped his body around and stepped back in the direction he'd just come from. Within seconds, his body was moving through the motions, punching, kicking, and blocking with smooth, practiced ease.

When the form was finished, Lei frowned. As good as

that routine felt, there was something wrong. He *shouldn't* be that good. His balance and precision were as fine as they were in his final days in the monastery, if not better. After years of drinking, that couldn't be true. He should have stumbled over his own feet and eaten dirt at least three times.

Curious now, he moved into the second form he'd been taught. The first two moves felt awkward, but as his conscious mind fell away, his body remembered. He was powerful.

Lei looked at his hands, uncertain that they were his own. The third form would tell him for sure. It was the first taught to the monks that incorporated the signs that focused one's energy. He hadn't dared form the signs more than a handful of times since his expulsion, and the methods, both mental and physical, took years to comprehend, even at a basic level.

As he flowed into the form, his fingers danced together. He formed the first sign for a shield, then launched a basic two-handed attack using the first sign. In his childhood, he'd been able to knock a wooden dummy back about five paces with the attack. His strike today, aimed at a small sapling growing in the center of the clearing, snapped it clean in half.

Lei shook his head, dumbfounded. He hadn't trained for years, and somehow he was stronger than ever, his control far superior to even his best days at the monastery. He pinched his inner forearm to ensure he wasn't asleep.

His hand traveled down to his sword. The blade had been drawn a handful of times in the past few years, but it had never been used. Its presence alone had always been sufficient to deter would-be assailants. And he'd certainly never tried to focus his power through it. His refusal to do so was the only reason he was still alive. Of that, he was certain.

Lei didn't dare, but his hand seemed to have ideas of its own. It grasped the sword and pulled, the well-maintained blade easily sliding free of its sheath.

He stared at the sword. Even though everything else in his life had fallen apart, this was the one object he had always kept pristine, had never considered selling for drink. The edge was razor sharp and the metal reflected hints of sunlight breaking through the leaves above.

The sounds of the world faded around him. Lei's curiosity, which had always led him around by the nose, wouldn't rest until he tried. He told himself it would be his final test. With one fluid motion, he snapped the blade into a high position, holding it over his head, parallel to the ground.

Lei didn't need much energy. The focus of the blade would be more than enough. He focused the smallest amount of his power into the blade and felt the sword respond, jumping to life in his hands. It was only an illusion, but a powerful one.

How fine had his control become? He chose a branch, no thicker than his wrist, about thirty paces away. He snapped the blade towards it, releasing his energy at just the right moment.

Energy couldn't be seen, but it could be felt by those who possessed the power. His aim was true, and the focused energy cut through the branch without even slowing. Twenty paces later it buried itself into a tree, cutting deep but stopping completely.

Lei sheathed the blade in one smooth motion, the only action he could take to prevent his jaw from dropping wide open. He walked toward the downed branch, holding the clean cut to his eye to inspect it. It was every bit as sharp as the cut on the rock far above him, but the energy hadn't gone too far, fortunately.

That shouldn't be possible. Not at all. He looked at his own hands, suddenly afraid of them.

He left the clearing quickly, almost running toward the Old Goat.

He really needed that drink.

ALTHOUGH HE HAD ONLY BEEN GONE a couple of days, it felt like a lifetime. Had it just been two days ago he had walked through these very doors, flush with new earnings? He felt like a different man now.

As he had hoped, Daiyu was tending the bar. She was perhaps the most beautiful woman Lei had ever met. Her beauty, at least in his eyes, went deeper than her perfect face and strong body. Her spirit, too, was unmatched for miles around. For a time, he had managed to court her. He would even say they had been in love. Perhaps they still were, but it didn't matter.

Those days together were the happiest that he could remember since the monastery. When he was with her, he drank less and worked more. She was in deep debt with the local triad, a curse inherited from her long-dead parents, and together the two of them had made progress in paying it off. But nothing he touched lasted.

Their relationship had always been tempestuous. Lei was prone to angry outbursts, and Daiyu alternated between being cold as ice and hot as fire, as the mood suited her. There had been love, but too many obstacles. Daiyu wanted out more quickly, and her determination to buy her freedom overwhelmed their chance at a relationship. At least, that was what Lei told himself.

Lei suspected a darker truth. He hadn't been strong enough to keep her. She needed a partner with a will equal to her own, and Lei, at least back then, had not been that man. When their relationship became difficult, he didn't work harder. He had turned to drink, as he always did when life became more difficult than he wanted to manage.

The relationship had ended, but they still saw plenty of each other. Daiyu had risen through the ranks of the triad and was now running the Old Goat. And the Old Goat was the only place that gave him credit, in no small part because of Daiyu. While their relationship couldn't be honestly described as warm, it was more than he had with anyone else.

She noticed something in him right away, her eyes studying him with unusual intensity the moment he stepped through the door. The tavern was empty except for two regulars, already sleeping loudly in the corner. Lei felt a surge of disgust. It was barely noon. Then he remembered his own naps on those very tables, naps that had often started earlier. Who was he to judge anyone here? In his own memory he had always been better than that, even if he suspected his memories were lies.

Daiyu's eyes never left him as he walked in. Her senses, honed from a life of survival on the streets, were as sharp as the sword he carried, and she used them just as effectively. He'd never known a more competent woman. When they were together, she had taken care of him more often than he repaid the kindness. Her voice was sharp, with just a hint of curiosity underlying it. "You're sober."

"Hopefully not for long. Beer."

She poured him a cup and slid it towards him, some of

the precious liquid spilling over the edges. He grabbed the cup greedily and brought it to his lips, eager for the comfortable numbness he knew so well.

But before he could take his first sip, a sudden revulsion came over him. He stopped the cup, held it just in front of his face for a moment, then put it softly back down. As he looked at the beer his stomach churned, rebelling at the thought of drinking it.

Daiyu's gaze never left him. He glanced at her, suddenly unsure of himself. Then a wave of hunger washed over him. He couldn't remember being that hungry for months. "Do you have any food?"

Without a word, she turned to the kitchen and came back a few minutes later with a steaming bowl of soup, filled with vegetables, meat, and noodles. He didn't even glance at his beer as he devoured the entire bowl. Out of habit, when he was finished he reached for the cup, but again, he felt no interest or desire.

Finally, Daiyu broke her observant silence. "Are you well?"

Lei picked up the cup and swirled the beer around, watching foam rise to the top. The sight, which had entertained and excited him for years, held nothing for him now. "I don't think so. I don't want this."

Daiyu's face was the very picture of disbelief. "You don't want beer that you've already paid for?"

He met her disbelief with his own. "No."

"Do you want me to call a healer?"

He knew she was mocking him. Her words were still sharp, and for the first time, he heard the hurt behind them. He searched his memory, trying to understand. Weren't they still close? He had thought so, but now realized perhaps he was wrong about that.

Something was wrong with him. Everything was just slightly off, as though he had turned his head sideways quickly and the world had never quite righted itself. He needed to make it right again.

He needed to find the man who had killed his brother.

At first, the thought had been a quiet one, one of a hundred racing through his head. But like a well-planted seed, it took root in his mind and suddenly exploded into bloom. As soon as he thought it, it was all he could think of. But why? He couldn't care less who had killed his brother. That was a problem for the monasteries.

He stood up and met Daiyu's gaze. Her long, dark hair was still gorgeous, and he wished he could remember what he had done to cause her to look at him with such anger. "I'm sorry, Daiyu. I'm sorry for everything. I'll see you soon."

He didn't expect her to accept his apology. If she had nursed a grudge against him since they broke up and been forced to see him almost every day, the damage would take time to undo.

But first, he had a compulsion that needed to be addressed, one he didn't fully understand. Somehow, he believed his life wouldn't be right until his questions were answered.

He needed to speak to the monks. It was time to make them talk.

8

———

Fang studied the compound below his perch with interest. As his master had predicted, the journey from their hideout to the residence had taken four days. Fang, conditioned as he was to long journeys on the road, covered more distance than the average traveler. He awoke early in the morning, started out at a fast walk, and didn't really stop until night had fallen. Still, it was impressive that the Silent Heart was so close. Although his master would never say, Fang suspected he had planned their location and the timing. In all the years he'd known his master, he'd never known the man not to have a plan.

Their good fortune was anything but for the monks. Fang didn't know what powers the object held. His master had been hesitant to tell him even the rumors, and his trust in him was absolute. He had only been warned not to channel his energy into the object and not to be afraid of it. The second command had only come as he'd been leaving, and Fang still puzzled over the meaning. Why should he fear a heart from a long-dead warrior?

His best guess was that the heart contained some

tremendous power. He was honored that he had been the one selected, that he had been found worthy by the order.

Stealing the relic wouldn't be easy. His master had forbidden him from using either the Dragon's Fang technique or any of his weapons. This way, it would look like the heart was stolen by a monk, and his master wanted the monasteries to suspect one another, sowing discord before their final fall. Although the prohibitions made the task more challenging, Fang almost giggled with childish delight as he imagined the monks accusing one another over nothing.

The man who possessed the Silent Heart was a minor noble. He was related to the emperor in some way, but Fang couldn't be bothered with the details. Once the monasteries fell in the glorious revolution, the nobles would soon follow. Why bother learning about a dead man?

For a minor noble, the man certainly protected himself well. Fang counted no fewer than eight guards patrolling the grounds. He suspected others were inside, but there was no easy way to see into the house without being spotted. He'd have to improvise as the evening began.

Fang took a thin leather cord and tied his dagger to its sheath. In the heat of combat he might attempt to draw the weapon, and this would prevent him from giving himself away. Then he donned a mask that covered everything but his eyes and nose. He might be outnumbered, but his opponents were outmatched.

His plan, such as it was, was straightforward. He would look for opportunities to kill a single guard at a time, but once the alarm was raised, he'd head straight for the house. Although he couldn't be sure from this distance, he didn't feel the presence of any monks, which meant this part of the task was relatively easy.

The residence sat outside the borders of a nearby village, surrounded by a forest Fang imagined had been planted just to provide the seclusion the noble was looking for. The home itself was two levels tall. The foundation was stone with painted wooden walls above. The sloped roof came to a point that towered over the nearby trees. Perhaps, Fang thought, if he had enough time he would climb the roof tonight and look out over the forest. He imagined the view was spectacular.

The space around the house had been cleared for well over a hundred paces. The grass was kept short and the guards remained constantly vigilant. Fang snuck to the edge of the clearing, hiding behind a tree as he more closely observed the guards.

They roamed in pairs, one group always in view of the group behind it. The area was lit by tall torches, burning brightly and eliminating any possibility of stealth. Fang sighed. He had hoped to winnow the numbers down a little before beginning, but as soon as any pair fell, the others would immediately sound the alarm. Despite his strength, he had been taught caution as well. There was no point in fighting more enemies than needed.

A few more minutes of waiting confirmed that he'd never have a better opportunity. He made a sign with his hand, focused his power, and aimed at one of the groups. He targeted one farther away, hoping to knock them down while he came in and killed the pair closer to him.

His aim was true, and the pair that had just come into sight went down. If he was lucky, perhaps he'd cracked or broken their ribs, but at this distance, using only the second sign, it seemed unlikely. The techniques he was limited to simply weren't as effective as the ones he was capable of.

Fang broke from the tree line as the guards came to alert.

Fortunately, the pair immediately in front of him didn't reach awareness quickly enough. He made the first attacking sign with each hand, feeling the energy swelling just beyond his palms. The guards were just turning around when he released the pent-up energy. At this range, the spells slammed into their chests and collapsed their lungs and ribs. Not a pretty way to go, but the dead didn't much care.

Should he break straight into the house or deal with the rest of the guards? He could make an argument both ways, but decided he would be safer if the guards on the grounds were dealt with first. They were converging on his location, but Fang didn't want to fight all six at once. He sprinted toward a lone pair, grinning as they drew their swords.

He formed the first shield sign with one hand and the first attacking sign with his other. Unlike when he'd fought the monk, the first signs were more than powerful enough against these weaklings. One guard swung his blade, a clean cut aimed right at Fang's neck. Fang blocked the strike by releasing his shield. From the guard's perspective, his blade had been halted in mid-swing, and he froze in confusion. Fang put his other hand next to the guard's face and snapped his neck with the blast.

The second guard of the pair was more fortunate. Fang had used up both his moves on the one guard, so he was unarmed as the second guard attacked. The guard's sword glinted in the moonlight as it came up, and Fang stepped into the attack.

The guard didn't react fast enough. He brought the sword down, but Fang was already inside his guard. Fang grabbed the guard's wrists and pulled him to the ground, and the sword slid away in the grass. Fang wrapped his hands around the guard's head and gave a twist, resulting in a sharp crack.

As he stood up, he instinctively dove toward the sword on the ground. He stopped himself just in time. The monks, curse their souls, would never resort to steel. Using the weapon would have made his life much easier, though.

The three final guards came at him, yelling until their voices were hoarse. Apparently one of the guards Fang first attacked had suffered injuries grave enough that he couldn't rise, making Fang's job a little easier. He was also assisted by the fact that the guards were running at him in a rough line, hoping to reach him at the same time and utilize the advantage of greater numbers. Fingers and mind worked together to weave his power into a new shape. Fang focused his will, pouring more of himself into the move. When he felt it was ready, and when the guards were close enough, he pushed his hands forward and released it.

The shape of the attack wasn't very thick, the force concentrated into a space less than the width of his wrist. But it was wide, and had it been visible, it would have looked almost like a large crescent moon. The guards couldn't see it and didn't stand a chance. The blast struck them all, snapping sword, armor, and bone as it passed. None of them would be rising soon, or ever again.

Not knowing how many guards were left in the residence, Fang didn't stop to savor his victory. He made it through a side door before anyone else arrived to help.

The residence was quiet. He couldn't hear footsteps or shouting anywhere. He frowned, sliding open some of the rice paper doors randomly to expose empty rooms. Not just unoccupied, but completely empty, lacking even the most rudimentary decorations or furniture.

The house could be a trap or a test, but either way, his mission was to obtain the relic. His master had highlighted areas of the house where the Silent Heart was likely to be, so Fang began his search with those places. The first two rooms he tried were also empty, and his senses were on full alert. An unsettling feeling sat in his stomach, and his hairs stood on end.

For a moment, he wondered if there was anyone else in the house. There were still no footsteps, no shouts or cries. He paused his search, allowing his breathing to settle. Still, he couldn't hear anything.

Then he felt another power in the house, strong and vibrant, standing in the middle of the next area he was planning to explore. Only one explanation made any sense, and Fang walked toward the other energy.

He slid aside the door and stepped inside, his hands hidden behind his back. One hand began focusing his power as a shield, while the other made the Dragon's Fang. This room was simple, but not empty. A bed sat against the far wall, and it had recently been occupied. An older man stood in front of him, probably at least fifty years old. He held himself well, Fang could see with a glance, and he was the source of the energy.

Fang frowned. "Are you the noble who owns this residence?"

The man settled into a fighting stance as he nodded.

"I didn't know you'd been trained by the monasteries." Fang needed more time. His attack wasn't ready yet, and it was challenging to focus his will in two spots while maintaining a conversational tone.

"It was deemed necessary to protect the Silent Heart." The monk took a step forward, his hands flashing signs.

The assassin looked around the room. He didn't see the

relic anywhere, but his next steps were easy enough to determine.

The monk attacked, throwing all his power into a single strike. Fang saw the move coming and was disappointed the monk wasn't more creative. Jian had challenged him, and he wondered if he would ever be challenged again. Fang's left hand, holding the shield, snapped forward and released just as the blast washed over it. Behind him, the rice paper walls tore into pieces as the energy dissipated.

For the entirety of a man's power, the blast seemed pitifully weak. Fang stepped forward as the older man collapsed to his knees. This was the man who was supposed to guard one of the monasteries' most sacred treasures? They didn't deserve it if this was all they would do.

He brought his other hand around, the moves for the Dragon's Fang completed. His will was focused on a point created between his thumb and his palm. He pressed it up against the monk's forehead. "I don't suppose you'll just tell me where it is?"

The monk didn't respond, anger flashing in his eyes. With a gentle push, Fang released his attack, drilling a neat hole through the man's forehead and all the walls behind it, including the stone foundation. He wondered idly how far the attack had gone before it dissipated to nothingness.

As the man dropped to the floor, Fang searched around the room. If this was the only occupied space, it stood to reason the heart would be kept nearby. After a few moments of searching, he found the hidden compartment beneath the bed. His power broke the lock and he was in.

The heart, for all this fuss, looked much the same as any heart Fang had ever seen. If he looked closely enough he could make out the three chambers. The heart was stored in a small glass jar with an airtight lid.

As soon as Fang grabbed the jar, a wave of revulsion passed over him, almost making him drop the relic. He tightened his grip, finally understanding what his master had meant about not being afraid. He set the jar down and his feelings returned to normal. But so long as he held the jar, he felt as though he was on the edge of vomiting.

As he left, he set fire to the building. His master had asked him not to use the Dragon's Fang, but they also hadn't expected a monk to be guarding the heart. Fire would burn away most of the evidence of his misdeed.

Fang wouldn't rest until he was rid of the relic. Some part of him recognized it as an abomination, and he was eager to return it to his master as soon as he could.

9

————

Lei's next few days fell into a predictable routine. He spent the mornings finding work and bringing in what coin he could. He had little need for money. So long as he could keep his cups full he was generally content. But he sensed a change coming, so he tried to save some up. In the midst of chaos, having coin always eased the way.

Work was surprisingly easy to find, though his memory argued against that. Before, he'd had to beg and plead for villagers to take him on. Now he found them more than willing to part with their coin in exchange for his services, especially after the first day or two back from the monastery, after word of his work had spread.

The work was almost entirely physical. Trees needed clearing, houses needed repairing, and gardens needed weeding. No matter the task, Lei threw himself into it, not because he enjoyed the work, but because he loved the exertion and the training. His muscles, once weak from their on-again, off-again use, hardened under the bright morning sun.

While he worked, he tried to understand the

compulsion that drove him. Logically, nothing had changed. He still hated the monasteries, and he hadn't forgiven Jian for what happened. So why did he feel such an overwhelming need to find out who had killed his brother? The need was stronger than any hunger Lei had ever felt, a desire that wouldn't be satiated until the truth was found. He fought against it, but every evening found him more tired than the last, exhausted more from fighting the compulsion than the labor he performed. Maybe it would just be easier to figure out what had happened.

As tempting as beer was in the evenings, he never drank, which also helped his coin accumulate. Two days after coming down from the monastery he had tried beer again, and again his desire had been pitifully weak. He had sipped half the drink, disgusted with the taste and with himself. It would have been so easy to dive back into his cups and forget everything, but he couldn't.

In the afternoons he trained, returning to the clearing he had known as a child. He ran through his forms, digging up his past and exploring what else he was now capable of. His development from before was no fluke. Every time he trained, his skills improved. Not only was he stronger than before, his control had improved several times over. Although he constantly questioned how it could be, he forced himself to accept the new reality.

Today he was feeling particularly bold. He had been hired by an older farmer who lived on the western edge of Two Bridges to bring down a large tree that had died the past winter. The farmer worried that if it fell the wrong direction in the wind it would crush his house. Lei had agreed to take the work, expecting to get at least a morning or two's worth of labor from the task.

But he couldn't resist. The tree, twice as wide as him, was

a perfect target. He began the work with the axe the farmer provided, but as soon as the farmer had moved out of sight and onto other tasks, Lei drew his sword. The cut would have to be just right, but he positioned himself so that if he failed, the damage to the surrounding area would be minimal.

He closed his eyes and focused his power into his sword. As it had for the past few days, the blade seemed to come alive in his hands. He took a cutting stance about ten paces from the tree and concentrated as he raised the blade up and over his right shoulder.

"Heeyah!" he shouted as he brought the blade down, releasing the energy as he cut. A crescent-shaped slice of power cut through the tree, the wound razor thin. Lei sheathed his sword, wondering if the move had worked. For almost a full minute he thought that it hadn't, but then the entire tree slid groaning toward the ground. Lei's diagonal slice had cut right through the tree, and when it slid down far enough it crashed to the ground, limbs cracking and leaves rustling, safely away from the farmer's house.

Lei thought he felt the ground shake with the impact, and the commotion brought the farmer running from the other side of the house. When he saw the tree downed already, his mouth opened wide in a silent "O."

Lei acted as though nothing out of the ordinary had happened. He smiled over at the farmer. "Job's done. But that's a huge tree. If you'd like, I'd be more than willing to chop it into pieces for you to use." The truth was, he wanted to practice this new skill, and the tree was ideal.

The farmer scratched his head. "I thought that would take you days, at least."

Lei shrugged. "Strong arms."

The farmer looked at him, then looked back at the tree,

as though confirming what he had seen. The man was as pragmatic as they came, and even if he couldn't find an explanation immediately, he couldn't deny that the tree he wanted down was lying in his field. Who cared how it came to pass?

"Sure," the farmer replied. "If you'd cut it down to size, I'd be greatly appreciative."

Lei picked the axe up from the ground and went to work. This time the farmer stood for longer and watched, seemingly disappointed Lei wouldn't finish the additional work in a few moments. Eventually he went back around the house to resume his tasks, and Lei smiled and drew his sword again.

THAT EVENING, Lei entered the Old Goat to a loud cheer from the assembled patrons. Word of Lei's tree work had spread far and wide, and being as he still visited the Old Goat every night, many had come to visit the hero of the week. Many drinks were offered, but Lei declined them all. Daiyu was working tonight, and she poured him a cup of water, for which he was grateful. Perhaps he was imagining it, but he thought the look in her eye had changed over the past few days. Instead of anger, now she seemed... curious, perhaps?

He never said how he had cut the tree, implying that the tree had been dead longer than people thought. His story was met with a healthy dose of skepticism, but the inquiries were good-natured; as the night went on, the retelling of Lei's feat became greater and greater, until even he was almost convinced he had felled an entire forest with the single swing of an axe.

Beyond the attention, Lei also received no small number

of job offers. Some were genuine, and some just wanted to get to the bottom of the mystery. Lei had covered his tracks that morning, hacking away at the trunk of the tree with the axe to make the cuts look less even and more natural. No one suspected he'd used his training from the monastery. Most of the patrons here probably didn't even remember that was where he'd once lived.

Eventually the attention died away as the men needed to return to their families and their beds. After midnight, only Lei, Daiyu, and the usual collection of snoring drunks remained in the tavern.

He would have given almost anything to know what was in her mind. Since he'd sobered up, his desire had only increased. But he'd done nothing, aware now of how poorly he'd treated her in the past. When she had needed him, he had been drunk. She deserved much better. But still, she was regularly in his thoughts.

At times, he convinced himself the interest went both ways. He swore that her eyes rarely left him, and more than once she'd even flashed him a genuine smile, far different than the one reserved for most patrons. Now, she cleaned cups and glasses as she stood across the bar from him. "So, how does it feel to be a local hero?"

"It's nice, but it won't last. It never does." He finished his water and held out his cup. She took it, filled it again, and passed it back.

She opened her mouth to say something, but stopped herself. Lei didn't dig, and he was comfortable with the relative silence, broken occasionally by the snores behind him.

"It's good to see you like this," she finally said.

"It feels good to be like this." He paused, afraid to admit what he'd learned. "I didn't realize how far I'd fallen. And I can't say sorry enough." He looked directly at her as he said the last line.

She didn't respond to that, letting the apology slide off her, her armor still intact. He hadn't really expected her to swoon over his apology, but he had hoped.

"I'm afraid of what will happen if I lose this feeling," he admitted, the confession surprising even him.

"Then don't. You have a choice."

"Daiyu..." he began, interrupted by a presence outside the Old Goat. What was a monk doing in town, especially at this time of night?

He'd been waiting for days for one to pass by, but this was the first one he'd seen or felt since he'd resolved to speak to the monks.

Across the bar, Daiyu was looking at him expectantly. He grimaced, torn between pursuing the monk and trying to repair the harm he'd done.

"I'm sorry, but I've got to go. Keep the change." He dumped far too much silver on the bar as he stood up and turned around.

"Where are you going?"

"To beat up a monk."

10

———

Fang slid to the ground, his back scraping against the rough bark of the tree, his stomach feeling weaker by the moment. How long had it been since he'd stolen the relic? Three days? Four? He knew he was becoming delirious from the combination of the prolonged effort, the influence of the relic, and the lack of sleep.

The monks, who up until his theft had been content to sit up in their monasteries and let the world pass them by, had suddenly swarmed the roads in large numbers.

Fang had come across the first of them the morning after his theft. He'd killed that monk, but then another and another had appeared, relentless.

The problem was that if he approached a monk, they'd be able to feel his power, the same way he could feel theirs. To his knowledge, there wasn't any way to conceal one's energy. His master seemed to do it, but that was the only person Fang had ever met who was capable of the skill. The sense of other gifted individuals allowed him to know when he was close to a monk, but they could also sense him as he approached.

Once he realized the monks were scouring the roads, he had taken to the wilderness, finding tracks that paralleled the road while maintaining a safe distance from it. There had been a few close calls, but he'd managed to avoid more violence thus far. The longer he went without discovery, the looser the noose around his neck became.

While he avoided the monks, he did manage to catch glimpses of their pursuit, often from a distance. Some of the monks wore the robes of their monasteries, easily identifying themselves. Others were dressed as average citizens. Fang saw one dressed as a beggar and another as a merchant.

His observations increased his curiosity. Did monks often hide in plain sight? In all his travels, he couldn't remember ever coming across a monk dressed in typical clothing, but it did raise the possibility that some of his enemies were hiding right in front of him. He was also surprised by the apparent level of cooperation between the monks. Typically, monks from different monasteries avoided one another, but he'd seen more than one meeting in which they seemed like old acquaintances rather than reluctant allies.

He didn't have time to worry about his observations. There was only one true obstacle remaining between him and his destination, a mountain pass currently occupied by no fewer than six monks. Under ideal circumstances, Fang would have considered attacking them directly and taking his chances. But his cargo was valuable, and he was beyond exhausted. The risk, both to his life and his mission, was simply too great.

His current perch allowed him to observe the pass freely. The mountain pass was plenty wide, with space for two carts to pass one another safely, if closely. Steep crags rose up on either side of the road. They weren't impassable, not this far into summer, but it would be incredibly difficult and slow going. If he slipped, he was done for. If he was seen, he was done for. Even a novice monk would be able to knock him from the high rock.

The easiest solution was to kill the monks guarding the pass, but how did he ensure his victory and the safety of the Silent Heart? When the idea finally hit him, he smiled at the simplicity of the plan. His path would be marked by those who pursued him, but by then it would be too late. He'd have the cover of the other side of the mountains and the forests beyond.

Fang stood, stretched, and walked down to the road. It was already early evening, with the sun setting behind him. Most of the travelers had already tackled the pass today, ensuring a room at the inns on the other side of the mountain by the time they finished. He and the monks had the road entirely to themselves.

As he approached the impromptu checkpoint, his eyes scanned the rock outcroppings. He'd never tested his strength to this extent, but his confidence was high. He made sure his dagger was sitting comfortably in its sheath and mentally marked his targets.

Fang wanted to gather his power early and funnel it into his blade, but restrained himself. The more he focused his energy, the more brightly he would shine to the senses of the monks he approached. It was better to remain relaxed and summon his strength quickly. Doing so was much more challenging, but it was for this very reason that he trained relentlessly. These were the skills needed to overthrow a corrupt system of rule.

He crested the pass a few minutes later, coming into full view of the monks on either side of the road. Every instinct demanded he turn around, but he kept putting one foot calmly in front of the other, as though encountering six monks was a daily occurrence for him. He kept his gait relaxed and his eyes sharp.

He was about thirty paces away when he first saw one of the monks tense. The gesture was minute, but Fang didn't dare risk losing his only advantage. As the monk's eyes widened, Fang flung all his power into the dagger. He drew the blade, holding it high above his head as he focused on his target. The weapon felt as though it was prepared to jump out of his hand at a moment's notice, almost alive in its zeal.

Part of his awareness registered the reaction of the monks. All of them were gathering their own energy, and in two cases, their strength was respectable. But he couldn't focus on them right now if he was going to pull off this attack. He swung his arm down, pushing his energy with all his will. The energy snapped off his blade with surprising zest, and Fang dropped to his knees, having put more of himself into the attack than he meant to.

The attack, razor thin, sliced through a section of rock above the pass. The newly created boulders immediately started sliding down the hill toward the monks.

Fang had to give them credit. They reacted faster than he'd expected. Some of them started to move out of the way, and one of them, a young man whose strength was considerable, turned his attention to the rocks falling above and tried to attack them with a blast of his own.

Fang imagined the young monk had been trying to push the largest rock away, but his blast didn't have the effect he desired. Instead of pushing it back, it shattered the huge rock into smaller boulders. Fang grinned to himself as he flung himself back. The monks who might have escaped were now caught, the boulders crashing down and over everyone.

He wasn't sure if it was imagination or not, but he thought he could hear the sound of bones cracking underneath the boulders. He also thought he saw a large, man-sized smear of blood on one as it continued rolling across the path.

The boulders raised a cloud of dust as they settled, and Fang covered his mouth and nose with his own clothes as he waited for it to settle. He couldn't feel anyone else alive, but in the aftermath of the attack, he wasn't sure he trusted his own senses quite yet.

Slowly, the dust cleared and he came back to his feet. The pass was no more. Fang guessed it would take the nearest villages days to clear the rubble and make it safe for carts once again. No doubt they would do so immediately. The pass was vital to trade between the towns, and it was high enough that it certainly closed for the winter. Every day of summer trade mattered.

He didn't see any survivors, so he climbed the pile of rubble, being exceedingly careful to test his steps before putting his full weight down. He couldn't afford to get caught himself, or even to twist an ankle.

As soon as he crested the rubble, he felt the sharp gathering of energy that preceded an attack. He panicked. Still spent from his own attack, he wasn't sure he could summon a shield, and certainly not in enough time. He'd been an overconfident fool. He launched himself to the side just as he felt the blast unleashed. He thought the power would send him flying, but the attack seemed to have missed. Even with the element of surprise, Fang had escaped unharmed.

At least, mostly unharmed. He'd still landed in the

rubble, and Fang cursed as sharp edges of rock dug into his sides. Groaning, he pushed himself up. The monk who'd tried to hit him had used the last of his energy, that much was clear. One of the monk's legs was trapped by the rubble, and he was struggling desperately to free himself. Unfortunately, he had no strength left.

Fang's side hurt as he stepped down the rubble pile, but he was otherwise unharmed. He could feel some blood trickling down his side, but he wasn't sure if that was his old wound reopened or an entirely new one. Either way, his movement wasn't hampered, so he wasn't terribly worried.

The monk's eyes were wide with fear. Like Fang, the monk had a shaven head, but the similarities ended there. The doomed monk blubbered, "Who... who are you?"

Fang put his foot on the man's neck and pressed down, watching the life slowly drain from the man.

"The death of everything you know," he answered.

11

Lei stepped out of the Old Goat and found the man he was looking for without a problem. He wore the white robes of a monk and was making his way quickly out of town, as though he was trying to escape without being seen.

There was no need for subtlety. Lei ran after the monk while trying to determine who he was. The monk turned around, no doubt alerted by Lei's power. For a moment, Lei thought the monk would try to run, but he didn't. The monastery was a long, hard run away. The monk stood tall, as though his posture would somehow protect him from Lei's onslaught of questions.

As Lei neared, he recognized the monk. It was Chen, a young man he'd been fairly close to during his own time in the monastery. Of all the monks Lei had ever known, Chen might have been the kindest. How much had changed in the years since they last spoke to one another? Chen hadn't come to visit him at the funeral.

Chen gave Lei a short bow. It wasn't much, but it was far more than he'd received from the others. He decided to take it as a promising sign. The Lei of a week ago would have fought against common decency, but today he offered a bow that was just slightly deeper.

"Lei, it is good to see you well," Chen said, his voice sounding genuine.

"And you as well, Chen."

Lei didn't see any reason to delay. Both of them wanted to get this confrontation over with. "What do you know about what really happened to my brother?"

Chen actually laughed, transporting Lei back to their time together. The monk had never taken his life or his training too seriously. Strangely, although Lei hadn't spoken to Chen in years, it felt as though he had just heard that laugh a few weeks ago. It was a difficult laugh to forget, coming from deep in the stomach.

"Still as direct as always, eh?"

"Saves everyone time, in my experience."

Chen's laughter slowly subsided. "I would love to tell you more, truly I would. It made my heart glad to learn that the abbot no longer suspected you. But we are all under strict orders not to tell you more than you already know."

Lei wasn't going to let up. "Why are you here? It's far too late for a monk to be in town."

"True. I was on a task for the monastery, but I was also asked to check on you. The abbot is concerned about your health."

Lei remembered Chen's ways well. The man hated lying, but he could twist the truth a dozen ways if given half a chance. His last answer stunk of a half-truth. "Why? He's never shown any interest in me over the past few years."

Chen's eyes darted back and forth, searching for something to look at that wasn't glaring back at him. "Lei, you know that I can't tell you more. Please accept my condolences and my apologies, but I must be off."

Chen turned to leave, but Lei grabbed his shoulder and turned him back around. "I'm not letting you leave until I have some answers, Chen."

Chen studied him. To his credit, he didn't dismiss the threat out of hand. "You're bluffing. You don't have the skill any longer." He turned again, and again Lei grabbed his shoulder.

Chen's arm snaked around Lei's. He'd anticipated the grab. Chen's hand latched onto his shoulder and pulled him forward and down. Lei let himself become the victim of the move, but wrapped his legs around Chen's arm as he rolled forward, pulling Chen down to the ground as well.

He let go and both of them were up in a flash, Chen's eyes suddenly more wary than they'd been before. Lei held up his hands, attempting to appear non-threatening. "I don't want to fight, either. And not just because I like you. But I need to know what happened to my brother."

"And I want to help you, but I won't disobey my orders."

They stared at each other, and Lei wondered if Chen would capitulate.

He didn't.

Without warning the monk practically leaped forward, a single fist flying for a one-hit knockout. Lei wasn't surprised by the attack, but he was by its speed and ferocity. He stepped backward as the punch missed by less than an inch. With his left hand he made the first sign for a basic attack as he deflected another punch with his right. He opened his left hand low, the blast catching Chen by surprise, lifting him off his feet and crashing him into a heap on the street.

"Come on, Chen. Just talk. I really, really don't want to do this."

Chen didn't say anything as he got to his feet, but this

time his stance was set. There really was only one way out of this, it seemed.

Lei waited for Chen to attack again. Had he taken the offensive, he probably could have ended the fight in just a few moves, but he absolutely didn't want to be the one to attack his old friend. If they had to fight, so be it, but it wouldn't rest on his conscience.

He didn't have long to wait. Chen came at him quickly, this time more cautiously. They exchanged a few light punches as they took the measure of each other.

What Chen didn't know was how much Lei was holding back. Lei found it hard to believe, but this fight against Chen was *easy*. Lei knew he'd gotten stronger, but until now, he hadn't realized just by how much.

Lei tossed Chen again, and when the monk rolled to his feet, Lei hit him with a blast that knocked him down again. He hadn't done anything to really hurt Chen yet, but the monk was becoming more upset by the minute.

As Chen returned to his feet once more, Lei could feel the energy building within his opponent. Chen had released all pretenses, and now he was fighting without holding back. He thrust his arm forward, the second sign complete, and Lei felt the wave of energy fly at him.

Lei formed the first shield with his left hand and slapped the attack away, aiming high. He felt Chen's strike go flying off into the distance, dissipating slowly as it drilled a hole through the clouds above.

Even he was impressed by that move. He had never learned how to do that; the defense had been pure instinct. Chen's eyes narrowed, and he set his feet as he moved into a new stance.

Lei recognized it at once. Chen's hands came together, making a triangle at chest height. Chen's will focused on that point, building with every second. It was the fifth sign of the two-hand-style attack the monks taught, and even though Lei had seen it done dozens of times as a child, he'd never been allowed to learn it. The danger had been too great. The attack was the most powerful the monks used, and to see Chen go to it was terrifying.

The attack was essentially a weaker version of the Dragon's Fang. The focus wasn't quite as tight, but such a concentrated burst of power was always a killing blow. For Chen to attempt the move here in the village was foolhardy, and extreme. Monks never killed unless forced to it.

Lei didn't attack. Reasonably, it was his strongest course of action, but he saw a way to end this fight for good. The risk was higher, but the potential reward was worth the cost. Again, he wasn't sure how he knew this technique, but he did. He started focusing his own power, forming the fourth sign for a shield.

Chen didn't even notice, focused as he was on his own attack. Lei felt the moment the attack was ready and braced himself.

The only warning he had was a slight shifting of Chen's stance and the exhalation of his breath. Lei held up his own shield as the full force of Chen's focused power shot at him. It slammed into the shield and Lei barely managed to keep his footing. That attack was even stronger than he'd expected.

The energies fought against one another for a moment, but this time Lei's defense didn't deflect Chen's attack. In the blink of an eye, his shield merged with Chen's blow, absorbing the wave of energy with ease.

The sensation that washed over Lei was overpowering. He felt as though he'd been kicked in the gut by a horse, but at the same time felt completely revitalized. He'd never had a similar experience.

Chen was wide-eyed. Lei couldn't tell if it was wonder, fear, or some other reaction, but it didn't much matter. The fight was over. The monk collapsed to his knees, his energy completely spent after the last attack.

"It's not possible..." the monk muttered to himself.

Lei took his time stepping forward. Chen was beaten, but he wasn't ready to talk, not yet.

"I'm sorry, old friend," Lei said.

He cocked his fist back, focused some of his will into it, then drove it into Chen's abdomen. The monk deflated as his eyes lost focus and he folded to the ground.

12

———

The room was pitch black, darker than any place Fang could ever remember being. Whether his eyes were open or closed, he could tell no difference. Beyond the darkness, there was little sound. It was impossible to completely shut out every sense, but this room came as close as possible.

Without light or sound, he had no clear picture of how long he'd been in the room. Perhaps only a few minutes, but more likely it had been a few hours. He could feel the hunger growing in his stomach, and he had eaten right before entering. So long as his body was behaving normally, his appetite was the best measure of time he had. His best guess was that he'd been in the room for six hours.

The room was the penultimate step in his initiation into the Order of the Serpent, the moment he'd been striving toward for years. Upon returning from the mountains with the Silent Heart, his master had informed him he had passed his final task as a novice.

The darkness did strange things to a person's mind. Given enough time, it warped reality and caused one's senses to turn within. Fang had been through similar trials before, although none for this length of time. Without inner peace, remaining in such a place would drive one mad, faster than many believed possible.

Fang had no such problem. His focus and his will were singular. Ever since he had been betrayed by the monasteries and left for dead, this was all he had worked for, all he had dreamed about. He took no lovers, abstained from almost all drink, and pursued no wealth. His life and his body were all bent toward one purpose, the purpose offered to him by the Order of the Serpent.

Together, they would burn this corrupt world to the ground and raise a new and better system. Criminals would no longer prey on the weak, as the punishment for any offense would be too great. Government would work for the people, bringing wealth to even the poorest of citizens. No longer would the rich be able to lord their coin over those who had none. The future shone brightly, and to achieve it, he would go to any end. His own life meant little when the stakes were so high.

So this darkness and silence were comfortable for Fang. He never doubted, never even twitched a muscle as he sat in silent meditation and focused on his breath. Breath was life, and life was his to either spare or take.

He heard a collection of soft sounds in front of him. Someone was removing the barriers in front of the door that blocked so much of the sound. When the door opened, the dim light from the single candle almost blinded him with its intensity.

His master stood there, silent, examining his novice one last time. He brought the candle close to Fang's face, and his dark eyes stared into those of his assassin. His nod of approval, when it finally came, was so small as to be almost nonexistent.

"Your will remains strong," his master said.

"Until all our enemies are vanquished," Fang replied.

"That time is sooner than you think, my son."

Fang felt the rush of blood to his cheeks, overjoyed by the recognition. The master gestured, and Fang stood and followed him into the main room of the house. A fire had been lit there, and a brand sat in it, glowing an angry red from the prolonged heat of the coals.

The master motioned for Fang to kneel, which he did without question. He knew what was coming. The knowledge that pain was near made him nervous, but he had come too far to show fear now.

They both knelt in silence for a moment, and then the master spoke, the words flowing like water, cooling Fang's fiery spirit. "From the moment you began your final meditation as a novice, this secret brand has been burning in the fire. It is infused with your spirit, a symbol of the dedication you will carry with you the rest of your life."

The master rolled up his own robes quickly, showing his own brand on the inside of his forearm, a serpent coiled around a sword. He quickly rolled his robes down again as he continued his recitation.

"The serpent represents everything we strive to become. It bends, so as not to break. It can strike quickly with poison, so quickly the victim barely has time to realize what has happened, or it can coil around and choke the life slowly from its prey. But its greatest virtue is its desire to remain close to the ground, to feel the tremors and the vibrations of the world. The serpent is humble but deadly.

"The sword is our country's symbol of life and death. Those who are corrupt use the edge of the sword to terrify those they rule over. But that same edge can also protect. That is our mission."

The master paused, focusing his gaze on Fang once again. "Beyond this, there is no more choice. Your obedience must be absolute, and even the smallest failure will result in your death. Our purpose demands nothing less. Are you prepared and willing to make these sacrifices, to fully immerse yourself in a cause much greater than you?"

Fang almost replied immediately, but the gravity of the moment was such that he paused. He had already given everything to the order, and there had never been even the slightest amount of hesitation. Had anything changed?

No.

"I am."

"Then present your right arm."

Fang rolled up his own sleeve, exposing his bare forearm. He held it out, fighting every survival instinct that yelled at him to run.

The master pulled the brand out of the coals and held Fang's arm tight. He pressed the brand into Fang's exposed flesh.

The pain was exquisite, and far beyond anything Fang had felt before. His arm screamed, but he locked his jaw shut. It felt as though every nerve in his arm was in agony, but then the pain was gone, leaving only the stench of burning skin.

The master removed the brand and set it off to the side. Fang fought the urge to vomit and was glad he hadn't eaten for hours. The pain faded, but the smell was almost too much to bear. Through it all, he hadn't uttered so much as a whimper.

His master nodded his approval. "I am proud of you

today, Fang. Get some rest, for in a few days, your real work begins."

Fang wasn't sure if he would be allowed to ask more questions now that he'd been initiated, but his curiosity was hard to stifle. "How do we start, Master?"

"By bringing the monasteries to their knees. Then we'll cut off their heads."

13
____

Chen came to a few minutes after he had been knocked unconscious. His eyes fluttered, then shot open. He patted himself down, then breathed a sigh of relief when he realized that other than some bruising he was unharmed.

Sitting only a few feet away, Lei almost laughed at the scene. Chen seemed so innocent, somehow.

He had considered tying Chen up and torturing him for the information if necessary, but he couldn't bring himself to fall that far. Chen had never done wrong by him. Lei didn't know what he'd do if he didn't learn what he needed, but hoped he wouldn't have to answer that question.

Chen noticed Lei and gave a start. He collected himself quickly. "You gave me a pretty good beating."

Lei wasn't sure what to say to that, so the two of them sat in silence. Chen looked as though he was debating something within himself. Lei gave him the time and space to make the choice on his own.

"Well, the abbot will be upset, of course, but I think

maybe you deserve more than you've been told," the monk said.

"Thank you."

Chen stared off into the distance. "Your brother had been sent out by the abbot to track down the truth behind some rumors. Word had reached us that some doomsday cult was plotting our demise, and the abbot found the stories disturbing enough to send Jian after the facts."

"Why my brother?"

Chen glanced across at Lei. "I know you two didn't keep in touch, but after you left, Jian threw himself into training. I think he saw it as repentance. He was the strongest and most skilled monk we had. The abbot believed he would be the safest of us if the rumors were true."

Apparently Jian hadn't been strong enough, but that remained unspoken.

"What do you know about this cult?" Lei asked.

The monk gave a little shrug. "I don't know much, and I'm not sure if the abbot knows much more. They call themselves the snakes, or something like that. The story was that a group of these snakes were cooperating with local triads to procure relics and destabilize monasteries. We didn't have any solid evidence to go on, but your brother spent a lot of time traveling, and said he had some ideas of where to look."

"That's all you know about Jian's death?"

Chen grimaced. As soon as he realized his mistake he tried to hide it, but Lei had seen the expression. Chen sighed. "Obviously, we know now they have at least one strong warrior. It would have taken a very talented monk to kill Jian, and you already know about the Dragon's Fang. But recently there has been other news. A very powerful relic that only the abbots knew about was stolen last week. In the hands of one as strong as the person who killed Jian, the weapon could cripple an entire monastery."

"What relic?"

"All I know is that it's called the Silent Heart. The abbot wouldn't tell us any more. But monks are swarming all over the land, trying to find the thief. A group was killed in the Pass of the Winds several days ago, but nothing else is known."

Lei considered the new information. Chen sounded sincere, but the news gave him a mixed reaction. He didn't care about the monasteries. They could all burn, as far as he was concerned. But one quality of the monasteries was without question: they controlled those who were gifted. The monasteries were the reason he spent his days cutting trees and shoveling manure, but they were also the reason he was still alive. If they fell, the entire empire was in danger.

What had Jian gotten himself into? And did Lei even care? His brother was dead, killed by a cult. He had his answers. Some insistent part of him tried to argue he should help, but that wasn't going to happen. Let the world burn. He would survive. He always had.

Chen spoke hesitantly. "You remind me of him, you know."

"We were brothers," Lei replied, his tone biting.

"Not in how you look, but how you fight. Those moves you used on me? The only time I've seen them before was when your brother performed them. I don't know how you learned them, but back there I thought I was fighting his ghost."

Chen was clearly waiting for some response, some explanation he could understand, but Lei was in no mood to share, and he didn't understand himself. He turned to leave.

"Wait! You should help us." The monk's voice was strained, as though getting those words out had been a physical effort. "Your brother deserves justice, and if you're this strong, you could be the one to deliver it."

Lei spat on the ground. "Jian deserves nothing. He left me utterly alone in this pit."

Chen looked aghast. "How can you even say that?"

Lei spun around and stomped toward Chen. "You can idolize my brother as much as you want. But don't pull me into your delusions."

Lei gave Chen a small, hard shove and then walked away. He stopped when Chen's voice broke the tense silence. "You know he saved your life, right? Every year."

Lei couldn't bring himself to turn around. But he couldn't walk away, either. What did Chen mean?

"You think the abbot would have let a boy with your temper and your strength just walk away from the monastery? You were supposed to be executed the day you killed that girl. But Jian begged and pleaded. He said he would watch you all the time to make sure you kept your word. Why do you think he traveled as much as he did? The trips gave him an excuse to check on you, every time he went through town. And every time, when he came back, he was proud to report you'd kept your word. Your brother saved your life more times than you know."

Lei didn't turn, but he heard Chen stomp away, felt the monk's presence diminish as he started up the mountainside. Lei cursed and walked the familiar path toward the Old Goat.

He needed a drink.

14

W henever Fang moved his arm, he still felt the pain lance up it, but he was finding it easier to deal with as time went on. Three days had passed since his initiation, and his master had been summoned on some matter of importance. Fang's first orders as an initiate were to relax and train. He wasn't supposed to push himself, but his master had made it clear Fang's skills were expected to remain sharp in his absence.

Like all orders, Fang took these to heart. He did conditioning every day, running through the woods, practicing his forms and various calisthenics. But he went no further, refusing to push himself to the limits he typically did. Because of the days of enforced rest, he was feeling better than he had in a very long time.

Nevertheless, he was excited to see his master returning from his journey sooner than expected. His master's face was grave, but his stride was quick and purposeful. Just watching his master move inspired Fang. What secrets would he learn when they were finally allowed to train together?

Master and student met in the yard to their house, Fang bowing all the way to the ground. His master rewarded him with a bow of remarkable depth. "You look well. Your arm is healing without problem?"

Fang showed his master the brand. The wound looked angry and red, but he could open and close his hand without problem. "Another few days and I will hardly notice it."

His master nodded. "That is good. I have spoken with my peers in the order, and since your mission was completed so successfully, we have decided to advance our schedule."

Fang fought to maintain his humility. His deeds had echoes that would reverberate throughout history. Of that, he was sure.

"What comes next, Master?"

"Come inside. Prepare me some tea and I will let you know about missions that must soon be undertaken."

The two of them walked towards the house together. The master sat down and began removing items from the bag he carried. Most were papers, some of them sealed with the black seal of the Order of the Serpent. As Fang stoked the fire and set the water to boiling, he risked a few glances at the papers.

Some looked to be in code. Fang didn't read well, but he recognized enough of the common characters to survive. Had he remained in the monastery longer, he would have been taught to read and write, but his master had labeled such skills distractions. Regardless, Fang could see that many of the symbols didn't even look to be in their language. They had to be a code known only to full members of the order.

There were also maps. Fang stole glances of mountain

ranges, forests, and plains, but never dared to look for more than a second or two. He still wasn't entirely sure what new privileges he had earned, but figured it was better to err on the side of caution.

The water reached a boil quickly, and Fang set about preparing the tea leaves. His master, a perfectionist in all things, would settle for nothing less than a superbly prepared cup, and for the next few minutes, Fang's full attention was on the task at hand. Once he was certain the water had reached the correct temperature, he poured the water over the leaves and let them steep.

When the tea was prepared he called for his master, who sipped at the cup with obvious delight. "Your tea is some of the best I've tasted. Every time I am on the road, I am reminded of just how far our people have fallen. Such a simple beverage, but so few take the time to prepare it correctly. I will miss your tea."

Fang's heart leaped. He had hoped to train directly under his master, but perhaps there was something else in store for him.

As usual, his master seemed to read his thoughts. "I know you were looking forward to training directly under me. However, it has been decided that you are more than prepared for the tasks ahead. In fact, it is in no small part because of your efforts that we are able to proceed so quickly. We had always feared the monks would learn of our plans before we could bring them to fruition, but you have guaranteed that they will not."

Fang bowed, partly to show his gratitude, but partly to disguise his excitement. The other masters also believed in him! While he had never met them personally, if they were even half the leaders his own master was, they were great indeed.

"The serpent teaches us humility, but you should be pleased with the work you have done, my student. You show tremendous promise, and you have my word that when our work here is done, I will show you all the secrets of our order. You will become even stronger than you are now."

Fang found himself nodding rapidly and forced himself to stop. He was closer than ever to the strength he desired, and the monks who had thrown him out would never know what they had lost. He would become the strongest warrior the empire had ever seen.

The master reached over to the pile of papers and pulled up a map. "After how well you performed, the order decided it was you who would be best suited to this particular mission. I can't tell you how important your success is. If you fail, the whole plan fails. Am I being clear?"

Fang nodded, his whole attention on the map. He recognized it as the area they were currently in, with the villages on the edges of the map being a solid month of travel apart. But more than villages and cities were marked. On the map was the location of all the monasteries nearby. Fang's heart raced even faster.

His master took a quill and sketched a path on the map. "Your mission is to follow this path, or at least to stay close to it. As you travel it, your only mission is to kill and injure as many monks as you can without hurting yourself. Make it so that monks are afraid to leave their walls. Those that do should fear closing their eyes, as they may never open them again. You will become an agent of chaos."

That mission was everything Fang could have dreamed of. He was honored that the other masters would trust him with the task he had trained almost exclusively for.

"Again," his master said, "do you understand? You must remain healthy. Even if it means allowing some monks to pass you by. If the pursuit becomes too intense, you are to run, even if that goes against your instincts or your own personal code. You must come first, and the monks must be secondary."

Fang fought a grimace and nodded. "May I ask why?"

"You have earned that right. Because you are absolutely vital to the next phase of my plan. And you'll need every skill and strength you have for that."

Fang agreed and poured another cup of tea for his master. "When do I leave?"

"If you are feeling well enough, tomorrow."

Again, Fang had hoped there would be more time with his master, but if their plan involved him leaving so soon, there was no room for him to question. He would leave.

The monasteries would crumble, and he would be the one who tore the walls down.

15

————

Lei stepped into the Old Goat, his mind in a dozen places at once. Part of him wanted to punch something, part of him wanted to get drunk, and part of him wanted to sit and weep. As he walked through the door, he would have put equal chances on any of those outcomes.

He sat down heavily on the first available stool and Daiyu gave him an inquiring stare.

"Beer," was his only answer.

She looked displeased, but she poured him a beer and set it down in front of him. "Rough day?"

"I've had better."

As he looked at the beer, the same revulsion came over him that had been present ever since his brother died. He cursed, grabbed the cup, and threw its entire contents down his throat. The beer felt both refreshing and sickening all at once. He'd never loved and hated anything at the same time to this degree.

He was about to ask for another when a wave of sickness passed over him. He felt everything coming back up his throat, but with a force of will, he pushed it back down. Had he become a lightweight in so short a time?

He took a few deep breaths through his nose and looked around the crowded tavern. Most of the faces he knew. There were two men in dark clothes that he didn't recognize, huddled around a small table in the corner. Maybe it was his imagination, but he thought they'd been staring a little too closely at him.

Lei shook his head and turned back to the bar. No one besides Daiyu had given him even a bit of attention in years. There wasn't any reason for that to change now.

He leaned forward to ask for another beer when another wave of sickness crashed over him. This time, he barely managed to hold it in. He stood up and walked quickly out of the tavern, turning a corner into a dark alley and throwing up violently. The acidic bile burned his throat as it came back up, but as painful as the vomiting itself was, he did feel better when it was over.

Something was happening to him. But what? Everything circled around his brother's death, but he didn't want to swim any deeper in that mystery. Let the monks worry about it. He fought another wave of revulsion and cursed.

Fine! If finding out more about Jian's death was the only way to understand what was happening to him, he would do it. But not with the monks. Never that.

He stood up, feeling immediately better. What was it Chen had said? That the snakes were working with criminal organizations? If anything like that was happening, there was one person he knew of who might be able to point him in the right direction. But would she?

He cleaned his face and returned to the tavern. He looked around, but no one, not even the men in the corner, seemed to have noticed either his departure or return.

Lei took his seat back at the bar. Daiyu served a few other customers before checking in on him again. "Are you sure you're well?"

"No, but could I get some water?"

She nodded and came back a moment later with a tall cup. He sipped at the water, amazed by how refreshing he found it. It was even better than beer. "Can I ask you something?"

She was only giving him half her attention, but when he put his hand gently on hers, her gaze focused on him. "Sure."

"Do you know anything about a group of snakes working with the underbosses here?"

Her reaction to his question was almost completely unreadable. She could be harder than stone if she needed to be, and he hated when she got that way. "Why?"

"Because when I questioned that monk, he told me something like that was happening, and that my brother was killed by them."

Daiyu's face was like a mask, and no matter how hard he stared, he couldn't seem to make heads or tails of what she was thinking. "No, I haven't heard anything," she said. "But if you want, I can ask around."

"Would you?"

She expelled a deep breath. "Sure. But only if you go home and rest. You're really not looking good right now."

Lei hated to admit it, but she was right. He felt horrible, and a full night of sleep sounded excellent. Part of him had hoped that tonight, like every night Daiyu tended bar, she would come home with him, but that wouldn't happen tonight. It probably would never happen.

He gave Daiyu a short bow and stepped out of the Old

Goat. As soon as he was outside he began to feel better, his stomach unknotting inside him.

He wished he understood what was going on with him, and he wished he had another chance with Daiyu. She treated him with kindness, and some days he confused her kindness for affection. But she never opened the door for him. Even if she loved him, she wouldn't let him in, and that knowledge hurt worse than any punch he'd ever taken.

Lei didn't make it far before he stopped and looked up at the stars. In the past, they'd always given him solace. No matter how horrible his life became, the stars were always there, constant companions. He couldn't explain why, but they made him feel small, and being small was sometimes all that he wanted. Maybe never more than now. He wanted to shrink to a size so small that no one would be able to see him again.

He heard the door to the Old Goat open behind him, and he glanced back, just to see who was leaving after him. He was surprised to find it was the two men he'd thought were looking at him. They seemed equally surprised to see him.

One of the men was a little taller and thinner than the other. He seemed to be the leader of the pair. "Looks like someone needs to learn to give women some more space. I heard her say that she wanted you to go home, and you're just standing out here."

Lei wanted to move, but part of him wanted the fight, wanted to release his frustration on anyone.

The shorter man snorted in laughter. "Looks like he's too scared to reply."

His partner said, "Looks that way. We'd better show him what happens when you don't show the proper respect to our boss."

Lei turned around, surprised by the comment. When he did, he saw that both men had drawn sharp knives, and they were stepping closer, ready to use them.

16

———

Fang walked slowly through the small village, allowing his eyes, ears, and nose to take in as much as they could. It was really no more than a small collection of huts, no doubt constructed by the local lord. A village was easier to protect than single homes scattered throughout the land, and the storage shed was large enough to hold the harvests from all the nearby fields.

But after giving the orders to create the village, it looked like the lord had done little else. Not even a single guard could be found for miles, and the village itself had no physical protection. It was open and exposed on the fields where the residents worked their whole lives to pay for their shelter. The very thought revolted Fang.

A group of small children ran around his feet, trying to catch one another in a game Fang didn't immediately recognize. He could hear their laughter, but all he saw was their skinny legs and arms, and skin darkened by long days in the fields. These children deserved better.

Several of the farmers sat together in the space that looked like it passed as the village square. They were gambling with one another, their entire pool of money less than what Fang carried in his own pouch as an allowance from his master. Did they even know how poor they were? Fang pitied the fools, but their miserable existence wouldn't last for much longer. Soon they would have all the money they needed.

The storage shed on the outside edge of the village attracted most of his attention. He received a few curious looks as he walked toward it. Like everything else in the village, it had no protection. There were no guards, no walls, and it wasn't even built of stone, just cheap wood that only needed a spark to be lit. It was a disaster waiting to happen.

He took no joy in being the person who would bring that disaster, but unless the people stood up to their oppressors, no one would enjoy the sweet taste of freedom. Sometimes people needed a kick to become better. He certainly had. Sometimes you were the foot, and sometimes you were the ass.

Fang sighed, depressed by the sights he saw. His original plan had been to wait until the evening, but he didn't see the point in wasting his time. His goal was to spread as much fear as possible, and what was more intimidating than realizing your entire life could be destroyed by one man in broad daylight? People usually believed the darkness of night held terror, but if they were afraid when the sun burned their skin, perhaps that was even more frightening.

Lighting the storeroom on fire would also catch the attention of the monastery nearby. The monks depended on the rice within, stored in large barrels that hadn't been moved up to the monastery yet. By itself, the fire wouldn't starve the monks, as promising as that was, but it would get them to leave their walls to search for the culprit.

Fang paused before he began. Years from now, when

they taught history to students, this village would be the place they pointed to. Here was where the revolution started. And all it would take was a spark.

He found a place behind the storeroom and out of sight of the entire village, then took out the materials from his pack to start a fire. Lighting a bit of kindling was no more than the work of a moment, and a few minutes later he had a healthy blaze started next to one of the walls.

Now there was nothing to do but wait. Before long, the villagers would recognize what was happening and would rise up. Their anger would be directed at the lord and monks who failed to protect them. The fire he lit here today would spread throughout the land.

Fang stood up and stepped away from the growing flames. He would remain for a few more minutes, just to ensure the fire grew large enough that it couldn't be extinguished by the efforts of the villagers.

He wasn't expecting the first person on the scene to be a young boy. The boy looked at Fang, looked at the fire, and immediately knew what had happened. The child couldn't have been more than eight or nine, but he drew a belt knife and charged at Fang.

Fang didn't even have to think, his instincts were so well ingrained in him. His right hand made a sign and a blast of energy shot toward the boy.

Fang's control over his strength had never been his greatest asset. He tended to put everything into every attack, but he tried to control himself. Apparently, he wasn't very good at it.

The blast slammed into the completely unsuspecting child, stopping his advance, lifting him off his feet, and flinging him back almost twenty paces. He tumbled limply across the dirt and grass to come to a complete and very still rest.

Fang wasn't sure if he had killed the boy or simply knocked him out cold. He supposed either would suit his needs. He took no pleasure in taking life. Such actions were only a means to an end.

As he walked around the storehouse to take his leave of the village, he came face to face with a pack of villagers. Men and women carried large containers of water, and one farmer had an old, rusty sword. When Fang looked at the weapon, he was more worried about infection than a fatal cut.

For a moment, they stood there, a frozen tableau, each surprised by the presence of the other. Then Fang took a single step forward and the entire village stepped back.

Anger snapped in him. These people were supposed to stand and fight! Even though he didn't want to harm them, he wanted them to attack, to fight for their village. He was outnumbered, but even the whole village working together wouldn't dare take a step forward against him, a complete stranger!

He summoned energy into both hands and threw it out. He didn't bother to focus or aim. He just released, a small shockwave expanding away from him. It flung the villagers off their feet, and they crashed to the ground as one.

Fang stood there, giving any of them the chance to fight back. If they wouldn't fight back against a single attacker, when would they rebel against an oppressive government? But no one stood.

Fang spit on the ground, cursing the village as he left.

Perhaps the monasteries would put up more of a fight.

17

Lei stared at the two men, unable to believe what he was seeing. Did they know who he was?

Of course they did. He was the local drunk, meddling in affairs he shouldn't. Rumor had reached an underboss, and these two had been watching the Old Goat.

He summoned his power into his hands, but stopped. Fighting these two would take only a moment, but he needed to consider the consequences. As good as it would feel to break these two in half, they were only part of something larger. If he fought them, more would come. And Daiyu would possibly be in danger.

He had made a lot of mistakes. He was only beginning to realize the extent of them. But he knew he could do better. He could be better.

So he focused his energy in his left hand. Lei refused to die just outside of the Old Goat, and so some level of protection was necessary. But otherwise, he did nothing.

"I'm sorry," he said, trying to sound sincere. "We used to be friends."

The taller man stepped forward quickly, and Lei almost released his attack. The man held the blade of his knife less than an inch away from Lei's throat. "We know. Everyone in town knows how you broke her heart. But for some reason she keeps letting you come here. So I'm going to make this clear for you. If you ever come back here again, you're going to really wish you hadn't."

"But I like the beer here."

Lei saw the attack coming, but didn't dare react too obviously. The tall man's foot came up between his legs. Lei shifted slightly so most of the force was absorbed by his inner thigh, but he didn't have to fake the blossoming pain he suddenly felt. He collapsed to the ground, still holding on to his energy.

"I think I've made myself clear," replied the tall man. He kneeled down and tapped the back of his knife blade against Lei's neck. "You won't live if we meet again, and the beer here isn't that good."

The man stood up and drove his foot into Lei's stomach. Lei curled around the blow, his focus still on the energy in his hand. It would be so easy. At this distance, with the focus he was capable of, Lei was certain he could create a fist-sized hole in the man's chest. But he held on. For Daiyu.

The men, apparently satisfied, went back into the Old Goat. Lei lay there, slowly releasing his energy and catching his breath. The beating, as far as beatings went, hadn't been all that bad, but he would still be sore for a day or two. Fortunately, he had plenty of experience being on the wrong side of a kick.

He stumbled to his house, desperate for sleep.

When he awoke, the sun was streaming through his open window, and there was a light knocking on his door. "Lei?"

He recognized the voice instantly. "One minute."

He sat up, groaning as his torso reminded him it had recently been assaulted. Fortunately, he had fallen asleep in his clothes, so there was little preparation required to answer the door. He rubbed his eyes, stood up, and opened the door.

Daiyu was there. Her face was concealed, and her clothing far plainer than what she normally wore. Even so, in Lei's eyes, she was still the most beautiful woman he'd ever met. How had he let her get away? Why hadn't he been a man worthy of her? Regret threatened to flood him, but he forced his mind down other paths.

She stepped into his room, taking in the austere environment with a single glance. "Still as clean as ever, I see."

"Habits die hard." In the monastery, cleanliness was considered a reflection of one's inner state, so dust was considered an offense against the spirit. He'd never quite lost the practice, and it was easy to keep clean a house that had no possessions.

She wasted no time in getting to the point. "I don't think you should ask any more questions about your brother's death."

After all their time together, she had to know there was no better way to pique his interest than telling him not to do something. "Why?"

"There's something big happening. I don't know what it is, but I've heard the whispers. The group you're looking for is called the Order of the Serpent. I'm not sure anyone knows much about them, but they've got connections with the local triad."

"That doesn't tell me anything I don't already know. How do I find them?"

She stepped toward him, bringing her hand to his face. Her touch was warm and familiar, and all he wanted to do was melt into it. "Don't. I don't know what you've been going through, but nothing is worth this. I don't want you to disappear on me, too."

When Daiyu was young, her father had left their family. Lei knew her father's absence was perhaps the deepest, most tender wound she possessed.

Their faces were close, closer than he'd dared in years. The soft scent of lilacs emanated from her, drawing him in. As he breathed in the familiar scent deeply, he knew what he wanted.

"Leave with me," he said.

She jumped back as though he'd stabbed her, her face shocked. A range of emotions passed quickly over her face, but she was too talented to keep any there for long. "You know I can't do that. My debt is too great."

It was his time to step forward. "I can protect you."

She looked up at him, appearing to consider the possibility. That she even considered it was enough to give him pause. Although the question had been the impulse of a moment, he'd meant every word. He would protect her and provide for her if she gave him the chance. She was the only person he had left.

He knew her answer the moment she turned her eyes from his. "I'm sorry, I can't."

He didn't even need to ask. The possibility had come up once before, long ago, and her answer and reasons were no doubt the same.

"Please, don't try to track down your brother's killer, and

maybe stay away from the Old Goat for a few weeks. That's all I can ask of you," she said.

Then she took two quick steps and was out the door, causing Lei to wonder just how many times she would leave him.

18

―――――

Fang crawled through the bushes, moving as silently as possible. He'd expected pursuit, but he hadn't expected the concentrated effort from what appeared to be several monasteries.

Pushing slowly, Fang lifted his head above the bushes, looking down the hill to where the path lay. There were almost a dozen monks conversing, deciding the best way to trap their elusive quarry.

Had he been more certain, he would have crawled closer to hear what the monks were saying. But even he wasn't sure he could overwhelm twelve of them at a time.

The village fire had drawn the monks like moths to a flame. Fang suspected the pursuit from his actions at the pass hadn't died down as much as he'd expected. There was plenty to hate about the monasteries, but they were persistent. Their hold on the land couldn't have lasted for so long without determination.

His master's map had him visiting a nearby monastery next, but if they were already alerted to his whereabouts, the wisdom of attacking the place seemed less solid. Attacking a monastery by surprise was one task, but attacking a monastery that was prepared and searching for him was entirely another.

Master had said that if necessary he could skip some of the targets. He'd emphasized Fang's safety over all else, and right now, Fang wasn't feeling very safe.

They'd come after him as he caught a few hours of sleep in the middle of the day. At least one of them was a skilled tracker, and Fang had been pursued relentlessly until he leaped into a river that had carried him miles downstream. The gamble had given him some space, but they'd caught up again. The monks were tireless, always stalking him.

Eventually he'd need to fight, but a wise warrior only fought battles he was guaranteed to win. He'd never fought that many monks before. Someday, maybe.

This group had come far too close to finding him. If he'd been walking on the path, he was almost certain he would have been spotted, or at least sensed. Fortunately, he'd already been walking about two hundred feet away, and had been able to sprint another hundred or so before they'd crested the small rise and come into view.

Fang had expected the monks to continue on, but they'd stopped down the path, discussing their task, he was sure. Hiding wasn't enough. If they somehow decided to spread out, he'd be noticed in short order. So he crawled, using the bushes as cover as he slithered toward the top of a small hill.

He kept his motions slow and deliberate. If one of the monks was paying attention, it was entirely possible they'd notice the movement of the grass in the distance.

Sweat was pouring down his face as he reached the top of the short rise. The sun beat down on him from above, but with his face to the ground, no breeze penetrated the grass.

He raised his head again, moving slowly so as not to attract attention.

There was a farmstead below. Fang couldn't see anyone moving, and perhaps it would be a better place to hide. The monks would be expecting him to keep to the open, he imagined.

Once he was safely over the hill, Fang stood up and ran toward the farmstead. One structure was clearly the home, while another nearby was the barn. Hopefully in the afternoon no one would be there. He kept his eyes fixed on the buildings as he ran, but he didn't see evidence of anyone. He ran into the barn, thankful to have found a place to hide and rest.

As soon as he was within the shade of the barn he saw the boy, shoveling manure out of one of the stalls. Fang cursed to himself. Was one break too much to ask for? The boy, who couldn't have been more than seven or eight, looked up, as surprised as Fang. Before the boy could so much as open his mouth, a blade came into Fang's hand.

The wise move was to kill the child. Fang wasn't sure how far away the monks were, but if the boy screamed loud enough, there was a chance the monks would hear, and then Fang would have on his hands the very conflict he was trying to avoid.

But he held back the knife. He held no illusions about his actions. Killing a child didn't sit well with him. Though some innocent casualties were necessary in a revolution, they should be prevented if at all possible.

"Quiet!" Fang commanded. "If you make a sound, you die."

The boy nodded, his mouth slowly closing. His eyes were wide and his hands gripped tightly on the shovel, as though he could somehow use that as a weapon against the assassin.

"I need to hide here for a while. If you help keep me safe, you have nothing to fear. I'll leave as soon as I can. But if you tell anyone about me, everyone you love will die." Fang glanced around the barn, making sure he hadn't missed anyone else. "Do you believe me?"

The boy nodded again, his tongue clearly unable to form words. Fang didn't blame him. Were he in the boy's place, at that age, he would have feared for his life as well. Trusting the child was a risk, but he didn't want the boy's blood on his hands.

Fang took up position deep in the shadows of the barn, halfway behind a pile of hay. The spot allowed him to look out on the fields beyond and the farmhouse. If the monks approached, he would see them. He squatted down so only the top of his head was showing. In the shadows, he was as good as invisible from the brightly lit outdoors.

He turned to the boy, who was still frozen in his place. "Well, go on. You don't need to stop your chores for me. I don't want you to get in any trouble on my account."

The boy seemed particularly confused by this, but after a few more seconds of standing and staring, he returned to his work, shoveling the manure into a cart with slow, hesitant motions. His fear was obvious. Every time he needed to turn around to shovel a new scoop, he paused as though he was afraid Fang would rise up and stab him in the back.

Fang had no such intentions, and his attention was soon turned to the view out the front of the barn. The entire group of monks approached the farmhouse. Had they somehow managed to track him this far? It shouldn't have been possible, yet here they were.

He cursed as a man stepped out of the house. The similarity to the boy was obvious even from a distance. He approached the monks, bowing deeply as he did. The monks and the farmer stood and talked for a few minutes. Fang had little doubt what the conversation was about.

He remained hidden, watching the exchange with a deep interest. Then another person ran out from the farmhouse. A young girl, younger than the boy in the barn, ran up to her father, her long, dark hair blowing freely in the breeze.

Another minute passed and the father turned towards the barn and pointed. Fang knew what came next, his stomach sinking.

"Boy," he said.

"Y-y-yes?"

"Do you love your family?"

"Yes."

"Do you want to keep them safe?"

"Yes."

Fang could see the boy puff out his chest, finding his courage as he did. "Good. Then you tell those monks you haven't seen anyone. And they better believe you. If not, I'll kill your father, and then I'll kill your sister, and then I'll kill you, but only after you've watched your family die."

Fang could see hope mixed with fear from the child. No doubt he believed the monks to be all-powerful, but Fang's threats certainly scared him. But Fang had put himself in a corner. He should have killed the child and moved on immediately, but he'd been soft. If the child didn't come out when his father called, the monks would be suspicious.

He had no choice but to trust the boy. But he had every intention of following through on his promise if the boy betrayed him.

As Fang expected, the father's voice called out for the child, who looked one last time at Fang. "Protect your family," was all he said.

The boy nodded and stepped out into the sunlight, Fang's fate in his small hands.

19

Lei paced his tiny room, the same debate running through his mind that had been going in circles since Daiyu's afternoon visit. At times, he figured he needed to leave his past life and problems behind. He would follow Daiyu's advice. He'd stay away from the Old Goat and maybe leave Two Bridges. There wasn't anything tying him here anymore. Daiyu's life would be better if he left.

But he couldn't do that, not quite. The other half of him wanted to walk to the door, throw it open, and charge out to the Old Goat. He knew that if he pushed just a little harder, Daiyu would crack. She would tell him what he wanted to know. There had to be some lead that would put him on the path toward the truth. He could rid himself of this strange compulsion and carry on with his old life.

The sun set and still he paced. His thirst, in addition to his own natural inclination toward doing the opposite of what people told him to do, decided the matter. Certainly Daiyu was doing what she thought was best for him, but he didn't need her protection.

Lei tied his sword to his hip, testing to make sure it

would clear the sheath easily. He took what little money he possessed and started toward the tavern, rehearsing exactly what he could say to make Daiyu listen to him.

The tavern was particularly busy that evening. There were a few games of dice being played around the tables, but Lei also saw a number of men he didn't recognize. All of them stood out, wearing clothing that was too dark and frowns that were too severe. Their presence disturbed the regulars, whose gambling was more subdued than usual.

Daiyu glared daggers into him, but he cheerfully ignored her. "Water, please."

He thought he heard her growl something under her breath, but he didn't catch what it was. He started to ask her to clarify but thought better of it. She turned around and slammed a drink in front of him.

He didn't have a chance to say anything before she twirled and stomped away, her face completely changing as she approached another customer. Her glare became a beaming smile, and her chosen target almost melted in his seat.

Lei felt an unfamiliar pang of jealousy. There had been a time when she had looked at him that way, a time when he thought he had even deserved her smile. But he had lost her affection, and that had been deserved as well.

He picked up his cup and took a sip, almost spitting it out when he realized she'd served him beer. He cursed out loud, but Daiyu looked as though she hadn't heard him, even though the tavern was fairly quiet. He raised the cup to slam it down and get attention, but stopped. Daiyu was his link to information. He couldn't risk her throwing him out, especially with the number of triads from out of town here.

So he masked his anger by taking another sip. The beer tasted dirty, somehow, and completely unpleasant. What had once been his favorite beverage held no pleasure anymore. He set the cup down on the bar, wondering again at the change that had so suddenly come over him. Had they done something to him in the monastery when he'd visited? It didn't seem likely, but he couldn't rule anything out. Very little made sense.

He looked up when he heard an angry hiss in his ear. This evening she smelled of jasmine, a familiar scent that brought back both pleasant and painful memories. "I told you not to come."

He met her gaze calmly. "I'm sorry. I don't want to fight or argue, but I will find out what happened to my brother."

The line wasn't rehearsed, but spilled out of him spontaneously. He wasn't even sure he meant it until he said it. But it felt true to him.

She backed away from him as though she'd burned herself. Her gaze was thoughtful, but still angry, when she turned to the other customers.

Lei wasn't sure saying anything else would help his cause, so he remained silent. He nursed his beer, unwilling and afraid to fall back into his old patterns. Fortunately, the desire to drink he thought he'd feel never materialized. Every sip was disgusting and he longed for a cup of water to wash it all down.

The hours drifted away, and Daiyu never said another word to him. She didn't even so much as check to see if his cup was still full or not. But every once in a while she would look at him as though she was trying to make the most important decision of her life.

He knew Daiyu might be putting herself at risk for telling him anything, but she was an adult, and one who could take care of herself. She would tell him when and if she decided.

The evening grew late, and he started to wonder if he had made a mistake by coming here. He had been so certain, but if he didn't receive the information he wanted, he might have risked everything for nothing.

There were still a few patrons in the bar when Daiyu came to him. He knew immediately she had made her decision, but she looked sorry to have made it. "Come with me. We can't talk here."

Fang looked around the room, seeing many of the faces he didn't recognize among the remaining patrons. He didn't know what she had planned, but he was willing to trust her. She deserved nothing less from him.

Daiyu led him out the front door, taking an immediate left and leaving town. Fang followed without question, keeping his eyes open for any of the faces he didn't recognize.

He assumed that Daiyu had used whatever influence she had to give them a little time. Gratitude welled up inside of him, knowing the risks she took for his sake.

His eyes narrowed when he realized something wasn't right. If she was leaving with him, they would've left in a different direction, either toward his place or hers. But the trail they were on led through some woods and out of town over one of the bridges.

"Where are we going?" Lei asked. He knew the answer, but wanted to hear her say it. She couldn't have hurt him much more if she'd stabbed him in the stomach and left him to bleed out.

She stopped at an intersection of trails surrounded by tall trees. "I'm sorry, Lei. I tried to warn you, and I tried to do everything I could, but you wouldn't work with me. You brought this upon yourself."

Half a dozen black shapes detached themselves from the

trees, creating a circle around the two of them. Daiyu gave him one last sad look before stepping out of the circle. None of the shadows tried to stop her, and she walked back in the direction of the Old Goat.

Lei had heard of such squads. Rumors had always circulated about assassination groups sent by the triads. When you saw a shadow like this, your life was over. The only people they didn't fight with were monks, and Lei certainly wasn't one of those.

Daiyu walked back toward Two Bridges without ever looking back at him. He wanted to call after her, but it would do no good. She had made her decision. Now he had to live through it. The strange thing was, even though he felt the pain of betrayal, he couldn't blame her. She was in deep with the triads, and this was her only way out.

He thought about his sword. If he drew it, summoning his power into the blade, he knew he would kill them. But he would also draw the wrath of the monks upon him. There was only so much they were willing to tolerate, and killing six assassins with a sword and his power was a step too far. Perhaps there would be a day where he could reasonably challenge that belief, but that day wasn't today.

That left defeating six assassins with just his hands, a feat he wasn't looking forward to. The big question, as of yet unanswered, was just how skilled these assassins were, and how much they knew about the powers he possessed. Would they be trained to fight against the powers of the monasteries? Lei didn't dare to guess. But he had no choice but to use the skills he had recently developed.

If he was going to test them, there was no better time. He took a deep breath, summoning a shield with one hand while summoning an attack with the other. Even though the movements came naturally, he struggled to understand how he had come to possess such skill. He'd never trained like this in the monasteries. And yet, as he held both moves, nothing could have felt easier.

The shadows shifted, and Lei couldn't tell if they could see what he had done, or if they were just preparing their attack. Either way, Lei didn't plan on giving them the time to ready themselves. Defeating six enemies, trained exclusively in the art of killing, was no small task. His attack would give him an advantage, and his defense would protect him in case of emergency. There was little else he could do.

Lei didn't even thrust out his hand. His enemies would receive no warning. The blast shot from his palm, knocking two of the assassins back into the trees, their dark clothes disappearing in the moonlit shadows. Lei didn't like that he wouldn't be able to see them, but with any luck they'd be knocked unconscious against a tree or two.

The attack only caused the others to hesitate for a moment. Then they were on him, swarming him and trying to open him up with their blades. Lei was forced to use his shield within the first few moments of combat, giving up ground by the yard so they wouldn't surround him. The forest had been replaced by a thick cloud of sharpened steel, all of it reaching out toward him, singing in the cool night air.

The defensive wall held for a moment, giving Lei enough time to prepare another attack with his free hand. As soon as the wall dropped and the assassins charged, Lei released his energy, throwing them all back several paces, tumbling end over end. The attack had been only a fraction of his power, though, and soon he saw that all six of his opponents were on their feet and ready for him. He swore loudly.

He looked down at his sword. Why didn't he just kill

them? No doubt that was their plan for him. Why should he take it easy? Something inside of him rebelled, the same feeling he was coming to recognize. It was the same feeling he got when he tried to drink beer.

It was his brother.

Lei didn't know how or why, but the moment the thought occurred to him, he knew it was true. Somehow, some part of his brother's spirit had lodged itself inside of him, guiding him... or perhaps forcing him to do what it wanted.

He didn't have time to work out the implications. But somehow, the knowledge allowed him to quiet the disease within. Of course Jian would never have wanted to kill. He had sworn an oath to protect life as much as he could.

But Lei had never taken such an oath. He'd been kicked out of the monasteries far before that time, and it was his life or the lives of the assassins.

Lei grabbed his sword, allowing his power to fill the blade. He listened for his brother, using one of his precious moments to ensure Jian wouldn't fight him. Lei could feel the stirrings of discontent, but whatever part of his brother remained seemed to understand there was no better way forward. It was the first time the brothers had agreed on anything in years.

All six assassins approached, creating a loose semicircle in front of him. Lei knew exactly what to do. He shifted his weight, moving so that the hilt of his sword was pointed at the assassin on his far left. Lei remembered cutting down the tree with one cut, remembered just how much energy it had taken. So little was needed.

Time seemed to slow down and expand, Lei's eyes taking in everything. The assassins prepared to attack as one, only paces away from him. The one on the far left, who would be the first to die, was raising his arms above his head in a classic overhead cut. Lei shifted his sheath, pulling it up so that his blade was parallel to the ground. With one smooth motion he drew the sword, allowing the focused energy to leap from the blade as he made a single, almost perfectly horizontal cut.

The crescent of sharpened energy sprang from the sword, eager for release. Lei completed his cut, and the tip of the blade stopped just beyond the assassin on his far right. The assassins all took another step forward, but Lei took no move to defend himself. The closest was almost near enough to touch, but Lei only checked to make sure his blade was clean before he sheathed it in the moonlight once again.

A dozen halves collapsed around him, a sickly mess of blood and guts that soaked into the ground. Lei took a few slow steps back, making sure none of the blood would touch him.

With one cut, he'd obtained an instant victory. Vicious pride and wonder fought against the terror he felt as he looked at his own hands.

He pushed all the feelings aside. Later, there would be time.

But now the chase was about to begin. Now, he didn't just have the triads after him.

The monks would be pursuing him, too.

There would be no safe places. Not for him. Never again.

20

Fang breathed softly through his nose, fighting the concern that welled up inside him. More than once, he caught himself beginning to focus his power, and he forced himself to release it gently. There was no telling how sensitive the monks would be to his presence. At their current distance, Fang could feel the monks' energy, but he was fairly confident that he was only able to because it was a large group. So long as none of the monks were more skilled than him, he should be safe.

He couldn't risk focusing his energy. The moment he did, he would shine like a beacon to the monks. So although it would have given him a level of comfort he didn't currently feel, he kept his hands still.

His attention was on the boy. Perhaps it was an exaggeration to say his life was in the boy's hands, but it felt that way.

He would have given half the coin in his bag to know what was being said. The boy appeared nonchalant, as though he was only disturbed that the monks were slowing him down on his chores. A few of the monks occasionally gazed in the direction of the barn and Fang fought the urge to dive behind the hay. Between the shadows and the hay he was plenty concealed. Although normal citizens often ascribed magical abilities to the monks, Fang knew none of them could see into the dark shadows.

The moments piled up slowly, and doubts raced through his mind. Surely by now the monks would have left if they didn't suspect anything? Were they trying to beg for their meal?

Fang centered his attention on his breath. His inhale, pause, and slow exhale became his world as he detached from the scene he observed. Control was the edge that separated life from death, and he wouldn't lose it.

When the monks turned to leave, Fang almost collapsed in relief. The farmer spoke briefly with the boy, then returned to whatever work he had been doing inside the house. The boy, looking as though he was second-guessing himself, returned to the barn.

The boy looked like he was walking to his own execution. His eyes stared furrows into the ground, and his pace was slow and lazy. Fang split his attention between the boy and the retreating monks. There was still a chance this was an elaborate trap.

When the boy returned to the shadows of the barn, Fang slowly stood up. "You convinced them?"

"Yes."

Fang stepped forward and grabbed the boy's chin with his hand. The boy recoiled weakly, but Fang's grip was tight. He lifted his chin up so their eyes were forced to meet. "Tell me the truth, boy."

"Yes. I told them I hadn't seen anyone. They didn't ask much of me. Most of their questions were for my father."

There was fear in the young man's eyes as they darted

from side to side, but Fang detected no duplicity. He believed the boy.

Again, the prejudices of the monks worked against them. Had they focused more on the boy they might have learned the truth, no matter the boy's efforts. But monks ignored the young unless they were gifted. It was one of a thousand ways the monks dug the pit that they would all soon fall into, never to rise again.

"You think that I will not honor my word?"

The boy said nothing, knowing either answer was a potential trap.

Fang considered killing the boy and his family. Most likely, their bodies wouldn't be discovered for a few days, meaning he would have that much more time when he wasn't being followed. He had no desire, but the action seemed prudent.

"You have no need to fear, boy. One day, my word will be law. Until then, you have my thanks." Fang pulled out his purse and gave the boy three silver pieces. The cost was a pittance to Fang, but the boy had likely only seen that much money on special occasions. The money wouldn't guarantee his silence, but the boy would think long and hard before betraying him, knowing it would probably cost him the silver.

Fang checked his surroundings one last time before leaving the barn. With luck, he had thrown off his pursuers to such a degree that he would be able to plan his next attack well. He was still alive, which would please his master, but there was much to accomplish yet.

After he had walked half the day without seeing anyone, Fang finally decided he was safe. He pulled out his map and studied the notations his master had made. The next monastery was the one above Two Bridges, the same monastery the monk he had killed was from. He felt a sense of satisfaction as he altered his course slightly. To him, it felt as though he was finishing a story that began with Jian's death and ended with the destruction of his home.

He walked throughout the day, figuring he would find a place to camp outside of Two Bridges sometime that night. The day felt full of promise.

Night had fallen several hours ago by the time he finally saw the glow of torches in the valley below. He picked up his pace, eager to rest. When he stopped, it took him a few moments to figure out why.

A sense of wrongness permeated this place, a sense of the natural order being disturbed. The feeling was indistinct, but it was similar to the sensations he felt after completing his own work. Violence opened a tear in the world. Most of the time it was too subtle to notice, but here a great degree of violence had happened in a short time, and not long ago.

Fang dropped into a crouch and opened up his senses. The moon had set less than an hour ago, so his eyes could make out little but the outlines of shapes. No unnatural sounds reached his ears, but he would recognize that smell anywhere. It was the smell of blood and viscera, the bitter smell of recent battle.

He allowed his eyes to adjust to the darkened clearing, and the indistinct shapes resolved into bodies. Or, parts of bodies, more accurately. Six. Six men had been cut in half, and it looked like it had happened all at once.

His eyes narrowed. Cutting through entire bodies, while popular in stories, was difficult for any swordsman to do, no matter how skilled. To cut down six, especially six at once, was impossible. Unless one was gifted.

Was there another like him somewhere nearby? This

didn't have the feel of a monk's work, but he was the only one he knew of who existed outside the monasteries. If one was gifted, one was a monk or dead. There really was no middle ground. The thought of another made his blood race and his heart pound. Earlier today, he had believed there was no one left to challenge him besides his own master.

As he crouched patiently, he began to notice even more details. The cuts on the men were sharp, too sharp to be made by any steel, or by any energy attack Fang knew. He also noticed the clothing the assassins wore. He had seen those clothes before. These men had been gang members. In a way, these men were his allies. Fang's knowledge was limited, but he was aware his master cooperated with the triads, both to obtain supplies and to coordinate the revolution. Whoever had crossed these men had crossed him, even if they were unaware.

He knew what his mission was, but this discovery changed everything. He couldn't allow a warrior like this to go unchallenged.

Fang stood up, a new plan forming in his mind. He would find the warrior who did this. They would fight, and Fang would kill him.

21

As soon as Lei left the field of battle he started plotting out his next steps. First, he needed to collect everything from his house that he wanted to take with him on the run. He owned very little, but there were a few items he couldn't bear parting with.

The journey didn't take long. Daiyu had only led him a half mile away from Two Bridges, so there was little ground to recover. The thought of her sent a stab of disbelief through him. Sure, he deserved what had come to him, but the betrayal still stung.

He shoved thoughts of her away as he opened the door to his house. He'd already made the list in his head of what he wanted. His pot, pan, and fire-starting equipment went into the bag, followed quickly by the tools he used to maintain his sword. His traveling clothes came next. There was little else he needed. With a start, he realized he didn't have anything to remember his brother by. If possessions indicated the impact a person had in the world, Jian hadn't even scratched the surface.

Lei's eyes stopped on a painting hanging on his wall. It

was the only decoration he possessed. The painting was fairly simple calligraphy, the artist's inexperience obvious even to someone whose eye was as untrained as Lei's. One of the symbols for peace was written in dark ink. Daiyu had created it, back when their relationship had meant something to them both.

He hesitated. He wanted to let it go, but he couldn't bring himself to do so. It was all he had of her. He grabbed the small scroll and rolled it up, tying it with the same string it had once hung from. The art was the last piece that went into the bag.

Lei looked around. His house wasn't much, but it was all he had in the world. Perhaps the triads would leave the place alone, but he doubted it. No one attacked the triads and survived the conflict. Examples had to be made. If Lei had had any family left, he would have feared for their safety. But there was only him. Daiyu might suffer, but he doubted it. She was a survivor. No doubt that was why she had turned on him. She'd make it out of all of this, her position probably improved somehow.

A wave of exhaustion crashed over him, his eyelids suddenly feeling as though they were heavy enough to drag his entire body to the ground. He needed someplace safe to rest. But where? No one in town would shelter him if he had offended the triads. It would mean the loss of all they loved if they were discovered.

An idea curled the edges of his lips into a smile. He certainly didn't need to sleep inside. He stepped outside, closed the door, and took in his house one more time. Truthfully, it wasn't much more than a small wooden hut surrounded by other huts, but it had been his. Then he crossed the street and climbed up the side of his neighbor's house. Mr. Wu was an old man, and cantankerous to boot.

His hearing was failing, but that didn't stop him from yelling at everyone for every action he considered inappropriate. If Lei was discovered, he didn't mind Mr. Wu suffering the consequences. A faint rumbling in his stomach indicated Jian's displeasure, but Lei was too tired to care. He lay down carefully on the tile, closing his eyes and falling asleep instantly.

He woke to the sounds of shouting from the street below. He opened his eyes, the glaring afternoon sun bringing tears right away. His long hair was sticky with sweat, the late summer sun having beat down on him for hours. Moving silently, Lei crouched and poked his head up so he could see the scene in front of his house.

Triads.

There were a lot of them. Far more than Lei would have anticipated. He'd really kicked the hornet's nest this time. They were led by a large man, a man Lei knew he had seen somewhere before. For all the man's size, he moved with power and control, his years as a martial artist immediately obvious. Tattoos ran up and down his arms, and Lei remembered.

The man's name was Niu. He was the local underboss, the highest-ranking triad member in the area. He lived in a compound between Two Bridges and Windown, managing the gang activity in both villages. Lei had never resorted to crime, but one didn't flirt with poverty the way he had without learning about the underworld. Perhaps Daiyu had mentioned him once or twice as well.

Lei had never met him personally, but the description certainly fit. He didn't look to be the sort of man one crossed willingly. The fact that he stood in front of Lei's house at all said volumes about the offense Lei had committed.

Crashing sounds echoed out of his place, and Lei

wondered idly what they were even throwing around. There was almost nothing left inside. Had they brought in loud items just to toss around and frighten the neighbors? The thought made him chuckle grimly.

There was more crashing and a handful of young triad initiates came out of the house, shaking their heads. Apparently they hadn't found him. Lei melted against the tiles. People rarely looked up, but remaining here was hardly wise. He glanced at the sword on his hip, and a violent revulsion came over him, far stronger than before.

Fine. He wouldn't attack the entire group, as appealing as that idea was to a part of him. He watched as they asked neighbors if they'd seen Lei anytime since last night. No one had, of course. They'd all been in bed when he'd gotten up to his mischief.

Niu looked like a man who'd been denied a feast. And given his size, Lei wasn't sure he'd even withhold a single grain of rice from the man. He gave a sharp order, and the triads brought the torches towards the house.

Lei cursed. It was one thing to know that they were going to burn your house, but it was entirely another to have to watch. He looked longingly at the sword, but his urge to vomit was too strong. He felt as though he'd throw up the moment he laid a hand on his blade. He couldn't fight if his brother's spirit struggled that much against him.

The blaze didn't take long to catch. The weather had been dry lately, and the walls caught after just a minute of being exposed to the flame. From there, it was short work.

Had the house been any other, Lei might have called the fire beautiful. It reached up into the sky, the flames appearing to tickle the mountaintops the monastery rested on. Even across the street, Lei could feel the heat emanating from the building that had once been his home.

The triads had been courteous enough to bring an incredible amount of water. Lei wondered if they had drained a well, but thanks to their constant dousing of the neighboring homes and their vigilance, the fire didn't spread beyond Lei's place. The triads were vicious, but they were fair.

When he had seen enough, Lei slowly crawled back to the place where he had slept. He wasn't looking forward to staying out all day in the sun, but hiding directly across from his house hadn't been the wisest decision. No doubt the triads would keep the place under observation for the next day, just to see if he would return. At night, he figured he could sneak out, but not before then.

His anger burned as hot as his house had. This wasn't just about his brother anymore. His house and life had been stripped from him, and he wasn't the type to forgive. The triads were going to suffer for this, starting with Niu.

Lei closed his eyes and tried to get some rest. Exhaustion took him sooner than he expected.

He didn't open his eyes again until he heard the screams.

22

───────

F ang slept near the bodies of the assassins. He was tired from a long day on the road, and his body demanded rest. He found a nice, quiet clearing about a hundred yards away from the site of the massacre and fell asleep without a problem.

Judging by the position of the sun, it was late morning when he woke up. Earlier would have been better, but he wasn't going to complain. A full night of rest did him far more good than an early start would have. He was certain he would have no problem tracking the man who had done this.

He gathered some food from the area and broke his fast. A clear stream, fed by the glaciers up high, quenched his thirst. As he ate, he decided on the best approach to track the other warrior.

Any investigation had to start in Two Bridges. Fang had contacts there within the triads, and if he needed further guidance, he could always send a bird to his master.

His path to the village took him back by the bodies of

the assassins. He paused, though, as he felt a grouping of energy nearby. Monks had arrived on the scene.

The presence of the monks gave him several pieces of information. The first was that the warrior who had done this definitely wasn't part of a monastery. If he had been, the monks wouldn't have bothered to investigate. Second, it meant that whoever was responsible was about to be hunted by both the triads and the monasteries. Neither was an opponent to take lightly.

Fang crept closer, slinking from tree to tree to gain an unobstructed view of the proceedings. As he had guessed, monks were gathered around the bodies, crouching over them to see better. He saw four of them and didn't feel anyone else nearby.

He crouched himself, wondering what was best. He'd never taken on four monks before, but the time was coming when he would have to. Avoiding them would only work for so long.

He was rested and ready, and had the element of surprise. There would never be a better time. He continued creeping from tree to tree until there was only one layer of trees between him and the monks. Part of him was surprised he was able to get so close without them noticing, but all their attention was focused on the bodies in front of them.

Fang made the gestures to focus his energy. One hand made the first sign of the attack while the other worked through the motions of the Dragon's Fang. He felt his attention divide as his power became two separate attacks. As expected, he couldn't remain hidden for long. The moment he started gathering his energy, the monks all looked up as though someone had dumped a bucket of water on them.

Fang slid out from behind the trees, thrusting out one

hand and blasting the monks backward. The two in the center of the clearing received the attack most directly and tumbled end over end, rolling smoothly to their feet. The two on the edge only had to shuffle their feet to stay upright.

He felt all of them gather their energy, which compared to his felt small and tiny. His heart leaped for joy as he realized just how weak the monks were. He wanted them to know it. His right hand continued to work on the Dragon's Fang while his left cast a shield.

All four monks seemed to default to the same attack, the second two-handed sign, which Fang considered to be the most noncommittal of attacks. It focused energy, but not too tightly. It was the attack one defaulted to if unsure of a better plan. Were he wise, he would have prevented them from even launching the attacks, but he was flush with confidence. The monks had nothing that they could do to him, nothing at all.

Fang stood still, waiting for the monks to release their attacks. It took them too long, but he was patient. Not only would he kill them, but they would despair as he did. It felt right, as though he had finally found the task he had been born to do.

Their attacks came in perfect, choreographed unison. Each of them finished their focus and thrust their arms out at him. As one, four waves of focused energy lashed out at him. Fang extended his shield and the energies collided.

He couldn't see anything, but he could feel the confluence of the forces. He could feel the wills behind the attack, could feel how insignificant they were. The monks still didn't realize the danger they faced. The will to survive was the strongest, and none of the monks in front of him had learned how to harness it yet. He would have to help instruct them. Unfortunately, it would be their last lesson.

Fang grunted as the monks redoubled their efforts. They had expected to blow him away, but he was equal to the four of them combined, and he was only using one of his arms. It was the first time he had tested himself to this degree, and he found his performance satisfactory.

The monks didn't seem to know what to make of these developments. One of the older monks yelled, a primal scream that tore from his throat. Fang felt the pressure against his shield increase, but he calmly held it. They didn't have the power to break him.

Finally, the attack dissipated. Of the four, the older monk who had yelled lasted the longest, but as they dropped off one by one, they knew they were beaten. Fang dropped his shield as the monks put their hands on their knees, bending over, struggling for breath. The older man, who Fang assumed was the leader, slumped to his knees. He had given more than he should have. These monks really knew little about the realities of combat. All their training was simulated. They'd never pushed themselves the way he had.

Fang raised his hand, the Dragon's Fang long complete. The older monk, staring his death down with courage, only had time to say, "So it is you."

Fang released the attack, his aim as true as ever. It blasted a small hole through the monk's forehead and into the trees and rock beyond. The leader's lifeless body collapsed to the ground.

The other three stared in shock. All of them were younger, none of them much more than twenty. Fang assumed they hadn't seen much of the outside world, and they certainly had never come across an enemy like him. He smiled grimly as they charged him blindly, losing all control in their grief and disbelief.

It was almost too easy.

When he was done, the monks joined the assassins on the ground. Fang looked around, thinking there had to be some greater meaning to what he saw. He couldn't decide what it was, though. The best he could come up with was that at the end, everyone's body came to the same unseemly fate. It certainly wasn't poetic, but he'd never had a way with words.

It seemed a shame to waste the bodies. His master had ordered him to spread discord and fear, and dead monks seemed to fit the bill admirably. Nodding to himself as a plan took shape, Fang went on a search for the tools that he needed.

The afternoon sun was beginning to set by the time Fang returned to the clearing with a cart. Fortunately, the area where the battle took place wasn't one frequented often. He assumed that was why the assassins had chosen it for their failed trap. For Fang, it meant he had the time to leave and return before the bodies were discovered.

He was sure the monastery above had noticed the battle. They had tools available to help them detect the use of the power. But they would be patient and wait for their monks to return. He had time.

Grunting, he picked up the monks and flung them into a wagon with less care than he'd shovel manure. Once all the monks and their various body parts were in, he positioned them just so, limbs folded at unnatural angles. Everyone who saw the monks needed to know they had died a violent, painful death.

When he was satisfied with his work, he grabbed the handle of the cart and pulled it toward Two Bridges.

The town came into view quickly. Fang's timing couldn't have been much better. It was suppertime, too late to be out working in the village square, but too early to be out for the evening. He passed one or two people, but the distance was great enough that they couldn't see what was in his cart, and the bodies hadn't begun to stink, not yet.

Fang left the monks in the middle of town, and making sure no one was looking, put down the back gate of the cart so that everyone could see his work. Then he darted off into a side alley. He knew the meeting place for the local triad. They would be able to tell him who the assassins had meant to attack, and Fang could complete his deadly goals.

23

―――

Lei heard the screams and his eyes shot awake, his heart pounding. At first, he thought he'd been discovered. Maybe somehow, he had picked the only day someone climbed high enough on a nearby roof to see him. As his senses caught up, he realized that wasn't the case.

The cacophony was coming from several blocks away, near the village center. Something disastrous had happened there.

Remaining cautious, Lei crawled to the edge of the building, seeing that the shouts had attracted anyone nearby. Lei pulled on a hooded cloak from his sack and dropped to the ground.

He knew he should leave and make his way out of town. No doubt it would have been the safest course of action. But like everyone else, he was drawn in by his own curiosity. The screams had been edged with terror, and if something was happening in the middle of town, there was a very real chance it affected him. He seemed to be at the center of the storm that was washing over this quiet corner of the empire.

When he reached the square, he stopped in his tracks,

knowing almost immediately what had happened. There were bodies in the cart, and from the way they were dressed, they were monks. Lei was fairly certain that if necessary he could kill a monk, but besides him, he could only think of one other: the man who had killed his brother. The assassin was close, and he was still at work.

Lei stepped a few paces closer, just to make sure he was seeing what he thought he was seeing. He was saddened when his glance confirmed it. There was a familiar face there, one he'd seen just a few days ago.

Chen.

Lei thought back to their fight. Chen had always been one of the best of the monks. Maybe not in skill, but in kindness, a gift that was in much rarer supply. Lei didn't care much for the monasteries, but Chen had deserved better. From the bruising on his face and body, it looked like he deserved much better.

Sorrow and anger wrestled for supremacy, leaving him feeling empty inside. All of it was meaningless. All of it was pointless. The Order of the Serpent couldn't bring down the monasteries; the system was far too powerful. It was violence for its own sake, a waste.

The townspeople didn't seem to see it that way. Many of them were on their knees, crying.

Sometimes Lei forgot what the monasteries and the monks meant to others. They were symbols of hope, protection, and more. They helped local militias patrol the land and keep travelers safe. Monasteries lived off the donations and extras of the towns they sat next to. Beyond that, the monasteries were considered almost infallible. It was a lie everyone bought into.

Everyone's attention was distracted, so Lei had no problem turning around and leaving the town square. He had better places to be, places where he could seek revenge. He remembered the face of the man he'd once been willing to call a friend, and he added it to the crimes of the man who had killed his brother. The murderer would pay for every drop of blood he had shed.

Lei found his way to the Old Goat without problem. The streets beyond the square were empty, and when he stepped through the door, he saw that everyone who wasn't a triad had heard the shouts. Those who remained were waiting for him. Of that, he had no doubt.

Daiyu's face froze like a rock when she saw him. Had she expected him to survive? When they'd been together, it had often felt like she understood him better than he understood himself. Had she suspected he would return, no matter the cost?

There was a scuffling of wood on the floor as chairs turned to face him. There were four triad members within the Old Goat, each one acting as though he was the toughest man on the planet. Lei fought the urge to laugh at them as he walked straight toward Daiyu, ignoring their angry glares.

Her face didn't move a hair as he approached, but everyone else did. Before he could even take three steps he was surrounded by men drawing knives and swords. He stopped, trying to keep the exasperation from his face and failing. He leaned to the side so that he could see Daiyu between two of the thugs. "Really?"

She shrugged, as if to say there wasn't anything she could do, and even if there was, she wouldn't help him. He sighed, fighting his mounting frustration. The first triad who moved instantly regretted it. Lei's energy attack flung him back against the far wall, his body going limp as it collided with tables and chairs on the way. The second fighter appeared confused as his sword struck Lei's invisible shield, but it was short-lived as Lei's spinning kick cracked against the side of his face. The third came in with a knife, stabbing straight at Lei's heart. Lei caught the wrist with ease, forced the man's arm around, and made him stab himself in the shoulder. The young initiate fell to the ground, his face a mask of pain.

The fourth was no fool. He came in slowly, but Lei was in no mood to dance. While making a sign with one hand, he tried to sweep the triad's feet. The man stepped back, which Lei had anticipated. But now Lei was on the floor, his hand pointing up at the criminal. He released his attack, flinging the man up against the ceiling of the Old Goat. Lei could have allowed the attack to dissipate, but he held it, pressing the man flat against the ceiling, his eyes wide with fear, pinned by an invisible force he could barely comprehend.

The third man, the one Lei had stabbed in the shoulder, got up. But when he saw his partner pinned against the ceiling, violating every force of nature he knew, he ran out the door, swallowing what little pride he had.

Finally, Lei had the quiet moment with Daiyu that he was waiting for. He stepped up to the bar, making sure never to release the sign that held the man pinned above them.

"Water, please."

Daiyu's smile might have been one of the most genuine he had seen in some time. Just looking at her was enough to make most of his concerns fall away. Suddenly, some of the pieces of the past few days fell into place.

"You've moved up, haven't you?"

She handed him the water. "I have. I report directly to Niu now."

"You can tell him that I'm coming."

He could never be sure with Daiyu, but she looked happy, as though relieved.

Lei had come to talk, to make sure he had made their relationship right before he left. Now, he saw there was no need. At times they might act like fools, but he felt that he knew her heart. His own was light.

"I will," she said.

He stood up, noting the way her eyes followed his every movement. He made a deep bow toward her. "I'll be seeing you soon, I think."

She gave the slightest of nods, almost imperceptible.

Lei stood up straight and stepped out of the Old Goat.

Moments later, he heard the *thunk* of the fourth triad landing on the dirty floor of his favorite tavern.

24

Fang remembered the location of the hideout from the instructions his master had given him. The journey only took him a few moments in the small town. He stopped when he saw the building he was looking for.

Perhaps hideout wasn't the most accurate term. The triads maintained an uneasy peace with the local militia. They provided goods and services that were illegal but necessary, and the militia turned a blind eye so long as the triads never stepped too far out of line. Fang had heard some rumors that suggested that the local governor was considering a crackdown, but it was a constant refrain from members of the court. Fang would believe it if he saw it happening with his own eyes.

The "hideout," as his master had called it, was a perfect example. The building was clearly one of the largest in the village, a single-story house with a solid, ten-foot-high wall around it. Based on the quality of the woodwork, there was no doubt it was one of the most expensive buildings in town, and it wasn't even the main headquarters of the triad.

Fang was admitted to the property with little fanfare. He

possessed all the correct passwords, and although he was a stranger to the men guarding the gate, they had been well-taught not to disobey or ask questions. Fang imagined they received plenty of unknown visitors.

He was surprised to see that the place was a hive of activity. From what little he knew of triad business, he had assumed it would be fairly quiet, but there were almost two dozen young men on the grounds. Fang guessed the assembled crowd made up most of the triad's strength in this area. Most likely the buildup had something to do with the dead assassins. They were all here in pursuit of the same man.

Eventually Fang found someone who had enough authority to make some sort of decision. Fang announced who he was and watched as the man turned pale. "You are in luck," the frightened man forced out. "Our boss, Niu, is here. I will take you to him."

Fang was led into the building. As they walked, Fang paid close attention to the paintings and decorations that adorned the walls. Many of the walls were painted with incredible scenes, filled with a detail he wouldn't have believed if he wasn't seeing it with his own eyes. He recognized several of the scenes from the well-known tale of the Foxcatcher, the name given to an ancient warrior of legend. The scenes depicted weren't of battle, which surprised Fang, who expected a more martial theme. They were scenes of the loyalty the Foxcatcher was so famously known for.

Loyalty above all else, he suspected. It made sense that his master cooperated with this particular triad. Fang also believed that loyalty to a master was necessary for a successful life. Lack of loyalty was but one of the reasons modern society was failing so terribly.

They reached a large room that Fang assumed was near the center of the building. A lone man kneeled there, enormous and yet completely peaceful. Fang immediately recognized a very dangerous man. Niu stood from his kneeling position in one smooth motion, his bulk flowing as though it was water in a stream. He gave Fang a bow of moderate depth. Unsure of his status, Fang returned the bow, slightly deeper. In his experience, it never hurt to be more respectful than necessary. He had no pride to save.

The giant straightened and spoke, his voice low and gravelly. "My name is Niu, and I am in control of this region. It is an honor to meet you."

"And my name is Fang, and I represent the Order of the Serpent."

"You come at an auspicious time, and word of your deeds has already reached my ears."

That came as no surprise to Fang. He had heard the screams not long after he left the square. No doubt Niu was aware of the event almost the instant it was discovered. However, he wasn't sure how much Niu knew of their plans, so he needed to be careful about what he said. "The monks were an obstacle to my mission, but they provided little challenge."

Niu didn't react to Fang's claim. Either he was an excellent card player, or he already suspected the extent of Fang's strength. "Perhaps we may walk together in life for a time."

"Perhaps. For now, I seek the man who killed the six assassins with one attack."

Niu studied him thoughtfully, his eyes wandering over Fang. "Such a man doesn't cause you to fear?"

"No."

Fang's simple answer did more to convince Niu than any explanation could have.

"Then our paths do align, although you may reconsider when you hear what I have to say." Niu gestured to some of the men standing near the walls, then indicated that Fang should come and sit down with him. Both sat, a small table was brought out, and rice wine was brought to both of them. Fang filled Niu's cup first, then Niu filled his. They raised their glasses, but Fang allowed Niu to drink first. The test wasn't foolproof, but it was better than nothing. Niu gave him a knowing smile and sipped his drink. Then Fang followed suit.

The wine was excellent. Fang didn't drink often, but this wine was the best he had ever tasted.

Niu spoke. "We know the name of the man who killed the assassins. His name is Lei, a local man who never seemed as though he would amount to much. His brother was a monk, the monk who I assume you killed a couple of weeks ago. Since then he has been investigating, trying to figure out who or what killed his brother. He was causing trouble, and so I decided to have him killed. Imagine my surprise when I learned the assassins had failed in such a spectacular fashion."

"There was never any evidence that he possessed the power?"

"No, it was known that he had the power. As a young boy, he was raised in the monastery with his brother. However, the story goes that when he was a young man he killed a girl with a weapon and was expelled. I never knew why he was allowed to live. For years he has been nothing but a drunk and a nuisance. His skill was unexpected."

Fang chewed on the new information. Something about this didn't make sense. The monasteries never ejected anyone. If someone committed an offense grave enough to merit the punishment, they were killed instead. The monasteries served as a leash on the power in society. They didn't allow those with the gift to wander freely, especially not a man with the strength of this one. Fang sensed a mystery to this man, a mystery he had no clues to.

"What steps have you taken?" he asked the boss.

"I made my way here as soon as I could. I brought some of my best fighters with me." He gestured toward the men who circled the room. Each of them was wary, and all looked like they knew their way around a sword. "Once here, we searched the village and his home. He was nowhere to be found. We burned his house, but received no response. The only explanation we can think of is that he escaped to the monastery to seek protection from us."

Fang wondered how true that might be. The course of action was certainly reasonable. He could think of several situations where the monastery would be the first place he checked. But still, something didn't quite fit, a fact he couldn't articulate even to himself.

It seemed as though Niu was waiting for a response. When he didn't get one, he continued. "Unfortunately, I do not have the strength to approach the monastery directly, and I must leave soon. If he did escape there, he is beyond my reach for the moment. However, if you are as strong as you imply, perhaps you could achieve what I cannot."

Fang had guessed that was the direction the conversation was going. He thought about his choice. Attacking an entire monastery was bold, and perhaps even foolish. If the man was hiding there, he would be formidable on his own. Combined with other monks, he might be undefeatable.

But Fang was attracted to the idea. His fight against the

monks had only whetted his appetite. They were so much weaker than he expected them to be. Maybe an entire monastery would be enough of a challenge? The idea made his blood race. What better way existed to prove his strength, and the strength of the serpent?

The words of his master echoed in his mind. He was supposed to choose safety, but the future wouldn't be won without risk. "I will."

Niu leaned back slightly, and Fang tried to decipher what the man was thinking. Was that a hint of fear he saw in the boss' eyes? It was there and gone before he could decide. Regardless, he could tell he had earned the giant's respect. This time, he filled both their cups, and they drank together.

"To the end of the monasteries," Niu toasted.

"To the end of the monasteries," Fang repeated.

25

Lei took most of the next night and day to reach Niu's compound, nestled deep in the woods off the main road between Two Bridges and Windown. The trip wasn't that long, but Lei moved with caution. He assumed his actions would attract the attention of the monastery in addition to that of the triads. He avoided the road and slept without a fire, unwilling to risk accidental discovery.

As he walked, he thought about his revelation. He had no physical evidence, nothing he could point to, but he was certain he was right. Somehow, some part of his brother's spirit now resided in him. Such possessions often happened in the legends the monks told, but he'd always dismissed it with the rest of their beliefs.

He didn't feel all that different. His skills were improved considerably and his power seemed stronger than before. Other than those changes, his body and mind seemed to function the way they always had. If he was possessed, it felt as though Jian's spirit was sitting on the front porch of his body instead of making itself at home in the bedroom.

The question was, if he was possessed, would he even

know it? As the old saying went, if you didn't know who the village idiot was, it was probably you. Were his thoughts even his own?

He couldn't allow himself to travel down those paths. That way was only confusion and despair. There was no way of knowing, but he could be fairly certain. He could trust his feelings. He had to if he didn't want to go mad.

Lei arrived at the compound in the afternoon, the day after the monks had been displayed in the village square. Despite everything, he had slept well and was feeling rested. A simmering cauldron of disgust sat squarely in his stomach every time he thought of Chen and the indignities that had been done to his body.

The compound was something between a fortress and a house. When it first came into view, Lei shook his head, almost unable to believe the governor would allow such a place to be built on his lands. The walls were stone, and several feet thick at their base. Lei could climb them, but he was pretty certain one of the dozen guards patrolling the walls would put a crossbow bolt in him before he reached the top. One downside of having to use hands to focus energy was that it made one as vulnerable as ever when climbing.

Between the walls and the house itself sat at least two hundred paces of open, treeless ground. There was a garden in one far corner, but it too was walled off, with the guards concentrating a fair amount of their focus there.

The house was beautiful, as well. It was two levels tall, with a sloped tile roof that was nearly as high as the tree tops. Lei had never been here before, but he remembered the awe in the voices of those who had visited. Niu's place had a reputation that was well-earned.

Lei squatted deep in the shadows and watched the

house. With his abilities, there were options. He could try slicing through the stone of the outer walls, or perhaps he could focus on the front gate. He ran through a few different scenarios, testing each to see if it would grant him success. Death was too high a price to pay for revenge. He kept thinking back to that last look Daiyu had given him. For the first time in years, he dared to hope.

As he watched, a caravan approached, and Lei recognized several of the faces. The most obvious, seated on an enormous charger that looked as though it would collapse under his weight, was Niu.

So, the underboss had remained in Two Bridges for an extra day. Lei had assumed Niu had returned immediately after burning his house. But he supposed the boss could have had other work to do.

Niu was greeted by many of his household staff, and Lei dismissed the idea of attacking immediately. Niu would die, but the others he was less certain about. The voice he recognized as Jian's rebelled against the idea of killing so many, but Lei didn't mind. If anyone decided to serve someone like Niu, they deserved what was coming to them.

An image of Daiyu floated through his mind, but he ignored the hypocrisy. She was different.

When Niu walked through the gate, another idea occurred to Lei. He could just walk in if he wanted.

The more he tested the idea, the better it sounded. Before he could begin to second-guess himself, he formed the sign of the third shield with his left hand. This sign formed a half-sphere around him, almost completely protecting him. It was another move he was certain he had never done before, and yet the weave of his power held without problem.

Lei walked down toward the path. As soon as he stepped

foot on the smooth surface, he heard a *whizz* as an arrow shot wide of his position.

"Halt!" screamed a guard above the gate.

Lei wasn't sure if the shot had been intentionally wide or a miss, but he didn't have any desire to sit and find out. He was confident in his shield, but he'd never tested it against a wave of crossbow bolts. Better to move forward and keep them guessing.

A few steps later, two more bolts shot from the walls. These two hit directly but bounced off his shield. The crossbowmen frowned. No doubt they had some idea what they were up against now. Suddenly, there were thirty men lined up against him.

The bolts came in waves. Lei guessed there were about ten at a time, but his shield held. He bowed his head. If this was just the beginning of what Jian had learned in the monastery, how much more powerful could he have become if he'd remained?

He didn't bother responding to the archers. He had an attack ready to go in his right hand, but that was in case of emergency.

Finally, everyone at the wall coordinated their efforts to release at once, but still his shield held with ease. The bolts clattered to the ground around him, and he stifled the urge to laugh at his enemies.

The gates began to close in front of him, but that wouldn't do. He focused more energy into his right hand, ensuring he didn't allow his shield to fall. The stray bolt still streaked towards him. When the doors were almost closed, he raised his hand and released his attack. The doors were slammed back, and from the screams coming from behind them, a few of Niu's men had been in unfortunate positions.

Lei stepped through the gate, looking around. One brave

soul with a sword charged at him, but he too bounced off the shield. Few things could look quite as foolish, in Lei's estimation.

The fight, or what remained of it, came to a stop as Niu himself stepped out of his house. He took one glance at Lei and seemed to understand the situation. "You."

Lei gave a mock bow. "I know you're involved with the group that killed my brother. I've come for answers."

Niu shook his head. "You're a fool for coming. But you've made my job easier. We can kill you right here." He gestured toward the wall. "You think we haven't thought about what to do if a monk comes here?"

Lei watched, curious, as a few of the guards tossed large rocks outside the wall. They seemed to be attached to something, but Lei couldn't make it out.

Suddenly, the very dirt underneath Lei's feet seemed to move. He thought for a moment it was the ground, but then realized that thin netted rope was being pulled underneath him. The slow movement suddenly accelerated, and he hit the ground hard and was pulled back. He shook his head, trying to clear out the cobwebs, when he realized he had dropped his shield.

The guards had all been prepared, and the dusty excess netting was thrown over him. He didn't even have time to react as a pile of guards drove knees and feet into him, knocking the wind clean out of him. The netting encircled him, and hands roughly pulled his arms behind him, through the netting and out of it. His wrists were tied together, followed by his thumbs, index fingers, and all the rest. When the guards were done, no matter how hard he strained, he couldn't make a single sign.

He was lifted up just in time to see Niu's meaty fist crash into his torso. Lei doubled over, coughing out the air he'd just managed to breathe. Lei had been in a fair number of fights before, but he'd never been hit like that. He thought he'd rather be run over by a boulder falling down a hill. He tried to stand, but his legs were convinced they were done, and he couldn't do it.

"Tie him to the post," Niu ordered.

He knew it was unwise, but he couldn't help himself. "Here I just thought we could talk about it."

Niu turned around, his fist smashing into Lei's abdomen again. Lei was certain the punch had gone through his stomach and hit his spine. He dropped again, not even trying to get his legs to work.

They didn't bother removing the netting. They just stood him up next to a post and wrapped straps around his chest, abdomen, and legs. When they were done, Lei couldn't move at all.

That was what he got for getting too confident. His skills and powers made him strong, but they didn't make him invincible.

He was trapped, and he wasn't looking forward to whatever they had planned for him.

26

F ang basked in the memories of his most recent trip up the mountain, stopping to reflect at the very place where he had killed the monk. The damage was still there. He could see the hole from the Dragon's Fang, could see the smooth slice he had made with his dagger. Fighting that monk had been the most alive he had felt in a long time.

The question was, would his brother be equally skilled? The early evidence was promising, but fighting took something special, something that couldn't be judged until the two of them met. The idea of coming across a true challenge excited Fang, pushing him past the scene of his previous victory towards his next one.

He didn't have a plan, nor did he worry about one. He would approach the monastery, break down their doors, and put everyone inside to death. The rest was in the hands of fate, if such a thing even existed.

Fang crested the top of the mountain in the early evening. No one stood watch at the gates, though they were locked. In fact, from what he could feel, there was very little power in the monastery at all. He frowned. Either the building was almost abandoned or the monks were weaker than he expected.

Once, he had thought about fighting the monks on fair terms. But that idea had quickly disappeared. If he was going to be outnumbered, he wanted every advantage he could get. He pulled his dagger from its sheath. Fighting with it gave him a tremendous advantage, but the monks should have known what they were getting into when they took their oaths. With two flicks of his dagger and a single energy push, the doors crumbled inward. If his history lessons were accurate, this monastery had never fallen before.

Until today.

Fang sprinted into the monastery, dagger ready and a shield cast in front of him. He expected the attacks to start at any moment, for the monks to surprise him from all directions.

The monastery was empty, without a soul in sight. Fang stepped forward cautiously, expecting each step to be the one that sprung the trap. But step after step, he revealed nothing. The cold breeze blew dust around the abandoned central square.

Fang cursed. His sense from outside the walls had been accurate. But why would they abandon one of their fortresses? And who was still here? Fang could feel the energy from at least one person, and someone must have remained behind to lock the door.

He stepped into the training courtyard, unprepared for the overwhelming sense of remembrance that attacked him. This hadn't even been his monastery, and yet he felt as though he had been here, training with the other initiates, running through the motions that were now as natural to him as breathing.

Flashes hit him, each one emotional. Bandaging one friend's training wound. Racing against another. The childhood crush he had on a local girl who delivered food to the monastery once a month. The force of the past almost brought him to his knees.

Then he thought of the fight on the cliff and the long fall to the river below, blood pouring from wounds given to him by the very adults he thought were his teachers. Adults he had trusted to protect him.

He wiped his eyes as another sharp breeze cut through the empty courtyard. He hadn't been here. His past was behind him. But others had grown up the same way he had. He could see the well-worn pits from hundreds of years of students standing in the same spots and performing the same movements, solid rock giving way to the inevitable power of time and repetition.

Fang felt an overwhelming urge to be methodical, to dismantle this monastery one rock at a time until no evidence of its existence could ever be found. Places like this were a disease, covering their land like blotches on otherwise healthy skin.

He walked toward the feeling of power. It was within the monastery's main building, whatever it was. He proceeded cautiously, checking corners and doorways for traps and finding none.

There was one old monk sitting in the meditation hall. Like the courtyard outside, Fang fought against the demons of his past, these ones falling easier. The meditation hall had held little emotion in his upbringing, except painful boredom.

The size of the hall, its wooden floor and walls polished to near-perfection, made the monk seem puny in comparison. Had one man been left to guard the monastery? The idea was ludicrous.

The monk made no move to indicate that he was aware Fang was even present. To introduce himself, Fang sent a wave of energy right beside the man. Floorboards exploded in a straight line from Fang's outstretched hand, right past the monk, and almost to the opposite wall. Debris stabbed into the monk, but still he didn't react.

Fang was preparing another attack before he realized how angry he was and what he was doing. He was searching for the monk's brother, and he doubted this old man was his suspect. He took a deep breath and slowly released the energy that had been building.

Still wary of a trap, Fang held a shield in one hand while letting his energy fill the dagger. Should it come to a fight, he would be prepared. Then he walked forward and stepped in front of the monk.

As he came around, he was surprised to see the monk had a look of peaceful serenity on his face. Small splinters from the floorboards stuck into the side of the monk's body, but he looked as though he wasn't concerned by them in the least. He seemed to be in a deep meditative state.

When the monk's eyes snapped open, alert and focused on him, Fang almost leaped back in surprise. Although he had felt the monk's energy, the look of sheer peace on his face made Fang wonder if he was dead.

"I've been wondering when you would come," the monk said with a smile on his face, as though greeting a long-lost friend.

"You knew I'd come here?"

"I guessed. Your goals, or more accurately, the goals of the organization you work for, aren't hard to decipher. Given that you'd made your presence known so loudly, it seemed reasonable to assume you'd attempt an attack of the monastery, especially if you've met with Niu recently. His distaste for our kind is well known."

Fang looked around the otherwise empty hall. "Then where is everyone? If you knew I was coming, why not mount a defense?"

The monk sat, as still as a rock in a river, and every bit as peaceful. "These are only stones. The monks within matter far more than this structure that divides us from the rest of the world. I sent them away."

So the monk was the abbot of this monastery. Fang had suspected as much, but hadn't dared assume. He didn't think the abbot was lying about sending the monks away, and he squeezed the dagger tightly as he thought about his missed opportunity. How dare they retreat before the fight even began. Did they have no honor? "I was taught that monasteries are sacred places, and yet you'd abandon one without even a fight?"

"Perhaps the monastery isn't the stones, but the teachings within. I'm sorry your own abbot never taught you that. Even among our leaders, there are mistakes. But you will find no fight here. You would have killed the monks, and that I could not allow."

Fang's anger at being lectured like a child gave way to a perverse pride. So even the abbot recognized Fang's strength? He *was* ready to take on an entire monastery, then.

His thoughts were interrupted by the monk speaking again. "Although I think I can understand why you feel the way you do, your goals are misguided."

Fang almost laughed. "Is that why you remained behind, to lecture me?"

The abbot nodded, and the import of that gesture hit Fang like a slap across the face. The abbot was under no illusions. He knew that when this conversation was over, he would die. And yet he had remained. Why? He had to know no simple conversation would change Fang's mind.

"It's a waste of your final breaths."

"I doubt it. Do you know why we ban the use of weapons in our training?"

"Because it makes us too powerful for you to control."

The abbot shook his head. "Control is part of it. But not like you think. Do you believe it is your strength that allows you to do the things you are capable of?"

That was a foolish question, and Fang hated that he was dragged into a conversation. But still, the abbot was willing to die to let him know this. Why? "Of course. Why else would I train every day?"

"Perhaps the mistake is our own. Maybe the message you bring is that we need to change our ways. But tradition is a hard yoke to break."

"Stop talking in riddles, old man. Why would you have me believe you don't allow monks to train with weapons?"

"It has little to do with us being able to control you. It has much more to do with you being able to control it."

"It?"

"The power that you summon even now."

"My power?"

The abbot shook his head. "I assume you left the monasteries at an earlier age?"

Fang's silence was answer enough.

"Suffice to say, it is not your power. It is something else entirely, and you are little more than the conduit. I wish I could explain more, but my point is we're trying to understand a power that is completely beyond us."

"It's not beyond my master," Fang blurted.

The abbot's look was skeptical. "Then you are a lucky man indeed."

Fang's head was spinning, but there was one question above all others that he still couldn't answer. One question colored everything the abbot said.

"So why are you here? Why sacrifice yourself if every monk's life is to be valued?"

"It is a distant hope, certainly, but I wanted to see if I could dissuade you from your path. Despite everything, you have a tremendous gift, and I would be more than happy to bring you under my tutelage. Your skill is impressive, and with your help, we could understand this power we have more clearly. By working with me, I believe we could guide you to an even higher level."

Fang couldn't believe the abbot's offer. "You want me to join you?"

The abbot nodded.

Fang stepped forward and whipped his dagger around, drawing a thick red line across the abbot's neck. The look of surprise on his face was almost worth all the blabbering Fang had just endured.

"Never."

27

Evening had fallen, and Lei was in exactly the same position he had been in hours ago. He'd strained against his bonds constantly, and so far his only reward was being able to move his fingers a little more than he'd been able to immediately after being captured.

He had no easy task in front of him. Not only was he tied tightly to the post, the net would hamper his movement even if he somehow managed to escape his bonds.

His only advantage, if he was feeling optimistic, was that he was still alive. They could have killed him, catching him as they had. They could still kill him. Any one of the triads wandering around the grounds could come up to him, stick a knife in his belly, and walk away. Lei would be powerless to stop it.

He wondered why he was still alive. The triads weren't known for their mercy, which meant something worse was probably in store for him.

Lei tried hard not to think about that. There was only the present moment. He couldn't allow himself the luxury of worrying about the future.

With the little extra give he'd been able to work into the leather straps tied around his fingers, he could separate his palms just a little. He experimented to see what he could do with the freedom. He was able to summon his energy and focus it between his palms, a slight variation on the first two-handed attack taught at the monastery. His thoughts on how he could use that ability stopped cold when Niu stepped back into the courtyard. He focused his gaze on Lei.

"I hope you've had some time to think about how hopeless your situation is, Lei," the boss said.

Lei wasn't sure what the appropriate response was, so he chose silence as his wisest course of action. He really, really didn't want to get hit by those meaty fists again.

Niu walked up to him and punched him in the stomach.

Lei convulsed, but his bonds held him firmly in place. He wanted to double over and gasp and try to catch his breath, but he couldn't move an inch.

Niu hit him again. Lei felt as though a giant had pulled an old tree out of the ground and was using it as a club against his stomach. He'd never felt blows like the ones he suffered through now. Had he come all this way to be beaten to death? He could think of many better ways to die.

The huge man stepped back. "Cut the net off him."

The men standing around leaped into action, their knives making short work of the netting. The moment they were done, Niu stepped forward and drove his fist once again into Lei. He gasped, trying to find any space in his lungs to get air. As Niu retreated a pace, he seemed satisfied, somehow. "That's better."

He motioned to the side, and another triad brought a small stool for Niu to sit on. As he did, Lei couldn't help but wonder what would happen if the stool collapsed. At least he would die laughing.

"Lei, I would like to ask you some questions."

He couldn't help himself. With the first full breath he could summon, Lei replied, "Aren't the beatings supposed to come after the questions? I think you're doing this wrong."

An overly zealous triad stepped in, fist raised, but Niu stopped him. "You're clever. That's good. It's the clever ones who always break first. They are used to drifting through this world, not willing to commit deeply to anything. If you're curious about my methods, I have found that providing a taste of what's to come encourages conversation."

Lei didn't have anything to say to that.

"Good. Now, I am curious about what you know and what the monasteries are planning. You may begin wherever you like."

Lei frowned. "How would I know what the monasteries are planning?"

Niu stood up and delivered another punch to Lei's midsection. Lei screamed and cursed, agony flaring across his body, blood flying from his lips as he coughed.

"Come now, Lei. We always thought it was suspicious when you managed to leave the monastery. No one leaves alive. But so long as you contributed generously to my taverns, I saw little reason to press the issue. But now you have shown us your skill, and your deception is over."

His stomach sank, and he would have laughed at the absurdity had he not clearly seen his immediate future. Niu thought he was a spy of some sort, sent by the monasteries to infiltrate the triads. Nothing could be further from the truth, but Niu already had the story fixed in his mind, and he would keep hurting Lei until he had the confession he wanted. Lei cursed again, wondering if he could come up with a lie that could save him.

Then he realized it would do no good. If Niu believed he had all the information Lei possessed, he'd kill him and be done with it. The fact that Niu thought he was a spy was the only reason he was still alive. He could lie and die, or tell the truth and suffer. Sometimes life seemed terribly unfair.

"I don't suppose you'd believe that I'm not working for the monasteries, and that I somehow inherited my brother's spirit when he died, would you?"

Niu's only response was another punch.

The evening became the longest of Lei's life. No answer he gave was good enough, and Niu had plenty of patience, and plenty of men who were more than willing to attack a defenseless man tied to a post for him. When Niu got bored, he let the others take turns.

Lei couldn't think of a single place on his body that didn't hurt. Bruises were forming up and down his torso. The leather straps holding him to the post had torn into his skin, and where he wasn't bleeding outright the skin was sore and chafed. Breathing hurt, and he wondered if he had cracked or broken any ribs.

Lei didn't know if an hour had passed or a week. He was in agony everywhere. Niu quickly tired of the entertainment.

"I must give you credit, Lei. I do not know what kind of training they provide in the monasteries, but you have more strength than I expected. Tomorrow, we will call for an expert."

With that, Niu walked back into the house, cleaning his bloody hands on a rag as he did so. Their evening's entertainment over, the rest of the triads went back to their normal duties. Lei would have sagged in his bonds, had they provided even the slightest amount of give.

His hands still had the same freedom they'd had earlier.

It wasn't much, but he could summon his energy and focus it, just a little. He glanced around the courtyard. No one seemed particularly concerned about him, and what he was about to do was invisible. There wouldn't be a better time. He wanted to rest, but he was worried if he did he would lose his only chance.

Lei focused his energy, feeling it form into a small ball between his hands. He focused it tighter and aimed at the leather strap holding his thumbs together. He released it and it cut through the bond. The leather fell to the ground.

Lei's restless eyes glanced around. But again, no one cared. He was tied and beaten.

Lei repeated the process, slowly cutting through every strap around his fingers. Twice he missed his targets, and his breath caught as he worried the attacks would raise an alarm. Once his hands were free, he had many more options.

Still, no one noticed. The straps around his fingers had been small, and in the dark it was difficult to make out details near his hands. His next test would be his wrists. The leather was a little thicker. He closed his eyes and focused, and the energy cut through the leather without problem. The straps around his wrists fell to the ground, and his arms were completely free. He still held his hands together, trying to sell the illusion for as long as he could.

Next were the straps lashing him to the post. He couldn't risk cutting them one at a time. Torchlight illuminated his front side, and one didn't have to be too observant to see the straps falling away. He searched his memory for a technique, finally finding one. The memory wasn't his; the technique was an obscure one he never would have studied.

Using his newfound mobility, Lei brought his hands close to the back side of the pole. He focused on his power, forming it into the weapon he would use to gain his freedom. Working by feel, he tried to position the attack correctly. Then he took a deep breath and released, the energy cutting towards the sky and the ground at the same time, running along the post.

His aim was true. The attack cut through the straps binding him to the post and he fell forward. He tried to catch himself, but was only able to keep his face from burying itself in the sand. His body refused to follow any commands. It had suffered too much damage.

Get up!

The voice, as clear as day, was Jian's. It was deeper and stronger than Lei remembered, but it was still his brother.

He pushed himself to his feet, stumbling as he did. Standing straight made it difficult to breathe, but his actions had been noticed, and he could see the archers turning their crossbows on him. There was no time to form an attack.

Lei flung out his arms and screamed, an unformed attack blasting from his hands. Such an attack was almost always a waste of power. Most of the time it dissipated within a couple of paces.

Icy hate filled him, though, giving him the power he needed. Even unfocused, the attack washed over the walls of the complex, sending men flying off backward or crashing into the walls behind them.

He could only sustain it for a few seconds, but it was enough to give him a clearing. His sword was nearby, resting against a wall where the triad had placed it after taking it off him. The door was there too, an easy avenue of escape.

Lei growled. His only way out was to go deeper in. He formed two attacks and sent them at the first people he saw stirring. Gradually, more of the triads worked their way to their feet.

But they didn't get him before he reached his sword. He let his power flow into the blade as he drew it, snapping off his first cut as he drew. He didn't bother to aim. His goal was utter destruction. His blade flung energy, cutting through wood, stone, and bone indiscriminately. Sections of the wall crumbled, men screaming as they were caught in the fall.

And Lei kept swinging, snapping off one destructive cut after another. A few seconds later he was done, and the walls and watchtowers were in ruins. It would take months, if not years, to repair what he had torn apart in moments with his anger.

The only structure undamaged was the house itself. Lei had questions of his own for Niu. No one followed him as he stepped into the building.

28

Fang made a cursory examination of the monastery, ensuring he was truly alone. He hadn't doubted the abbot, but everything seemed so strange. The abbot hadn't made the slightest effort to save himself, but why? Why sacrifice himself just for the opportunity to speak to Fang?

His mission was complete, and he knew his task was to keep moving, to spread even more discontent. But every time he looked at the destroyed gate he, found another reason to stay. At first it was to make sure everyone was gone, but that quickly became nothing more than an excuse.

The abbot's words disturbed him more than he cared to admit. The power they summoned wasn't their own? The idea was counterintuitive to everything Fang knew. Why else train the body to the degree they did? Why did people feel exhausted after giving everything they had in an attack or a defense?

Maybe he shouldn't have killed the abbot as quickly as he had. As the head of one of the monasteries, the man would have been privy to secrets. With more time, who knew what Fang might have learned?

A clap of thunder brought him to his senses. He found the highest point in the monastery, a stone tower that rose above the rest of the structures. He climbed it quickly, welcomed by a vicious, cutting wind as he reached the top. He could see a storm front racing toward him, dark and ominous, a thin veil of grey rain drifting toward him. Lightning spiked across the sky.

That changed his plans, then. Mountain storms were nothing to be trifled with. Fang had expected to head back to town tonight, or perhaps even to Niu's stronghold. Although he'd probably survive the storm if he decided to walk, the risk didn't seem worth it. Besides, perhaps there was more information in the monastery that would be valuable.

A rumble in his stomach reminded him that food would be necessary as well. He hadn't eaten since beginning his hike up the mountain, and he could use a good meal. The kitchen was easy enough to find, but he was disappointed to find that very little was left for him to eat. Apparently, the monks had taken most of the food when they left.

A bit of scrounging turned up enough to make a meal, though. He found some rice in the bottom of a sack, a few strips of dried meat, and some less-than-ideal greens in the monastery garden. Nothing that could be called a feast, unfortunately.

He was content, though. Running from the monks meant he'd had little time to hunt, and he didn't dare show his face in most villages where he might be remembered. He'd eaten hardly anything for days, and even the meager scraps he was able to scavenge from the kitchen were enough to provide him a treat by his standards.

He boiled the rice and the vegetables together, collecting water from the drizzle of rain outside. While the food cooked, he gnawed his way through the dried meat, his mouth salivating to soften the food. The meal was hardly what his stomach demanded, but it would have to be enough. Hunger was an old friend of his.

By the time he finished, the storm crashed against the monastery walls. Safe by the small cook fire he had made, Fang felt contentment like a warm blanket covering him. He loved storms, and listening to the rain pound relentlessly against the roof above made him grateful for the shelter.

Fang stood up from his meal and went to the kitchen door, opening it to observe the storm from relative safety. The door was on the lee side of the structure, so little rain found its way into the building. The fury of a storm at this altitude, with nothing to tame it, was remarkable. Rain as sharp as needles blasted through the narrow corridors between buildings. The wind howled and whistled as its fingers pried for weaknesses between stone and wood. And Fang was the only one here to observe the raw majesty of nature.

He took off most of his clothes, leaving only his undergarment on. He folded them quickly and left them near the fire to remain warm while he stepped outside into the driving rain. The storm lashed at him angrily and the wind picked up, as if personally challenged by his defiance. Fang walked to one of the walls and climbed it, allowing the full force of the storm to whip across his body.

The power of the storm vibrated in his heart. He felt the claps of thunder in his chest as bolts of lightning arced overhead. Rain sliced at him as the wind screamed, and Fang opened himself to all of it. There was so much power in nature, so much force to deal with.

Then he formed the sign for a shield with both hands, throwing it up in front of him. The gale became a swirling breeze, and although he couldn't see his shield, the rain ran into it and slid around him. Fang grinned childishly as the rain streamed past his invisible barrier. He could feel the force of the storm pushing against his defense, and he dropped it.

The tempest hit him again, and after another moment of enjoyment, he came down off the wall. Back in the kitchen, he sat next to the fire and dried himself, then put his clothes back on. He felt at ease, the revelations of the abbot now more of an annoyance than a constant worry. He enjoyed being reminded that there were forces far greater than him that walked across the world.

Fang lit a torch and stepped out of the kitchen, forming a shield to protect himself from the rain. The previous experience had been enjoyable, but now it was work that called him. There was no need to get soaked. Rain washed down his shield as he made his way toward the library. It was one of the smaller buildings in the monastic complex, a stout, single-level structure that could have been a prison if it wasn't filled with books. Fang believed the comparison was apt.

He opened the door and stepped inside. After lighting a few small torches along the walls, he could see clearly. Wooden shelves had been built, and many of them held scrolls. Near the back he saw a few precious books, clearly the gems of the collection.

With a sigh, Fang started opening the scrolls and trying to read them. After he'd opened a few, though, he realized the size of the problem he faced. While he was familiar with quite a few words, he could only read maybe one out of five in each scroll, and the words he could understand were unimportant ones.

He clutched more tightly at each scroll as he opened

them, his grip finally tearing one in half. The situation was made worse by his awareness that there was knowledge within these scrolls. Several of them had images. Fang recognized a number of hand symbols used to focus energy, and saw a few he had never seen before. He vowed to try them when he got the opportunity.

But the sign was only half the technique. The signs helped focus the mind, which focused the power. A child could mimic the same signs Fang did with ease, but without access to the power and the mental fortitude to wield it, the signs did nothing.

Was the answer to the abbot's riddles in here? Fang felt certain it was, but he couldn't access it. He had climbed the highest mountains of knowledge, only to find the final door locked because he couldn't read. His master had promised he would teach Fang someday, but that day hadn't yet come. For the first time, Fang considered the possibility that his master had made a serious mistake.

He tried a few more scrolls and even two of the books, but the result was the same. They might have been written in code for all the good they did him. Fang left the library and returned to the kitchen, determined to get a good night's rest. In the morning, he would think more clearly. He was tired from the long day.

The next morning, he awoke to the cool smells of fresh rain and silence. Alone on a mountaintop, there was nothing. No people were going to work or trying to sell their goods. He was a hermit from the world, and he found he didn't mind at all.

His decision was a lot easier to make in the light of day. The library was no use to him, and Fang suspected it was only a matter of time before the monks returned to reclaim what was theirs. He couldn't stay, not when there was so much more to be done.

When he came into the library, one of the torches from the night before was still flickering. That would be good enough. He pulled the torch from its mount on the wall and tossed it among the pile of scrolls. For a few seconds, nothing happened, and Fang wondered if the monks had somehow managed to protect their collection. But then the flames caught and spread, and Fang had to back out of the library, surprised by how quickly the small building filled with smoke.

Fang left the library door open to let more air in. Today he would return to the task he'd been given. Without a backward glance he began walking down the trail back to Two Bridges. Behind him, the monastery burned.

Fang hoped it was the first of many.

29

Lei stepped cautiously through the large house. Already, two triads had jumped out at him around corners, and both times he had relied on the sword to cut them down. He hadn't even used any power, relying instead on traditional swordsmanship. He worried about what would happen if he made a cut with his energy inside a house. Being crushed to death sounded barely more appealing than getting beaten to death.

This time, he heard the triad before he saw him. There was the sharp intake of breath and the sound of a foot pivoting on the wooden floor. Lei crouched low as a triad spun around the corner, swinging his sword parallel to the ground. Had Lei been standing, the cut would have sliced right through his chest. It was a pretty poor strike, all things considered.

From his crouch, Lei released the attack he'd been holding on to, the blast catching the triad from below and lifting him up and across the hall, crashing through a rice-paper wall. The boy would live, so long as Lei didn't bring the house down later.

Even though Lei couldn't sense his enemies, he knew he was getting closer to his goal. The attacks became more frequent, and more desperate. They were trying to keep him from something, or more likely, someone. Niu was their employer, after all. If he died, who would put food on their table?

Two more triads went down after being hit with a strong blast, and then he was in a large room. Part reception hall, part practice ground, weapons of all shapes and sizes lined the walls of the room. Inside, gathered together, were five men. Niu stood in the center, and the four men surrounding him kept adjusting their distance, apparently struggling to decide who was more dangerous—their boss or the man who had torn down the stone walls.

Lei approached, wary of traps but eager to fight. Niu seemed to be in the same mood.

"Kill him," he ordered.

The command was enough for the men to overcome their reluctance. They charged forward as one, a variety of edged implements raised. Lei raised his hand and pushed, his energy flowing freely towards the men. The blast caught them squarely, throwing them backward. As they fell, Lei pushed his energy toward Niu, who braced his feet and took the blast full in the chest.

Lei saw Niu's clothes ripple as though they were caught in the wind, but the giant didn't move. Lei assumed too much of the energy had broken against the men who had charged him. He began the same sign again.

Niu had no intention of letting him finish. He sprinted forward with impossible grace, his feet seeming to float over the boards. Lei was too surprised to react quickly, and Niu's body slammed into his own, wrapping him in a deadly embrace.

Lei panicked. He barely knew how to grapple, and Niu clearly intended to make this fight as close as possible. Lei squirmed, fighting his way free of the embrace. As soon as his head slipped under the giant's arms, he started trying to make a sign.

But Niu grabbed him by the wrist and lowered his weight, forcing Lei to the ground. He couldn't focus enough to release any energy. All he needed was a second or two of time, but Niu was aware of that as well. Lei kicked desperately, and the blow bounced off the side of Niu's head.

It wasn't much of a hit, but Niu relaxed the pressure on Lei's wrist for a moment. Lei pulled his wrist away and scrambled back, trying to get his feet under him.

He stood up just in time for Niu to attack him again. Lei gave up ground, looking for space. But Niu was offering none. He mirrored every movement Lei made, giving him nothing to work with. Lei dodged and ducked, but all Niu needed was for him to make a single mistake and it was over.

The mistake came when Lei tried to punch wildly at Niu's face. He'd panicked, the giant's face too close to him for comfort. Niu grinned as he caught Lei's wrist, the grip so tight Lei thought his wrist was going to break just from the pressure. How could a man be so strong?

Caught, Lei didn't know what to do. How could he overcome such a man?

As his mind blanked, his instincts took over, giving him the answer he was looking for.

Lei had no experience in grappling. But suddenly, his body knew what to do. He didn't seek to understand. He just let go, allowing instinct and reaction to work for him.

Niu was pulling him in by the wrist, driving his right elbow toward Lei's face. Lei grabbed, twisted, and ducked, pulling the giant's weight down and over his extended hip. For a moment, he wasn't sure he'd be able to support the weight of the massive man, but then Niu rotated completely over the hip, landing flat on his back against the hard floor. Lei felt the floor vibrate under his feet.

But Niu's grip pulled Lei along. Lei fell forward, also landing on his back beside Niu.

Niu let go as he attempted to get to his feet, and it became a race to stand.

Lei won the race. He drove his knee into Niu's face as he was on hands and knees, dropping him back to the floor.

But Niu was fighting for his life, and wouldn't be beaten so easily. As Lei struggled to his feet, one of Niu's meaty hands came up and pulled him back down, ensuring he didn't have the time to collect his energy and end this fight. Lei fell toward the boss, managing to turn the fall into a tackle, landing on top of Niu and forcing him back to the floor.

Lei ended up in a top mount position, straddling Niu and trying to choke him. Niu was far too strong for such a technique to work, though. He reached up, somehow calm even though he couldn't have been able to get any air into his lungs. He grabbed Lei's wrists and dislodged them from his throat as though playing with a child. Lei knew that in a moment Niu would throw his hips and toss him like a ragdoll.

He couldn't let that happen. Lei grunted and threw his head forward, his forehead cracking into Niu's nose. He felt the cartilage give way under the blow and flung himself around Niu's neck, wrapping his right arm around it and grabbing his right wrist with his left hand and pulling. All he needed to do was hold on long enough to bring the man down.

The task wasn't going to be as easy as he'd hoped. Niu roared and rolled over Lei, knocking some of the wind out of him. Lei focused on nothing but holding on as Niu found his feet and sent the two of them crashing against every solid surface he could find.

First Niu tried a wall. He turned and smashed Lei into the wall twice, each blow leaving Lei feeling like he was being flattened by a cart rolling down a mountain. Lei's vision went red, but he held on, knowing that if he let go, his life was very likely forfeit.

Then Niu tried a square pillar. Lei got a glimpse of it coming, giving him just a moment to dread the impact.

His body cracked against the pillar, bending at an unnatural angle as his spine turned in ways it was never meant to. He tried to hold on, but his arms and hands wouldn't obey the orders he gave. He dropped off of Niu, collapsing against the ground.

Lei's eyes traveled over to Niu, who had apparently been closer to passing out than Lei had expected. He was struggling to get his breath, his face still red from the lack of air.

Lei didn't want to do anything but go to sleep. His body was done for, and didn't have much left to give. But a small, insistent voice told him to get up. If he fell asleep here, he would never wake up. If he did wake up, he would wish he hadn't.

So Lei struggled to his feet as Niu panted for breath. They both staggered like drunks, the once-pristine practice hall now filled with debris from their fight.

Lei kept his right hand behind him, out of Niu's sight. Drawing his sword was tempting, but he needed Niu alive, at least for a few more moments. He needed whatever answers Niu was willing to give. He signed the third attack, focusing his energy as tightly as he was able, praying it would be enough. He wasn't capable of more at the moment.

Niu recovered faster than Lei hoped. As soon as he had his breath back, he charged, bringing the fight in close again.

Niu took three steps, then four. He was reaching his fastest speed, barreling at Lei like a bull. Lei only needed to make one more sign to finish the technique, but he wasn't sure he'd have the time. But now he was committed. The idea of remaining still and in front of Niu's charge terrified him, but he forced his feet to remain planted.

He thrust out his hand less than a second away from impact and released his attack. Niu stopped like he'd run into a wall, and Lei crouched down to get a better grip against the floor. He could have sworn he saw the air bend between them as Niu's physical power clashed directly against Lei's more esoteric strength. Niu's feet clawed at the ground, trying to gain better purchase. His hands raked the air inches in front of Lei's face, unable to grab Lei and crush him, and Lei was throwing everything he had left at the man. If he'd been fresh and rested, he didn't think it would even be a contest. But he was fighting for every breath, every muscle screaming against the agony.

He had to have more. In spite of the imminent danger, he closed his eyes and focused, trying to tap into his will to survive. He pushed with everything, wondering if his will or Niu's strength would give first.

When he opened his eyes, Niu had been pushed back several inches. The veins in the boss' forehead were bulging as he strained against the invisible force pushing against him.

Lei thought of Niu standing in front of his house,

watching it burn with contempt. Anger burned within him as he screamed, his throat raw. Energy welled up inside him and darted towards Niu.

For a moment, Lei thought it wouldn't work. Niu held out, still fighting against the force. But then his feet lifted off the ground, and once that purchase was gone, the fight was over. Niu's body picked up speed, his giant limbs windmilling around until he crashed into a pillar with a thunderous crack.

Lei collapsed to his knees, utterly spent. Fortunately, Niu wasn't moving either. Lei took a couple of deep breaths. He could rest later. He stood, shakily, and walked over to Niu. He found a dagger lying nearby, dropped by one of the triads. The weight and balance were perfect.

Lei stood over Niu. The giant's eyes were open but glazed, and blood trickled out of his mouth.

Lei didn't waste words. Niu was in pain, and Lei wondered if some of his internal organs had been punctured by broken ribs. "What can you tell me about the Order of the Serpent?"

Niu gave a grim chuckle, blood trickling out with every little cough. "They pay well."

"What are they after?"

"To end the monasteries."

"Why my brother?"

"He could stand up to them. Most couldn't."

Lei cursed. This was pointless, he wasn't learning anything he hadn't already known. "Where can I find them?"

Niu laughed again. "I sent one of their warriors to kill you up at the monastery, just yesterday. You don't need to worry about finding them. They'll find you."

Lei wanted to throw it back in his face, but he recognized

the truth of the statement. He wondered what had happened to his abbot and the people he'd once known at the monastery, but couldn't bring himself to care too much. He needed to worry about himself.

He had more questions, but Niu had closed his eyes, and his breath wasn't coming anymore.

Lei swore again. He needed to leave. Otherwise someone would find him, and he was in no place to fight again.

Some torches were burning in the corners of the room, and Lei smiled. He supposed it was only fair.

A few minutes later he stumbled away from the destroyed walls, while flames licked at the remains of Niu's house.

30

Fang laughed as he looked at the scene of destruction in front of him. A day and a half of travel had taken him from the monastic heights to Niu's home and fortress. He'd never been here before, but based on what he'd seen back in Two Bridges, he'd assumed it would be ostentatious.

He would have been right, if he'd been here a day or two earlier. He laughed again, a harsh bark that echoed among the ruins. At the same time Niu had sent him up to the monastery to kill Lei, it looked as though Lei had taken the fight to Niu.

Lei's work had been more thorough than his own, though. He'd simply set fire to the monastery and left. The wooden portions would burn away, but the stone walls and foundations would stand, and if the monks ever decided to, they'd be able to rebuild easily enough.

Niu's fortress was an entirely different story. At best, the stone that lay scattered in all directions could be used again, but nothing of the old home really remained. Fang walked over to the remnants of the stone walls, observing the sharp cuts in the rock that had brought them down. He was intimately familiar with such cuts, and he had believed he was the only one in the world with that skill.

The picture forming in his head wasn't quite right. The colors didn't exactly match. Niu had said that Lei was a monk who had become a spy, trying to infiltrate the triads. But the walls of Niu's home told a different story. Fang couldn't imagine a single monk willing to break their taboo on weaponry. Until today, he had been confident he was the only one who'd pursued such training. It required a basic understanding of how to harness one's gift, which could only be taught in the monasteries, as well as the willingness to break a very strong cycle of conditioning. Such people didn't exist in the world.

But if Lei wasn't a monk, Fang couldn't imagine how he possessed the skill he did. Even among the debris and the bodies Fang could recognize the marks of a master. Lei's aim and control had been impeccable, the sort of skill that only came from a lifetime of practice. This work hardly looked like it came from a man who spent most of his money on drink.

Fang searched the wreckage for a few more minutes, listening for any sounds of life he might have missed. But he was greeted with nothing more than the sounds of the forest. Lei hadn't left anyone alive.

That, too, was unlike a monk. Most hated the idea of using their gift as a weapon. Their martial philosophies talked about the "Spring of Life" and other such nonsense. They trained in the skills of violence, but they didn't see their techniques as violent. Perhaps the monks would argue that the difference was only philosophical, but Fang disagreed. Killing another person, up close, tested your spirit and your will. Most monks never prepared for such a test, pleasantly naive behind their thick stone walls.

Lei was different. Lei could and had killed. At least in some cases, Fang assumed he'd done it without hesitation. If he had hesitated, Lei would be dead.

If he had any idea how, Fang would have attempted to track Lei. But he knew little about the man, except that his brother and his monastery were destroyed. He itched for another battle that would challenge him, but his master's orders had been clear. He needed to continue working his way towards the capital of the region, Jihan, sowing as much panic and destruction among the monks as he could.

That being said, his master would want to know what happened here. Niu had been in charge of delivering essential supplies for the operation. Fang knew very little of the big picture, but he knew enough to know that Niu's death affected their plans. The fastest way to reach his master was by bird, which required a trip back to Two Bridges and the triad house there. If he happened to run into Lei on the way, so much the better.

F ANG KEPT his ears open and his senses peeled, but he didn't detect any trace of Lei. No one gifted was anywhere near the road that led from Niu's home to Two Bridges. Fang kept turning corners, fingering the hilt of his dagger, hoping against hope that Lei would attempt to ambush him.

But the road was quiet and pleasant. Most traffic traveled the other way, in the direction of the regional capital, preparing for the harvest festival in less than two weeks. It was a reminder to Fang he should be heading that direction soon as well.

He found the triad's hideout without problem, entering upon a scene that was as somber as any funeral he'd ever been to. Apparently, word of what happened to their boss had reached them. Fang didn't pity them. Those who joined the triads were weak, searching for a community that supported them because they didn't feel like they could survive this life on their own. They needed strength, not other people.

Fang looked around the room, trying to decide who he should talk to. No one present seemed to be in any hurry to claim leadership, their eyes darting back and forth, as if the first one who made eye contact would be the new boss.

He was about to speak when the door opened behind him, and someone stepped in. Fang turned around, surprised to see a woman there. She was fairly tall, and beautiful, but even from a single glance, he could tell that she was colder than the snow-capped mountains in winter. He might have been attracted to her, if he wasn't immediately concerned she would slip a knife under his ribs.

Instinctively, he knew this was the person he needed to speak to. He gave a short bow.

Her voice was gentler than he expected. "You are with the Order of the Serpent?"

Fang gave another short bow and bared his forearm to her in reply.

"My name is Daiyu. Until we hear from our bosses, I am the highest ranking member here. How may I help you?"

"I must send a bird to my master. He must be informed of recent events."

Daiyu nodded. "Is there anything else?"

There wasn't, but all he could think about was facing Lei. What kind of man would he be to cause the destruction he had? "Have you seen or heard from Lei?"

Fang couldn't believe it, but her gaze became even colder. "He has not been seen for several days."

Fang knew that he had no desire to be Lei at that moment. Daiyu was not a woman to be crossed.

She must have sensed he had nothing else to add, because she turned to leave the room. "When you write to your master, you may also let him know that the shipments will proceed as planned. Our supplies were here, not at Niu's. He may rest easy on that account."

"He will be happy to hear it," Fang replied to her retreating back.

He couldn't be sure if it was his imagination or not, but he could have sworn the room became warmer when she left. She was definitely not a woman he wanted to anger.

31

Lei groaned and opened his eyes, blinking away the harsh rays of sunlight.

Where was he?

The world around him was quiet, almost as though he had fallen asleep under a blanket.

One by one, his senses returned to him slowly, as if finding their way back to his body and reluctantly settling in. Sight was first. As his eyes focused, he saw that he was in the woods somewhere, tall pine trees swaying gently in a strong summer breeze. A few seconds later, the sounds that had once been muffled cleared up. He heard the birds chirping to one another and the soft whistle of the wind through the needles of the pine.

Then came pain and memories, unwanted guests that he would have been happy to do without.

His brother's spirit fought against the memories, upset at the loss of life and the destruction Lei had committed. The queasiness of his stomach was another layer of discomfort to add to the bruises and aches he felt all over.

Lei sat up, still not quite sure where he was. What had

happened after the fight? He remembered leaving Niu's house burning behind him, but what else happened? He had stumbled into the forest and that was all he remembered.

A small but consistent wisp of smoke helped him identify where he was. He assumed it was the remnants of Niu's house, and from the direction of the sun, it looked as though he had stumbled away from the house and from Two Bridges. Had he tried to go toward Windown after the fight? If so, why?

His memories were indistinct. Whenever he tried to hold on to them, they slipped like sand through his fingers.

Looking back on what he could remember, he wasn't sure he had ever given as much of himself in a fight. Niu hadn't even been gifted, but his strength was still almost enough to overcome the power Lei possessed. And Lei had thought the fight would be easy.

He knew better now, though, and he wouldn't make the same mistake again.

The queasiness in his stomach, the feeling he identified as his brother rebelling against some thought he was having, grew.

A sudden rage came over Lei. He swore loudly, even though there was nobody nearby to hear.

"Stop! Why do you keep tormenting me?"

There was no answer, of course. His brother wasn't there, not in any way that mattered, at least. His only response was that Lei felt even sicker. What did he even have to vomit? His stomach was trying to remind him he hadn't eaten for some time.

The urge to throw up became overwhelming. Lei turned over and retched, but nothing but a little bile came out.

Twice he vomited onto the forest floor before the feelings subsided.

"Jian, we weren't brothers. You turned your back on me and embraced the monastery. Why are you trying to make me do this?"

There was no response. But at least this time, the queasiness didn't increase. As near as Lei could tell, his brother was silent.

He dismissed the small ball of regret he felt. The past was in the past. Jian had made his choice, and had no right to haunt Lei now, however he was going about it.

"Get out, Jian! Just. Get. Out." He grunted every word, wondering if this was what madness felt like. It felt like Jian had somehow become part of him, but who knew?

His sickness subsided, and as he struggled to sit up straight, he wondered what would happen next.

The truth wasn't pleasant. He had started on a path that only led in one direction. Destroying Niu and the local center of triad activity would paint a target on his back. The triads would hunt him as far as they could, and their memory and reach were long. There was no chance of him returning to the life he'd once known.

But this quest for justice for his brother was equally foolish. In the clear light of day, covered in bruises and cuts, he realized just how much of a fool he was. What had he possibly hoped to accomplish? He had destroyed what little he had left of his life.

There was only one connection remaining in his life. As irresponsible as it was, he needed to see Daiyu. She had chosen the triads over him time and time again, but that final look she had given him when he last left the Old Goat haunted him more than Jian did. He wouldn't forgive himself if he ran without knowing. He needed to see if she would choose to come with him and go on the run together or if she would continue to walk her own path. Of course, thanks to him, she might be up for another promotion. Perhaps she would be the one who led the hunt for him.

Lei knew of only one way to discover the truth. He needed to see her one last time before he left his home for good.

VISITING Daiyu proved to be no small challenge. First, he needed time to heal his own body. The moment he tried to stand, he realized he was in worse shape than he believed. His bruises were more than cosmetic. They went deep, making him struggle to even walk naturally. His muscles ached, and weariness hung over his shoulders like a heavy, rain-soaked cloak. Every step was a test of will.

Lei didn't dare walk on the road. He didn't know how many people would be looking for him, and he was in no condition to wrestle a child, much less defend his own life. His safest choice was to cut through the fields and forests that surrounded Two Bridges. He tripped over branches and stumbled frequently, especially as he began his journey.

In one corner of his mind, he realized he wasn't in any state to meet Daiyu. He looked and felt like he'd been on the road for months without bathing, and a quick sniff of his armpits confirmed his suspicion.

Then he laughed. He'd just killed a triad underboss and no small number of foot soldiers. His odor was the least of his problems. But still, he should probably try to clean up a little before his meeting with Daiyu.

He observed his surroundings carefully as he walked, but the few people he passed in the fields seemed to have little interest in him. He knew most everyone who lived just outside of Two Bridges, and while his reputation was hardly stellar, he at least was considered harmless. Once the triads began their hunt, they'd be able to track him, but he assumed he had a little time yet.

Lei stopped on the banks of the Kuyo, the major river that ran outside of Two Bridges. He stripped naked and waded into the cold, clear water that traveled from the mountains above. He fought the urge to tense up, but breathed deeply and stepped in deeper. The freezing water felt like needles in his skin, but for a few minutes he was able to forget the never-ending throbbing of his bruises.

He dunked his head under the water, holding his breath for as long as he was able. Then he waded back to shore, picked up his clothes, and did his best to wash them in the river. He didn't have the tools he needed, but anything was better than their original state.

When he was done, he threw his clothes back on, letting them dry against his skin as he walked. He felt refreshed. While his bruises still ached, the pain was diminished and he was able to push it to the back of his awareness. He shook out his long hair and tied it back up as he walked.

As he approached the main road and the bridge that led to his hometown, he tried to decide where he would find Daiyu. The day was getting late, so he might find her at the Old Goat, but by now word of the destruction of Niu's home had to have reached town. He didn't think Daiyu would be bartending tonight. She would have more important issues to take care of.

He didn't want to spend too much time in town. Returning at all was a risk, and although he felt as though a great deal of his strength had returned, he had little doubt he was in no condition to fight. His first guess needed to be right.

Lei predicted she would be at the triad's hideout. Daiyu was many things, but above all else she was a survivor, and surviving the chaos Lei had just caused would require her presence at the manor. He hoped he wasn't wrong.

Lei kept to the alleys and the side streets, avoiding what people he could. He also kept his senses open. If the man who was out to kill him was near, Lei was doomed. If the man was strong enough to kill Jian, he'd make short work of Lei in this condition.

He came to the wall that surrounded the manor in short order. Since he couldn't use the front door, he decided to climb the stone wall from an alley. He poked his head over the edge, trying to get a glimpse of Daiyu. He wasn't foolish enough to attempt sneaking onto the grounds themselves, but if he could see her, he could work out some sort of plan.

What he saw almost caused him to drop off the wall. The grounds were a hive of activity. Men were moving barrels into carts, and the barrels looked heavy. The grounds had the appearance of a caravan about to leave.

Lei took all that in with a few glances, but his attention was distracted by the woman at the center of it all. Daiyu stood there, fierce and proud, the men surrounding her seeming to shrivel under her gaze. That was what he loved about her. He couldn't think of another woman who could take control of a local triad with such ease.

But he also wasn't going to have a chance to speak to her. He saw that immediately. Everyone surrounded her, and a constant stream of people kept returning to her with new questions. Lei was too far away to hear what was being said, but he knew Daiyu wouldn't have time to see him anytime soon.

Lei descended the wall, considering his choices.

The smart one was to leave town immediately. The

farther away he could travel, the safer he'd be. With a head start, he could find a new home, settle down perhaps.

Memories of Daiyu focused his attention. He couldn't leave, not without an answer from her. They had a chance once before, and he couldn't leave without knowing.

Which meant patience. Daiyu would have to be alone soon enough.

It meant risking his life, but he would wait.

32

F ang watched the two monks as they walked casually along the road between Windown and Jihan, the capital of the region. Windown wasn't much more than a day behind him, and he figured at the pace he was keeping, he could be in Jihan within the week. It all depended on how much he dallied, and if the monks ever began a true pursuit of him.

He had sensed these two ahead of him about two hours ago. They seemed to be deep in conversation, no doubt arguing some small philosophical point that meant the world to them. He had heard similar arguments all the time growing up. When you didn't want to face the challenges of life, arguing over the small bits that didn't matter was the first alternative.

They were so oblivious, Fang didn't even bother trying to leave the road. He traveled a few hundred yards behind them, keeping well out of sight through the bends of the lightly wooded forest. He was waiting for a moment when he was certain they were unobserved. Not only would it offer him extra protection, it would ensure no innocents were harmed when he attacked.

Fortunately for the monks, the road was busy. The harvest festival in Jihan attracted citizens from all over the region, and already merchants were beginning the journey toward the capital. Heavy carts pulled by tired horses were a common sight, with virtually every merchant appearing frustrated with the lack of progress, as though success would only come to those who arrived earliest.

As the afternoon faded to evening, Fang decided the time had come to act. The monks would pull off the road soon to find a place to rest, and Fang wanted their bodies on the road, where everyone could see and the word would spread. He didn't want to be seen, but if he must, he must.

His break came just an hour before sunset. They came upon a long stretch of path that was abandoned as far as the eye could see. Once Fang was certain, he ran.

By the time the monks noticed him, it was already too late. He had gathered a small bit of energy in his dagger, and he snapped it at both of them. One of the monks reacted quickly enough to dodge the cut, falling backward in his haste. The other turned and had begun to make a shield sign when the attack hit. The cut sliced right through him, the top of his body continuing to rotate as the legs collapsed underneath.

The second monk looked at his fallen friend, scrambling backward as fast as his unresponsive limbs would carry him. He finally had the sense to gather his energy into an attack, but his signs were sloppy and his focus was clearly lacking. Fang gathered some energy in his hand and slapped the attack away as if it were a mosquito out for blood.

The monk's eyes became even wider. Fang could imagine the thoughts running through his mind. Monks were supposed to be the pinnacle of society. They were the wisest and the strongest. They couldn't imagine being prey to people like him.

Fang considered stabbing the monk and letting him bleed to death, but he didn't really want to clean his dagger. Instead, he gathered a small amount of energy and made another cut. The attack was a test of sorts, to see just how much control he could exert with the dagger. A narrow slit opened up on the monk's body, revealing the organs inside.

As Fang approached more closely, he bent over to see how deep his cut had gone. He had no doubt the attack was fatal, but it appeared not to have gone clean through the body. Fang nodded to himself as the monk whimpered in agony. He'd never used such a controlled, shallow cut before. He practiced the technique on the monk one more time, ensuring he had the amount of power just right. Fang checked the body again and smiled in satisfaction. Perfect.

He continued on the path, whistling softly to himself.

THE NEXT DAY, he continued walking. There was little traffic behind him, no doubt because of the bodies he had left behind.

Fang had expected there would be some sense of satisfaction, but that was far from the truth. This wasn't the first pair of monks he had killed since leaving Two Bridges. Over a dozen had fallen to his attacks, from lone monks to a group of four. His master had wanted him to spread terror, so that was what he did. No doubt he was the talk of the entire road at the moment.

He had always thought that overthrowing the monasteries would be his life's work. So why didn't he feel more excited by what he was doing? The end was finally in sight.

He thought back to his fight with the monk on the mountain path. Fang had been confident, but still, the battle had been close. Had he been any weaker, he might have lost completely. But in the course of that fight, he'd felt truly alive for the first time in as long as he could remember.

Despite the success he'd had, there was only one thing on his mind as he walked. He wanted to fight Lei, to test himself again. The rest of the monks didn't matter. He only wanted to prove that he was the strongest.

Fang heard the sound of a galloping horse far behind him. He tensed up, expecting to see pursuit of some sort. He hadn't sensed anyone, but it seemed hard to believe no one would come after him.

Logically, he knew he had little to fear. No one had seen him kill the monks, and he looked as unremarkable as a traveler could. He didn't even carry a sword, his dagger the only visible weapon he possessed. No one would suspect him.

Fang was shocked when he turned around to see a man who was unmistakably his master in the distance. His master was riding at full speed, and it looked like the horse was on its last legs. The beast was slow to obey his master's commands, and it was panting heavily as it finally slowed to a sluggish stop.

Fang bowed deeply. "Master."

His master was flushed, clearly exhausted from his own long ride. "I saw your work on the way here. It has attracted no small amount of attention. I am impressed."

Fang's bow went even deeper. Compliments were rare from his master. "Thank you."

"I received your missive, and I'm afraid that I must change our plans."

Fang straightened up, focusing on his new instructions. He hoped his master would ask him to focus on finding and killing Lei.

"I need you to return to Two Bridges. There is a large shipment making its way from there to Jihan. Niu's death has pushed up our timetable, and we must move immediately. I fear that someone will make an attack on the shipment, ruining all of our plans."

"You fear the man named Lei?"

His master nodded. "Not only him, but what he might represent. If the monasteries have been infiltrating the triads with spies, there may be others we don't know of. If they attack the caravan, we might lose everything. Do you understand?"

Fang tried to hide the frustration he felt. Guarding the caravan was undoubtedly important work, and he was honored that his master trusted him with a task of such enormity. Certainly there were others more worthy than him. But still, all he wanted was a chance to fight against Lei. Everything else had become far less important in the past few days. But his face was a careful mask. "I do, Master. I will leave immediately."

"Thank you. I must travel on toward Jihan. I must put the pieces in place, but if you succeed, Fang, our glorious mission is almost complete."

Fang bowed once again, upset that he would have to delay his hunt. Perhaps once the monasteries had fallen, he could track Lei to the ends of the land.

33

Lei hadn't expected the caravan to move out so quickly, nor had he thought Daiyu would travel with them. He was somewhat aware of her involvement with the triads, but she'd never been asked to leave the region of Two Bridges. Her departure meant she really was moving up in the world.

He knew he was being foolish, but he figured a caravan would be easier to infiltrate than the triad's hideout. He was planning on leaving town anyway, so from one perspective, Daiyu's trip was fortuitous. That was the way he chose to look at it, at least.

The caravan left in the middle of the night. Lei thought the time odd, but he supposed it meant fewer curious eyes watching the train of carts leave town.

He followed the caravan without problem. Carts didn't move fast, and there were only two roads out of town they could take. After only a few minutes, Lei knew they were heading in the direction of Windown. They would pass the remains of Niu's house on their way to their final destination.

Lei kept an easy pace, staying far behind the caravan. He

figured he could wait for them to stop, then try to find a way to meet with Daiyu. Until then, there was no point in him risking discovery.

The triads traveled throughout the night and through the next day. Wherever they were going, they were trying to make good time. By mid-afternoon, Lei could feel the ache throughout his body. He was exhausted, but soon he would rest.

If there was one bright spot in their travel, it was that Lei couldn't feel his brother's presence strongly anymore. The feeling was still there, like a tickle in the back of his mind, but he could go long stretches of time without noticing the disquiet in his heart.

The sun was setting by the time the triads decided to set up their camp for the night. Tents came up in short order, and Lei found himself impressed by the organization the triads displayed. Based on his previous interactions with them, he had guessed them to be somewhat inept. But this group displayed an almost military precision in everything they did. After a single long day on the road, they were already over halfway to Windown, an impressive distance by anyone's measure.

Lei worked his way closer to the camp, alert for any dangers. He snuck off the road and into the woods, approaching the camp from the side. When he found a position where he could watch the camp without risking discovery, he settled in.

He watched Daiyu eat her evening meal, apparently giving some orders as she did. The men deferred easily to her, and Lei realized Daiyu felt comfortable in her new role. In fact, she looked more at ease giving orders among the triads than she did pouring drinks behind the bar at the Old Goat.

Uncertainty knotted the pit of his stomach. After their last meeting he'd thought he understood where they stood. Truth be told, he had taken this risk because some part of him was sure he'd succeed. When they'd met in the bar the last time, he'd remembered the look she'd given him. It was a look that promised everything he dreamed of.

But she hadn't been the boss of the local triad then. Had his actions created the opening she'd never have been able to make for herself? The thought twisted his gut.

Eventually she settled into her tent for the evening. The triads stationed a few lookouts, but they didn't have the men needed to do a proper job. Lei traced a mental route through the sentries to Daiyu's tent. Assuming he didn't make too much noise, he thought he could succeed without too much problem.

He could sit and worry about Daiyu's answer, or he could go and ask her. He figured in the worst case she would yell and he would have to fight his way clear. He wasn't feeling invincible, but with his sword he was confident he could escape, even if it cost another group of triads their lives.

From his hiding place, Lei slithered toward the camp. He advanced slowly, clearing the ground in front of him of twigs, dead leaves, and anything else that would make enough noise to give away his position. The evening was half passed before he made it to Daiyu's tent. With one quick motion he slid inside, only to be greeted by the gleaming point of a blade reflecting the single lit candle in the tent.

He held up his hands slowly in a gesture of surrender, and Daiyu got a glimpse of his face for the first time.

"Lei!" Her voice was hushed, but it sounded relieved.

He didn't have time to respond as she dropped the short

sword and wrapped him in a tight embrace. All thoughts fled his mind as he returned the gesture, feeling her body relax against his own.

They knelt together for some time, and Lei could feel the tension draining from Daiyu's body. She was the first to speak. "I thought for sure one of them was going to try to kill me tonight."

From what little he had observed, Lei was confused. He thought the other triads appeared deferent almost to the point of obsequiousness. But perhaps what he saw wasn't what was true. "From outside the camp, it looks as though you have them under your thumb."

They broke apart. "You know life in the triads is a game of appearances. I must appear to be in control, and they must act obedient. But they chafe under the rule of a woman. If not tonight, the knife will come soon. I couldn't sleep for fear of who would come through those tent flaps."

Lei hadn't ever fallen in with the triads, even in his darkest moments. Call it pride or foolishness, but after the monasteries, he couldn't see himself ever beholden to anyone else again. He knew more about the triads than most, but still not enough. His heart raced, though, knowing that Daiyu might be looking for a way out.

For the first time since he'd entered the tent, she took a moment to study him. "I'm glad to see you alive, but you look like death."

"Thanks. I feel like it, too."

"I've heard the stories of what happened at Niu's place. Your work was impressive."

"It felt more desperate than anything else. I almost didn't survive." He gestured around the camp beyond the tent walls. "But anything to get you a promotion."

"You kept me alive. I'm almost certain Niu would have

had me killed after you were dead. But with him out of the way, there was no one higher in the area."

That led Lei to think about the caravan. "What is all of this, anyway?"

"Our partnership with the Order of the Serpent. We're ferrying hundreds of pounds of black powder to Jihan."

Lei's eyes bulged for a moment. They were sitting near enough powder to blow all of them into pieces. He'd never even heard of so much gathered together. "To what end?"

"I don't know. We're just following orders, orders that come from Jihan. After you killed Niu, we were almost immediately ordered to get on the road with whatever we'd collected. They weren't supposed to leave for another five days, but I think you forced their hand."

Lei fell back into a sitting position. Daiyu had given him too much to think about, and his head wasn't clear enough to understand everything. He realized he still hadn't even asked her the question he'd come all this way to ask. He needed rest.

She came to his side immediately. "You're exhausted. Come, I'll make sure you get your rest tonight." She started peeling his clothes off him. He thought about fighting it, but he didn't want to. In only a few moments she had him undressed and lying down on her bed, and he relaxed into the moment, smiling as their lips met.

Lei fell asleep easily that night, Daiyu's body curled up against his. For one evening, everything in his world was just the way he wanted.

He woke up before the sun, startled awake by a sensation he couldn't immediately place.

Once he did, his heart sank.

He sensed another gifted warrior, walking toward the camp.

34

Fang may have grumbled about his task to himself, but he made good time back the way he'd come. When his master wanted something done, Fang did it. If he was deemed worthy, he would gain his master's instruction, and he would become stronger than ever.

He slept little, allowing himself only a few hours of rest a day. He walked until well after the sun went down and woke before it rose. Still, it took him a couple of days to reach the caravan.

As he approached, he thought something was off about the caravan. He'd run into them earlier than expected, and the sun wasn't yet up for the day. By sight, everything seemed normal, but from a distance, he thought he caught a sense of another warrior with the gift. Fang stopped and observed, looking for anything untoward. The camp seemed normal, a few flickering torches lighting most of the perimeter. There were gaps, but not many.

Fang chewed on his lower lip as he considered what he should do. From this distance, he couldn't be certain. The feeling of someone being close came and went, never quite solidifying into absolute certainty.

He didn't think he'd be able to surprise whoever was near the camp. Standing alone, Fang's own presence would give him away first, unless the man was actually asleep in the camp. That seemed unlikely. With few other options, Fang decided charging in straightforward was best.

As he approached, the few sentries that were on guard came alive. They called for others, and soon Fang was facing a line of guards. They stopped him about fifty yards from the camp.

The closer distance resolved the sense of the other warrior. He was on the other side of the camp, off deep in the shadows where Fang couldn't see. For the moment he was still, but Fang didn't think that would last long.

The guards recognized him, but wouldn't let him come close to the caravan. They were wary, even of those they knew, approaching in the dark like this. In only a few minutes the woman came out of her tent, giving him the same cold glare she had a few days ago.

"Fang," she said.

He bowed. "My master has asked me to escort you to Jihan."

She eyed him frostily. "Very well. We will welcome your assistance."

"Did you know you are being followed?" As he said the words, he could feel the presence of the other man diminishing as he retreated through the woods.

Her face looked as though it was made of stone. Too hard, in his mind. "No."

"I believe Lei is trailing behind you."

At that, she turned around, as though he would be right

there. When she didn't find him, she turned back to Fang. "You're certain?"

He nodded.

"Then go kill him. We'll wait here until you return."

Fang bowed again. Although he knew few women, this one was like none he had ever met. She had a warrior's heart.

He took off, striding through the camp in a few moments and coming to the other side. Lei's presence was weak, but not gone. No doubt the man was on the run.

Fang stepped into the woods, fighting the urge to sprint after him. In the woods, in the dark, there were too many dangers. Lei might have set traps, or Fang might make a mistake as simple as tripping over an exposed root and spraining an ankle. Caution was wise. His pace was quick, but he didn't break out into the sprint he desired.

The other man kept moving away. When Fang didn't feel like he'd closed any distance between the two of them after a few minutes, he knew the man was trying to get away. It was fortunate he'd shown up just when he had. If he'd been much slower, Lei might have already destroyed their work.

Fang was becoming more certain that Lei hadn't set any traps, and he picked up his pace, jogging lightly but carefully. He came into a small clearing in the woods just in time to see Lei enter the woods on the other side. Fang quickly summoned an attack and flung it at the fleeing monk. A tree cracked in half, but the attack missed its intended target. Fang let out a small curse and broke out into a full sprint.

He tried to pull up the geography of this area in his memory. He knew the road more or less followed the Kuyo River on its path between the elevation of Two Bridges and the lower-lying Jihan. Beyond that, there was little that he remembered. There wasn't any place for Lei to run that he could think of.

When Fang heard the sound of rushing water, he understood what Lei was trying to accomplish. The man was escaping, and the river would provide the means. Fang pushed harder, his legs burning as he sprinted as fast as he could.

By the time he sensed the attack it was already too late. The blast of energy caught him full in the face, and at a full sprint, the effect was devastating. His head snapped back and his back slammed into the ground as his feet were flung out ahead of him. He saw stars dancing in his vision, and for a few moments, his mind went blank.

He almost died as a result. This time, his senses returned just in time, and he sensed the sharp wave of energy slicing toward him. He rolled to his side and the ground opened up where he'd just been. Fang's eyes went wide as he saw the nature of the cut. He focused on Lei and saw just what he expected: Lei was holding his sword, and Fang could feel the energy within the blade.

Lei cut again, the energy snapping from his blade as Fang desperately drew his dagger, slicing madly at the incoming wave. The energies cut into one another and shattered, the first time Fang had ever felt anything of the sort.

Fang found his footing and darted behind a tree, realizing his mistake too late. Another cut lashed out at him, and Fang rolled away, the energy slicing through the tree as though it was nothing. The entire forest wouldn't provide him cover from those attacks.

His combat sense also told him that something was wrong. Lei had every advantage. Fang had run straight into the first attack, his bloody nose proof enough of that. Lei should have advanced, but he didn't, instead choosing to remain close to the river. Why?

He didn't have time to answer the question before another attack came flying at him. Fang was losing ground, but he still felt as though he should be losing more. If Lei was as good as Fang suspected, why wasn't he seizing this advantage?

The attacks stopped, and Fang stepped out from behind the tree he was crouched behind. Lei stood there, his face impassive, his sword in a high guard position, the tip pointed right at Fang.

Fang focused a shield in his free left hand. He might stand in the open, but he'd never allow himself to be caught without a defense. After days of circling around one another and seeking one another, the two of them had finally come face to face.

Fang had expected... more, he guessed. While Lei was clearly strong, he didn't look like the sort of man who had the physical strength or fortitude to cause such problems. In Fang's imagination, he had visualized Lei as a giant.

He could see the resemblance with the brother, though. If Lei had the sense to cut off some of that long hair, he and his brother would have looked almost identical.

"So you're the one who killed my brother." Lei's voice had a calmness to it that was intimidating. There was no fear there.

"He gave me the best fight I've ever had. He was a worthy warrior, which can't be said of many of you monks."

A strange look passed over Lei's face, but it settled quickly.

Fang studied his opponent's stance. It was obviously one that wasn't taught in the monasteries, given the sword, and it looked to be entirely unique. Lei's weight was balanced, shifted just a hair forward in anticipation of an attack. But he looked loose and confident. His shoulders were relaxed and his breathing was even.

Fang's heart raced in anticipation of the conflict. He summoned a small amount of energy into the dagger, wondering how best to approach a fight with another warrior with the same skills. He'd never considered such a fight before, and he wasn't even sure how the energies would interact with one another.

Before he could decide, he realized that Lei had also summoned energy. A pinpoint of power, focused just at the tip of the blade, was aimed directly at his heart. Fang frowned, trying to understand exactly what he was feeling. The attack was perhaps even more focused than the Dragon's Fang.

Lei unleashed the attack, an almost impossibly tight weave of energy stabbing out. Instinctively, Fang brought up the shield he had prepared, getting it in front of himself just in time for the attack to smash against it. Fang's feet dug into the ground as he slid backward from the force of the strike.

The actual amount of energy expended wasn't great, but it was so tightly focused it took everything Fang had to fight against it. Lei's attack drilled into his shield, the energy trying to find the way to his heart. His pulse raced and his muscles strained as he fought to keep his shield up.

A second later, or maybe a lifetime later, Lei's attack finally dissipated against Fang's shield. Fang fell to his knees, exhausted by the attempt to prevent his destruction. When he looked up, Lei was gone.

He blinked in confusion before guessing what had happened. Lei had used the attack as a distraction. He must have jumped in the river.

Fang fought his way to his feet and jogged toward the

outcropping of rock Lei had stood on. The river narrowed here a bit, the current speeding its way between two walls of granite. In the dim light of the very early morning, Fang thought he could just see Lei's head bobbing around the corner and out of sight.

He started to pursue, sprinting alongside the river in an attempt to catch up to his prey. But the trees were thick in places and he needed to detour. He also tired quickly, his store of stamina almost exhausted from the desperate defense.

Finally, he ran gently into a tree and stopped. Chasing Lei down the river was a fool's errand, with no guaranteed chance of success. Besides, his orders were to protect the caravan. If Lei had tried to attack it once before, he almost certainly would again. And when he did, Fang would be there, eager to end this fight.

35

Lei coughed and gasped as the freezing cold water of the Kuyo River forced its way down his throat. He'd never been the strongest swimmer, and trying to stay afloat while his sword and clothes tried to drag him down exhausted what little energy he had left.

The current slammed him against a rock hiding under the water's surface, and for a moment he was flung up, his face breaking through the surface of the water. He took a deep gasp of air before he was plunged below once again.

The worst part was not being sure which way was up. The only time he was certain was when he was dragged against the riverbed, but the moments never lasted long enough for him to take advantage of. All he could do was take breaths whenever he got the chance and ride the current.

Eventually he felt the current slow. The Kuyo was fed by the snow up high in the mountains, and at times was a truly fearsome river, crashing through the rocky passes as though it could crack the granite. But here, beyond Windown, the river began to widen and calm.

Jumping in had been a desperate gamble, but he hadn't seen many choices at the time. The last attack had taken almost all the energy he had, and although he was hopeful, he doubted it had killed the man. In all his life, he'd never met anyone who looked more fearsome.

Lei managed to half-swim, half-claw his way to shore, pulling himself up on a grassy bank, his boots still in the water. He wasn't sure he had the energy to finish pulling himself out.

The whole situation had been too close. He guessed he'd sensed the man—Fang, Daiyu had called him—before he'd been sensed. Being part of a crowd was a bit of a mask in that way. He'd had just enough time to dress and scurry out of the tent, slithering just beyond the perimeter by the time he was certain Fang had sensed him.

The sight of Fang had awakened his brother's dormant spirit. Lei had burned for the fight, hungered for the opportunity to kill the man who'd killed his brother. But he just didn't have the strength. Even using the sword to focus his energy, he hadn't been able to penetrate Fang's defense.

Lei somehow found the strength to crawl entirely out of the water and poke his head up above the tall grass. As near as he could tell, he was in the middle of nowhere. He couldn't see any sign of the road, which was good enough for him. He lay down his head and let exhaustion claim him.

When he woke up, he was surprised to see that the sun was high in the sky. He'd expected that after everything, he'd sleep longer than half the day, but he wasn't disappointed. Although he hadn't seen any sign of the road, there was no telling just how close it was. If Fang followed the road and got close to Lei, the hunt would continue.

In the light of day, Lei wondered what he should do next. Until now, he'd been driven by the desire to see Daiyu, to know if she would go into exile with him. Now he was certain that she would, but because of him, her situation had become even more delicate. The question was, how soon had he been discovered by Fang? If it was on the outskirts of the caravan, Daiyu would probably be safe. But if he'd been sensed in Daiyu's tent, she was as good as dead.

Lei stood up and tested his body, opening and closing his fists and making a few tentative punches at the air. Everything seemed to be more or less in proper order, but he was sore and tired. And hungry, his stomach reminded him. It had been far too long since he'd had a proper meal.

Should he attempt to rescue Daiyu and fight Fang and the collection of triads all at the same time? He wanted to, as unwise as that would be. He didn't care about his brother's death anymore, and he didn't care about the enormous amount of black powder making its way to the capital city. Those weren't his problems. All he wanted was Daiyu in his life.

But before he did, he needed to take care of himself. In his condition he'd never win a fight, maybe not even against the triads. He started with his own possessions. He took his sword from its scabbard and made sure it was dry. When he got into Jihan, if he got the chance, he'd have to be sure to polish it to make sure it stayed protected. There wasn't much he could do about his clothes, but the weapon needed to remain as pristine as possible.

His eyes ran over the smooth steel, the gentle waves that rippled up and down the length of the blade. The sword had a history, and he would only be a part of it. It had fought in wars that were now the gardens of legends. He wondered idly if this chapter in its life would be remembered, or if future generations would simply try to forget these years when he had wielded it.

He pushed the idle thoughts away. None of them did him any good. He needed food, and then he needed to find a place to lay an ambush. Perhaps he could come up with some way of attacking Fang before Fang even realized he was near. If he could, the rest of the battle should be fairly straightforward.

Stretching, Lei started walking toward the road. He was certain he had come out of the river on the same side he'd jumped in from, which meant if he walked away from the river, he'd eventually find the road. Once there, he would decide which direction seemed wiser. He wasn't sure how far downstream he'd been swept, but once he found a road sign, he'd know where he was.

The forest was deceptively peaceful here. It was beginning to thin, turning into the pasture and plains that marked the terrain around Jihan. As the capital of the region, this area had abundant access to resources, from the mountains in the south to the Kuyo River and the surrounding farmland. It was the center of trade for hundreds of miles, and for good reason.

Lei reached the road after only ten minutes of walking. It never strayed too far from the river. Here, the road was busy, with almost everyone traveling toward Jihan. The Harvest Festival was the second largest festival of the year, second only to the New Year. Most of the travelers were merchants, their carts piled high with goods to be sold. In about a week, Lei assumed the road would be filled with families.

He supposed that if the triads were going to strike, the Harvest Festival was the best time to do so. The militia would already be overwhelmed by their duties. He wanted to kick himself for not asking Daiyu what the triads were hoping to accomplish, but then he reminded himself that it wasn't his problem. He was like Daiyu. All he needed to do was survive.

Lei headed north, towards Jihan. Although there wasn't any way of being certain, he assumed the triad caravan hadn't passed him while he slept. The river had carried him several miles, and he didn't think he'd been asleep for more than a few hours. Caravans didn't move that quickly.

Besides, if he was going to escape the caravan with Daiyu, it made more sense to do so closer to the city. There were more chances there, more openings than on the open road. He only had to hope she'd make it that far.

He didn't know why he didn't sense them. Perhaps his mind was more tired than his body, or perhaps he was distracted by thoughts and memories of Daiyu. But when the first energy wave crashed against him, he was completely unprepared.

As far as attacks went, it was fairly unremarkable. Had he any warning, he would have easily defended against it. But it still managed to knock him a few feet off the road, where he found himself surrounded by five monks.

Before he could get his feet under him, four of them launched simultaneous attacks, pinning him tightly in place, their energy crushing him between their combined forces. No matter how hard he tried to move, he could only wiggle at best.

Gritting his teeth, Lei started forming the sign for a basic attack with one hand. Every movement was slow, and he had trouble concentrating. But his hand strained against the force that sought to hold it in place. In just a moment, he would break this attack without problem.

He lost his focus when the fifth monk stepped directly in

front of him, fire in his eyes. Before Lei could say anything, the monk's foot came around in a roundhouse kick aimed squarely at his face. Lei tried to dodge, but there was nowhere for his head to go. The kick connected, and for the second time that day, Lei's world went black.

36

F ang stretched his arms high over his head, fighting a yawn as the caravan approached the first checkpoint toward Jihan. He'd hoped that Lei would attack the caravan again, but the trip had been as boring as it was long. There hadn't been the slightest sign of the man.

He saw Daiyu leading the column, and memories of their last conversation grated against him.

"Did you kill him?" she'd asked.

"No. He escaped downriver."

"I thought you were the best. Is he too strong for you?"

He had contained his anger at that. "No. Just lucky."

His rage couldn't melt the ice in her gaze. "Then don't let it happen again."

Since then, they'd been traveling and the two of them hadn't shared a single word. Every time he looked at her, the question of being the strongest echoed in his head. He clenched his fists and thought about the revenge he would take on Lei once he had the chance.

For two days he'd been alert as a fox, but he hadn't noticed anything out of the ordinary. As they got closer to

Jihan, there were more people on the road, to the point where the caravan had to move slowly to stay together in the press of merchants.

The first checkpoint was about ten miles beyond the outskirts of the city. Given the lateness of the evening, Fang expected that Daiyu would stop one last time. The gates to the city were closed in the evenings leading up to the Harvest Festival. The governor found that it prevented some of the chaos if citizens knew there was no coming or going after a night of causing trouble.

Although he knew that the triads had arranged everything regarding the transportation of the powder beforehand, he still tensed up as they neared the checkpoint. His dagger wouldn't raise any suspicions, but there were hundreds of soldiers in the area. Even though he was much stronger than them, he'd be outnumbered. It would be a hell of a fight if that was what it came to.

Fang kept a close eye on Daiyu, studying her as the caravan slowed to a stop. A handful of guards approached, and Daiyu stepped forward, projecting an air of authority even he wanted to obey. She spoke to the head of the guards, passing over a few slips of paper.

Something about Daiyu tingled his senses; there was something that seemed off about her and he couldn't put his finger on it. While the soldiers wandered up and down the caravan, pretending to do their job, he walked up to one of the triads, who looked particularly nervous.

At first, Fang's presence did nothing to alleviate the other man's discomfort. He shifted his weight from foot to foot and his eyes darted around nervously. For most of their time together, Fang had avoided the triads, and none of them had gone out of their way to make him feel welcome. The situation had been to his liking.

Fang bobbed his head towards Daiyu. "Is she always like that?"

The triad started, looking as though he'd been considering any question but that one. But he eventually collected himself. "No. She used to be in charge of the Old Goat, a tavern in Two Bridges. She did accounting and provided private spaces when needed. There, she always made you feel welcome."

"She didn't make you feel as though all the warmth had gone out of a room?"

The triad chuckled softly. "She could, if you crossed a line, but no, not often."

Fang watched Daiyu as she conversed easily with the head of the guards. If appearances were true, they would be moving on through the checkpoint soon, a flawless passage. Cold or not, she had been efficient in transporting their goods. He might be looking for problems where none existed.

The triad looked like he wanted to ask Fang questions, but Fang had no interest in answering any. He stepped away before the two of them could strike up a real conversation. The triads were useful, but they were as weak as the soldiers who imagined they were keeping the people safe.

The captain of the soldiers waved them through the checkpoint, and Daiyu remained behind as every member of her caravan passed. Once everyone was safely through, Daiyu said her farewells to the captain, passing him a small purse. If Fang hadn't been watching closely, he never would have seen it.

Daiyu caught up to the rest of the caravan and was making her way toward the front when Fang stopped her. As much as he disliked the idea of making conversation with her, he needed to understand why he was uncertain about her.

As she approached, he noticed that her eyes watched their surroundings closely. Was she waiting for something, observant, or nervous? But when her eyes locked on him, he swore they froze over.

"A smooth passage," he observed.

"Niu had his weaknesses, but his preparation was excellent. The guards were prepared for our arrival."

"And what about you? What weaknesses do you have?"

When her gaze hardened, Fang could almost believe that his blood froze. "Impatience."

Meeting her stare required as much courage as Fang could muster, but he refused to be intimidated by anyone. What was it about her that didn't sit well with him? Was it just that he'd never come across anyone like her before? He'd never met a woman with the determination to run a triad, nor the cleverness to stay in such a position for more than an hour.

"What plans do you have once we reach the city?" she asked.

"I will escort the shipment until it reaches its final destination. Then I will receive new orders from my master." He realized he hadn't hesitated to answer her question at all.

"You have my gratitude for your escort. Your arrival was... fortuitous."

With that, she increased her pace and made her way toward the front of the column.

Fang gave his head a barely perceptible shake. She said all the right words, and acted in all the right ways, but he didn't trust Daiyu. When they reached Jihan he would ensure the shipment was safe. But once that was done, he thought that maybe he would turn his attention to the new leader of this triad. At this stage in their plan, they couldn't risk even the smallest disturbance.

There was a chance he was wrong, but if his master had nothing else for him, he would get to the bottom of what it was about Daiyu that made him so distrustful.

37

When Lei woke up, he almost immediately wished he hadn't. The light stabbed into his eyes, and when he tried to wipe away the tears that formed, he found that his hands were tightly bound behind his back, each hand wrapped tightly around the opposite forearm, preventing him from making any signs.

Beyond that, his head pounded, each beat of his heart making his head feel like a door being attacked by a battering ram. His throat was parched, and within a few seconds of waking, his stomach reminded him that he still hadn't eaten in quite some time. The chair he was sitting in wasn't comfortable either.

His vision slowly cleared as he came to his senses. The first fact he recognized was that he was in a monastery. Not one he'd ever been in before—he didn't recognize the walls, but the feeling of a monastery was the same no matter where it was. He could feel the energies of dozens of people nearby, and he was in a room with no small number of white-robed monks. There were three that he could see in front of him, but there were more behind him. The monks in front of him certainly didn't look happy to see him.

Before he could even say a word, one of the monks drove a fist into his stomach. Lei coughed violently. He was sick and tired of getting tied up and beaten. Anger burned brightly in his chest, and he considered the possibility of releasing his energy without even a hint of focus. The gesture wouldn't do much more than cause the monks to step backward in surprise, but even that would feel like a victory.

A severe tightness in his stomach ensured that finding the focus to do anything against his captors would be difficult. He cursed his brother for his attitude toward the monks.

Another monk, standing behind Lei's assailant, spoke, his own voice full of vitriol. "Why did you kill those monks?"

Lei spat and cursed, anger and frustration boiling over what little control he had left.

The punching monk stepped back and chambered a kick. Lei, knowing what was coming, braced himself against the impact.

The kick pounded into his arm, sending him crashing sideways. Rough hands picked him up and threw him back in his chair.

"Why did you kill those monks, Lei?" The monk in charge repeated.

Lei glared at the monk, hoping his gaze would kill. He breathed through his nose, forcing himself to calm down. His anger would do no good, especially if he couldn't fight.

"I might be a murderer, but I've never killed a monk. Not for lack of desire, though."

The monk in charge stopped the bruiser from swinging

again. His gaze was impassive but constant, as though he hoped answers would come if he simply observed for long enough.

A voice behind Lei spoke up. "I believe him."

The voice was familiar, but Lei couldn't quite place it. He sensed one of the presences behind him coming around to face him.

Taio. The monk sent to fetch him right after Jian's death.

Despite their past animosity, any face he recognized that was still alive was a relief. Lei wondered if his reaction was his own feeling or if his brother was trying to assert himself again.

"I'm glad to see you survived," Lei said.

"Most of us did. The abbot suspected something was coming. He didn't think we were safe huddled together at the top of the mountain, so he sent us away. He faced the destruction of the monastery alone."

Lei bowed his head. His past with the abbot was complicated, but he'd always acted fairly, even if Lei hadn't been able to see that at the time. Still, a small part of him believed the monks deserved what was coming to them.

Taio turned to the monk in charge. "Our abbot believed in him. As do I."

A tense silence settled in the room. Lei tested his bonds to see if there was any give, but if there was, he didn't notice it. He was still defenseless.

The monk in charge finally agreed. "I can detect no lie in him. Untie him."

Lei suffered through the process of being untied, upset they weren't going to apologize as well. But a monk never would. Despite all their talk of service and sacrifice, if you weren't one of them, you were beneath them and not worthy of consideration.

The monk in charge turned to Taio. "Learn what he knows. Report to me when you are done."

Taio bowed. "Yes, abbot."

A few minutes later, Lei was free and alone with Taio in the monastery room. Taio looked him over. "Food or bath first?"

Lei's stomach answered that question in a moment. "Food."

Taio grimaced. "I'd hoped you would choose bath."

Taio led them toward the kitchen, and Lei got to see more of the monastery. He had vague memories of visiting other monasteries as a child, but none of them were vivid. The similarities between this one and his own were striking. Most of the monks practiced their techniques in the courtyard, while others scurried around on one errand or another.

Lei noticed that while he was free, he wasn't safe. All of the monks were paying attention to him, and he had no doubt that if he tried to focus his power he'd be attacked from all directions. He was still a prisoner, just one who was free to walk around.

The dining room was a simple room with bare white walls and several long tables. Taio motioned for Lei to sit while he poked his head into the kitchen to request food. Lei hadn't thought to check the position of the sun outside, so he wasn't exactly sure what time it was. Clearly, it wasn't mealtime yet.

Taio returned moments later with two huge bowls of rice and vegetables. Lei wasn't sure how long it had been since he'd seen so much food set aside just for him. His stomach rumbled in anticipation and he grabbed the chopsticks before Taio even had a chance to set them down. Before a single word could be uttered, Lei was deep in his food.

Taio was wise enough, or at least patient enough, to allow Lei to finish the meal before he started quizzing Lei about what he knew. Lei finished both bowls of food, and with a contented sigh, leaned back. Now that his stomach was full, he felt as though he could take on any challenge, including answering Taio's questions.

"What happened to you?" Taio asked.

Lei considered how he should answer. Saying too much might almost be as dangerous as saying too little, but the only way to clear his name was to tell more of the truth than he was comfortable with. He had little choice but to put his future in Taio's hands. The two of them might be alone now, but Lei was still aware there were dozens of monks surrounding them who had orders to prevent Lei from leaving the monastery.

"Something happened to me on the day of my brother's funeral," Lei confessed.

For the next few minutes, Lei talked about the changes he'd experienced, from his sudden distaste in beer to a level of skill he'd never possessed. He didn't leave anything out.

"And you say the triads attacked you?"

Lei nodded. "At first. I asked too many questions, and they became uncomfortable. But I attacked Niu's place on my own."

Taio nodded gravely. "We've heard stories of the destruction there from travelers. I won't pretend to regret Niu is gone, but all the same, to use our gifts in that way..." His voice trailed off.

Lei forced himself not to say anything. The monks held a deep reverence for the abilities they'd been gifted with, but at times, Lei wished they'd be more willing to express themselves in the world. He respected the monastic life and values, but one of his greatest complaints was that the monks did too little.

"What do you know about what the triads are planning?" Taio asked.

"Not much," Lei admitted. "I've met the man who killed my brother, and he's strong. I was fortunate to escape. If he's any indication of the strength the triads are assembling, it must be an impressive force. I know they are bringing in hundreds of pounds of black powder, and I suspect they will use the Harvest Festival as cover for their activities."

Taio absorbed all the information without so much as nodding. Lei knew there was something more that Taio knew that he wasn't talking about. "What do you know?"

Taio didn't hesitate to answer. "We are very concerned. With your brother's connection, do you have his memories?"

"No. At best, I get his feelings."

"In the past few years, some of the monks in the Tenno region have made some fascinating discoveries. Their practice is much more internal than even our own. In short, they've discovered that our abilities do not originate within ourselves. It is perhaps more accurate to say that we are conduits to something greater."

Taio's neutral tone masked how shattering this revelation was. For all the years of his training in the monastery, Lei had understood that one's strength came exclusively from one's own efforts. Why else would they spend so much time in training not just their bodies, but their minds? Had all those days and years been so fundamentally misguided?

"Something greater?"

Taio shrugged. "A realm of spirits? A deity? There have been as many theories as there are monks, it seems, but no one knows."

"How long have the monasteries known?"

"About six years."

The entire room that Lei sat in seemed to shift just a bit, a whole new worldview opening up to him. Though his memory was sometimes clouded by the amount of drink he'd consumed over the years, it had been about six years since the monks had begun keeping more and more to the monasteries, leaving the roads and villages more unprotected. Now he could put a reason to the change. They had become uncertain of their own abilities.

It also meant he didn't understand his own training anymore. How could it be that the strength wasn't his own? What was the point of the physical and mental training? "So why did the monasteries' training work if the ideas behind it were all wrong?"

"We're still not sure. You need to understand, everything is being rewritten as we speak. The last six years have been both impossibly difficult to grapple with, but also tremendously exciting. However, we do believe that people's innate ability to act as a passage for this energy is due in no small part to their physical and mental health."

"And how does all of this relate to the triad's plan, and this Order of the Serpent?"

"We don't know. I was hoping you would know more."

Lei gestured back toward the door of the kitchen, and the two of them stood up and left the building, wandering the monastery slowly. Lei watched the training of the new monks, wondering how different their education was than the one he'd gone through. His eyes also ran over the walls, studying the monastery's defenses. Would they hold against Fang?

Taio seemed content to wander for a few moments. They stopped on a small rise overlooking the courtyard, where the monks were lined up in perfect rows for one of several meditative sessions. Even after everything, he still felt a sense of peace within these walls. There was order here he could rely on. He only wished he could be sure the feelings were his own and not his brother's. He hadn't felt anything resembling peace for years when it came to the monasteries. But who was wrong? Him or Jian?

"What comes next?" Lei asked.

Taio looked down at his feet, as though that was the one question he'd hoped never to have to deal with. Lei imagined he wasn't going to like the answer.

"The abbot has ordered that you remain in the monastery. Even if your cause has been noble, you've broken your agreement, and you know the punishment for that."

"And now that you know I don't know anything useful, my life is forfeit?"

Taio looked up, angry. "Don't play the victim, Lei. You've had plenty of chances. Everything you've suffered is your fault. Jian might have felt sympathy for you, but no one else did."

Lei met the angry stare, surprised at the emotion behind it. Even after all these years, they still felt so strongly? They would kill him, when he was the only person who'd faced Fang and lived? That same queasiness haunted him again as he thought about how the monasteries deserved their retribution, the two souls within him warring for dominance.

"I'm sorry, Taio. I can't understand your anger, but I regret causing it."

Taio's shoulders relaxed, and Lei realized the monk had been ready for a fight.

"Perhaps your sentence will be delayed. There are

legends of possessions, but your case is unique, and I have no doubt there are monks who would be honored to investigate further."

Lei's voice was quiet but firm. "Taio, do you really think you can stop me? I have my strength and Jian's control. I'm no longer a monk, and I refuse to submit to your judgment."

Taio stepped back as if he'd been stung. Lei felt the monk gather his energy and focus it into an attack. In that moment, his mind was made up. Taio, one of the monks in charge, could barely summon enough energy to be a threat to him. After so long away from the other monks, Lei didn't realize how much stronger he was.

Lei held up a placating hand. "I don't want to fight, Taio. You and I disagree, but that's not worth fighting over. But I can't submit. For one, I like my life. But you have no chance against the forces arrayed against you. You need me."

Lei watched as anger distorted Taio's features. The man hadn't liked him much back when he'd been in the monastery, attached to the rules as he was, and it appeared that anger had only grown in time. But Lei wouldn't be moved. He was glad to hear that the monasteries were changing, but they still had a long way to go.

For a moment, Lei believed Taio was actually going to attack. Doing so inside the walls would quickly escalate into a fight Lei didn't want. But looking at Taio's hand, quivering with the effort of holding his energy, Lei thought he might do it. He refused to summon his own energy, though. He wouldn't be drawn into this fight.

Finally, Taio relented, releasing his energy and dropping his hand. "What would you have us do?"

Lei looked at the monks training below. If Taio's energy was any indication, they would be worse than useless. They would get in the way and make it more difficult for him to track Fang.

"I'll make you a new deal for my life. Stay here. It's what you monks are good at, anyway. I'll find Daiyu, and she'll lead me to the powder. Then I'll finish your fight for you."

38

Fang watched with careful attention as the final barrels were unloaded from the carts. Here in Jihan, the triad maintained a network of safe houses that were being used to store the powder. From here, the triads would slowly place the powder in the positions they had agreed on.

As far as Fang was concerned, his work here was almost over. He didn't bother sending a message to his master. His master would find him sometime before the festival. Fang was to stay in one of the safe houses until he heard from him.

But the prospect of remaining within the walls of a safe house chafed. Besides, his suspicion of Daiyu continued unabated. She had fulfilled the terms of their contract admirably, but still, he couldn't shake his feeling that there was more to her than he knew. Her underlings might be too afraid of her to suspect, but he wasn't.

As the final cart was unloaded, she came over to him and gave a short bow. "Thank you for your assistance. If there is anything further you require, any of my men will be able to find me. I hope you find your stay in Jihan pleasant."

He returned the bow, unable to detect anything except cold formality in her tone. "Thank you for your services. I will report the excellence of your work to my master."

Her face remained perfectly expressionless. No one was made of stone, but Daiyu seemed to want people to think she was.

She turned to leave, and for a minute, Fang watched her go. When he was certain she didn't suspect him, he turned to one of the triads from the safe house. "I must go on errands for my master. If I receive any messages, I will return for them."

The triad bowed, not caring one way or the other.

Then Fang turned and began following Daiyu. Perhaps it was all nothing. Maybe he was just unaccustomed to women in positions of authority. But with the plan this close to completion, they couldn't risk a problem. Her behavior tickled some part of his intuition, and until he was certain she wouldn't betray them, he would keep an eye on her. At the very least, it was more interesting than having nothing to do in the safe house.

The triad boss wasn't hard to follow. She was taller than average, especially for a woman, and although she occasionally checked around her to make sure she wasn't being followed, Fang had no problem melting into the crowd when she did. Her path wandered back and forth, but the streets were so busy with the approach of the Harvest Festival that she had little hope of spotting anyone.

After perhaps a half hour of walking, Daiyu came to an estate that was walled and patrolled by guards on the inside. From the outside, Fang couldn't make out any signs that would indicate what the building was. But since it was the first place Daiyu visited upon the completion of their mission, it could only be one place: the local and most likely regional headquarters for the triad. Given the appearance of the place, Fang was willing to risk quite a bit of coin that his guess was correct.

There was no easy way for Fang to follow her into the estate, and he figured it was more than likely she was going to report all the recent news, including the completion of her mission. He wouldn't learn anything about her while she was inside. He spotted a small restaurant that had tables where he could keep an eye on the front gate of the estate. His stomach growling, he walked to it and sat down, his mouth watering at the menu choices he knew how to read.

As he carefully ate the delicious food, he kept an eye on the streets, trying to gauge the mood of the city. Jihan was a major center for trade, and one of the largest cities in the empire. How people felt here would reflect shifts around the empire.

Unfortunately, to Fang the day looked entirely unremarkable, without even a hint of revolution. People scurried about their petty business, certain that whatever they were working on was the most important thing in the world. There were some greetings as neighbors ran into one another, and the whole street felt as though it was preparing for a celebration, which it was. Even the dust from the carts and horses couldn't wipe the smiles off the people's faces.

They would all learn soon enough, though. The society they relied on would be revealed as a façade soon enough. All they needed was more time.

Fang was done with his food when Daiyu came out of the compound. Given the nature of her sudden promotion, Fang figured she was lucky to have come out at all. He tried to guess what had happened inside, but her face was as much a mask as ever, completely unreadable. She could have been given a sack of gold or learned her entire family had been killed for all Fang could tell.

He paid his bill while watching Daiyu go farther down the street. He gave himself plenty of distance, trying to just barely keep her in sight. The crowds were still thick.

Almost immediately he realized something had changed. Before, Daiyu had tried to see if she was being observed, but she hadn't worried much. Now, if he didn't know better, Fang would say she was trying to ensure her privacy. As she walked, she checked over her shoulder repeatedly, and she often stopped at some of the vendors to look at goods. But even from a distance, Fang could see she was checking to see if anyone was following.

She went down an alley, and as Fang allowed the pull of the crowd to move him in front of the opening, he saw that she was simply standing there, watching the opening. Fang didn't think she'd spotted him, but he crossed the street and waited to see what she would do next.

Eventually, she came out of the alley.

Her actions over the course of the next hour convinced him she was trying to hide something. She circled blocks, doubled back, and tried a dozen other tricks to reveal any pursuers. Twice Fang thought he was almost spotted, but both times fortune favored him. Had Harvest Festival not been approaching, Fang would have had no chance of remaining unobserved.

No matter how long the chase lasted, Fang had no plans of giving up. This was the first real evidence that Daiyu was more than what she seemed, and he wouldn't let this thread vanish. He followed her into one of the more upscale districts in Jihan. The streets were less crowded here, and those who walked the streets wore robes made of finer materials. City guards forcibly removed any beggars from the streets, and the district as a whole seemed quieter than before. He put more distance between the two of them to keep himself safe from discovery.

Finally, she came to a small building and entered it. Fang waited at a distance, but when she did not reappear, he decided it was worth the risk to see what the building was. He walked up to it, his eyes studying every inch. The building was as nice as anything else in the area, and perhaps even nicer. It was larger than he'd initially thought, the wooden walls reaching back far from the street. He recognized the symbols for the word "inn," though he'd never seen an inn of this quality before.

Fortune was with him. As he walked past the inn, he saw movement within one of the windows. Daiyu was there, being shown a room by an older gentleman Fang assumed was the innkeeper. So, now Fang knew both the purpose of the visit and where exactly she was staying.

He looked around, seeing a tavern across the street. It was a risk, but he'd have to get his nicer clothes and more money to come back to continue watching Daiyu. As it was, he worried he would attract attention. But he knew where Daiyu was staying, and he would be back. He would find her secrets, no matter how long it took.

39

After another meal and a full night's rest, Lei felt like a completely new man. Some of his injuries still ached, but they were easy to ignore. Once he had stretched and warmed up, he felt as strong as he ever had.

Taio was waiting for him within the monastery's courtyard. The monk's white robes looked so clean it was as though they'd never been worn, and Taio stood almost as stiff as his robes. Although Taio believed Lei's story, he made no secret of the fact that he thought the path they walked on was misguided. He believed Lei should remain so they could observe and study him. But Lei's combination of threats and promises had secured his peaceful exit from the monastery, even if the cost was higher than he wished.

Taio held his sword, which Lei took off his hands without ceremony.

"You should keep the monks within the walls," Lei warned.

"And you should stop meddling in our affairs," Taio replied.

Lei shrugged. There would be no cure for the animosity

between the two of them. The pain was too deeply rooted, and Lei felt like if he claimed that the sky was blue, Taio would disagree on principle alone. But Taio wasn't his problem. None of the monks were.

Lei didn't have anything else to say, so he turned to the gate of the monastery. With his sword, there was nothing they could do to stop him, but all the same, it was a relief when they allowed him to pass outside the walls without a challenge. He could feel their stares on his back as he left, but he didn't mind.

The monastery he'd been taken to was located on the outskirts of Jihan. Although the space immediately surrounding the walls was open, huts and a few shops stood not more than a few hundred paces away. The Jihan monastery was one of the oldest in the region, and when it was built it had been well outside the city. But the city had grown and was coming close to swallowing the monastery.

When Lei was in training, he had overheard conversations between monks discussing the relocation of the monastery to someplace more remote. But as was often the case with the monasteries, tradition bound them to poor decisions. Apparently, even after all this time, the monastery stood where it always had, even though it was only a few years away from being completely surrounded.

While the decision might have been a poor strategic one, it did simplify one of Lei's problems. In his mind, he only had one goal. He needed to find Daiyu, and together they were going to escape their former lives. Nothing else mattered to him, not even his promises to Taio. Jian's presence in his stomach threatened to upset him as the thought crossed his mind, but he would have said anything to escape the monks. The triads, the Order of the Serpent, and the monks could all fight among themselves, but he wanted no part of it. Maybe he and Daiyu could open up a tavern or an inn at the far reaches of the empire.

The dream was pleasant, but first he needed to find Daiyu, and in a city the size of Jihan, that would be no small task. Lei had tossed the problem around his mind last night, but he'd been too exhausted and too contented by multiple bowls of food to think clearly. He'd drifted off to sleep almost immediately.

Once he was beyond sight of the monastery, Lei searched for a teahouse. Fortunately, they were fairly common in the area, and within a few minutes he was sitting at a low table, waiting for his tea to steep while he considered the problem.

It wasn't until he sighed in pleasure at his first sips that he realized what had happened to him. He'd never been a tea lover, but his brother had been. The feelings and the queasiness had mostly passed, but it seemed his brother's spirit was influencing him in more subtle ways now.

The realization shook him. He hated not knowing what was really him and what wasn't. He hadn't thought anything about stepping into a teahouse to consider his options, although that was a choice he never would have made weeks ago. Lei preferred loud taverns. Would his brother sabotage his efforts to find Daiyu? Was that the real reason he'd fallen asleep so quickly last night when trying to figure out how to find her?

He took a deep breath, held it, and released it, an old trick he remembered from his monastic training. He sipped at the tea again, finding it delicious, the grassy notes giving way to a slightly sweet aftertaste. In all the times he'd had tea, he'd never tasted it quite like this before.

Perhaps he was looking at his situation with his brother incorrectly. Whatever had happened, maybe there would be a way for them to live in peace? Despite his injuries, he felt more at ease than he had in years. His anger, which had simmered underneath the surface for the better part of a decade, was diminished to the point where he didn't really feel it anymore.

A slight queasiness passed through his stomach once again. Knowing his brother, Lei didn't have any trouble deciding what he meant. His brother wanted justice. He wanted Lei to fight Fang, to save the day and the monasteries. But he'd chosen the wrong body for that. Lei wanted nothing more to do with anything.

The slight sickness receded, and Lei wondered if his brother was giving up. Ultimately, it was Lei's body, and he would use it as he saw fit. His attention undivided, he put his mind toward solving the problem of finding Daiyu in a city this large.

Lei didn't know where in the city the triads kept their headquarters, and those were certainly not the type of questions one wanted to go around asking.

A memory surfaced, unbidden.

He and Daiyu were lying in his bed, the morning sunlight streaming through the open window. Their talk had wandered for hours.

"If you could do anything," Lei asked, "what would you do?"

Her answer was immediate, a smile playing across her face. "I've always wanted to run my own inn. Welcome weary travelers from the road, give them good food and a place to rest."

He returned her smile. He tried to imagine her running her own inn and found he had no trouble doing so. Although she didn't show it often, she was a natural leader, often issuing commands and expecting others to follow them. He'd seen it often enough with rowdy patrons at the Old Goat. There was something about her that caused others to follow, even if there was no need. Besides, she had excellent taste in wine and beer. No doubt she'd have quality drinks for thirsty travelers. Her cooking skills were a bit lacking, but that could be hired out.

"What about you, what would you do?"

He shook his head. Since the monastery, he'd had no real goals.

"Just be with you, I guess."

Her bright eyes darkened for just a moment, but she rarely chided him on his lack of ambition.

Lei changed the subject, hating to see the disappointment in her face. "Is there an inn you would model yours after? Surely you'd do better than anything in Two Bridges."

Her eyes lit up again. "Have you ever been to the Heron in Jihan?"

"No."

"It's a small, beautiful inn. I had to meet someone there once, and it felt like a home."

Daiyu didn't often speak of the tasks she'd had to perform to reach her rank in the triad, but Lei was no fool. Daiyu's past was just as cloudy as his own.

Seized by an impulse, he'd replied, "Someday, when we have more money, we'll go to the Heron together."

She rolled closer to him and ran her hand through his hair. "I'd like that."

The memory dissipated, and Lei ran his finger thoughtfully around the edge of his cup. Perhaps he was foolish, but it made sense. They wanted to run away together, and where else would she wait for him to find her?

If nothing else, he had nothing to lose. He stood up and paid his bill.

The Heron wasn't difficult to find. After asking for directions twice, he found his way to the inn. It was just the way Daiyu described it. He stepped inside, searching for the common room.

The room itself was empty, but only because the day was gorgeous, and he could hear voices coming from the other side of the wall. He found a door and stepped out into the skywell.

Lei wasn't sure he'd ever been in a more peaceful place. Each of the plants was immaculately cared for, and the thick walls of the inn kept out any noise from the street, even though that wasn't much. The clouds drifted lazily overhead, keeping the parts of the space that were open cool.

As soon as he walked in, he saw her. She was sitting alone at a table, reading a book. How often had he come across her in that very pose in their quiet times together? For a moment, past and present melted into one.

Somehow, she became aware of his presence. Her eyes came up and saw him, and a slow smile spread over her face. Lei wanted to live in that one moment forever. He was certain he would die content if he could.

He walked slowly over to her table and sat down. Almost immediately, an older woman who Lei assumed was an innkeeper came to him. "The young lady doesn't want company, young man. Now, leave her alone!"

Daiyu laughed. "He's fine. This is the friend I've been telling you about."

In the space of a moment, the innkeeper's demeanor changed entirely. Where before she couldn't be rid of him soon enough, now she took interest in him as though he was going to become her own son-in-law.

After plenty of questions, the innkeeper left them alone.

"You remembered," Daiyu said.

"I did. Although I think if we're going to stay here, you're going to have to pay."

"I already did," she said with a mischievous grin that could only mean one thing.

They didn't remain long in the common room.

Later, as they were lying together in her room, she ran her hands through his hair. "This is the cleanest I've seen you in some time."

"The monks let me bathe before I left."

"I'm still surprised they let you leave."

"As am I."

Both of them were dancing around the subject they needed to discuss.

"I—" they both started at the same time.

She motioned for him to go first.

"I was just thinking these beds are as nice as you said they were," he said, cursing at himself for his sudden lack of courage.

She gave him a tight-lipped smile. "We need to talk about what happens next."

"We run, as far and as fast as we can. Do you have money for horses?"

Daiyu frowned. "I have gold, but not enough. However, there will be more if I return to headquarters soon. They have decided to give me Niu's share of the profits, which they should have by tonight."

"So Fang is in the city, too?"

"He is. He's staying at one of the safe houses until his master comes for him."

"His master must be some warrior to keep Fang's loyalty."

Daiyu looked like she was about to disagree, but she didn't say anything. But long ago, Lei had learned to trust her instincts. "What?"

She bit her lip before speaking. "There's something wrong with this 'Order of the Serpent.' I've only ever heard of the master and Fang, and the master doesn't strike me as a warrior, at all. I'd expect him at least to look like an older monk, but he really just looks like an old man. I don't get the same sense of danger from him as I do from you or Fang. He is clever, though."

Lei chewed on her thoughts. By themselves, the observations didn't mean much, but they were interesting nevertheless.

"So you want to go back to headquarters tonight?" He tried but failed to keep the displeasure out of his voice. It felt too risky when they were this close to freedom.

"I think I need to."

"We could travel light, and I could hunt for our food."

"I know, but think about how much easier more money will make the trip. And there's no need to worry. The triads don't suspect anything. I'll get the money and we can leave this evening."

"I could come with."

"You could, but that would be foolish. It's safer for you here. And anyway, you look like I've tired you out."

He pulled her toward him. "Not quite yet, you haven't."

40

———

When Fang saw Lei step into the inn, he almost couldn't believe his eyes. Not only was Daiyu betraying their cause, she was working with an undercover monk. All the behaviors he'd seen from her in the past few days were suddenly explained.

His impulse was to run into the inn and attack Lei, no matter the consequences. If he could just beat Lei, he was convinced he would be the strongest. He came as far as standing from his table before he realized what a mistake he would be making.

Fang wasn't entrusted with the entirety of his master's plans. According to his master, not even others in the order knew everything. The knowledge of the plan rested entirely within his master, so as to be completely safe. As much as Fang wanted to fight Lei, their mission was bigger than a feud between the two warriors. Before he could act, he needed his master's advice. Only his obedience to his master allowed Lei to live.

Fang waited for a while, just long enough to confirm that the two of them had gone to Daiyu's room. He didn't need to guess what they were doing. They would give him enough time to seek the advice he needed. He left and returned to the safe house.

When he arrived at the house, he saw that a message was waiting for him. He had one of the triads read it. His master would be in a commercial district nearby, waiting for him. Fang went straightaway and found his master at a well-respected teahouse, sipping his tea silently while his eyes studied the room.

Fang gave his master a short bow and knelt at the table. He jumped right into his story, beginning with his suspicions and the discovery he'd made. When he was done, his master was impressed.

"As always, Fang, your work has been all that I could ask for. I could not have done better myself, and you displayed great wisdom in coming to me first. We must find out what the woman has given away. I'm disappointed the triads trusted her as far as they did, but we will make it right. If they separate, take the woman and bring her to the safe house. If they remain together, follow them and report back. If they remain together and try to leave, you have my permission to kill them both."

Fang could feel his heart begin to pound in anticipation of his fight with Lei. Even if he abducted the woman, Lei would come after him. Either way, this only ended with the two of them locked in combat. Nothing would make him happier.

His instructions clear, Fang returned to the inn. As far as he could tell, the two of them were still in Daiyu's room. He'd been gone less than two hours, but still, he was impressed. He settled back into his position to wait. Now that he knew conflict with Lei was inevitable, patience came easily.

The sun was setting and his restaurant was about to close when Daiyu stepped out of the inn. She looked around carefully, but she didn't spot him tucked into a corner of the restaurant. She took off down the street, her pace quick.

Following her presented more of a challenge in the early evening. Many shops had closed for the day, and while the streets were still busy, they weren't as packed as they had been earlier in the day. Fang relied on longer shadows to hide himself from her roving eyes.

Fortunately for him, she wasn't as careful this time as she had been earlier. Only once did he worry that he might have come close to being spotted. But soon enough, he knew where she was heading: back to the triad headquarters in the city.

His nostrils flared as he thought about the betrayal she was involved in. She would wear that mask, hiding her true nature from the world as she brought down all of their carefully laid plans. But not anymore. Thanks to him, she'd be stopped, and for good.

He decided to take a risk. If he knew where she was going, he could scout ahead to find someplace to ambush her. His odds of taking her without a commotion increased if he could take her by surprise. Letting her out of his sight was hard to stomach, but he was confident he knew her destination.

Fang darted onto a side street that paralleled the street Daiyu walked on. He picked up his pace until he was moving at a very fast walk. In a few blocks, he found an alley that appeared perfect. He glanced around and saw a cart, abandoned from the day's work. He wouldn't find a better spot.

Fang crept to the opening of the alley facing the street Daiyu was walking on. He barely peered around the corner, looking just long enough to ensure that the traitor would walk right by him. He melted into the shadows and waited for her to arrive.

The wait crawled by, but eventually she stepped in front of him, never even seeing him. He reached out and pulled her into the alley, deep into the shadows. One hand clamped over her mouth while his other arm snaked around her throat, putting pressure on the blood vessels there.

She fought for a second before she realized she wasn't going to break his hold. For the space of a heartbeat, Fang thought this would be easy.

Then she bit his hand and drove a dagger into his inner thigh. He hadn't even noticed her going for a weapon, but her strike was true all the same. Another few inches in and he wouldn't have been able to chase her. Surprised, he lost his grip and she stumbled forward, pulling the dagger out of his leg as she did so.

Daiyu made it two steps towards the entrance of the alley before Fang's anger took over. He refused to let her make a fool of him! He focused his rage into his hand, unleashing his energy, smashing it directly against the back of her skull.

Without a word, she fell forward, unconscious. Fang hadn't meant to hit her as hard as he had, but there was nothing to be done for it now. He bundled her up and put her in the cart, covering her with some rags found within. Then he picked up the handles and started pulling, eager to find out what the traitor had done to destroy their plans.

41

───────

After Daiyu left, Lei fell asleep instantly. Even though he was greatly recovered after his recent adventures, sleep still called to him. His slumber was deep and dreamless.

When he awoke, the sun had long set. The streets outside their windows were dark. He came to his senses slowly, a creeping unease working its way underneath his contentment as he did. He wasn't sure exactly how long he'd been asleep, but Daiyu should have returned by now. She hadn't expected her task to take more than a few hours.

Lei forced himself to remain in bed. Daiyu was one of the most capable women he knew. He had nothing to worry about. There were a hundred reasons why she wouldn't be back yet, and only a handful of them meant disaster.

Still, he worried. For the first time in years, he had something to lose. Daiyu had taken him back, and the thought of losing her again threatened to break him.

Unable to remain in bed, Lei climbed out and worked his way through some of the practices from his days in the monastery. One by one he practiced the forms he remembered, as well as some he was sure he had never learned, forcing his mind to focus on his movements. The practice provided relief for a little while, but the later the night became, the more distracted he was.

It was well after midnight when Lei decided that something had happened. A small whisper in the back of his mind told him that he wasn't worthy of Daiyu. He'd had his chance once and blown it, and she had finally realized he didn't deserve a second chance. Every time he tried to ignore the whisper it returned, a little louder.

Maybe she had left him again, or maybe something had happened, but either way, his response was the same. He needed to find Daiyu. He could always go searching and return here later. She had the room for a few days, so perhaps he would come back and find her here, laughing at his worry.

Lei left the room, not sure how to begin his search. Daiyu had gone to the triad's headquarters. However, she hadn't been kind enough to let him know where that was. In a city this size, he could look for days and never have a chance to find her.

His only solution was to try to work his way up the triads. If he could find any triad, he could eventually work his way up the chain until he found someone who knew what was happening and where the headquarters were. Without a better solution, he followed his instincts and walked the city, his eyes open for triad business. At this time of night, he could only think of one starting point, and that was to find a gambling hall.

Lei had never been much for gambling. He'd gone out a few times, back when people had been more willing to be seen with him, but he'd never much seen the point. It was rare to leave with more money than you came with, and he never felt the thrill so many of his friends had. But that was unusual, he figured, as almost every village and town had some place for gambling, even if it was only in a shed behind someone's house.

Not only did gambling exist everywhere, it was also always controlled by the triads. No one attempted to run gambling without them. Those that did ended up with broken bones more often than not, and that was if they were lucky. And halls were often open late into the night, making them perfect for his purposes.

It took Lei nearly an hour of wandering to find a gambling hall. The building itself didn't draw much attention, but the two guards posted outside did. Even back in Two Bridges the gambling was always guarded. The triads kept some people out of the halls, but also ensured that no one tried to run away with money that wasn't theirs. Lei had heard no shortage of stories telling how uncompromising the triads were about such matters.

He decided it was safer not to approach too closely. He felt no threat from the triads themselves, but if possible, he didn't want to announce his presence to Fang. So he would remain quiet and hidden for as long as possible, and tonight that meant waiting until one of the triads left the hall.

Fortunately, he didn't have long to wait. After only five minutes in the shadows, Lei watched a young man leave the hall, his steps purposeful. He also had a tattoo on his hand, a symbol many triads wore. The man walked alone into the night, and Lei would never have a better chance.

Lei detached himself from the shadows, stepping out into the street and following the young man. There were a handful of other people in the streets, but not nearly enough to provide cover and protection. Lei simply followed, hoping the man would never turn around.

Fortune favored him. The man had no concern about being followed, walking through the streets with a slight spring in his step. Lei approached closer, waiting for any moment to strike when he wouldn't be seen. His hand made a sign that focused an attack. It wasn't very strong, so it wouldn't be felt by anyone too near, but it would be enough to knock the man down.

The triad turned a corner and Lei knew he had his opportunity. He quickened his pace. The triad had been about thirty paces ahead, and Lei didn't want to lose him. Lei turned the corner, raising his hand as he did.

The triad was standing in the street at the door of a building. Just as Lei arrived, the door opened and a young girl came charging out. "Father!"

The triad bent down and swept the girl into a hug, picking her up and spinning her around.

Lei still considered attacking the man. He was completely unprepared, and his daughter would keep him distracted. Lei aimed his attack, a moment away from releasing it, when an overwhelming feeling of nausea rolled over him.

He hadn't felt his brother this strong in days, but Lei stumbled and caught himself against the wall of a house. His stumble drew the attention of the triad, who doubtless saw a drunk in the street. The triad took his daughter and went into their house, closing the door.

"Let me do this," Lei growled under his breath. All he could think about was Daiyu and the trouble she might be in. But the moment he stepped toward the triad's door, the same sickness struck again, this time driving his last meal back out.

Lei gave one last glance at the house, anger flooding him. This was so much like the brother he'd known. Jian wanted justice, but he wanted it his way. Lei just wanted to be done, tired of his body not being entirely his own.

He remembered a time, back in the monastery, when he and Jian had argued. Looking back on it, that argument might have been the beginning of the end for the two of them.

Lei had taken Jian to an unobserved corner of the monastery, a place the monks rarely came, holding a long stick in his hand that he'd carried up from Two Bridges the day before.

"Look," he whispered excitedly. Narrowing his eyes in concentration, Lei let some of his energy seep into the stick. He used only the smallest amount, making sure he didn't focus enough to draw the attention of the monks. Jian looked at the stick, dividing his attention between his brother and their surroundings.

"What happens?" Jian asked, his curiosity about the taboo overwhelming his usual reluctance.

"Feel this. It'll hurt a little." Lei pointed the stick at Jian and let the energy go. It shot out of the stick and hit Jian in the chest, causing his eyes to open wide. Lei knew exactly how his brother felt. He'd barely used any energy, but he'd tested the attack on himself the day before, and knew how hard the blow felt.

Lei was getting excited. "Can you imagine what you could do if you put all of your energy into something like this? I bet you'd be the strongest monk who ever lived. No one would be able to defeat you."

A sudden look came over Jian's face, a look that Lei knew all too well. If Lei wasn't careful, Jian was about to report him to the other monks. "Jian! We could do this together! Think of how strong we could become!"

That was Lei's real hope. Both of them were strong. The

monks told them often enough. But Jian was disciplined. He always did all his work, and sometimes did extra just because he believed it would make him stronger. Lei could never see the point. If he could do the tasks set before him, why bother with extra effort? Perhaps this way, they would have something they could work on together again, something that would draw both of them.

Jian shook his head. "If the monks told us we're never supposed to do that, there must be a good reason."

"Maybe they just don't want students who are stronger than they are."

As soon as the words came out of his mouth, Lei knew they were the wrong ones. Jian practically venerated the monks, giving them all the thanks for keeping the two of them fed and safe after their parents died. Where once his brother had been wavering, Lei knew he'd lost the argument for good now.

Jian stood up taller. "I'll let you get away with this, Lei, but if I ever see you with a weapon again, even a stick, I'll tell the abbot everything. You need to understand, it's not just about getting strong, but being strong in the right ways."

Perhaps that had been the beginning of the end. Lei didn't know. There seemed to be a dozen points or arguments that had led to their final falling out, but that was one that always stuck with him—Jian's insistence not just on doing something, but on doing it right. They'd never quite seen eye to eye on that. They didn't now, either, it appeared.

"Fine," Lei said, taking one last look at the triad's house. "If you don't want this, just leave me alone. I'll find her another way."

Lei turned back down the quiet street, wondering how he'd ever find Daiyu in a city so large.

42

Fang watched Daiyu as she came to. He'd been watching her for a while now, waiting for her to wake up. In his mind, she was more beautiful as she slept. Her eyes weren't cold, freezing him in place every time they met his.

Her eyelids fluttered and Fang straightened. She'd be awake soon. When her eyes opened she took in her surroundings, including Fang, in a single glance. He thought that maybe he saw her flinch, but for the most part she was as cold as ever. He shuddered, impressed that even when captured she didn't break. She had more courage than most of the men he'd met.

"What did you do?"

"I've been following you since you made the delivery. I saw you with Lei. When you were alone, I ambushed you."

"And brought me back to your room in the safe house."

Fang nodded. He wasn't surprised that she recognized her surroundings as quickly as she had. Her eyes met his, and he received the distinct impression she was calculating, deciding what to do next. Emotion had no place in those decisions.

"What do you want?" she asked.

"Information. I need to know how far you've betrayed us. How much do Lei and the monasteries know? What are they planning?"

Fang had more questions, but was stopped cold by Daiyu laughing. It was a soft laugh, but her rock-hard mask had slipped, and Fang wondered for a moment if he had somehow captured the wrong person.

He waited for her to finish, waiting for her to tell him what she found humorous about her situation. Her laughter lasted for almost a minute, grating against his confidence. He was supposed to be in control of the situation, but it didn't feel that way to him. She was as calm as ever.

When she finally stopped laughing, she was transformed. The woman he'd known in Two Bridges and on the road was gone, replaced by someone else entirely. Daiyu sat relaxed, and while her face was still expressionless, it wasn't cold. "I'll tell you whatever I can, as I see no reason to lie, but I do not think you'll like the answers."

He gestured for her to go ahead. "I'll be the judge of that."

Daiyu gave him a small shrug of her shoulders. Had Fang not been the one who had abducted her, he would never have guessed the stress she'd just experienced.

"First, Lei isn't working with the monasteries."

Fang stopped her immediately. "That's not true. My master told me that Lei is working as a spy, trying to infiltrate the triads for information about what we're doing."

Daiyu laughed again, this time the laughter firmer than before. "I don't know where your master is getting his information, but I can't think of anything further from the truth. Lei hates the monasteries almost as much as you and your master seem to. He was kicked out of one years and years ago and has carried the grudge ever since."

"Maybe that's what he wants you to believe."

"He killed a girl."

Fang was just about to retort when he realized what she had said. Niu had said the same.

"He did what?"

"Killed a girl. A merchant's daughter. I've never heard the whole story, but everyone in town knows it happened. After that, he was banished from the monastery, and has been trying to survive ever since."

"If he killed anyone, the monasteries would do more than banish him. They have no mercy."

Daiyu shrugged. "I can't tell you why he's alive. I suspect his brother, the monk you killed, had something to do with it. He reached some sort of bargain with the abbot. Regardless, Lei lost the only home he had, and he's never forgiven them. If you asked, he'd probably more likely join your movement than cooperate with the monasteries."

Fang tossed the ideas in his head. He wished his master were around. Fang couldn't detect a lie in Daiyu, but his master had a better nose for truth. But the story was so outlandish that he struggled to believe it could be a lie. Lies had to be believable. This was not.

But questions still remained. "If he wasn't working for the monasteries, why did he kill Niu?"

"Because Niu tried to kill him first. Lei was asking questions about you, trying to find out what happened to his brother. Niu figured it was safer to kill Lei than to let him get too close. But Lei fought back."

Fang thought about the bodies he'd seen, both the

assassins and the triads within Niu's compound. Lei had fought back, certainly. He could see how Daiyu's story might be true, but he wasn't convinced. There was still something missing.

"Then why is he here? Niu is dead, and he should be safe, and yet he's followed us all the way to Jihan. That doesn't strike me as a man who is only trying to survive."

A smile spread across her face. "That's because of me."

Fang gave her a quizzical look. If he'd had any doubt she believed she was telling the truth, it vanished after that claim. No one in their right mind admitted to their interrogator that they were responsible for something.

"Many years ago, Lei and I were together. It didn't work, but now that he's trying to run from the triads, he is trying to bring me with him."

The pieces clicked into place. "And you've agreed. You were going to headquarters to collect your final payment and run away with him."

She nodded.

Fang fought the wave of disgust that washed over him. He didn't care one way or another about the triads, but he did believe in loyalty. The idea that she would so casually turn her back on the organization she was sworn to cut deep. The little sympathy she'd managed to create by telling him the unvarnished truth vanished.

He paced the room, past and future colliding. He was surprised at how similar he was to Lei. They were both strong, both haunted by a past in the monasteries. Both of them had been banished, and now Lei was the only one who stood between him and the title of the strongest.

Ultimately, none of it mattered. Lei was a threat to their plans and needed to be dealt with. Daiyu would be the bait that brought Lei out of the shadows. They would have their fight. The thought of it brought a smile to his face.

Daiyu seemed horrified by the sight of his grin. "What?"

He turned to her. "If you want to have even the slightest chance of seeing the sun rise, you need to write a letter for me."

She hesitated, but agreed. Fang understood her now. Daiyu was a survivor, her own life coming before even those of her closest friends.

He grabbed some parchment and told her what to write.

By the time Lei returned to the inn, he was in a dark mood. He was almost certain something had happened to Daiyu, but a soft, malicious voice kept whispering to him that he was a fool to trust her. He'd known her for years now, and if there was one fact he knew, it was that Daiyu looked after herself first. It wasn't selfishness, exactly, but an awareness that if she didn't, no one else would. Although Lei blamed only himself for the dissolution of their relationship, if there was any fault that was hers, that was it.

He knew the reasons. She'd been abandoned early on, forced to survive by her wits and her looks. She had a past almost as dark as his, but that had been something they'd shared: plenty of regrets. So tonight, while he remained almost entirely convinced that something had happened to her, the voice of doubt was too strong for him to ignore. This wouldn't be the first time she'd broken his heart.

Their room at the inn was still empty, although Lei hadn't really expected otherwise. He lay on the bed, then immediately stood up as the scent of her flooded his nose.

What to do next? He wanted to find her, to ask what had happened, to at least have some certainty in his life. But that same whisper in the back of his mind told him he was better off without her. He could travel faster, not have to worry about protecting anyone else, and only need to support himself. The idea was tempting, but he couldn't bring himself to do that, either.

So he sat in the room, undecided, torn between equally unsatisfactory options, hoping against hope that she would walk through the door and solve all the problems for him.

When there was a soft knock on the door, Lei almost tripped over himself with how quickly he answered it. His face fell when he saw that it was the old innkeeper, holding a message for him. It was unsealed and unremarkable. The innkeeper gave a slight bow. "I apologize for the late interruption, but I received this from a young man and was told that it was urgent."

Lei grabbed the note, trying to keep his hand from trembling. "Thank you very much."

The woman left and Lei closed the door, opening the note immediately. It was written in Daiyu's handwriting, the flowing script easily recognizable. The tone was matter-of-fact. She'd been abducted by Fang, and he would be waiting for Lei in a building near the outskirts of town. The two of them would finish this.

Lei paced the room. He could feel the spirit of his brother, shouting for a rematch. Lei himself wanted to run out the door and get directions to the building, but he couldn't, not right away. His feet felt as though they weighed as much as a horse. He couldn't get them to move.

He realized with a start that he was afraid. Very afraid.

Lei had tasted Fang's strength once already. True, he'd already been in bad shape, but the difference had been substantial. And this was the man who had managed to kill Jian, the strongest monk Lei knew of. He wanted to run in and save Daiyu, but the truth was, he wasn't certain he could.

He slapped himself across the face. Thinking like that was detestable. Lei took several deep breaths, calming himself. The feeling he recognized as his brother surged through his body, but Lei pushed it down. He needed to make clear choices, and he couldn't be influenced by his brother's desire for revenge.

Lei tied the sword tightly to his side and took one last deep breath before stepping out into the night air.

LEI FOUND the building Daiyu's note had directed him to with little difficulty, massive as it was. The foundation was made of heavy stone, with brick laid on top. Lei wasn't sure what the building was used for, but he suspected there wasn't a force of nature that could bring it down. Through an open doorway he could see shadows of torchlight dancing within, but in the dark of night, the building felt ominous. Although that could just be the way he felt, he supposed.

There was no point in delaying the inevitable. He could feel Fang's energy inside. Hopefully Daiyu would be in there as well. The only way to know was to step inside.

He tried to feel confident. This time, he was healthy and rested. Fang might be strong, but Lei was no weakling either. And he owed Fang a debt he would delight in repaying.

His heartbeat pounding in his ears, Lei stomped toward the door, passing through it without hesitation. The building looked to be almost barren inside, Fang and Daiyu the only occupants.

Even though Fang was the greater danger, Lei's eyes and attention immediately went to Daiyu. "Are you all right?"

She nodded, though she made no move toward him. It was only then he saw that a thin rope was tied around her neck, the other end of the makeshift noose held tightly in Fang's hand. "He hasn't harmed me, yet."

Lei could feel the anger building within him. He could also feel his brother's spirit, begging for attention, but Lei refused. This was a fight between him and Fang. His brother had his chance and had lost. He would be the one who would save Daiyu.

Lei had been expecting some conversation, some threat, like there always was in the stories he'd grown up with. But Fang must have grown up with different stories, because the battle began all at once.

Fang made a sign and attacked Daiyu. The attack wasn't very strong, nothing more than the equivalent of a strong shove, but it threw Daiyu forward onto her knees, causing the noose around her neck to suddenly tighten. Her eyes went wide as she tried to breathe and couldn't find any air.

Lei stepped forward, trying to come to her rescue, only to become aware of Fang's open hand making another, more focused symbol. Lei cursed and dove, completely unprepared for the sudden range of threats and problems he had to deal with. He'd expected a simple duel, not this.

His first concern was saving Daiyu. Without her, all of this was meaningless. But he wasn't sure how to reach her. The slim rope kept her near Fang, and Fang kept tension on the cord, depriving her of air. Lei figured she didn't have more than a few moments left, but every time he tried to approach, Fang would send a furious blast of energy his way.

Worse, Lei couldn't respond. Fang kept rotating, keeping

Daiyu between the two of them. He only stepped aside to attack, not giving Lei any chance to counter. Even if he did land an attack, Lei worried that Fang falling backward would choke the last of Daiyu's air off. For now, he was helpless.

In the end, Daiyu saved herself. She reached down and pulled a small, thin knife from her inner thigh. Even after all these years, Lei hadn't forgotten that small blade she always carried in addition to the dagger at her hip. When she got the chance, she sliced the rope away. She stumbled forward, gasping for breath, her trembling hands trying to untie the noose.

Lei didn't waste the opportunity. He sprinted forward, summoning a powerful attack with both hands. As soon as he was certain he wouldn't hit Daiyu, he attacked, the wave slashing away from him and toward Fang.

Fang met the attack with a hastily signed shield. He hadn't had enough time to prepare, though, and Lei's attack punched through his shield after only a brief pause. The blast hurled Fang back, rolling and kicking up dirt from the dusty floor.

Lei stepped toward Daiyu, but realized that Fang was already standing back up. The blast hadn't been enough to do much damage. He saw the assassin forming an attack with each hand, and he knew he wouldn't have enough time to form his own attack. Lei set his shield just in time for Fang's assault. The energy crashed against Lei's defense, flowing around it and smashing the rock wall behind Lei. Dust shook from the rafters above as the entire building rattled.

Lei considered drawing his sword, but they weren't far enough outside the city. He'd be tempted to use all his power, and focused to a point, there was no telling how far the attack would travel. He didn't want more innocent blood on his hands.

Fang seemed to feel the same. They'd traded a few blows, and so far Lei felt confident. Judging by the way Fang moved about the room, though, it seemed he felt the same.

Lei formed an attack with each hand, taking the time to focus his energies. What was it Taio had said? They were conduits of a larger power? Was there some way he could turn that to his advantage? He didn't know. Right now, everything felt like it was coming from somewhere inside him, the same way it always had.

Fang attacked first, but Lei met the incoming energy wave with one of his own. The attacks bit into one another, and Lei grunted with the effort of holding his. Through the attack, he could feel the rage that drove Fang.

Little by little, the confluence of the attacks moved toward Lei. The difference wasn't much, but Fang's power was greater than his own. There was nothing to be done, though. If Lei let go, Fang's attack would strike him, unimpeded. Lei pushed harder, searching for any scrap of power that he wasn't already putting into his attack.

Inch by inch, Lei knew that he was doomed. He had nothing left to give, and Fang's attack was relentless, pounding and pushing against Lei's until he was worn down completely.

It had to end eventually, and Lei finally gave up. If he hadn't, he would barely have the strength to stand again, and he needed to keep this fight going.

Fang's attack blasted into him, lifting him off the ground with the force of the impact. Lei crashed into the stone wall behind him, the breath slammed out of his chest, the back of his head cracking hard against the unforgiving foundation. He was held there by Fang's invisible force for a moment before the wave dissipated, dropping him to the ground. Lei barely had the presence of mind to break his fall.

The room spun around him. He struggled to catch his breath, and he couldn't tell if the room was loud or quiet. He coughed, and blood mixed with drool dripped from the corner of his mouth. His whole body ached, as though he'd climbed a mountain and then tumbled all the way back down.

In the corner of his vision he saw Fang step toward him.

Lei cursed. He knew he had to get back up. He knew he had to summon his energy and fight, but he couldn't find the strength. His legs refused to move, and no matter how much he shouted at his body, it seemed content to relax and let its end come unopposed.

Daiyu. He wouldn't leave her with that monster.

He pushed himself to his feet, wobbling as he did, extending his hand to the wall to brace himself. Fang watched him, allowing him the opportunity to stand, a gleam of pleasure in his eye and an attack already prepared in each hand. The assassin had a smug look on his face that Lei wanted to wipe off, but the moment he removed his hand from the wall he wobbled and almost collapsed again. He took a deep breath, steadying himself.

He couldn't beat Fang in a contest of pure strength, especially not now. But there were other ways to win a fight. Lei considered his sword once again but rejected the idea. If he went for it now, Fang would attack before he drew the blade. What he needed was an opportunity to distract Fang, then draw the sword and finish the fight with one cut.

Fortunately, Fang seemed to be reveling in the joy of his victory. As soon as Lei managed to find his balance, Fang directed another wave of energy at him. The attack wasn't strong, but it was aimed at one of Lei's legs. The blast knocked his leg out from under him, sending him crashing to the ground again.

Lei embraced the dirt floor. Perhaps he'd never get up again, but that didn't sound like that horrible of a fate, not right now. If he just closed his eyes, it could all be over...

He opened his eyes as he heard a shout. The voice was familiar, even though it sounded like it was coming from far away. Lei's eyes focused and he saw Daiyu charge at Fang, her short thin knife leading the way.

Fang didn't even turn around. Without looking, he aimed his second hand at Daiyu and released his attack, flinging her onto her back.

Lei didn't even realize he'd gotten back on his feet in less than a moment. Fang's eyes widened, surprised by the sudden change. Without even thinking, Lei formed a strong two-handed attack and released it, drilling into the unsuspecting Fang. The assassin had used both his attacks and hadn't bothered to prepare any more. He was caught completely off guard. The attack sent him crashing back, rolling again and again in the dirt as he tried to protect himself.

Lei's success did nothing to cool the boiling rage bursting in every muscle. He opened his mouth and screamed, a primal roar that came from deep in his chest and exploded from him. Fang could attack him all he wanted, but he would never let that man harm Daiyu.

As Fang struggled back to his feet, looking dazed, Lei's hands danced an intricate pattern, weaving a tight focus of energy. He didn't know the technique, and yet his hands felt as though they had run through the pattern hundreds of times. He felt the energy gather and grow the more it was focused.

Fang must have felt the growing attack as well, because his eyes widened and his hands rushed to create a shield. The moment Lei finished, he flung his hands out in front of him and released the attack. In the back of his mind, he realized something about this attack felt different, in a way he couldn't quite explain. Somehow he knew this wasn't coming from him.

The attack sliced through the space between the two warriors, and Fang met the attack with his hastily constructed shield. Lei's attack washed over the shield and crashed against the wall behind Fang, blowing a hole in it. Rock and brick flew outward, the explosion letting loose a giant crack that set Lei's ears ringing.

He pressed the attack, feeling suddenly invincible. He could keep pushing and attacking for days and never run out of this incredible source of strength. The amount of power was intoxicating, and Lei let more and more of it funnel through his attack. Fang's shield eventually cracked, and the blast flung him through the new hole in the wall and out into the street.

Lei released his attack before he did any more damage. What Fang had just been hit with was far worse than the blow Lei had taken earlier. The assassin had to be dead.

But Lei's first priority was Daiyu. He rushed to her side, surprised again at the energy he felt. His entire body felt bruised, but he still felt as fresh as he did when he first woke up in the morning. Never before had he been able to attack with so much energy and have so much left when it was over. Perhaps there was something to what Taio had said about the new discoveries the monks had made. Had Jian been on the verge of discovering the techniques that allowed one to tap into a new source of strength? When there was more time, Lei would have plenty of questions to answer.

He reached Daiyu's side, but she brushed his hand away. She stood up on her own power, and although it looked as though she was a bit unsteady on her feet, Lei couldn't see any permanent damage. He breathed a sigh of relief.

She was the one who came to her senses first. "We should get out of here before the patrols arrive."

Lei nodded, still trying to understand everything that had just happened.

Then he felt energy building up outside the storehouse they were in. He cursed. Daiyu, unable to sense what he felt, looked at him strangely, a question half formed on her lips.

Lei didn't have time to explain. He'd never felt this level of energy before. It felt like an entire city was going up in flames right beside him, and he resisted the urge to check his skin to see if it was burning. Never had he thought a single person could be so strong. He grabbed Daiyu's wrist and pulled her toward the exit and away from the power.

Behind him, the power continued to swell, and his feet felt as though they were running through thick mud. No matter how fast he ran, the door never seemed to get closer. When the power stopped growing, a new sun right outside the building, he knew he would never have enough time. He let Daiyu go, his hands beginning the fourth sign for the most powerful shield he knew. He braced his feet, trying to find that same energy he'd tapped into just moments ago.

"Get under me!" he yelled, not even having the time to see if she was listening to him. Daiyu wasn't the type to hide behind a man, no matter the circumstances, but her life depended on it now.

The attack was unlike anything he'd ever experienced before, like nothing he'd even imagined. It didn't feel focused, at least not in any traditional sense. And yet he had the vague feeling that it was heading his way, a wall of energy that consumed everything in its path.

The huge, sturdy walls in front of him, the walls he had once believed could handle any force, crumbled as the energy of one man's will pushed against them. First the stone cracked, sharp resounding echoes stabbing into his ears. Then the mortar and the brick gave way, all of it rushing toward him.

His eyes were pulled skyward as the ceiling collapsed, tons of wood and tile collapsing in slow motion. And still, his shield wasn't quite ready. The world moved slowly, and Lei believed he could make out individual bricks as they shot towards him. He couldn't remember if he'd finished the shield, or if it would be nearly strong enough, but there was no more time. He released his energy just as the entire building collapsed around them.

44

Fang dropped to his knees, unsure of what to make of what had just happened. After their first exchange, Fang thought the battle was his. The monk's brother wasn't even as strong as the monk had been. All this chasing, all this hope, and it had all been for nothing. But then the battle had turned in a way he'd never expected.

Fang didn't know where that devastating series of attacks had come from, or what had come over him afterward. All he remembered was being in the street and feeling a power unlike anything he'd felt before wash over him. The attack had seemed to come from somewhere deep inside him, another level he'd never reached before. The whole sequence felt unreal, like a dream he couldn't quite wake from.

Regardless, the battle was over. Dust settled slowly in the street, the building before him little more than rubble. He'd never imagined possessing such power. Using his dagger, he could have eventually achieved the same result, but to know he took that building down with his bare hands? What was his limit? Was there anyone alive who could challenge him, or was he the strongest that had ever lived?

The sounds of the surrounding area slowly penetrated the fog that blanketed his senses. People were coming. The local militia would be on their way soon. As weak as he was, fighting again was out of the question. He'd be defeated in almost no time, even by regular soldiers.

Fang got to his feet, his knees shaking as he did. One step at a time, he stumbled away from the scene of devastation, dazed beyond comprehension. The only thought planted firmly in his mind was the knowledge that he needed to get away, he needed to stay safe. His master required it.

WHEN FANG WOKE UP, he couldn't remember how he had returned to his safe house. After the fight, everything was dark and hazy. He remembered stumbling for what seemed like forever, but no more.

He'd made it back, though. The walls of his small room were familiar, and his gear was stowed neatly in the corner, just the way he'd left it. As soon as he lifted his head, he regretted it. A pounding pain beat in time to his heartbeat, and although his body didn't hurt, there was a weariness in every muscle so deep that it felt as though it had always been a part of him.

The hunger stabbing into his stomach was the only reason he even worked up the effort to move. As soon as he was out of bed, the desire to return was almost overwhelming. Once he had some food, then he could go back to rest.

The safe house seemed to be alive with activity. In every corner, young men were collecting the items scattered around the house and packing them up. It looked as though the triads were preparing to leave. Questions swirled through Fang's mind, but he couldn't summon the energy to seek answers. Food was his only concern.

The kitchen was as busy as any other place in the house, and the woman who cooked was directing several men as they removed her tools from the area.

Fang sat down on a stool, grateful for the rest. He was exhausted from his walk from the room.

"Food?"

The cook gave him an angry glare, but she managed to pull together a bit of a meal from the various scraps in the kitchen. On another day, Fang might have been offended, but every leftover crumb looked and tasted like a feast. He devoured everything put in front of him, and when she finally told him there was nothing more, a profound disappointment washed over him. After all that, his stomach still rumbled.

But the cook wouldn't be budged, and Fang was ready to drift off into sleep once more. He stumbled back to his room and fell asleep the moment his head hit the mattress.

WHEN HE WOKE UP AGAIN, there was only the barest hint of sunlight breaking through the window. Fang's first realization was that the house was quiet. He'd never noticed before, but the house had always possessed an undercurrent of activity, no matter the time of day or night. There had always been quiet voices or the sounds of footsteps in the hallway. Now, there was nothing.

His second realization was that his master was in the

room with him. Fang didn't start, as surprised as he was. On any other day, he would have rushed to stand up and bow, but he was still too tired. The weariness had faded somewhat, but he still didn't feel his usual self.

"Master."

"I saw your work on the outskirts of town. I assume you found Lei and fought him?"

"The woman from Two Bridges, Daiyu, was cooperating with him. Once I found out, I used her as bait."

"They are both dead?"

Fang realized he'd never made certain. In his confusion, the thought hadn't even occurred to him. But why should it have? "I dropped a building on them. They won't bother us again."

Fang didn't intend for the comment to sound disrespectful, but he realized it could be taken as such. "I apologize, master. After the fight, I was more exhausted than I'd ever been. My only thought was to escape. But I find it hard to believe they would have survived."

His master looked at him, his glance appraising. "Very well. We have more important obstacles as it is."

Fang fought to summon his attention. "What must be done?"

"I need you to mount an attack on the monastery in Jihan."

Fang was about to mutter a curse but caught himself just in time. He must be tired, to be as disrespectful towards his master as he was. In his condition, mounting an attack against a monastery was the same as committing suicide. The monks were weak, but he was even more so at the moment. "May I ask why?"

He didn't think his master would give an answer, so he was surprised when his master spoke softly. "The plan is coming together perfectly, but the monks are beginning to suspect the truth. We need a diversion, and if you attack the monks, they'll believe they are the targets."

Fang's mind couldn't keep up. He heard the words that his master spoke, but he couldn't seem to figure out what they meant. His lack of understanding must have been obvious, for his master stood up. "Walk with me, Fang."

Fang grumbled to himself but stood and followed as his master went out the hallway, up the stairs, and climbed a ladder onto the roof. The safe house stood high above many of the others in the city. Fang didn't find the short journey as exhausting as he'd expected, but he was still looking forward to returning to bed.

The view from the roof was magnificent. From up high, Fang could see the patterns that made up the city of Jihan, concentric circles stretching out for almost a mile in any direction. From up here, the seething mass of humanity, lit by the early morning rays of the sun, almost made sense. Almost.

His master spoke without prompting. "The time is close enough at hand. You should know what you've worked toward." He took a deep breath before continuing. "You know I've spent years studying ancient texts, manuscripts that have been thought lost to time. The skills the monks practice today are weakened versions of what our ancestors were capable of."

The blasphemy was profound. In Fang's own time in the monastery, short as it was, he had been taught that the skills he acquired as a child equaled those his ancestors achieved in a lifetime of study. Had they been so wrong?

"There was a theory, never proven by the monks, which I believe in. Some monks, long ago, believed that their gift wasn't an internal one, but a manifestation of a power greater than themselves."

Fang frowned. He had the idea of an uncomfortable echo, remembering the abbot of the monastery above Two Bridges saying almost exactly the same thing. Had his own master discovered the truth as well? Fang pushed the question aside to focus on his master's continued explanations.

"Furthermore, they believed that there were places where this power gathered, places that were important, although they never could explain why. From my research, I believe that Jihan is one of those places. All of our great cities might be."

Fang shook his head, trying to clear the remaining cobwebs. His master, for the first time, sounded like he had lost his mind. Everything he was saying went against what Fang knew to be true. But it couldn't be coincidence that this idea kept reappearing. Had so many been so wrong for so long?

"These monks speculated that the places where this power built played a role in their ability to use their gifts. They claimed to feel stronger in the area surrounding Jihan."

Fang's eyes locked on his master. Could he possibly be speaking the truth? Was he stronger just because of where he stood? Was that why he'd been able to drop a building as strong as the one he had?

His master didn't even seem to notice Fang's confusion, lost in thought as he was. "The speculation ended eventually when the monasteries were reorganized, but one monk believed that the life above and the power these places possessed were somehow linked. He argued that the monks needed to pay special attention to places like Jihan, because if those places were lost, so too would their power be."

Fang gaped at his master, his mind finally putting the pieces together.

"My plan is to use the black powder we've scattered around the city to light all of Jihan on fire during the night of the Harvest Festival, when the most people are present. If the monk was right, perhaps we will break the strength of the monasteries once and for all!"

Fang hesitated. If the monks lost their powers, wouldn't he lose his as well? The concern gnawed at him, but he didn't dare ask another question when his master was already being so generous with information. But what if his master was wrong? What if these monks of long ago were wrong? Had all of this been for nothing?

His master seemed to be reading his mind, as he often did. "And if it's all wrong, the monks will still have failed to protect the capital of this region. They are charged with the defense of these lands from the threats inside it. If they fail so spectacularly, the monasteries will still fall. So long as Jihan burns, the monasteries are over."

Fang finally understood. A part of him worried about losing the strength that made him who he was, but his trust in his master was absolute.

"So, you see, the monks cannot discover the plan before it comes to fruition. They know enough to suspect something is coming. If you attack the monastery, they will think the attack is directed at them. They won't know the truth until it's too late."

Fang nodded, an idea coming to light. "You only need the monastery to think they are under attack, correct?"

His master nodded, curiosity evident on his face.

"I have a plan, then. I just need to find another high

place with a view of the monastery, preferably at least a few blocks away."

"You will have it."

Fang ran through the symbols of the Dragon's Fang in his head. It was time to see just how strong he'd become.

45

Lei groaned under the pressure of the beams and stone, their weight endlessly pushing down, threatening to squeeze what small space they had left. Beneath him, Daiyu lay as frozen as stone, her eyes wide and her chest heaving.

Lei's shield had barely come up in time. One stone, bigger than his head, had hit before the shield came up. The stone was now inches from Daiyu's face, a constant reminder of how close they had come to dying. How close they still were to dying.

He breathed in deeply, his mind as frozen as Daiyu's body. They needed a way out, but he couldn't even get his mind to begin working on the question. All he could think about was keeping his shield intact, keeping the rocks above their heads. It wasn't enough, though. He needed to move the rocks, push them above or away.

Dust gathered in his mouth as he tried to get enough air, and he kept coughing. He collapsed to his knees, exhaustion threatening to consume him.

Where was the power he'd once felt?

Strangely, as he fell even lower, the rocks crunching against one another above him, his thoughts turned to his brother. For the first time, he was sorry he hadn't done more with his life. He was sorry he hadn't ever worked things out with Jian.

Lei felt a glimmer of energy build inside him. It wasn't much, but it was more than he'd had before. Still managing to hold the shield with his left hand, he used his right hand to form an attack. Moving his hand felt like climbing up a mountain, but his fingers formed the signs, and he focused his will more and more. He made it through the first three signs, but couldn't summon the fourth. The third sign would have to be enough, then. He launched the attack in a random direction. Rocks and brick shattered and flew away, leaving a small hole, big enough for someone to crawl through.

"Daiyu!"

She was still frozen. Her limbs didn't move, and her eyes were wide with fear.

"Daiyu!" He tried to get her attention, but he couldn't break whatever mental fog was obscuring her thoughts. He needed to shake her or something, but he had no energy, no strength left.

"Daiyu!"

Finally, she blinked her eyes, and he saw them focus on him. He nodded toward the hole. "Get out!"

She scrambled toward the hole, turning towards him before she got in. "What about you?"

He shook his head. "I can't hold this much longer. Go!"

For a moment, he worried Daiyu wouldn't listen, that she'd refuse to go until he had joined her. Then she turned and slithered through the opening. Lei waited until she was through, then crawled forward himself. Once he was near the edge of the shield, he had to let it drop. He had no idea how to maintain a shield he wasn't behind or under.

With an ear-splitting roar, the rest of the building collapsed behind Lei. He scrambled as fast as he could, knowing the narrow tunnel was collapsing behind him. The entrance of the tunnel seemed so far away, but he could see Daiyu at the end of it. He just kept going, as fast as he could, crawling toward the only person cared about.

After what felt like an eternity, he felt his wrists being pulled, dragging him out just as the last of the building settled behind him. He collapsed, sucking in clean air greedily. Daiyu, seemingly recovered from her momentary paralysis, pulled at his armpits, dragging him from the last of the wreckage.

Lei turned around, looking at the ruin they'd just escaped. There was no sign of Fang anywhere, and people in the city were already gathering to watch. Lei lay on his back and closed his eyes, just grateful to be alive.

By the time evening fell, Lei and Daiyu found themselves at the monastery. The fight between Fang and Lei had awakened all the monks, and they'd made their way down to the collapsed building in short order. The local abbot had offered them shelter, and after everything they'd been through, they were both happy to accept. The monastery was far safer than the Heron at the moment.

They'd been questioned briefly, but there wasn't too much to say. Eventually, they were allowed to rest, and they sat on the bed together, each of them trying to understand what had happened.

Lei only had one question on his mind, a question that seemed out of place after everything he'd just been through.

He thought he should be wondering how they were going to escape the clutches of the triads. He should be worrying about how they would finance their travels. But none of that consumed his attention.

"What's bothering you?" Daiyu asked.

Lei gave a bitter chuckle. After the fights, the escapes, and the close calls, any number of things were currently bothering him. But he knew she was watching him, aware that there was a problem on his mind that he couldn't solve. He forgot sometimes that no one alive knew him better than she did. Even if he tried to hide from her, he wasn't sure that he could.

"It's my brother's spirit, I think," he finally replied.

A slight frown was the only indication of her surprise. He suspected few other people would have even noticed it.

"I know that it wants revenge. He wants me to fight Fang. But I don't think I'm strong enough."

She slid closer to him and ran her fingers through his hair. He breathed deeply as he relaxed. "All I want to do is leave. I want to take you and get as far away from here as I can. But if I do, does that mean his spirit is going to be a part of me forever? I don't want that, either." Daiyu shifted her weight, and Lei could tell she wanted to say something but was afraid of the consequences. "Yes?"

"Do you think that maybe this is more about you? I'm not saying I don't believe you, but maybe all of this has been your reaction to your brother's death. Maybe the secret is just to let him go?"

Lei tore himself away from Daiyu as he stood up and started pacing the room. He'd never handled talking about Jian well. When Daiyu mentioned him, he felt as though she'd ripped a scab off a wound that was barely healed, and she was someone he cared for.

Her eyes got colder as she watched him, and he felt himself slipping into the past again. He knew this Daiyu well, the one who became harder and sharper than any sword. How many times had they had a similar argument? Over the years he'd lost track of the number.

Icy fear washed over his rage, erasing it quickly. He imagined Daiyu leaving, just as she had before. If she did, he wasn't sure how'd he react. There wasn't much else to live for.

He sat down next to her and grabbed her hand. "I'm sorry. I'm still not over Jian. Even now, whenever I hear his name, all I can think of is the betrayal."

She leaned forward. "What really happened that day?"

He sighed and finally gave up. He'd never told anyone the full truth before. Enough people knew the major points that the details didn't much matter. And some part of him thought that if he never had to speak about that day, he would get over it more quickly. But that hadn't been the case. He still wasn't over anything. Maybe it was time to tell someone. And if anyone deserved the truth, it was Daiyu.

"Do you know why it is considered taboo for monks to use weapons?"

She shook her head. "I always just assumed it had something to do with being dishonorable. Monks are already so much stronger, using a weapon would just be too much."

"If only that were true. First, most monks have a hard time imbuing energy into weapons. I don't know why, but most can't make it work. By some accident of birth or skill, I've always found it a simple task.

"The real problem is that for those who can, the power is difficult to control. Much of the strength of a monk's attack comes from the amount of focus they can achieve. The symbols we make with our hands help guide our thoughts. In theory, the symbols are unnecessary, but in practice, I've never known a monk who could use the power without the symbols. By using a weapon, we can achieve tremendous focus with little effort. Even the weakest monk could slice through a rock with his energy if he could use a weapon. For someone stronger, like myself, there's no telling how far one of my attacks could travel. It's conceivable that an attack I made on one end of the city could cut through the entire populace."

He paused. Daiyu's attention was completely focused, but he didn't get any impression of fear from her. She sat as close as ever, and that gave him strength.

"That is why the monks don't allow the use of weapons. In fact, in most cases, it is punishable by death. That type of power, it's too much for anyone to possess."

He could see the questions behind her eyes, but she remained respectfully silent, letting him tell the story as he saw fit.

"I discovered I could imbue weapons with energy at a young age, even though I didn't realize the implications of my discovery. Within the first year at the monastery, I found I could use a stick very effectively. I knew about the ban on weapons, of course, but in my youth, I didn't think of a stick as a weapon.

"The only person who knew was Jian, and he convinced me to keep my ability secret. For the most part, it wasn't a problem. Both of us thrived in training, and I felt little need to use anything besides my own skills. That began to change when we graduated to the upper training levels."

"How old were you?" Daiyu interrupted.

Lei stopped to think. "Thirteen, I think? Jian and I were two of the youngest to ever be promoted. Most monks don't make it to that level until sixteen or seventeen. I'm not sure of the exact age, but thirteen sounds about right."

She nodded, and Lei continued his story.

"Once our training became more intense, the differences between Jian and I became more apparent. I didn't take as well to the discipline of the monastery, and the truth was, Jian just learned faster. I'm not sure which of us would have ended up being stronger, but in training, at that age, Jian was clearly superior. His quicker learning allowed him to obtain techniques I couldn't achieve, which meant he was stronger."

Lei's voice trailed off. He'd thought a lot about who would be stronger, had they both had the chance to complete their training. It might have taken him longer, but he longed to know which of them was truly the better warrior. But now there was no way of knowing.

He took a deep breath and continued. "There's a lot I could say, but the truth is, I was angry. I was upset at being less than my brother, and there was always a friendly animosity between us. Our fights became passionate.

"One afternoon, Jian and I were training. He was beating me, but my anger was destroying me. My attacks were wild, and he was batting them away as though they were meaningless. In one blow, he knocked me back, and as I slid, my hand clasped a nice, thick stick that had fallen from one of the trees."

Memories threatened to overwhelm him, but he forced himself to continue. "I didn't even think anything of it. I grabbed the stick, flooded it with my power, and flung it at him. Jian didn't know how to fight against such an attack. With the ban on weapons, defending against such an attack was beyond even our teachers. He jumped out of the way, not realizing there were people behind him."

Lei couldn't speak anymore. The moment was as bright in his memory as the day it happened. He saw Jian leaping out of the way, and saw one last glimpse of the young girl before his attack cut her down. The moment when part of her body collapsed while the other part held on to her father's hand was frozen in his mind, and even today he felt like vomiting.

Daiyu finished the story. "That was how she died?"

Lei nodded, unable to say anything at all. The memory played, again and again, and finally completely broke him.

She rested her head against his shoulder. "Lei, it sounds like an accident."

"NO!"

She backed away from him, surprised at the sudden burst of anger. He shook his head, clearing a few tears from his eyes. "Whenever someone means well, they tell me it was an accident. And maybe it was. But it was my fault. I could have told a monk what I could do. I shouldn't have been so angry. I made a hundred small choices that led to that final one."

The silence in the room was thick.

"Do you wish you had killed Jian?" she asked.

For a moment, he was shocked. Then he understood. "No. I'm not angry at Jian because he dodged. Everything would be far worse had I killed him. I'm angry at Jian for what happened after."

Once he was sure he wouldn't choke up, he continued. "After, of course, I was confined and guarded. Jian, as one of the strongest warriors, even then, was one of the people who guarded me. My own brother helped to imprison me.

"I assumed that I would be executed. There is no leniency for a crime like mine. But then Jian came into my cell and told me that I would be free to leave, so long as I promised never to use my powers again.

"I didn't want to die, so I agreed. But I figured that Jian would come with me. We'd always been close. But he abandoned me completely."

Daiyu's hand grasped his more tightly.

"I was fourteen, with no idea how the world worked. I'd been in the monastery since I was six. But he didn't even care. They kicked me out of the monastery without so much as a copper, and I wasn't allowed to use the only skill that made my life worth living. And the one person who cared for me let me walk away, without even a word of condolence. I know now that he made some sort of deal with the abbot to help keep me alive, but he still left me completely alone."

He broke into tears again, and this time he felt as though there would be no stopping them. She embraced him tightly, continuing to hold him as he sobbed silently.

46

In a strange twist, Fang's master now refused to leave his side. Finding the right building had proven to be a challenge. Fang wanted to be far enough away that they would be able to escape, but needed to be close enough that his attack would cause plenty of damage. They settled on a building almost ten blocks away from the monastery, a tall inn whose roof provided them the line of sight Fang needed.

Although his master seemed certain, Fang was filled with doubt. He had no doubt in his master's skills, but it was likely their actions would conclude in a footrace, and he'd never seen his master run.

"Master, are you sure you want to remain? I do not know how the monks will react, and I would rest easier if I knew you were safe."

His master shook his head. "I have worked in the shadows long enough. There is nothing the monks can do to me, and I *want* to see the destruction of the monastery. It is time the monks learn how fragile their throne is."

Fang still felt uneasy about the arrangement, but there

was no point in arguing with his master. The man's word was law, and he'd made his wishes clear.

"Fang."

He looked over at his master, whose intense gaze stripped away any pretense.

"Remember what they did to you. They knew what strength you possessed, what skill you held, and they tried to kill you for it. They threw you off a cliff and left you for dead, all because of what you could do."

A cold rage settled over Fang. There weren't many days where he didn't reflect on the monastery trying to execute him. He fingered the dagger at his belt, feeling the symbolism of the weapon. The blade had been a gift from his master. Under his master, Fang's gift had been considered just that, a gift—not a reason to execute a child. In his years of training at the monastery, he'd only made one mistake, and that was letting the monks realize he could imbue weapons with his power.

He remembered coughing and sputtering in the cold river that had run below the cliff he'd been thrown off. They thought he'd already died, that he'd lost too much blood. The monks had detested him so much they hadn't even burned his body as tradition demanded. They had let the swift current dispose of their mistake for them. But his will and his power were indomitable. He'd dragged himself, frozen and pale, out of that river and had never looked back.

He never would.

"Are you ready, master?"

His master nodded, and that was that.

Fang began preparing the Dragon's Fang, his hands guiding his mind through the necessary steps to focus the attack. He prepared it within the space of a few breaths. One last look at his master confirmed the order. With a final breath, he aimed his attack at the monastery wall and released it.

He'd never put so much into the attack, and had never seen it travel such a distance. He felt the attack meet the resistance of the wall. The force of his will pressed against the weight of the stones. For one heartbeat, and then another, nothing happened. The wall stood, unyielding to his assault.

Then he heard the mortar begin to crack, a loud splitting sound that echoed in the narrow alleys that separated them. He didn't put any extra energy into his attack, but let it work at the wall, like a river eroding a bank. With a groan that could be heard from the rooftop, the wall blew inward, no doubt showering the monks with stone and debris.

Fang didn't waste a moment. He summoned the attack again, aiming at an adjacent point in the wall. This time the wall collapsed more easily. It had already been broken; now Fang was just finishing his work.

From his vantage point, he saw monks running about wildly. Fang summoned one last attack, smiling at the thought of the monks falling like flies. He aimed carefully, picking out one monk in particular who seemed stunned, wandering around in circles aimlessly. With a soft exhale, he released the Dragon's Fang.

Before it could strike and kill the monk, a shield appeared in the hole in the wall. The Dragon's Fang struck it just as it had the wall, but the shield held against the assault.

Fang pushed more energy into the attack. He wasn't trying too hard, but the shield held up against the extra force.

The longer their energies interacted, Fang got a better sense of who he was fighting. There could be only one person, and the energy felt exactly the same. He cursed. Lei had survived the most powerful attack he'd ever summoned. For just a moment, he felt the first trickle of fear, of doubt in his mind. Maybe he wasn't the strongest warrior to walk in the empire.

He cut off his attack. From this distance, he wasn't certain how effective the Dragon's Fang would be, not against Lei.

His master looked at him. "I was expecting more."

Fang shook his head. "Lei is there. He's blocking my attacks."

"He's that strong?"

Fang hadn't thought so, but how else could he explain the fact that the man was still alive? Twice now they'd met, and twice the man's heart continued to beat. "Yes."

His master didn't seem as upset as Fang had anticipated. "Well, we've probably done enough. Our mission is accomplished. Let's go."

Fang studied the monastery walls. From where he stood, he couldn't make out Lei, but somewhere down there was the only challenge he'd ever faced.

Then he heard the bells and saw the monks begin to pour out of the monastery, heading straight toward them.

He turned around and followed his master off the roof. The chase had begun.

47

Lei felt the Dragon's Fang being formed, somewhere off in the distance. It shook him out of his funk. He'd never felt the technique before, but there was no doubting what it was. It felt as though an enormous amount of power was being drawn to a single point. There could only be one explanation, and he cursed his poor luck.

The first blast tore the wall away not five feet from where they lay. Daiyu looked at the sudden open space with wide eyes, but quickly came to her senses. She dove to the floor, trying to present as small a target as possible.

Lei took longer to respond. He'd been in his own head, running in circles around the past, and even the violence of the present wasn't enough to bring him to immediately. The second attack did the trick, though. He felt the energy rip through the building, just a little farther away, sending stone shooting off into the courtyard.

The screams of the monks finally came to his ears. He peeked around the corner and saw a scene of devastation. The monks had been caught by surprise as much as he had, and stones and debris had landed on and around them. The legs of one monk twitched underneath a boulder that had once been part of the wall, and another monk wandered back and forth, muttering to himself.

Lei felt the attack forming again. With his better perspective, he was able to see the silhouette of two men on a rooftop, many blocks away. He didn't know who the second man was, but the first had to be Fang. Lei couldn't determine much by sight, but there was no other explanation.

Lei looked back at the devastation behind him and started breathing quickly and deeply through his nostrils. He was tired of this endless cycle of meaningless violence. The monasteries were far from perfect, but they didn't deserve this. Almost without thought, he formed a shield, using both hands to focus his power. The Dragon's Fang spit out from the rooftop in the distance, but Lei had plenty of time to place the shield.

The powers crackled as they met, but Lei had been through worse, even just recently. The attack was strong, but wasn't nearly the power it could have been. Lei didn't question whether or not that was due to distance, injury, or some other reason he couldn't fathom. He just knew he could protect the monks.

When the attack faded, he felt a bit of pride at his work. He'd done some good, at least.

He shook his head, wondering if that thought had come from him or his brother. And just like that, it was decided. He was tired of being uncertain of who he was or who was in control of his actions. Whatever was happening with his brother's spirit, it was time to end it.

He turned to Daiyu, to make sure she was unharmed. She was already back on her feet and had rushed to the courtyard to give what aid she could to the monks. As always, he was impressed by how cool she could be when the situation devolved into chaos.

The dust was settling in the courtyard, and Lei risked another glance toward the rooftop where Fang and the other unknown assailant were. They were scrambling down from their perch, and he quickly lost them to the shadows. But Fang, with his strength, should be easier to track. So long as they left soon, they would find him.

Lei found Taio, who was directing some of the rescue efforts. "We need to track them down," he said.

Taio shook his head, a hint of disbelief in his face. "Look around you! Can't you see what they've done? We need to heal what monks we can and shore up our defenses. Obviously we're their target! Their next attack could come at any time."

Lei wasn't sure he agreed, but there was no time to waste on debating. "I saw where the attack came from. At least give me a handful of monks, and I'll hunt them down for you."

Taio looked undecided. After a few heartbeats, Lei had waited enough. The monks needed to act more quickly. "Fine. If you won't help, I'll be back soon!" He turned to walk through the wall.

"Wait!" Taio yelled after him. "I can't spare many monks, but give me a minute."

The senior monk was as good as his word. A few moments later, he had corralled several monks who were dazed but otherwise unharmed. "Follow him," Taio commanded, "and return as soon as you are done."

Lei knelt by Daiyu's side as she bandaged up a monk who'd been cut across the neck by a piece of debris. Fortunately for the monk, the cut didn't look too deep. "I'll return soon. Remain here until I do."

He could see she wanted to argue, but she saw reason quickly enough. This was a battle between those with the power, and she would only be in the way. At the monastery, at least she could do some good. She kissed him full on the mouth, and he smiled as they separated. "Now I have to come back."

He barely saw her smile as he turned and led the monks away from the monastery. He broke out into a light jog and the others followed shortly after.

"Keep your senses open for someone with the power. Outside of us, there shouldn't be any monks in the city right now. But if you see him, don't try to attack him on your own. He's too powerful. Just send an attack into the air so that we can all come and join the fight."

The monks yelled their assent, but Lei wondered how many of them would actually follow his directions. There was murder in their eyes, and most of them were too young and too untested to know wisdom. But there was nothing else to do, and he needed the extra monks to cover more space. By himself it would be too easy for Fang to get away.

As they neared the building that the attack had come from, Lei gave directions to each of the monks. They spread out, covering several blocks and then jogging in parallel. If there was more time he would have tried to put together a better plan, but every second they wasted planning was one more that Fang was speeding away.

The monks and Lei ran, and Lei stopped every block or two to focus on his sense. The other monks quickly faded away, and for all the world it seemed as though he was simply running through the city without a purpose.

Several minutes passed, and Lei was beginning to fear that their quarry had managed to evade them. Just then, he felt a haphazard attack shoot into the air, several blocks away from him. He turned the corner and sprinted, pushing through the confused masses of people.

Fortunately, the streets weren't as full as they might have been this close to the Harvest Festival. After two buildings had been damaged, Lei imagined residents were staying inside, nervous about whatever was happening outside their door.

He felt another energy source, only about a block away, also running toward the beacon that had been launched. He formed an attack with one hand, just to be safe, but was relieved when he saw it was another one of the monks. They ran together, not saying a word.

Three blocks away, Lei suddenly felt two surges of energy. One was another attack, launched into the sky. Lei and his companion turned sharply, skidding into an alley and changing direction. They were getting close. The other energy, Lei had felt before. It was Fang.

Lei felt one of the energies fade away, and he cursed. Either the monk had tried to attack, or had followed too closely and become a target for Fang. It was another life the assassin would have to pay for.

Lei and the other monk turned a corner that opened up onto a wide street, deserted after the previous attacks. For the second time in as many days, Lei came face to face with Fang. The other man with Fang had wide eyes and a look of panic on his face. Lei assumed the man was the one Fang referred to as his master. Even this close, Lei couldn't feel a shred of power from the man, but he had to have some skill if he'd trained a man like Fang. Perhaps killing him should be the first test.

Lei summoned an attack as Fang did the same. Lei dove to the side, and Fang's attack passed through the space where he had just stood. Lei aimed at the master and let go, never expecting what happened next.

Lei's strike was perfectly aimed, but as it approached the master, it was diverted by another force Lei couldn't sense. All he could feel was his own attack flowing around the master like water flowing around a rock in a stream. It was as though the master was able to shield himself without effort. Even as Lei's attack passed harmlessly by, he couldn't feel the smallest pull of power from the man. If Lei hadn't just felt what had happened, he would have said the man had no power at all.

The monk next to Lei seized the opportunity and lashed out with his own power at Fang. Compared to the strength Lei and Fang possessed, the monk was like a candle next to a bonfire. Fang didn't even bother to block the attack. He took the blow and returned it fivefold, sending the monk flying back into the alley.

Lei still wasn't sure he could beat Fang in an even match of strength. Every time he'd tried, he failed. But that didn't mean the man was invincible. Lei drew his sword and charged the assassin. He allowed some of his power to seep into the blade, but he held it there, unwilling to let it go. Here, inside the city, it was far too easy to let an attack get away from him, killing an innocent. He'd never allow himself to do that again.

But the sword could still act as a defense. Fang unleashed a powerful attack, but Lei sliced through it as though it was a sheet of silk. Fang's wave of energy dissipated, and then they were close enough for Lei to physically attack with the sword.

When he'd been expelled from the monastery, he'd taken some lessons. He had figured that if he couldn't use his power to defend himself, he would need to find another way. With his years of monastic training, he'd taken quickly to the practice, but had run out of money soon after starting. Unaided, against a master swordsman, Lei didn't think he'd have much of a chance. But he was still better than the average militiaman.

He kept his balance as he struck. Fang danced backward and gave up ground. In response, the assassin attempted to unleash several close-range, almost completely unfocused attacks. Lei spun away from them one at a time, frustrated that Fang was doing just enough to keep him from getting a clean attack.

They were both distracted when the monk who'd come with Lei entered the fray once again, sending another attack at the master. The result was exactly the same as Lei's. The attack broke around a shield that by all accounts shouldn't have been there.

Lei was confused and angry. If they could destroy the master, it would be much easier to take down Fang. But the master was an unknown, and their attacks were useless. Fang also seemed concerned about his master, his attention constantly divided.

Lei didn't see the kick coming in time, his own attention wandering over too many aspects of the battle. Fang's foot crunched against his chest, sending him stumbling backward.

"Master, come!"

The two of them turned and ran, Fang leading the way. Lei regained his balance and was about to chase after them when he realized he was looking at a long, uninterrupted stretch of street that ran to the outskirts of town. He had a completely open attack on the fleeing fugitives. Judging his power carefully, he focused his attention on his blade. He would have preferred to aim at Fang, but the master was the easier target, and Lei was going to take as few risks as possible. It was time to see if the master's powers could protect him from a weapon attack.

As Lei snapped his sword down, Fang must have felt the attack coming. He turned around, his face set with a mask of determination. Lei saw the assassin form the first symbol for a shield as he pushed his master out of the way. Fang barely got his shield up in time, and Lei's attack sliced into it.

Fang was strong, but not strong enough to fight against the force Lei had struck with. The shield collapsed and a gash opened up in his chest, immediately soaking his tunic in blood.

As the master bent over his student, Lei attacked again, his second strike as true as his first. But again, the tightly focused wave simply washed around the master and dissipated. The master didn't seem to react at all to the attack. Lei cursed. Apparently, any energy attack would fail against this man. But there were other ways to kill a person.

The master was pulling Fang to his feet. Lei hoped that his attack had been fatal, but he couldn't tell how deep the wound was. Fang hobbled away, definitely injured, but not dead.

The chase resumed as the pair of criminals started down a side alley. Lei chased after them, sword in hand. He'd never had a better chance to end this all.

It didn't take him long to close the distance between them. The master looked out of breath, and Fang was hurt. The assassin who'd once been so feared was now the one slowing the pair down, the master pushing him ahead, apparently goading him on. As they ran down the alley, Lei heard the master tell Fang to keep running. The master paused, just for the space of a breath, to pull a few market stalls down.

Amidst the shouts and curses, Lei crashed through the fabric and goods, barely slowed at all. He caught up to the master and pulled him to the ground. The master fell, and it occurred to Lei, just for a moment, that it never should have been that easy. Lei pulled the man up to his feet, prepared to fight, only to realize there was nothing to fear. The master made no symbols with his hands, and his eyes were as wide as teacups. The man was literally quivering with fear. Now that Lei had a chance to look at the man, he was more confused than ever. The master's balance was poor, as though he'd never had even an hour of martial training in his life.

Lei and the master were at the mouth of the alley opening out onto another wide street. Fang had just crossed and gone into another alley when he glanced back to find his master missing. The assassin's mouth opened in shock when he saw what was happening behind him. Lei saw Fang's hands begin to form the symbols for an attack.

The way Lei saw it, there was only one way forward. He was tired of these fights. His gut churned at the thought, the now-familiar sensation of Jian's spirit protesting what was about to happen. But Jian had protested too often, and Lei was able to ignore the nausea as he made a single cut with his sword, drawing a deep gash across the master's neck. The master's eyes, already wide, went even more so, as though it had never occurred to him he might be facing his death. He dropped wordlessly to the ground, the contents of his pockets spilling out across the ground.

Lei looked up and met Fang's gaze. The man was in shock, and Lei braced for an attack.

Even braced, Lei wasn't ready. The attack swept past his shield and knocked him back several feet. As he got to his feet, another attack washed over him. Lei was standing up to fight when he saw Fang approaching, drawing his dagger.

Panicking, Lei retreated out the alley and around the building. The structure wouldn't protect him, but it would make it more difficult for Fang to aim at him.

Lei forced himself to take some calming breaths. Fang was injured, and Lei had a sword of his own. He drew it, imbuing it with energy as he did. He snapped back around the corner, ready to finish this, but Fang and his master's body were both gone.

48

Fang grimaced as the needle slid through his skin. The woman who mended his wound either didn't notice or didn't care, and Fang wasn't sure which was worse. He'd returned to the triad headquarters, the only place he could be certain of finding help and remaining safe.

Although the building had barely been staffed, he'd been able to find someone to tend to his wounds. From the uncaring look on the woman's face, Fang guessed she'd seen no shortage of cuts and injuries. Her hands worked quickly, but she didn't seem to care about the discomfort her patients experienced. Fang supposed he should simply be grateful that he was receiving attention.

The memory of his master being killed thrust itself into his consciousness, as it had over and over all day. The look on Lei's face matched that of the woman who currently stitched Fang's cut: completely uncaring.

Fang had more questions than answers. For one, how had his master managed to defend against all Lei's attacks without using energy of his own? Fang had always believed that his master had mysterious powers, but what he had sensed earlier was beyond his comprehension. He'd never felt anything like that defense before. Under other circumstances, Fang would argue that it was all the evidence he needed of his master's skill.

But if he'd been so skilled, how had Lei killed him so easily? That was the question, more than any other, that haunted Fang's thoughts. Of all people, his master should have been able to kill Lei, but it had turned out the other way.

The death played in his mind again, his master dropping dead in the alley. Fang couldn't be certain of his own perception, but he thought he'd seen his master's face for a moment as the body collapsed. The face was frozen in fear.

Fang figured he was in shock. He should be angry, should be furious at his master's demise. But he felt shallow and empty, as though he had already poured out all his emotion.

The question he needed to answer was what to do next. His master had confided his plans, so Fang knew what came next. The Harvest Festival was two nights from now.

For the better part of a decade, Fang's every task had revolved around his master's wishes. Without guidance, what should he do?

He wanted to kill Lei. That man, monk or not, had taken more from Fang than anyone else. Not only would Fang kill him, but he would make it slow and painful and give the man something to regret.

But his master's wishes should come first. Fang knew enough to be able to finish the plan.

The woman finished her work, cutting the string with a sharp knife. Fang looked down. Despite her unconcerned appearance, her stitches were among the best Fang had ever seen. Far better than what he would have accomplished on his own.

After putting a clean shirt on, Fang went to the room where he had brought his master's body. He hadn't had the strength to face Lei, but he'd managed to escape to pay a final debt of respect to his master.

The body was being prepared for burning, and young men were clothing the body after cleaning it. Fang watched, feeling as though he was nothing more than an observer in this life, as though he was watching the scene through a window.

He remembered when he first met his master. He had been young, no more than seven, and had made his way to a small village, stealing the food he needed to eat. He'd been celebrating his most recent acquisitions quietly by a stream when his master had come up to him.

"I know that you are a very special young man," he started.

Fang was surprised. He had never seen the man before. Out of instinct, he started making a sign with his hand, but his master grabbed it before he could finish the process. "You shouldn't show your skills in public that way."

He'd asked Fang questions, the first adult who had done so since the monastery. Fang told him everything, how he'd been a star student in the monastery and how they had tried to kill him when they discovered he could use weapons with the power. The man who would become his master listened with startling intensity.

"What if I told you I also had powers?"

Fang scoffed. The man didn't look anything like the monks. His clothes were fine, and underneath his robes he appeared to have a bit of a belly.

"You don't believe me."

Fang shook his head.

"What if I told you that I know you have an apple and two silver pieces in your left pocket, and you have a wound on your right side that hasn't healed properly?"

Fang's eyes widened. He'd just stolen the apple and silver earlier that morning, and the shopkeepers hadn't had a clue. And his right side still ached when he moved too fast. Sometimes the cut, given to him as a parting gift from the monks at the monastery, opened and bled.

From that moment on, Fang had been the master's servant. The longer he served, the more he learned. His master had been rigorous, reading texts to him from all around the world to teach him. His master never demonstrated techniques, but forced Fang to learn on his own. By doing so, Fang was convinced he was stronger than any other monk.

Fang watched as the young men preparing the body rolled up the master's sleeves. When they did, Fang saw something that stopped his heart. The mark of the Order of the Serpent was gone, as though it had never existed. Fang stepped forward and had one of the young men hold out the arm. Fang stared, but no matter how close he got, he could find no evidence of a mark ever having been there.

He looked at his own arm, wondering what sort of magic caused a brand in the skin to disappear. The order kept its secrets, even in death.

Perhaps it was a small detail, but it solidified his resolve. There was no doubt he would finish what his master started. The man had saved his life, and completing his life's work would be Fang's crowning achievement. After that, he could find the rest of the Order of the Serpent and continue his training, becoming stronger than ever before.

His decision made, there was little for him to do besides

wait for the Harvest Festival and heal. He considered hiding in the triad headquarters, but decided against it. The monks would be sufficiently angry that if they were certain he was inside, they would attack. He and his master had upset the balance, and the monks wouldn't feel kindly about it.

It was outside the city, then. He would set up camp somewhere, rest, heal, and prepare. On the night of the Harvest Festival, he would bring down the tower in the town square. Then the entire city of Jihan, and soon the entire empire, would go up in flames.

49

Lei squatted next to the items that had fallen from the master's body as the monks studied the area. There was so much blood in the area, splattered all over the walls. Lei was grateful he'd been behind the master when he made the cut.

What held the attention of most everyone, including himself, was the small jar sitting in the middle of the street. Lei had never come across anything like it before, but every time he came close, he felt an illness trying to take him. It wasn't the same queasiness he felt from Jian, but a wrongness, twisting inside his stomach, more like a disease than anything else.

Inside the small jar was a small object that looked like a human heart.

Taio came up to him, displeasure on his face. "Monks aren't supposed to kill."

"And I'm not a monk, so your reputation is safe."

Taio shook his head but didn't pursue the argument. The monk's restraint was a sign of how seriously they were taking the threat of the order. By all accounts, Lei had expected them to try and kill or capture him half a dozen times by now. But no matter his actions, they put up with him as the lesser of two evils. "You said that none of your energy attacks worked?"

Lei nodded.

"Then we are indeed holding the Silent Heart. I have only ever heard about it, but seeing it so closely makes me think its reputation is well-deserved."

Lei frowned at the heart. "That was what protected him?"

"Yes. It's a rare artifact. We've never come across anything else like it. It protects everyone within about three paces from any energy attack. You remember I told you it had been stolen several weeks ago?"

Lei vaguely remembered, but that conversation felt as though it had been years ago. How much had happened in the past few weeks?

The monk and the rebel exchanged looks, and Lei knew what was coming. It was the speech he'd been expecting for some time now.

"We'd like you to come in and resume training with us," Taio said, making it sound as though he was extending the greatest honor in the world.

"Thank you, but no." Lei's stomach churned a little, but he ignored it.

"Do you think you have a choice?"

"I always have a choice."

Taio cursed under his breath. "I was beginning to think you might be less difficult to work with."

"I'll help you find and kill Fang, but then I'm leaving."

"I just told you that monks aren't supposed to kill."

"Then you can watch." Lei was trying to keep the anger from his voice, but was struggling. The world was a harder place than the monks realized. Sometimes a man just needed killing, and Fang was one of those men.

Lei knew he was placing Taio in a hard position, but he didn't much care. Taio was less flexible than their abbot had been, and he had been a man who placed tradition quite high. No doubt, had Taio been abbot a decade ago, Lei would now be dead. The monk thought he'd made a great offer by allowing Lei to return, but Lei wasn't having any of it. He wouldn't return to the monasteries, and if they tried to force him, he would be just as much a problem as Fang was.

There was another fact in his favor, and it was that he was the only one capable of fighting Fang, and they all knew it. Taio had no choice but to capitulate, at least until Fang was taken care of. Then the monk might find a stronger backbone.

Lei turned his attention to the other scattered debris. "Did you find anything else?"

Taio shook his head, a look of disappointment on his face. "If you didn't tell me Fang had called this man 'master,' and if we hadn't found the Silent Heart, I would never have believed you. We've spoken to several witnesses, and no one remembers feeling intimidated by the man at all."

"It doesn't make sense," Lei said. "When I snuck up on him, he didn't fight at all, and I got the impression he didn't even know how. But if so, why would Fang look up to him?"

"You'll have to ask him, I suppose."

Lei agreed. Maybe it was money, or something else that Fang saw in the man, but Fang's master—as far as Lei was concerned—was a nobody. He had no skill and no strength.

Taio ordered all the monks to return to the monastery, then turned to Lei. "What will you do next?"

Lei gave a snort. "I was going to ask you the same."

Taio shrugged. "It's obvious that the monastery is going

to be the focus of the order's attacks. I'm sending all the monks back to rest and prepare as well as they are able. When the next attack comes, we're going to be ready."

Lei rolled his eyes, and a couple of curious passersby stepped away. They'd never seen a monk treated with such blatant disrespect. "Fang isn't attacking the monastery."

"You can't be sure of that."

"But I am certain. Daiyu told me that they were spreading the black powder all around the city. I think the attack on the monastery was a diversion."

Taio looked down at the blood. "It was a pretty expensive diversion. And there's no reason to trust Daiyu. She's a known triad. Have you ever considered you're the one being manipulated?"

The crowd that was already backing away practically ran in terror as Lei grabbed Taio by the neck and slammed him against a wall. Taio tried to sign an attack, but Lei slapped his hands away contemptuously. "Don't you ever, ever, question Daiyu in my presence again! Do we understand each other?"

Taio nodded rapidly and Lei let him go. After Taio caught his breath, he looked at Lei with disgust in his eyes. "We should have killed you then."

"But you didn't and now you can't. I'm not out to harm the monasteries, and the sooner you realize we're on the same side, the better off we'll both be."

They glared at each other for a few moments, but Taio was the one who broke first, as Lei knew he would be. The monks had all the power, but none of the strength needed to wield it.

"You need to send your monks into town. They need to be patrolling for Fang. If they find him, we can attack and finish this."

Taio just glared, and Lei threw up his hands in frustration. "Look, if you want, put more of your monks around the monastery, if that's so important to you. But make them patrol the entire city, too. It's the only way we can stop him before his attack begins."

"Fine," Taio finally said, gritting his teeth.

Without another word, the two of them turned and began walking back to the monastery.

Lei and Daiyu lay together, the moon providing all the illumination their room needed. She gently ran her fingers through his hair.

"What are you thinking?" she asked.

He turned to face her, disappointed to have to end the massage. "Nothing makes sense. Who was the master? If they are part of this big order, where's everyone else? Why is Fang the only person we're coming up against?"

"What if it was all a lie?"

He started. "What do you mean?"

"I only met the master once, but he struck me as a very intelligent man. What if he was the one who put this all together, on his own? Fang is determined, but he's not the kind of person who could plan an attack this big. Maybe everything is just a scheme made up by the master?"

Lei considered. He supposed it would make sense. Perhaps the master had found some way to convince Fang he was far more powerful than he was. Or perhaps he had some other hold on Fang. Either way, Lei needed to kill Fang to put everything to rest. Thankfully, his gut gave him no problems when he considered that particular killing.

"I don't suppose there is any chance I could convince you to leave the city?" he asked.

She shook her head. "We've gone over this. I'm not leaving without you."

"But what if I fail?"

"You won't. Don't forget, you've got your brother on your side."

He frowned, upset even though he realized she was just making some good-natured fun of him. "I just want you to be safe."

"I will be. You'll make sure of it." She smiled, and any arguments he might have thought about making vanished with the wind.

50

____

There was a part of Fang that wanted to take part in the Harvest Festival celebrations. The Harvest Festival had been important to his master, and every year they took a break from their daily routine of training and chores to take part in the feasting. Unfortunately, he suspected that as soon as he entered Jihan, his final mission would commence. No doubt the monks were out in the streets looking for him.

Even from the distance he was hiding at, he could feel the energy of the city. A loud rumble, the sum of thousands of voices singing, laughing, and cheering, was nearly constant in his ears. Occasional fireworks launched into the sky, and Fang laughed at the idea of one of them accidentally lighting one of the stores of black powder hidden throughout the city. He could not begin his mission until close to midnight. That was when the triads would be in position, waiting for the signal that meant the city was ready to burn.

Fang didn't know what else to do. He assumed that his master had taken many factors into account, but Fang had no idea what they were. He hadn't earned that level of trust. So, no matter what, he would bring the clock tower down at midnight, and the explosions around the city would destroy the regional capital.

Night had completely fallen by the time Fang began working his way down toward Jihan. Sights and sounds threatened to overwhelm him as he approached. Even as he entered the outskirts of town, vendors shouted at him, practically throwing their wares in his face. He smiled and carried on, sliding through the crowds without a problem, a ghost on the most festive of nights.

He had one advantage, thanks to the festival. It was more difficult to detect someone's energy in a crowd, and the streets had never been more packed. Fang guessed a monk would have to be within a block or two to notice him, and there was a lot of Jihan to cover.

Eventually, part of his exterior shell crumbled. After all, he'd made good time into town and didn't want to show up to his destination too early. He didn't want the monks to know where he would strike. One vendor in particular promised a cut of beef grilled to perfection, a rare treat. Fang gladly handed over his money in exchange for the meat on a stick.

The first bite practically melted in his mouth, a mixture of sweet, savory, and salted meat. Fang closed his eyes and allowed the treat to consume his full attention.

His master used to buy him this dish during every festival. The two of them usually lived an austere existence, but on those days, he treated Fang almost as if they were related. Fang felt the weight of sorrow in his heart as he chewed, but it lacked the edge it had a few days ago. He would complete his master's work, but that was all. Then he would move on and complete his training. He suspected there would be much work to do as the monasteries fell.

The food finished, Fang continued on his way, wondering how long his luck would hold out. He had only advanced a little ways into the city, but he hadn't come across a single monk yet.

Almost as soon as the thought crossed his mind, he felt an attack, blasted into the sky, about a block away. Fang tried to sense the monk who'd sent up the beacon, but he couldn't sense anyone in the crowd. He supposed his energy probably burned brighter, but it was still unfortunate he'd been spotted.

Fang didn't run. It would only draw more attention to himself. The attack, as bright as it was to his senses, was invisible to everyone else. He turned away from the beacon, finding an angle that would allow him to continue approaching the center of town while avoiding the monks.

He still hadn't sensed the monk when the beacon went off again, this time about a block behind him. Apparently he hadn't been able to evade so easily. Fang picked up his pace, moving more quickly through the crowd. There was still plenty of opportunity to lose the monks. He had no problem fighting them, but every moment he paused would give them time to converge on his location. He was confident in his ability to fight multiple enemies, but the more attacks that came his way, the more likely it was that one of them would find him. There was no point in taking foolish risks.

Fang cursed when another beacon went up, this time in front of him. The monks were managing to converge on him. He stopped and debated. The price of getting stopped was still too high, so he turned away from his destination and continued walking. He was almost certain he wouldn't be able to get away without a fight, but he had to try. Any commotion raised too early could doom his chances of success.

Beacons continued to go up all around him. But Fang realized something. None of them had gone up any closer to him than a block. He frowned, wondering if it was a coincidence or not. He stopped completely, waiting to see what would happen.

A few minutes later, a set of beacons went up all around him, but none of them were close.

Fang guessed their intent quickly enough. The monks, after all this fighting, were starting to learn their lessons. They knew they couldn't attack Fang and live, so they were only acting as spotters. There was only one person he would have to face, and it was the same person who'd haunted him since the moment he'd killed his brother.

There was something fitting in it, Fang supposed. The two of them had circled each other for weeks, and it could only end tonight. He suspected that Lei probably felt much the same. As Fang watched a pair of children brush by him, running and laughing, he decided he should find a more suitable battleground. He wanted a place where both of them could unleash their full potential. The warehouse district not far away would do.

Fang changed his direction, and as the crowds thinned, he could feel the faint hints of the monks who followed him. As he had suspected, he was surrounded, but none of them made any effort to get close to him. He had been caught by a net of watchers, not hunters. Fang gradually moved from the more commercial areas of the city to those that were dominated by industry. The buildings here were for making and storing goods. Their walls were made of stone and brick instead of wood, but the streets were quiet. Here was a place they could have a fight on fair ground.

He pulled out his dagger and studied it. The weapon was one of the first gifts his master had given him, and it had been at his side through countless missions, trials, and adventures. In this whole world, his master was the only one who had ever shown him kindness, no matter how small. Fang wasn't sure he'd ever be able to repay the man for the gifts he had given.

As soon as he stopped, the monks sent out beacons all around him, calling the only man who could put an end to this. He waited patiently. He didn't figure it would be long now. He let himself be filled with memories of the past, of all the times he had spent with his master, the life they had made together. Perhaps the master wasn't Fang's father, but no one else could claim the title more strongly.

Fang felt Lei before he saw him. Compared to the monks who surrounded him, Lei was a bright light in the darkness. The monk's brother was the only person who made Fang feel alive, like there was a challenge worthy of being conquered, a reason to keep improving.

A few minutes later, Lei stepped around a corner and into the small square that Fang rested in. Fang stood up and bowed. He'd never be able to tell the other man how much this duel meant to him, but somehow he suspected Lei understood him better than almost anyone else.

Only one of them would leave alive, and there was no place in the world he'd rather be.

51

Lei studied Fang. At least two dozen paces separated the two of them, but neither made a move to advance. Both were perfectly capable of killing the other at this distance. Despite the awareness that this might very well be his final fight, Lei didn't feel his heart racing at all. His breath was strong and even, unshaken by the threat standing in front of him.

His eye was drawn to the dagger on Fang's belt. There was only one reason that dagger was there. Like him, Fang could use weapons.

In another life, the two of them might have been friends. He hated the idea, but there was almost more that brought them together than separated them. If only Fang hadn't killed his last remaining family and set this all in motion.

This fight would finally rid him of his brother. If he won, then he could live his life on his own terms and allow his brother's life to fade into obscurity, as it should. Only one man stood in his way.

Fang bowed, and Lei returned the gesture.

Lei watched Fang begin to form an attack with one hand

and a shield with the other. Perhaps he was waiting to build up to his full strength, but Lei had no such intentions. Fang was stronger than him. Their previous battles had proven that well. If he was going to win, it was going to be through ferocious, unstoppable attacks. That meant only one solution.

With a yell, Lei focused his energy into his sword and drew it, snapping the point of his blade toward Fang. He'd never put as much energy into a blade as just then. A deep gash opened up the ground between them, the earth splitting in a razor-sharp line toward the assassin. Dust, leaves, and small stones shot off to the side like small, deadly arrows as Lei's attack flung them out of the way.

Fang wasn't expecting an attack of such magnitude, not so soon. He threw up his shield, but Lei's attack threatened to shatter it. Lei felt Fang summon more of his energy, pouring his strength into the barrier. He didn't think Fang would be able to hold out against the attack, but he saw no reason to make it easier. He made another attack, this one the horizontal companion to the first vertical cut. His power whipped out, and Fang's eyes bulged with awareness of what was coming.

Lei charged, closing the distance between them, willing to add his own physical blade to the mix of attacks.

Fang's reaction happened almost too quickly to perceive. He let go of the attack he'd formed with one hand, grabbing his dagger instead. At the moment his shield collapsed, Fang swung his dagger at both attacks.

There was a tremendous clap, as though a bolt of lightning had struck right between the two warriors. Lei felt his body being pulled toward Fang, then suddenly an invisible explosion slammed into him, throwing him backward, skidding across the ground. His head struck the road and his vision swam for a second before focusing again.

Fang wasn't where he'd stood before either. Whatever the blast was, it had knocked both of them well away from each other. Lei grunted as he got back to his feet, swinging his sword and launching more attacks at Fang. He kept his power contained, conscious both of the need to conserve his energy and the disaster that could befall the city if their power got out of control.

Fang met each of his sword cuts with one of his own. Small explosions rippled between them as their focused blasts met, one after the other.

After a handful of swings, Lei realized he was dealing with a tremendous problem. A dagger was smaller than a sword, and faster. Soon, Lei wasn't attacking, but was defending against Fang. The reach of the sword, so useful in a physical fight, was quickly becoming a liability. The two of them stood their ground, but Lei could see that the explosions that marked the meetings of their attacks were creeping toward him. In a few seconds, there wouldn't be anything he could do.

As much as he detested the idea, he needed to move. Dodging the blasts risked the rest of the city, but the rest of the city was at risk anyway if he failed. Lei scrambled to the side as a series of quick cuts flew toward him. They sliced into the building he'd been in front of, cutting through the stone walls as if they were nothing more than paper.

Lei closed the distance between them. The sword had been a gamble to begin with, and it had almost worked. But again, with both of them armed, the fight had turned in Fang's direction. If he could just get close enough, though, the length of the sword might once again become a benefit instead of a handicap. He could hope, anyway. He funneled some of his energy into the sword, ready for whatever came next.

Fang sent another few cuts his way, but Lei stepped around every one. With a clever smile, Fang swept his dagger about in a wide, horizontal arc. There was no way Lei could sidestep such an attack.

Unfortunately, with over half the distance closed between them, he didn't have many options. He held up his sword to cut through the attack, and to his surprise, it worked. He felt the resistance as the sword met the cut, but he sliced through it, unraveling the attack. Lei didn't have time to consider the implications, though. He was already too close to Fang.

Lei swung his sword, being careful to keep the power contained within the blade itself. Fang blocked with his dagger, the sound of steel on steel amplified within the walls of the small square. Lei twisted to make another cut, but was knocked backward by a wave of power.

He barely had time to regain his balance before another attack was released. He threw up a hasty shield, a single-gesture defense that was good for little but emergencies. Fortunately, Fang hadn't had much more time to form his attack, so the shield was enough to keep Lei safe.

Lei tried to close the distance again. If Fang was stronger, Lei's best chance at victory was getting close and killing him the old-fashioned way. He thought he felt a small rumble in his stomach, but he couldn't be certain.

Lei cut down with his sword, and Fang responded by trying to block with his dagger once again. Lei changed his cut at the last moment, directing it away from Fang's body. Fang's block met only empty air, throwing the assassin slightly off balance. Lei spun and put his full weight behind a spinning kick that knocked the dagger from Fang's hand.

Lei wasn't expecting the way Fang reacted. With a primal roar of rage, Fang lowered his shoulder, heedless of the fact that Lei had a weapon and he didn't. He charged directly into Lei, tackling him to the ground. Lei tried to cut at him with his sword one-handed, but Fang grabbed his wrist and pinned it to the ground at the same time that he smashed his forehead into Lei's nose.

Warm blood poured out of Lei's nose, but he had enough sense to keep his wits about him. He lashed out with his open fist, trying to drive it into the side of Fang's head. But again, Fang was too fast. The other man caught the punch, and it became a struggle of strength against strength.

Unfortunately, Lei had two things working against him. First, he was trying to push up, using only the strength of his arms. Fang was on top and could utilize the weight of his upper body. Second, Lei simply wasn't as physically strong as Fang. Fang's body was rock hard, no doubt conditioned by years of daily training. Lei wasn't weak, but all the same, there had been plenty of days where the only work he'd done was bringing his beer to his lips.

Lei gave up trying to overpower Fang. There was almost no chance of succeeding. Instead of pushing toward Fang, he suddenly grabbed Fang's wrist, holding his punch and pulling it down toward the ground while thrusting and rolling with his hips.

Fang hadn't felt the move coming, and the two of them rolled across the ground, ending with Fang now on his back and Lei on top. Lei returned Fang's headbutt with one of his own, cracking the assassin's nose open as well. Now that he was on top, he managed to get both hands on the hilt of his sword and push it toward Fang's neck.

Fang wrapped his hands around Lei's and the two of

them fought for control of the blade. Fang might be stronger, but now Lei was able to put his entire weight behind the work, and inch by agonizing inch, the sword crept towards Fang's exposed neck. Fang tried throwing Lei, but Lei wouldn't let him get the leverage, and every time Fang gave any attention to something that wasn't the sword, it inched ever closer.

The two of them were face to face, grunting and straining against each other, the blood from Lei's broken nose dripping onto Fang's snarling face. For a moment, Lei dared to hope.

His hope was immediately shown for being as foolish as it was. Fang released one hand from the sword hilt, and while the move cost him two of the remaining three inches, he held out long enough for his free hand to focus an attack.

Lei cursed, throwing all of his weight onto the blade, unsure of what else he could do. If he could just cut Fang's neck before the attack happened...

Lei's blade cut into Fang's flesh the same moment the attack was released. The wave lifted Lei into the air, blasting him backward. Lei managed to get his feet down, but couldn't land on them. He stumbled back and fell.

Fang gave him no time to recover. Another attack washed over him, sending him skidding along the ground. Lei's only thought was that he needed to hold onto his sword. So long as he did that, he had an advantage.

This time, it was Fang who was charging, trying to prevent Lei from using that very advantage. Dazed, Lei cut at Fang, but Fang dodged easily and the attack flew off into the distance, cutting a hole through a cloud high above, letting more moonlight illuminate the battleground. Lei swung again, this time just trying to cut Fang, but Fang had closed the distance. He grabbed Lei's wrists and ripped the sword away, sending it clattering about fifteen paces away.

Lei felt the energy in Fang's punch and rolled to the side as it passed his head, energy uncurling from the attack. He heard bricks crack behind him, but he was too focused on exchanging a quick series of strikes between them.

Lei saw an opening and struck, kicking Fang back several paces. The move gave him time to return to his feet. The two warriors stood there, neither one leaping again to the attack.

"You're stronger than your brother."

Lei shook his head. "It really doesn't matter."

Fang frowned, as though Lei had spoken to him in a foreign language. "Strength is the only thing that matters."

Lei laughed, exhaustion giving his chuckle a sharp edge. "What has strength ever done for you? Has it made your life better? Has it made you happier? Strength for its own sake is meaningless."

"Your weakness will mean your death."

Lei didn't have a response to that. He just settled into his stance, forming an attack with each hand. It was more aggressive than was wise, perhaps, but this felt like a battle in which defense had little role.

Fang opened up, releasing one attack and then another. Lei felt them coming, slid to the side of each of them, and heard the building groan behind him as its supports were weakened. He responded by launching his own attack, but only one. The other would be held in reserve until he had need of it. He attacked, formed another attack, then repeated the process.

As they launched and dodged, they closed with one another, dancing on the edge of disaster. Closer distances meant less reaction time, less time to form an attack or a defense if needed. With his left hand, Lei used one symbol, then attacked, then repeated the process over and over. In his right hand, he was up to the fourth symbol, but wasn't sure he could go much farther. Already, he felt the effort of maintaining such focus.

One of Fang's attacks grazed Lei's arm, spinning him around. When he finished rotating, he was face to face with Fang, who held an attack, pointed right at his head. Lei smiled. Fang had forgotten about the attack in Lei's right hand, the one now pointed at his torso. Lei released the attack before Fang could, and the blast tossed Fang like a dead leaf in a windstorm. Fang tumbled across the road, coming to a sudden stop against a building.

Lei felt a surge of satisfaction, pride greater than he'd ever felt. He'd done it!

The thought died in his mind as Fang started coming to his feet. Lei didn't understand. A blast that strong should have killed the man. His internal organs should be a soupy mix right now. Standing was as impossible as the sun not rising the next day. And yet he stood, shuddering but whole.

For the first time, Lei knew true fear, the fear one feels when facing the unknown. His stomach clenched, and even though his fingers ran through the motions of focusing his energy for another attack, his mind was blank and helpless. His energy remained unfocused.

Fang didn't seem to have that problem. Lei felt the energy focusing, drawing tighter and tighter. Fang reached the third symbol and released his attack, punching Lei in the chest and knocking him backward. Lei's feet skidded across the street as he tried to find purchase, but he was slammed into the wall behind him, pressed against it, squeezed against it, as though a boulder had crashed on top of him. He struggled to breathe, and darkness swam across his vision.

His mind screamed, but there was nothing to do. He was pinned, the force too great and his focus too distracted. Fang couldn't be standing, couldn't be breathing, couldn't be attacking him with the strength that he was. This was a dream, or a nightmare, that he couldn't wake from.

The blackness became deeper, tinging the edges of his vision, swirling until he couldn't make anything out.

Eventually, the darkness consumed everything.

52

———

Fang found himself surrounded by crowds soon enough. The Harvest Festival was so loud that even their fight hadn't disturbed the revelers. As the night wore on, more fireworks launched into the sky, exploding in reds and blues that cast deep shadows on the ground.

Fang didn't feel well. Although he'd had a few days to heal from his last battle, fighting against Lei was taking too much of his strength. The cut on his chest was mostly closed, but the blows he'd taken had snapped a few of his stitches, and he could feel a gooey mixture of blood and pus creeping down his stomach. His movement wasn't hindered, but he could feel the pull of newly created flesh when he fought.

He hadn't bothered to check if Lei had lived or not. Midnight was closing in, and he still had a fair amount of distance to travel before he reached the center of the city. If he didn't make it, the triads would disperse without lighting the black powder, and his master's final plans would be unrealized.

He truly wanted to kill Lei, but he'd beaten him, and

that would have to be enough. All that really mattered was that Lei was out of the way.

The crowds were thicker than Fang had expected. He fought his way through them, trying to move quickly while not drawing too much attention to himself.

With the fireworks above, the crowds jostling him, the exhaustion, and the exotic scents from dozens of stalls, Fang's mind began to shut down. He felt as though he was walking through a dream. The only fixed point was the tower, like an anchor that kept him grounded.

He wondered if his fight with Lei had done more damage to him than he thought. Perhaps he was dying and didn't know it. The idea didn't disturb him much. He was tired, and he felt as though he'd been fighting for his entire life. Resting, even forever, wasn't without its appeal. Only the fear of disappointing his master in this final task kept him moving forward.

At times, he felt like he wasn't even in charge of himself anymore, but was driven forward by a power stronger than anything he could summon. He could feel the power coursing below his feet, like a giant heartbeat underneath the city. Was this what his master was talking about, the power that he was supposed to destroy? Doing so felt wrong, like killing for the sake of killing.

Fang lacked the words to describe the sensations he was feeling. The power coursing through the city, for lack of a better term, felt like a life. A life more valuable than any other.

He shook his head, trying to clear the delirium from his thoughts. Too much had happened, and he needed rest.

He didn't see the group of monks until it was almost too late. Five of them had worked their way in front of him, their white robes a marked contrast to the bright colors that surrounded them and lit up the sky. Fang felt the energy of their attacks gathering; a deep anger, one that had never been quenched, exploded in his chest. These were monks, the same people who had tried to kill him as a child, simply because of what he could do. They deserved no forgiveness, no mercy.

He felt the same power he'd experienced once before, when he fought Lei inside the abandoned building. The five monks attacked in unison, their attacks converging on him, seeking his blood once again.

Fang made the first sign for a shield, a sign so weak it shouldn't have had a chance against the five monks combining their strength. But when he released the defense, he knew it was more than enough. Far more. The attacks struck the shield, and Fang thought it felt as though he was being tickled, or perhaps attacked by flies. The monks weren't even close to being able to penetrate.

When their attacks dissipated, three of the monks fell to their knees, exhausted from their single attempt. Fang's hand went for his dagger, only to realize he'd forgotten to pick it up after he left the square where he had battled Lei. He frowned. He would have to pick it up on his way out of town, if he could.

The loss pained him more than he expected it to. That dagger was the last piece of his master, and now he felt completely alone, completely cut off from the rest of the world.

The monks started forming the signs for another attack and brought Fang's attention to them once again. He held his shield with one hand, then formed a basic attack with the other. He aimed at the first monk on the left and released the attack. It struck the monk, throwing him far back. His head crunched against the street, and even at this distance Fang could hear the crack of the man's neck snapping.

He moved to the next monk just as they attacked again, throwing all their energy into the attacks. Fang felt as though he could have fought off the attacks for days. Nothing could stop him. While he was blocking the monks' attacks, he released his own, hitting the next monk in line, who still hadn't found the strength to stand. The strike knocked the monk back, and he skidded across the street. Fang wasn't sure whether or not he'd killed the man, but he certainly wasn't going to stand anytime soon.

The third monk, also on his knees, suffered the next blow. The results were largely the same. These monks didn't have the slightest chance against him. They were ants, and he was the boot that stomped on them and the broom that swept them from this reality.

By now, the crowd must have realized what was happening. They couldn't see the waves of energy that shot from monk to assassin and back, but they could see the results of those strikes, the bodies flying through the air and skipping along the ground. The crowd panicked, trying to find a way out, not knowing where the danger was. One poor soul walked into a monk's attack, and it knocked him back as though he'd been punched across the face. People screamed and ran in all directions, creating more of a danger with their stampede than the fight between Fang and the monks.

Between the chaos in the street and the sight of the bodies of their comrades, the two surviving monks finally realized that they had no chance against Fang's strength. They turned and ran, trying to find shelter. Fang made sure they wouldn't find it in time. He allowed his shield to drop so that he could form an attack with his second hand. He focused to the third sign, not because he needed the strength, but because he needed the additional accuracy.

The first monk was hit in the back and sent flying through a market stall. Hot oil spilled all over him and caused his robes to catch on fire. Fang grinned as the monk went through the stall and into the house beyond, lighting that on fire as well.

The final monk was almost free when Fang attacked. Like the other coward, the attack caught him full in the back and sent him flying into a house. Fang didn't have any need to see if he was dead or not. They were out of the way, and if his master was right, they would be easy enough to kill later on, when they could be picked off one at a time.

Fang looked at his hands, feeling the same power course through him. What was this new skill that he'd unlocked, and how had he acquired it? He had so many questions, but no answers. All he knew was he had more power than he'd ever dreamed of having, and that was enough for him. The tower was getting close, and now his path was clear. His master's plan was almost complete.

53

———

Lei came to and immediately regretted it. Miraculously, he seemed to be in one piece, and still breathing. He pulled his tunic up, just to see what his torso looked like. Mottled bruises were already rising, but they wouldn't be at their worst for another day or so. Breathing deeply hurt, but the pain was an ache and not a sharp stab, so he was pretty confident that his ribs were intact. He was healthier than he should have been.

There was a flurry of footfalls in the distance, and Lei grunted and summoned an attack and a shield. He didn't want to move, but that didn't mean he shouldn't be prepared. He released the weapons when he saw that it was a group of monks with a single woman among them.

Taio led the way. "What happened?"

Lei groaned. "We fought."

"And?"

"You don't see his body, do you?" The answer should have been obvious enough to anyone with eyes and the sense to use them. Taio glared at Lei, then turned to the monks he'd come with. Daiyu took the moment to break from the group and kneel next to him.

"How are you?"

"I've had better days."

She looked him over. "I'll say. You look like a whole line of horses ran over you."

"Thanks."

She offered her hand and Lei took it gratefully. He was fairly certain he could stand on his own without falling, but not so certain that he was willing to try in front of the monks.

"What are you going to do?"

Lei sighed softly. "Find him again, I guess."

"Can you beat him?"

Lei thought for a moment, then gave a small shake of his head. "I fought better than ever, tried tricks that should have killed him, and hit him harder than any man should be able to take. I'm exhausted, and everything hurts."

"Then why do it?"

Lei fought against the tightness in his stomach. The liar inside him wanted to tell her that he was the only one who could stop Fang, was the only one who could stop whatever they'd planned for Jihan. The statements were true, but the intent was not.

He wanted his life back. As grateful as he was for the skills he possessed, he hated not knowing if he was acting of his own accord. He had lived for the better part of a decade hating his brother for sending him out into the world on his own. Now, all he wanted was to forget his brother and leave him behind with the debris of this past life.

"I need to be rid of him," was all he could say.

Daiyu seemed to understand. "Is there anything I can do?"

"No. The farther you are away from this city, the safer I feel."

She stared into his eyes. "Then I'll be at the Heron, waiting for you."

He thought about arguing, trying to tell her that he'd feel better if she was outside the entire city, but from the set of her jaw and the fire in her eyes, he knew that was a losing battle before he even began. But he had to try. "If I lose, you'll suffer and die with everyone else."

"Then don't lose."

With that, she turned on her heels and began walking away, in the direction of the Heron.

Despite himself, he was amazed. Daiyu had always survived in the past. This decision seemed very much unlike her. Before, she would have been gone in a moment. But she'd given him another reason to fight.

Taio stopped him before he could take more than a few steps. "What are you doing?"

Lei stopped himself from cursing, barely. "Going to fight Fang."

Taio's hand on his shoulder prevented him from stepping forward. "You can't do that. You don't know where he is, and you don't have a chance against him. Look how much damage was done here." He gestured to the cut in the street and the damage to the buildings in the area.

Lei glared. Everything that needed to be said already had been. There was nothing more to add. Taio tried to stare him down, but eventually his eyes turned down. He knew the truth as well as anyone else.

Lei scooped up his sword and sheathed it. Taio had one fact correct: he didn't know where Fang had gone.

That problem was solved by explosions of energy off in the distance, near the center of Jihan. Lei's eyes traveled to the tower that stood over the center of the town. That would be his destination. Something in Lei knew it would be true. He started walking.

As he was about to leave the square, he saw a simple dagger left on the street. He'd seen that dagger before, in Fang's hand. He picked it up and tucked it safely away. Now he had all the weapons.

WHEN HE GOT to the center of the city, he was surprised to see how busy it was. Despite the devastation all around the city this night, most people still didn't seem to know just how much danger they were in. This was no place to fight. With a deep sigh, Lei released his energy without a symbol, without any focus. A wave passed through the revelers, knocking people to the ground, tipping over beer mugs, and collapsing tables.

For a second, everything was silent, but then people started running. Most people had never felt power like that, and it only took a few of them realizing what was happening to start the panic. Within a few minutes, the square was mostly clear.

Fireworks lit the sky as Fang stepped around a corner and into the square. If he was surprised to find Lei there, his face didn't show it at all. "You can't kill me," he said.

"And you can't be allowed to live for the murder of my brother."

Fang stepped closer, until they were about twenty paces apart. "That's what all this is about?"

"It always has been."

"Your brother would have played the hero."

"He always did."

Fang smirked. "I think we could have been friends."

"You're probably right." Lei didn't lie. Despite everything, he felt a certain kinship with the assassin. The man was strong, and had made his own way without the monasteries. More than anyone, Fang understood the way Lei felt, the way they had both been wronged.

"Well, let's finish this, then, shall we?"

Lei nodded. There was something different about Fang. He seemed to be positively aglow with power, more than Lei had ever sensed from another person. Where did all this strength come from? The way Lei felt, he wasn't sure he could even brush away a fly with his energy.

Lei's fingers started dancing, forming the first, second, and third forms of the attack. He aimed the attack at Fang, but the assassin seemed completely unconcerned. The other man didn't even attempt to protect himself. Lei wouldn't waste any advantage that he was given. He released the attack, and the wave sprinted toward Fang.

In response, Fang made only the first sign for defense, throwing up a hasty shield between them. Lei's attack struck the shield and broke instantly. Lei opened his mouth in surprise. Had the last battle weakened him that much? Fang shouldn't have been able to deflect that energy with just the first sign. Not only that, Lei hadn't even felt like he'd gotten close to breaking through. What had happened to Fang?

The assassin seemed to read his mind. "I told you, you can't kill me. I've found a power, greater than before. I'm not sure there has ever been anyone as strong as me."

Lei's left hand starting making the signs for a shield. He was at the fourth sign when Fang finished his sentence and made a single sign.

Lei's eyes widened as the attack swept toward him, like a tidal wave of power. He threw up his shield, grunting as the energies collided and he fought to keep his balance. Maybe it took an eternity, or maybe just a second, but eventually the wave broke, right before his shield would have. Lei collapsed to his knees, breathing hard. They'd only had two simple exchanges, and he felt as though he could sleep through the better part of a month. And that had only been a first-level attack.

For the first time, despair threatened to drive him flat to the ground. He'd always known this would be a tough fight, but somewhere in the back of his mind, he'd always thought he'd find a way to win. He and Fang had always been close in the power, but no longer. The gulf between them was vast.

But he only had one option, especially now that he was here. He thought of Daiyu, waiting for him at the inn, and he found the strength to stand back to his feet. He wobbled for a moment, but his hands on his knees prevented him from falling. Fortunately, Fang seemed to be enjoying his moment in the spotlight.

"I'm impressed. No one else could have withstood this power for so long," Fang said. "But it is almost time, and I do want to be ready."

Not knowing what else to do, Lei drew his sword.

Fang laughed. "Yes! What better test!" He started forming the signs for a shield, his fingers sliding through the first three so fast that Lei almost couldn't follow them.

Lei pushed all the power he had left into the blade. This was his last effort, and there was no reason to hold anything back. If this failed, it was all over. He felt the sword almost grow hot in his hands, burning to be used. When he didn't think he could channel any more into the blade, he swung.

The cut was a clumsy one, resulting in a wide, arcing blast of destruction. Had Fang decided to step to the side instead of blocking it, there was no telling what damage the cut would have done. A deep gouge opened up in the square, brick and packed dirt simply disappearing from the force of the strike.

Fang released his shield, then watched as Lei's attack neared. He didn't make any attempt to move. How strong had he gotten? Lei didn't know, but the air around Fang looked like it almost warped with his energy. It seemed so powerful, Lei was certain even those without the gift could feel the power. His own hairs were all standing on end.

The energies met with catastrophic force. Lei tried to get a sense of what was happening, but the magnitude was beyond his comprehension. His attack was the strongest he'd ever released, and Fang's shield was the strongest defense he'd ever encountered. When the explosion hit, Lei didn't have any strength to resist. His only thought was to keep the sharp blade in his hand but away from his body. He didn't know if he hit a wall or the street, but he felt the bone in his upper left arm break, the agony just another part of the roar that deafened his ears and buffeted his body.

For a few seconds, his whole world was filled with the blinding glare of energy, as white as the cleanest sheets. Slowly, his vision returned, spots still in his eyes. Buildings all around the square had collapsed. The only one still standing was the tower on its firm foundation. He couldn't see what had happened to Fang, but given the strength of his own attack, there was no way the man could have survived. Lei was glad. After everything, he wasn't sure he'd be able to stand for a week.

He sighed, trying to feel if his brother's spirit was still somewhere inside. It had gotten harder to tell as of late, as if the spirit had become a closer part of him.

He knew he needed to stand up. Daiyu was waiting for him, and in his condition, he feared what the monks would do to him. Taking a deep breath, he rocked to his feet, the world tilting worse than when he'd been a drunk. He blinked rapidly, trying to clear his vision. His left arm hung useless at his side, but that was neither here nor there at the moment. He would get it set and give it time to heal. He had no plans to do anything else for a while.

The only warning he received was a hint of movement in the settling dust in the corner of his eye. He turned, but there was never really a chance. Fang slammed into him, grabbing him by the throat and lifting him into the air. Lei kicked feebly, the blows not having any effect on the assassin.

Lei's eyes rolled back in his head, only to remember that he still had a sword in his hand. He swung it haphazardly, hoping at least to cut through most of Fang's arm.

Fang responded by dropping Lei to his feet and blasting him away. Lei screamed in agony as his left arm was crushed between his body and the street. He stood up, only to realize he'd somehow dropped the sword. Then Fang was on him, raining down punches and kicks that were enhanced by his power. Lei felt more of his ribs crack and he coughed up blood.

After a few seconds of that, Fang delivered a crushing kick that sent him stumbling backward. Somehow, he managed to keep his feet, but it took everything he had. There was nothing left to give, and although Fang looked like he'd taken quite a bit of a beating, it was nothing compared to Lei's own condition.

He would miss Daiyu. He would miss beer. Truth be told, he'd miss his brother, at least a little.

Lei's attention was drawn to Fang, who was forming the signs for an attack with his right hand. The power the man was focusing was incredible, even stronger than what Lei had sensed before. Even after everything, he still had so much more to give. Lei never had a chance.

Fang moved through the first four signs without a problem. The fifth one required more concentration, and then he performed the sixth, the Dragon's Fang. The same attack that had killed Jian would kill him, too. Lei supposed it was fitting.

"You were stronger than him, you know. Considerably."

Lei knew Fang meant the comment as a compliment, a last bit of respect between two enemies who understood each other well. But all Lei could think about was how disrespectful it was that the last words he heard had to be about his brother.

His anger wasn't great. The rage he'd once possessed that had driven him to drink every evening and most days had burned out. But there was still a little. There was no point in hiding his gestures. Fang would sense the attack as soon as he began to form it.

Lei raised his own right hand, forming the first and second signs for an attack. Fang smiled. "A fighter until the end. I shall always remember you."

Lei formed the third sign, but could feel his focus slipping away. Why even bother? Even if he could make it all the way to the sixth sign, which he didn't know, Fang had demonstrated, frequently, how much stronger he was. But Lei refused to stop.

He made the fourth sign, sweat breaking out as he concentrated on focusing his energy. One more. Then he could die knowing he had done everything that was possible, that he left nothing of himself behind. His fingers felt as though they were moving through thick clay, but he formed the fifth sign and aimed it at Fang. Compared to the attack aimed at him, his own felt pitiful, like he was a cup of tea trying to put out a house fire.

Lei attacked, releasing his energy, putting everything he had left into it. Just as it was about to hit Fang, Fang released his own attack, smashing Lei's as though it was nothing. Lei still pushed, giving everything for the last few moments of peace.

The Dragon's Fang darted toward him, and in his final moments, his memory seemed to disconnect from the present moment. He saw his evenings with Daiyu, back when they had been younger and happier. He saw his training sessions with his brother in the woods, their laughter echoing straight into the present.

They weren't all happy memories. He saw his greatest mistake, the girl unaware her life had been taken from her far too early. He felt the overwhelming rejection that came from his brother telling him that he had to go alone. Even now, the memory tore his heart in two.

Then a new series of memories, subtle ones, flowed through his thoughts. He heard Chen telling him how Jian had made a deal to keep Lei alive. He remembered all the times Jian had wandered through Two Bridges, while most of the monks only came through every few months. Like a fool, he had always assumed it was just because Jian had more missions than the rest of the monks.

Clear as day, a single memory floated to the surface. He was outside the Old Goat, feeling his own energy inside the tavern. With a start, he realized this memory wasn't his own. Lei felt his energy grow in anger, and the overwhelming sadness his brother felt at that moment, and a determination to make things right. It was the last strong memory Jian had before he died.

His entire perspective shifted, as though for almost a

decade he had been seeing the world from a different angle. At that moment, he knew Jian would have given anything to stay by his side. But to keep him alive, the cost had been high. And in return, Lei had given his brother nothing but hate.

How could he not have seen the sacrifice Jian had made? All this time, and he'd been too blind to realize both he and his brother had always wanted the same things. A profound sense of regret washed over him, disappointment in years of actions that had torn him and his brother farther apart. Actions that could never be undone.

"I'm sorry, Jian," he whispered.

With a start, he realized that the Dragon's Fang had stopped. Not that Fang had stopped attacking, but that the attack itself was held in check by his own power. The Dragon's Fang was only a handful of inches from his own outstretched palm, but there it remained.

Then he realized just how different he felt. He felt a connection, much like he had back inside the abandoned building, as though the power wasn't coming from him, but through him. But there was something else in the power, a presence that enveloped him and strengthened the connection. A presence that had been trying to break through to him for weeks.

Jian.

Even after death, his brother continued to protect him.

Lei's attention moved beyond the wild energies clashing in front of him to Fang, standing about ten paces away. The assassin was wide-eyed, a grimace on his face as he realized that his strongest attack hadn't yet found its mark. The man who killed Jian gritted his teeth and pushed, but all Lei felt was a slight increase in pressure. He didn't feel as if he had to work harder; he just had to become more open to the connection.

"I'm sorry, Jian. I understand." He felt a tingling warmth surging through his body. Jian built the bridge between him and the incredible source of power, and Lei gave himself over to it, surrendering, trusting his brother for the first time since he'd left the monastery.

The momentum of the struggle changed in an instant. The extra power flew through Lei toward Fang, driving the Dragon's Fang attack back several feet before it reached a new equilibrium.

The longer the two of them fought, the more Lei understood. Like him, Fang had some sort of connection to the same power Lei was drawing on. But the nature of the connection was subtly different. Fang didn't seem to be able to access it the same way Lei could.

Lei knew there was more power available.

He didn't feel any hate for Fang. The two of them were two sides of the same coin. But he couldn't be allowed to continue. Lei imagined Jian in front of him and gave him one final embrace; his connection opened wider, and the power overwhelmed even the Dragon's Fang.

Unlike before, there was no explosion, nothing to mark the powers that had been unleashed. The Dragon's Fang unraveled, leaving Fang completely exposed. Lei's attack slammed into him, and almost instantly, Lei cut it off. Without control, the blast would have torn through the city.

Lei sagged forward, but the exhaustion wasn't quite the same. Yes, he was tired, and his left arm stabbed at him every time he moved it, but he could walk. He stumbled over to Fang, picking up his sword on the way.

Against all reason, Fang was still alive. His body looked unnatural, as though the bones that supported it had been turned to pulp. He looked to be in complete agony, his eyes darting around but his body unwilling to respond to commands.

There wasn't anything to say. But as Lei raised his sword to end Fang's misery, Fang saw his dagger tucked in Lei's waistband. The assassin stared at it longingly, and somehow managed to raise his arm enough to point at it. "Please?"

Lei nodded. He could still feel his connection and knew he had nothing to fear. Fang would never harm another again. He put down his sword, far enough away that Fang couldn't reach it. Then he drew the dagger, flipped it so he was holding onto the blade, and extended it down to Fang.

Fang grabbed the handle, the effort seeming to take all of his focus. Then he clutched it to his chest the way a child would hold on to a doll or toy.

Lei felt the pity welling up in him as he picked his sword back up.

He met Fang's eyes, and Fang mouthed two words to him, blood bubbling up from between his lips.

"Thank you."

Lei nodded again and swung his sword, separating Fang's head from his body.

EPILOGUE

Lei woke up inside the monastery walls, and his first reaction was one of panic. After everything he had done, how could they be so callous as to detain him?

Then his memories returned and he relaxed. Daiyu sat near the door to the room, partly to watch over his recovery and partly to do what she could to protect him. Although he had dozed off and on for the past several days, she had told him the entire monastery was in an uproar, as he imagined it would be. Under other circumstances, he might even care.

As it was, all he cared about was sleeping and recovering. His stamina had been battered by the fights on the night of the Harvest Festival, and his broken arm was also slow to mend, even though it had been set and cared for by the best physician the monastery had.

Before he and Daiyu could exchange so much as a word, he sensed the presence striding toward the room, a determined aura that could only belong to one man.

There was a sharp, confident knock on the door, and Lei nodded at Daiyu to open it. He noticed she had a dagger in her hand, concealed well behind her back. She opened the door, revealing Taio on the other side. His eyes took them both in, and Lei guessed he knew Daiyu held a weapon. It was a mark of how much things had changed that the offense caused nothing worse than a raised eyebrow.

Lei broke the stalemate before someone did something foolish. "Come in, Taio."

The monk slid into the room gracefully, and Lei imagined the monk in his element, the master of the small spaces of the monastery. Some things would never change. Taio gave Daiyu a disdainful glance, then turned to Lei. "How are you feeling?"

"Weak, but better."

"It's time we talked about the future."

Lei nodded. He had guessed as much. "I have some questions, first."

Taio raised his eyebrow again, indicating the extent of his feelings about the rudeness of Lei's request. "Go on."

"What happened after the fight? Daiyu won't tell me anything beyond it all turned out for the best."

"She's right. Your suspicion turned out to be correct. There were barrels of black powder scattered throughout the city. Although we don't know for sure, it seems reasonable to conclude Fang was responsible for setting off the first barrel within the tower, and the others would have followed his lead. Being as he was unable to, the other triads abandoned their mission. While there have been dozens of injuries and a couple of deaths, thanks to Fang's actions, the worst of the crisis was averted."

"Did anything happen elsewhere in the empire?"

Taio frowned, not expecting that question. "There has been no news."

"And the monasteries?"

"Shaken, to tell the truth," Taio admitted. "Your case was

always unique, but to know that there was someone else who escaped the system, who grew to such a power… well, there are many questions that we have to face."

Lei could imagine. "And our monastery?"

"We will rebuild. I will be officially installed as abbot once it is completed."

"Congratulations."

"Thank you."

There was a cold silence in the room as the men studied one another.

"That brings me to the subject I came here to speak about," Taio began.

"I'm not staying."

"You don't have a choice."

"Of course I do. I was allowed out once before, and I did no harm to the monasteries or to others."

"That agreement existed only because of your brother's sacrifice. His agreement and regular participation were all that kept you alive."

Lei started. He'd figured it out for himself, in that final battle with Fang, but to hear it confirmed was still a surprise. "What do you mean?"

"Jian fought like mad to leave the monastery with you. He didn't want you out in the world on your own, but the abbot could never allow you both to leave, not with the power you'd already demonstrated. After days of arguing, your brother agreed to remain at the monastery to train. I think you knew this. But he also agreed that if your power ever got out of control, he would kill you himself. He was the only one strong enough to do so, and the deal allowed the abbot to keep at least one of you. Otherwise, he would have had to kill both of you. But you see, without Jian watching over you, there can be no deal."

Lei absorbed the new information, completing the new picture of his brother. He could listen to others talk about Jian without anger now.

"You can't keep me here."

"Maybe not, but you're injured, and if you left, all the monasteries in the empire would hunt for you. That's no life to lead. We're willing to welcome you back with open arms, and that's a deal you'll never get again."

Lei left most of his accusations unsaid. He knew the monks would be desperate to study him, to understand what he had been able to do. Perhaps his life wouldn't be filled with suffering, but it wouldn't be very pleasurable either. And unlike his brother, he wouldn't be able to leave the walls very often.

Taio didn't look like he wanted to start an argument. Instead, he pulled a small flask out of his robes, with two cups. "I'm told this is some of the best wine in Jihan, given to you by a tavern keeper after she discovered an unexploded barrel of black powder outside her building. Drink up and enjoy, and we'll talk soon enough."

Without a glance back, he swept out of the room. Daiyu slammed the door behind him.

Lei rested again, this time with Daiyu nestled on his uninjured side. When he woke, dusk was falling. He tried to move without waking Daiyu, but she was alert the moment he moved.

"How are you?" she asked.

He thought for a moment. "Good."

They sat up and looked into each other's eyes. She truly was gorgeous, he thought. And strong. One of the strongest women he'd ever had the pleasure of knowing.

"Can you still feel Jian?"

He shook his head. "There's one way to be sure, though," he said as he looked at the flask.

She gave him a dubious look, and he understood. She knew where that path led.

"I think I'll be okay, but if not, you're welcome to your revenge."

Still looking worried, she went to the flask and poured them each a drink. They clinked their cups together and sipped. Fruity flavors exploded on his tongue, and Lei grinned. "That's some of the best wine I think I've ever tasted."

Daiyu was busy finishing her cup, but she nodded her agreement. "Another one?"

He turned his cup over, an action that took almost as much willpower as fighting Fang had. But there was too much to lose.

"No."

She looked relieved at his decision, but she still helped herself to another cup of wine. Lei watched longingly, but knew he couldn't go down that road, not again. It had been cruel of Taio to leave the flask here, no matter how good the wine was.

"Can you feel him?"

He shook his head. "Nothing at all."

Lei watched Daiyu sip the last of the wine, feeling the old longing for alcohol but able to resist it.

When she finished the wine, Daiyu looked at him. "So, what comes next?"

"I don't want to stay here, and I want to be with you."

"Is there a question there somewhere?"

"Will you go on the run with me?"

"With no money and all the monasteries hunting us?"

Lei shrugged. "We'd have each other."

She laughed. "Absolutely. I was wondering when you were going to get around to asking."

They both smiled and laughed, and that night, they slipped away from the monastery, dissolving into the shadows beyond Jihan.

THANK YOU

Before you go, I just wanted to take a moment to thank you for reading. I had a lot of fun writing this story, and I hope you had a lot of fun reading it.

If you enjoyed this story, reviews mean a lot to authors today. If you could take a moment and review the book wherever you purchased it, I'd be very grateful.

With gratitude,

Ryan

ALSO BY RYAN KIRK

The Nightblade Series

Nightblade

World's Edge

The Wind and the Void

Blades of the Fallen

Nightblade's Vengeance

Nightblade's Honor

The Primal Series

Primal Dawn

Primal Darkness

Primal Destiny

Primal Trilogy

The Code Series

Code of Vengeance

Code of Pride

Code of Justice

ABOUT THE AUTHOR

Ryan Kirk is the bestselling author of the Nightblade series of books. When he isn't writing, you can probably find him playing disc golf or hiking through the woods.

www.waterstonemedia.net
contact@waterstonemedia.net